Amish
COOKING CLASS
BOOK 2

———⟡———

THE BLESSING

Amish
COOKING CLASS
BOOK 2

—◦∞◦—

THE BLESSING

WANDA &
BRUNSTETTER

BARBOUR
PUBLISHING

The Blessing © 2017 by Wanda E. Brunstetter

ISBN 978-1-63609-124-2

Adobe Digital Edition (.epub) 978-1-63609-435-9

Scripture quotations are taken from the King James Version and the New International Version of the Bible.

Scriptures marked NIV are taken from the Holy Bible, New International Version®. NIV® Copyright © 1973, 1978, 1984, 2011 by Biblica, Inc.™ Used by permission. All rights reserved worldwide.

All German-Dutch words are taken from the *Revised Pennsylvania German Dictionary* found in Lancaster County, Pennsylvania.

This book is a work of fiction. Names, characters, places, and incidents are either products of the author's imagination or used fictitiously. Any similarity to actual people, organizations, and/or events is purely coincidental.

For more information about Wanda E. Brunstetter, please access the author's web site at the following Internet address: www.wandabrunstetter.com

Cover Design: Buffy Cooper
Cover model photography: Richard Brunstetter III, RBIII Studios

Published by Barbour Publishing, Inc., 1810 Barbour Drive, Uhrichsville, OH 44683, www.barbourbooks.com

Our mission is to inspire the world with the life-changing message of the Bible.

Member of the
Evangelical Christian
Publishers Association

Printed in the United States of America

To Pastors Jim and Pam Merillat. Thank you for the many blessings you bestow on others. Your dedication to God and others is appreciated!

———✦◦∞◦✦———

"The things which are impossible with men are possible with God."
LUKE 18:27 KJV

Chapter 1

Walnut Creek, Ohio

Heidi Troyer's skin prickled as a gust of wind blew into her kitchen. After peeling and cutting an onion to go in the savory meat loaf she was making for supper, she'd opened the window a few minutes ago to air out the room.

Glancing into the yard, Heidi watched as newly fallen leaves swirled over the grass. Across the way, freshly washed laundry she'd hung on the line a few hours ago fluttered in the unseasonably cool breeze. Even the sheets made a snapping noise when the wind played catch and release.

They'd soon be saying goodbye to the month of August, and Heidi was glad. A long dry spell had caused some of the trees to drop their leaves early, and the rustling of those still clinging to the branches sounded like water rushing down a well-fed stream after a heavy rain.

"I wish it would rain. Even a drizzle would be nice." Heidi looked toward the sky, but not a single puffy cloud was in sight. September was a month of transition, teetering between warm, summer-like days and cool, comfortable nights, so maybe the rain would come soon. She looked forward to its fresh, clean scent, not to mention it removing the necessity of watering her flowerbeds and garden.

Heidi glanced at the plot where she'd planted a variety of vegetables in the spring. The potatoes and other root vegetables still needed to be dug and put in the cellar, and she wanted to get the chore done before Kendra's baby was born and the adoption became official. Once the infant came, Heidi would put her full attention on raising the child. She'd already made the decision not to teach any more cooking classes—at least not until her son or daughter was older and didn't require round-the-clock attention. Heidi certainly couldn't teach and take care of the precious baby, and she didn't want to juggle between the two—especially after waiting so long to become a mother.

Heidi's senses were heightened, and she giggled out loud as she visualized herself holding the infant while stirring a batch of cookie dough. After being married to Lyle for eight years and finding herself still unable to conceive, the idea of soon becoming a mother was almost more than she could comprehend. In a matter of weeks, her dream would finally come true. How thankful she was that Kendra had moved into their home and agreed to let them adopt her child. Once the baby was born and Kendra got her strength back, she would find a better-paying job and move out on her own. It wouldn't be right to ask her to leave until she was physically and financially ready.

Heidi sighed. *What a shame Kendra's parents turned their back on her and she felt forced to give up her baby. But then if they hadn't, Lyle and I would not have been given the opportunity to raise Kendra's child.*

Satisfied the onion smell was gone, Heidi took one more breath of the late summer-scented air, then closed the window and took a seat at the table. She owed her aunt Emma a letter and would start writing it while the meat loaf cooked. Maybe by the time supper was ready, Kendra would be back from her doctor's appointment, and Lyle from Mt. Hope, where he'd put his auctioneering skills to good use most of the day.

I can hardly wait for us to be sharing a warm meal at the kitchen table, so I can hear about the events of their days. Heidi was most eager to get updates on Kendra's doctor's appointment.

She'd offered to go with her this afternoon, as she had several other times since Kendra moved in with them. Today, however, Kendra had said she had a few stops to make after seeing the doctor and didn't want to take up Heidi's day.

I wouldn't have minded. I enjoy being with Kendra. Heidi's nose tickled, and she rubbed it, trying to stifle a sneeze. Smelling onion on her fingers, she wet her hands under the faucet, then rubbed them along the sides of their stainless steel sink. After a few seconds, she smelled her fingers again and was amazed the onion scent was gone. Heidi didn't know how it worked, but she was glad her friend Loretta had recently given her this unusual tip.

"I'll have to keep this in mind to share with my students once I decide to start up the cooking classes again." Heidi wrote a note to remind her, since it would be a good while before she taught more classes.

After she stuck the note in her recipe box, Heidi turned her attention to a daily devotional book lying near her writing tablet. She read Psalm 9:1, the verse for the day, out loud: " 'I will praise thee, O Lord, with my whole heart; I will shew forth all thy marvellous works.' "

Closing her eyes and bowing her head, Heidi prayed: "Thank You, Lord, for Your many blessings. I praise You with my whole heart for all Your wonderful works. Thank You for this day, and for my family and friends. Protect us, and shower Your people with many blessings. Amen."

Heidi had no more than finished her prayer when she heard a car pull into the yard. She went to the window and looked out, smiling as she watched Kendra get out of her driver's car. Since Kendra didn't have a vehicle of her own, she'd hired one of Heidi and Lyle's drivers to take her into town. If Heidi had gone with her, they might have traveled by horse and buggy; although it would have taken them longer.

Keeping an eye on Kendra as she made her way toward the house, Heidi couldn't help noticing her slow steps, and how she pursed her lips, while holding her stomach, as though in pain.

Heidi's shoulders tightened as she rushed to open the door. She hoped the doctor hadn't given Kendra unsettling news today.

"Sorry I'm late." Kendra entered the house, avoiding eye contact with Heidi, and took a seat at the kitchen table. "We need to talk." She pushed a lock of auburn hair behind her ears.

Heidi pulled out a chair and sat. "What is it, Kendra? Is everything okay with the baby?"

"Yes in a physical sense at least." Kendra's brown eyes looked ever so serious as she took the seat next to Heidi.

"What do you mean?"

The young woman's shoulders curled as she bent her neck forward. "The whole way here, I thought about how I should tell you this." Kendra took a shuddering breath. "And still, I don't know where to begin."

Heidi held her hands in her lap, gripping her fingers into her palms. "Please, tell me what it is you need to say."

"Well, the thing is. . ." Kendra shifted in her chair. "Miracle of miracles—my dad called my cell phone this morning. He asked if I'd be free to come by his office this afternoon." She paused and drew a quick breath. "I went there after I left the doctor's office, and. . ." Her voice faltered, and she paused to swallow before continuing. "He said it had been a mistake to kick me out of the house after I told him and Mom I was pregnant."

Heidi smiled. "That's good news, Kendra. I've been praying for it to happen. I hope things will be better between you and your parents from now on."

"Yeah, well, Dad wants me to move back home so he and Mom can help raise the baby."

"Raise the baby?" Heidi blinked rapidly, her breath bursting in and out. "Does this mean you've changed your mind about Lyle and me adopting your child?"

Kendra gave a slow nod. "Since my parents are willing to

help, there's no reason for me to give up the baby now. And since the contract the lawyer drew up says. . ."

Heidi held up her hand. "I know what it says; although I never expected you would go back on your word."

"I. . .I wasn't planning to, but things have changed." A few tears trickled down Kendra's cheeks. "I never wanted to give up my baby; you have to know that. I only agreed to it because I had no support and knew I couldn't take care of a child by myself." She touched Heidi's hands: both of them had turned cold. "I can see you're disappointed, and I'm sorry, but I hope you understand."

Understand? Heidi's stomach clenched, and she pressed the wad of her apron against it. She sat in stunned silence, unable to form a response. The tension felt so strong, she could almost touch it. It didn't seem possible, after all these months of Kendra living with them, that she had changed her mind. Heidi wanted to be happy for the young, pregnant woman sitting at her table. It was good Kendra had reconciled with her parents and been invited to move back home. But Kendra's decision to keep the baby put a hole in Heidi's heart—one she felt sure would never close. Her dream of holding a tiny baby she could call her own was just that—only a dream. The walls in this house would not echo with the laughter of children. Tiny feet would never patter across the floor. No chubby arms would reach out for a hug. Heidi fought for control. The ringing in her ears was almost deafening.

She glanced toward the hall, knowing the nursery that had already been set up would have to be dismantled. All the baby blankets and clothes would have to be packed away. The crib would be disassembled. She'd have Lyle haul it out to the barn, for having the crib in the house would be a painful reminder of their loss. Heidi didn't even want to look at it now.

She thought about the scripture she'd quoted several moments ago and wondered if she would ever praise the Lord again.

Less than an hour later, Heidi checked on the meat loaf, decided it was done, and turned the oven temperature to low. It was all she could do to get supper ready for when Lyle got home. Kendra's shocking announcement numbed her mind. She wondered what Lyle's reaction would be when he heard the news.

Kendra came into the kitchen and stood watching as Heidi took a sack of potatoes from the pantry. "Would you like help getting supper ready?" she asked.

"We need a kettle for boiling the potatoes." Heidi could barely make eye contact with the young woman. Truth was, she wished she could be alone to deal with her grief.

Kendra went to the lower cupboard and took out a medium-size pot. "I'll add water to the kettle and set it on the propane burner to heat."

Without a word, Heidi slid over the jars of home-canned beans she'd taken out earlier. After removing the lids, she dumped the contents into a kettle and sprinkled some leftover onion bits on top. She stirred them around a bit, set the lid in place, and put the pan on the stove. She felt like a robot, merely going through the motions of preparing their meal.

"Is there anything else I can do?" Kendra waited by the stove.

"We'll have iced tea to drink. Could you make that while I cut up a few carrot and celery sticks?" Heidi glanced at Kendra. *This meal will be so awkward. I'd give anything if Kendra's decision wasn't absolute.*

Her hands trembled as she took out the carrots and began slicing them. She wished it was still morning and things were as they had been before Kendra's shocking announcement. *Is there even a chance she might think things over and change her mind? Is it right to cling to that hope?*

"When I'm done making the tea, I'll set the dining-room

table." Kendra put the tea bags in the pitcher of hot water.

"Okay." Heidi washed celery stalks and cut those as well, pausing briefly to glance at the clock. Lyle would be home soon, and he'd be hungry. Her insides twisted; she had no appetite at all.

Silently, Kendra got out the plates, silverware, napkins, and three glasses. She placed them on a large tray and headed for the dining room, elbows tucked into her sides. This had to be difficult for her too. Heidi and Kendra had become close during the months she'd been living here. Heidi felt sure the young woman did not want to hurt her. But she had, and Heidi needed to come to grips with it, despite her disappointment.

A few minutes later, as Heidi watched the water bubbling over the potatoes, she heard the familiar sound of Lyle's horse and buggy pull in. She glanced at the timer on the counter. The potatoes had ten more minutes to go. It felt like it was a countdown to the moment she would give Lyle the news. *Should I tell him before supper or wait until we've finished eating?* Either way, there simply wasn't a good time nor an easy way to say it.

The back door squeaked open and clicked shut. A few seconds later, Lyle entered the kitchen, carrying his lunch box. He placed it on the counter, then pulled off his straw hat and smoothed back his thick auburn hair. "How was your day, Heidi? Did everything go well here?"

She moved away from the stove and gave him a much-needed hug. At the moment, Heidi felt so overwhelmed she could barely speak.

"You're trembling, Heidi. Is something wrong?" He patted her back gently. "Wasn't Kendra supposed to see the doctor today?"

"Jah." Heidi's voice sounded muffled as she held her face close to his chest, hoping to draw strength from his embrace.

"There's nothing wrong with the *boppli*, I hope."

"No, Kendra's baby's fine."

Kendra came into the room just then. "Are we about ready to eat?"

"Almost." The timer for the potatoes went off, and Heidi stepped back to the stove to shut off the burner. The beans were also well heated, so she turned them off too. "I'll set everything on the dining-room table, and we can take our seats." She'd already decided not to tell Lyle about Kendra changing her mind regarding the adoption until they were alone this evening. It would be too difficult to say it in front of Kendra.

"Okay, just let me get washed up." Lyle gave Heidi's arm a tender squeeze before he left the room.

Kendra picked up the amber-brewed tea sitting near the refrigerator. She also got out a tray full of ice before turning to face Heidi. "Lyle doesn't know about me moving back with my folks, does he?"

"No, I haven't said anything yet." Heidi's voice caught in her throat. She picked up a pair of pot holders, opened the oven door, and brought out the meat loaf. After placing it on a platter, she sliced up their main course.

Kendra paused a minute, blinking rapidly, then without a word, she made a hasty exit with the tea and ice cubes.

Soon Lyle returned from washing up and offered to carry the meat loaf to the table. Heidi gave a brief nod and followed him with the beans and potatoes. Then, remembering the carrots and celery that had been sliced, she returned to the kitchen to get the container. When Heidi returned to the dining room, she took a seat across from Kendra, and they all bowed for silent prayer. Lyle sat at the head of the table, and he cleared his throat when he'd finished praying. Heidi took this as a cue, and she lifted her head. It had been difficult to even formulate a prayer. Although she was thankful for the food on their table, she felt no gratitude for the fact that her hopes and dreams of being a parent had been crushed. She couldn't let it defeat her, though; she had to be strong.

After the food was passed around, Lyle looked over at Kendra and smiled. "I was asking Heidi about your appointment earlier. How did it go?"

Kendra picked up her iced tea and took a drink. "Umm… It went fine. The doctor said the baby and I are doing okay."

"Good to hear." As if sensing Heidi's gloomy mood, Lyle reached over and lightly touched her arm. "You're not eating much."

Her lips quivered. "I–I'm not really hungry tonight."

"How come?" He reached for the bowl of potatoes and helped himself to several pieces. "Did you have too much to eat for lunch?"

Before Heidi could respond, Kendra blurted, "I believe it's my fault Heidi's not hungry. She's upset." She paused and looked at Heidi before continuing. "I can't blame her, and I'm sure you'll be upset too with what I have to tell you."

Lyle's brows drew together. "What is it, Kendra?"

"I've changed my mind about giving up my baby."

His eyebrows shot straight up. "What?"

Kendra explained the situation and said her parents wanted her to move back home. "I'll be packing up my things and leaving in the morning."

Heidi wished Kendra hadn't said anything—especially during their meal. Her shoulders slumped as she dropped her gaze and stared at her uneaten food. Heidi felt her husband's eyes upon her, and she couldn't help wondering what Lyle must be thinking right now. Her heart felt like it couldn't sink any lower. *It's so unfair. How could this be happening to Lyle and me?*

Chapter 2

Lyle placed his hands on Heidi's shoulders, where she stood at their bedroom window watching the remaining colorful leaves swaying gently in the trees. "Are you all right? You've been staring out the window for the last ten minutes. If we don't get ready for church soon we're going to be late."

"It's our off-Sunday," she reminded. "We can stay home today and do our own private devotions."

"I realize that, but I thought we were going to visit a neighboring community today, like we often do between our own church district's biweekly Sunday services."

Groaning, she flopped onto the bed. "I don't feel like going. It would be hard for me to sit and watch other women holding their *bopplin*."

"There are babies in our own district too. Are you going to stay home from church every Sunday because of that?"

Heidi blinked several times, willing herself not to cry. She'd had enough tearful spells since Kendra had moved out two weeks ago.

The bed creaked beneath his weight as Lyle took a seat beside Heidi and clasped her hand. "Don't you think it's time to let go of your grief and get back to the business of living?"

She pulled away from his grasp. "That's easy enough for you to say. You never really wanted to adopt Kendra's baby. You only agreed to it because of me."

He shook his head. "Not true, Heidi. It may have been

the case at first, but I changed my mind, and was looking forward to being a *daed*." Lyle pressed a hand to his chest. "I'm hurt by Kendra's decision as well."

She tipped her head. "Really? You haven't shown it that much."

"I keep busy with my work and try not to dwell on what happened. Don't you think it was hard for me to take the crib down and haul it out to the barn? Like you, I couldn't bear looking at it." Lyle leaned his head against Heidi's. "We can't change the situation; Kendra's moved out and gone back to live with her parents." He paused and drew a deep breath. "I've reached the conclusion that the adoption must not have been God's will for us."

Heidi stiffened. "So are you saying God doesn't want us to become parents?" Her throat felt swollen from holding back tears, and she swallowed hard to push down the lump that had formed.

"I don't know if God wants us to have children or not, but if it's His will for us to become parents, then we'll be given another chance to adopt."

"Oh, so you think some other pregnant woman is going to show up at our doorstep and ask us to adopt her child?" It wasn't right to speak to her husband in such a sarcastic tone, but Heidi couldn't seem to hold her tongue this morning.

"That is not what I meant."

"What then?"

"We can put our name in with the adoption lawyer, and..."

"I don't want to." Folding her arms, Heidi shook her head stubbornly. "Not now, anyway. Even if the lawyer found another birth mother seeking adoptive parents to take her child, she might change her mind at the last minute, like Kendra did." Heidi's voice cracked. "I can't deal with another disappointment, Lyle."

He slipped his arm around her waist. "Let's wait a few months, then we can talk about this again. Okay?"

She lifted her shoulders in a brief shrug. What choice did she have?

"Have you thought about teaching another cooking class? You enjoyed the last one you taught, and your students learned a lot more than cooking from you. It would give you something meaningful to do, and teaching six more classes might prove to be fun."

Heidi couldn't deny having enjoyed teaching her first set of students. During the six classes she'd taught, some wonderful things had happened. She would never forget how Ron Hensley turned his life over to Christ and went back to his hometown to make amends with his grown children and ex-wife. Then there was Loretta Donnelly, who'd formed a relationship with their friend and neighbor, Eli Miller, and was preparing to join the Amish church this fall. Heidi had been pleased when Charlene Higgins, engaged to be married, learned how to cook under her tutorage. The young school teacher had gained more confidence in the kitchen, which in turn, gave Charlene a better relationship with her future mother-in-law. Even Kendra Perkins had changed during the time she'd been in the class, focusing on the positive, rather than letting negative thoughts fill her mind.

Despite Heidi's disappointment over not being able to adopt Kendra's baby, she wished the young woman well. "Maybe it is time to teach another class," she murmured. "At least it would keep me busy."

Lyle patted her arm. "Good for you."

Drawing strength from deep within, Heidi turned toward the closet. "I'll change into my church clothes and be ready to leave for church by the time you have the horse and buggy ready."

He smiled and leaned down to give her a kiss. "You'll be glad you went once we're sitting in church and singing familiar hymns from the *Ausbund*."

"Jah, you're probably right. The songs of old, as well as our ministers' sermons are enough to lift anyone's spirits."

Coshocton, Ohio

"Hey, buddy, what's for breakfast? You're not gonna give us any leftover stew, I hope."

"No, Andy, I'm certainly not. We're gonna have cold cereal this morning." Bill Mason ground his teeth together. He and a couple of his buddies had gone camping at his cabin for the weekend, and as usual, he'd gotten stuck with all the cooking.

Andy, Russ, and Tom wrinkled their noses. "Come on, Bill," Russ said. "Can't you do better than that? If I wanted cold cereal for breakfast, I could have stayed home."

"Maybe you should have then." Bill poked Russ's arm. "Whenever we go camping you guys always want me to cook, but then all you do is complain."

Tom shifted on his canvas camping stool and leaned toward the fire he'd recently built in the pit outside Bill's cabin. "Know what I think?"

Bill shook his head. He had a mind to throw his gear in his rig and head for home. *Let 'em fend for themselves and see how they like it.*

"I think you oughta take some cooking classes. If you started on 'em right away, by the time deer season starts, you might be ready to cook us some decent meals."

"Humph!" Bill folded his arms. "Maybe you should be the one to take cooking classes." It was hard not to let his so-called friends get under his skin this morning. Bill hadn't slept well last night, even though his was the only bed inside the cabin. The other men had bedded down near the fireplace with their sleeping bags on fold-away cots.

Tom shook his head. "Nope. Out of the four of us, you're the only one who likes to cook."

"Tom's right." Andy gave a nod. "Even if I took classes, it would do me no good."

Bill grunted. "Well, you'd better get used to my cooking then, 'cause I ain't takin' no cooking lessons—end of story." He grabbed a box of cereal and set it on the metal folding table he'd set up near the fire pit. "And by the way, I don't actually like to cook; we just wouldn't eat if I didn't do it, 'cause none of you guys can do much more than boil water."

Tom threw another log on the fire. "You're right about that, but even if we could cook a decent meal, you'd probably still do it." He pointed his finger at Bill. "'Cause you like to be in control of things, since this is your hunting cabin."

Bill massaged his temples. *I wonder if it would have been better for me to go to church today instead of camping with this bunch of ingrates.* The truth was he hadn't been to church in a good many years. More than likely, he'd never step into a church building again.

Millersburg, Ohio

Clutching a plastic container, Nicole Smith ambled across the room and placed it on the table. "Here you go, Tony. Are you happy now?"

Nicole's freckle-faced, nine-year-old brother looked up at her and frowned. "Is that all I get for breakfast—just some boiled eggs?"

She pointed to the plate in the middle of the table. "You can have some of the bread I toasted too."

Tony squinted his blue eyes and wrinkled his nose. "You don't have to be so bossy, Nicki."

She shook her finger at him. "Don't call me that. My name is Nicole. Do you hear me, Tony? N–i–c–o–l–e. Nicole."

He puffed out his cheeks and grabbed a piece of toast, then slathered it with strawberry jam. "Mama calls you Nicki."

"That's right, and she knows I don't like that nickname." Nicole looked at her twelve-year-old sister. "Are eggs and toast okay for you, Heather, or do you want a bowl of cold cereal?"

"I don't want either." Heather shook her blond head. "I want pancakes this morning."

Tony bobbed his head. "Yeah, that'd be a nice change."

Nicole felt like telling her siblings if they wanted pancakes, they should get out the ingredients and fix them, but that would be a mistake—even worse than if she made them herself. "Listen, you both know I'm not good at making pancakes. The last ones I made turned out all rubbery." Nicole plopped both hands against her slender hips. "I'm tired of you both wanting something different every day. Can't you eat what I fix for breakfast without complaining?"

"I don't like cold cereal." Tony wrinkled his nose again.

Heather clutched her throat, making a low-pitched gagging noise. "The taste of boiled eggs makes me feel sick to my stomach. You oughta learn how to make somethin' else for a change."

"All right you two; don't give your big sister a hard time. Nicole does the best she can." Dad came into the kitchen and took a seat at the head of the table. He paused long enough to add some cream to his coffee, then helped himself to a piece of toast.

"She needs to learn how to cook somethin' besides cold cereal, boiled eggs, and toast." Heather looked at Nicole. "Maybe you should take some cooking lessons. Then you can make us some yummy-looking stuff like that lady on TV who has the cooking show."

"Dad doesn't have enough money to pay for cooking lessons." Gritting her teeth, Nicole grabbed a hard-boiled egg and cracked it open. *Cooking meals for my sister and brother, as well as Dad, shouldn't be my job anyway. It was Tonya's responsibility, and she oughta be here taking care of us right now.*

Nicole tried not to dwell on it, but there were times, like now, when her anger bubbled to the surface. She was a sophomore in high school and should be having fun during her teen years, not babysitting, cooking, cleaning, and doing all the other things her mother used to do before she started drinking and ran off with another man. The high hopes Nicole once had for her high-school years had died. Everything she did now was an unappreciated chore.

Nicole couldn't fault Dad for agreeing to the divorce Tonya asked for—especially when she said she didn't love him anymore and had started seeing another man. But that didn't make it any easier to deal with the disappointment Nicole, Dad, and her siblings all felt. The responsibilities on Nicole's shoulders had increased this past year, and it was hard not to feel bitter and let anger take control.

Nicole had given up on her dreams of going to the upcoming homecoming dance that would be held the night before the big football game against her school's biggest rival. Win or lose, after the game there'd be a big bonfire. Guess she'd be missing all that too. Well, what did it matter? She had no one to go with anyhow. She couldn't really blame the few friends she used to hang out with for not wanting to include her when she always turned down their invitations to go places and do things with them. Even after-school clubs like being on the yearbook staff, which she wouldn't have minded joining, were out of the question now. Nicole always had to get home right away, do several chores, and of course, get dinner going before Dad got there.

Nicole rubbed her forehead and heaved a sigh. Becoming a cheerleader was an even bigger pipe dream—a far-fetched hope that would never come true.

She jumped when Dad placed his hand on her shoulder. "You know, your brother and sister could be right. Taking some cooking classes might be a good idea, Nicole."

Her eyes narrowed. "You're kidding, right?"

He shook his head. "It might be fun and even good for you. I think I'll start looking around to see if there are any classes being offered in our area."

Lips pressed together, Nicole slunk down in her chair. She hoped if Dad did start looking, he'd come up empty-handed, because the last thing she wanted to do was take cooking classes, with some stranger telling her what to do. Besides, when would she have time for that? Nicole was already on overload.

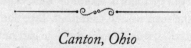

Canton, Ohio

Kendra gripped the grocery cart, as she pushed it down the baby aisle. Since moving in with her parents, she'd tried to make good use of her time and help wherever, and whenever, she could. Her mother needed a few groceries, so Kendra had volunteered to go—if for no other reason, than to get out of the house for a while. Now, she wondered if it had been such a good idea.

Since early this morning, she'd been having what she thought might be the early stages of labor. A dull, persistent pain throbbed through her lower back, but not bad enough to stop her from doing anything. Kendra wanted to keep mobile and stay busy, to help keep her mind off things, and grocery shopping would do just that.

As the time drew closer to her due date, Kendra grew increasingly apprehensive. What was labor like, and how long would it last? Could she withstand the pain? Would she have any complications? Would her baby be born healthy? Kendra had all the normal questions of a first-time mother, but she had even more important things to ponder. *Did I make the right decision to move back home? Would it have been better for my child to be raised by the Troyers and not under my parents' influence? Mom can be so spineless, and Dad. . . Well, he's impossible to please most of the time. He may have invited me back, but I don't think he's ever forgiven me for bringing shame on my family.*

Already, Kendra's folks had been suggesting things they thought would be best for their first grandchild. But Kendra

23

did not commit to anything. She placed her hand on her stomach. "This is still my baby, and I have the final say, no matter what Mom and Dad might suggest," she huffed under her breath. Kendra kept walking when a shopper looked quizzically at her.

"Didn't you ever talk to yourself?" Kendra mumbled low enough so the man wouldn't hear her. Then she stopped at the diaper section, which took up a large part of the shelves. Kendra didn't realize how many selections there would be, and how many different brands of disposable diapers were available for purchase. It was a bit mind-boggling.

Pulling an envelope from her purse, Kendra flipped through the coupons inside to see if any hadn't expired yet. "Oh good." She took out a dollar-off coupon. "Here's one I can use." Thankfully, this store carried the brand, and she could save a dollar, at least. After realizing she'd need to buy two packs of diapers to qualify for the coupon, Kendra made room in the cart to put them. When she grabbed the second pack off the shelf, a sharp pain stabbed from her lower back all the way to the front of her swollen middle.

Grasping her stomach, the pack of diapers fell, and she shuffled over to her cart to hang on. At the same time, a young woman, who was also pregnant, but not as big as Kendra, stopped to see if she needed any help.

"Are you okay?" the kindly lady asked. She picked up the diapers and placed them in Kendra's cart.

"I—I think so." Kendra remained still until the pain subsided. "It's not my due date yet, and I'm hoping these aren't labor pains I've been having."

"By the way, my name's Delana." The woman rubbed her stomach. "I'm not due until the beginning of December, but in the last maternity class I attended, we learned about false labor. Do you think that's what you might be having?"

"I'm not sure. I've had a backache all morning." Kendra reached around and rubbed the small of her back. "But then, since I've grown larger, my back always hurts, so who knows?"

"Okay, well, maybe you'd better finish your shopping and get back home, just to be on the safe side," Delana suggested. "Would you like me to call your husband or someone else?"

"No, that's okay. I only live about fifteen minutes from here." No way would Kendra admit to a stranger that she had no husband. Her situation was no one's business but her own. Kendra hadn't even bothered to introduce herself—not even after the woman had said her name.

"Well, if you're sure." Delana hesitated a minute. "It was nice talking to you, and good luck."

"Same to you." Kendra pointed to the diapers in her cart. "Thanks for assisting me."

"Sure, no problem." Delana moved on.

Looking at her mother's list, Kendra headed for the frozen food aisle. *Let's see. . . Mom wants four packages of mixed vegetables.* This morning, her mother had mentioned wanting to make soup for supper. Luckily the store was having a sale on a well-known brand this week. *Ten packages for ten dollars. Sounds like a good deal.*

As Kendra held the freezer door open to get the frozen vegetables, another pain, worse than the last one, made her scream. This time, the cart's support did no good, and she doubled over and crouched on the floor, barely able to deal with the pain. By this time, several patrons gathered around, including the young pregnant woman she'd spoke to minutes ago.

Delana didn't ask any questions. She got out her cell phone and called 911. An older woman took her sweater and bunched it up to make a pillow for Kendra's head. "There, there dear, lie down on the floor and try to relax. Help will be here soon."

By then, Delana had made the call and hunkered down next to Kendra, taking her hand and patting it gently. "Looks like you might be having your baby a little sooner than you expected. Just breathe deeply and think positive thoughts. The paramedics will be here soon."

Delana looked up at the other people gawking at Kendra, and said, "She'll be okay. The ambulance is on the way. No need to hover all around. Please, just give her some space."

A few people hesitated, but then they finally dispersed and went about their shopping.

When only Delana and the older woman were kneeling beside Kendra, she didn't feel quite so intimidated.

Delana leaned closer. "I never got your name."

"It–it's Kendra." She tried to get up, but the older lady told her to stay put.

"But the pain is gone now, and I feel okay. My water hasn't even broken yet, so I don't think the baby's coming right away."

"Still, you should get checked out." Delana placed her hand on Kendra's shoulder. "What if you were driving home and had another bad contraction? You don't want to have an accident and get hurt or injure the baby."

"I guess you are right," Kendra relented, even though the floor was hard and uncomfortable.

As she remained there, trying not to think about her situation and willing herself to relax, Kendra looked toward the end of the aisle. For a fleeting moment she saw a man who'd been looking her way, turn quickly and scurry around the corner.

Was that Dad? If it was, then why didn't he come see if I was okay?

Millersburg

Later that evening, Nicole reclined on her bed, working on a math assignment. She laughed out loud, thinking about her dad's silly idea of her taking a cooking class. "I can't believe he'd even suggest such a thing."

Soon, her bedroom door opened, and Heather walked in. "I heard you laughing. What's so funny in here?" She flopped on the end of Nicole's bed.

Nicole rolled over and sat up, swinging her legs over the side of the bed. "You heard me laugh?"

Her sister gave a nod. "Were you talkin' to yourself too?"

"Yeah. I was thinking about Dad saying I should take a cooking class. Can you imagine me doing something like that?"

Heather shrugged. "It's not a bad idea, you know. We get tired of eating the same old things all the time."

"You can take over for me anytime you want." Nicole stretched her arms over her head. "It's not easy being in my shoes, you know."

"It's been hard for all of us since Mom left." Heather's chin quivered. "I wish she'd come back, Nicki."

Nicole gave a quick shake of her head, choosing not to make an issue of her sister calling her Nicki. "Not with her drinking problem, Heather. That's what got her messed up in the first place." Her gaze flicked up. "Besides, she's married to someone else now." *And he's a big creep,* she mentally added.

Heather sniffed. "Don't know why she'd want to leave Dad. He's a great guy, don't you think?"

"Absolutely. He works hard and does the best he can for us. We're lucky to have a dad like him." Nicole gave her sister's arm a pat. "You'd better get ready for bed, and I need to finish my homework."

"Okay." Heather scooched off the bed. "See you in the morning."

Nicole smiled. "Yep. I'll have your cold cereal ready and waiting."

Her sister paused at the door and wrinkled her nose. "If Dad can afford it, I think you'd better take a cooking class." Heather hurried out of the room before Nicole could form a response.

Nicole picked up her math book and stuffed it in her backpack next to the bed. She was too tired to do any more problems. If she got up early tomorrow maybe she could finish then.

Yawning, she stretched out on the bed again and closed her eyes. A vision of her mother popped into her head—scraggly blond hair she sometimes wore pulled back in a ponytail, and blue eyes often rimmed with red. *Why'd you have to ruin things between you and Dad? How come you chose your new husband over us? He's not even a nice man.*

Chapter 3

Walnut Creek

The sun's announcement of morning cast an orange tint to the dimly lit kitchen, where only a small, battery-operated lamp had been turned on. "You look *mied*, Heidi." Lyle poured himself a second cup of coffee and took a seat at the kitchen table. "Are you sure you're feeling up to teaching a cooking class this morning? We can still go out to supper this evening, but maybe you should take it easy the rest of the day."

Heidi yawned. "I didn't sleep well last night, but I'll be fine."

"Did you have a bad dream?" He added a spoonful of sugar to his cup and stirred it around.

Heidi poured hot water over her tea bag and sat in the chair across from him. "*Jah*. It wasn't really bad though—just unsettling."

"What was it about?"

"Kendra's *boppli*. Only in the dream, the baby was ours. At least it seemed that way. She was beautiful, Lyle, with golden hair, so soft and downy." Heidi lowered her head and massaged the back of her sore neck. "We were in the nursery with her. I watched while you held the precious infant tenderly in your arms. You wore your Sunday clothes, and I needed to finish getting ready for church. It was our first service with the baby. I was thrilled to show her to everyone."

29

Heidi lifted her head and looked at Lyle. Sympathy showed on his face as he lightly stroked her forearm. "All at once, we were at church," she continued. "I sat on a wooden bench, holding the baby and singing a hymn from the Ausbund. Then I noticed a woman I'd never met before, sitting next to me. She leaned over, and whispering, asked what I had named the baby." Heidi paused and took a sip of the herbal tea, then set her cup down. "I stammered and hesitated with what to say, not knowing what the infant's name even was. I looked across the room, where you sat beside your friend Eli, hoping to get your attention, but that didn't work."

Her brows furrowed. "I excused myself to the woman and rushed out of the barn where the service was being held. Holding the boppli close, I gulped in some air." Perspiration beaded on Heidi's cheeks, remembering the stress she'd felt in the dream. "The next thing I knew, there was no baby. I was standing in our kitchen with my first cooking class. Kendra was there, wearing an apron, like my other students. Smiling, she stepped up to me and asked what we'd named the baby. My jaw dropped. We still hadn't named her yet." Heidi began rubbing her neck again. "Then I woke up."

"Sounds like quite a strange *draame* you had." Lyle took over massaging her neck. "No wonder my *fraa* seems deprived of her rest. After having such a night of strange dreaming, who wouldn't be?" His tone was gentle and soothing. "Once more I have to ask—are you sure you're up to teaching the class today?"

"I'm tired, but I'll be able to teach my students." Heidi released a lingering sigh. "I have to follow through with this, Lyle. Five people have signed up for my class, and I won't let them down." Squinting her eyes, she turned to face him. "Besides, as I recall, it was your suggestion that I teach another group of students."

"True." He took a sip of coffee and set his mug down. "But I could have been wrong. You might not feel up to it yet."

"I'm fine physically, and keeping busy will help to ward off my depression." She glanced toward the door leading to the hall and grimaced. "It's still hard for me to look at the empty room that would have been our baby's nursery without thinking about Kendra and how she went back on her word. It seems so unfair."

He touched her hand. "But can you really blame her? Kendra's back with her folks again, and you were praying for that."

"Jah." Heidi pushed away from the table. "I wonder if she's had her baby yet."

"Didn't she promise to let us know?"

She gave a slow nod. "Maybe she changed her mind about notifying us, the way she did about giving us the boppli. Guess I'm overreacting. The baby's not due until next month."

"Well, October is only about two weeks away." Lyle left his chair and pulled Heidi into his arms, gently patting her back. "I'm sure Kendra or someone from her family will give us a call after the baby is born."

"Maybe so. I hope you're right." Heidi tried to remain positive. It wasn't in her nature to carry a grudge or think negative thoughts, but she hadn't fully come to grips with them losing out on the opportunity to become parents. Somehow, she would need to work through it, though, and the only way she could think to do it was to stay busy and keep her focus on something else.

Heidi glanced at the clock on the wall near the stove. In one hour her new students would arrive, and then she'd have something else to concentrate on.

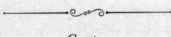

Canton

Grabbing his notebook and pen, Todd Collins rushed out the front door of his condo. Today he was going to test the limits of his palate—or at the very least, attempt something he hadn't tried before. As a food critic, Todd had learned to try almost any food he came across, no matter how strange or foreign it might seem. He'd been in many different restaurants—Italian, Chinese, Mexican, and several others, critiquing countless entrées and various meals. Some small, ordinary places served delicious dishes, while some high-end locations were not so good. Todd had even traveled to food festivals and become obsessive in his search for new food trends and ideas. He'd also researched other food critics and chefs, and taken a few cooking classes as well. Today, however, Todd was about to embark on something unique.

Normally, when he was critiquing a restaurant, Todd had to go incognito—never meeting the owners or getting to know them personally. A few times, however, he'd introduced himself and even made a few acquaintances. This morning, though, he could just be himself, as he was sure no one would recognize him. Besides, even with other people there taking the class, he didn't plan to broadcast his profession. It would be better that way, since the Amish teacher might be offended if she thought someone was critiquing her. And she probably wouldn't like it if she knew Todd eventually planned to write an article for his column about his experience of taking a cooking class in an Amish home.

I'm not really being dishonest, acting like a dumb schmuck who can hardly boil water. That part is actually true. I can say, however, that I'm one of the best at discerning good food from bad. Tasting all kinds of fare that I hope to write about is my goal with the job I currently have.

Todd kicked a stone with the toe of his shoe as he approached his flashy red car. He stood close to the side mirror, gazing at his reflection. *I'm not such a bad guy, really. Just misunderstood, that's all. It's an Amish lady teaching the cooking classes, and those attending with me are probably a bunch of little old ladies who are bored and need something to do. There's no way Heidi Troyer will know who I am or figure out the reason I signed up for her class.*

New Philadelphia, Ohio

Allie Garrett had never been a morning person, and rushing around to get the kids ready to drop off at the babysitter's only added to her frustration today. Nola, age five, and Derek, who was nine, had been pokey eating breakfast, and now sat in the backseat of Allie's minivan squabbling over some nonsensical thing. Allie was tempted to pull over and have Derek move to the third seat, all the way in the back of the van, but she was running late and didn't want to stop and take the time to separate the two. Her kids would just have to work things out themselves.

She blew out an exasperated breath. *Such things kids find to quarrel about.* The latest, being the pull-down arm rest between her daughter and son, which somehow had become a boundary line. When one had even a finger on the other's side, the bickering instantly flared up, and a shoving of hands and arms followed. Then, every time Derek said something, his sister mimicked him, which only made things worse.

Resisting the temptation to scold them, Allie clasped the wheel even tighter, and concentrated on the road ahead. She hoped by ignoring their childish attempts to win out, they would eventually quit.

She looked forward to attending Heidi Troyer's cooking class today, if for no other reason than to get away from the children for a few hours. She was a devoted mother and loved

33

Nola and Derek very much, but sometimes they got on her nerves. One of the reasons could be because Allie worked as a receptionist for a pediatric dentist and had to deal with whiny children four days a week. But the biggest reason Allie felt overwhelmed when her kids acted up was because she shouldered most of the responsibility for their care. Her husband, Steve, was a policeman and worked odd hours, so he often wasn't around when Nola and Derek were home. To make matters worse, Steve frequently filled in for others on the force when they needed time off.

Allie felt like a widow sometimes, and knowing how dangerous his job was, she worried she might become one. Any time the phone rang at odd hours, her fears heightened, and she always thought the worst.

Pulling up to the babysitter's house, Allie turned off the engine and went around to the side of the van to let the children out, thankful they had finally settled down. It was fortunate for Mrs. Andrews, their babysitter, who never hesitated to report how well her children got along. *Why is it that kids are usually on their best behavior for someone else?* Allie wondered.

Switching mental gears, Allie thought about the cooking classes her husband had paid for on her behalf. If nothing else came from taking the classes, at least she would learn how to cook some traditional Amish meals, and it might even prove to be fun. Maybe she would come away with some new ideas for what to fix for supper. Steve might be impressed with her cooking—at least on the evenings he was home and could join her and the children at the table. It had been some time since he'd complimented Allie on anything she'd made. Maybe the gift of the classes was his way of letting her know she needed to improve her cooking skills. Either that, or Steve wanted her to do something fun and creative so she'd stop complaining about him being gone so often. Well, no matter the reasons, she was committed to giving these classes a try.

Dover, Ohio

Lisa Brooks stood in front of the bathroom mirror, staring at her dark circles and red-rimmed eyes, accentuated by her fair skin. In addition to meeting with a client about the five-tiered cake, as well as the meal she would be catering for the couple's wedding reception next week, she'd stayed up late last night, reading a book she'd recently bought about the Amish culture. Since Lisa would be attending a cooking class this morning, taught by an Amish woman, it was a good idea to learn what she could about their lifestyle. The last thing she wanted to do was embarrass herself by saying or doing something foolish or that went against the teacher's customs and religious beliefs.

One thing Lisa had been surprised to learn was that some Amish who lived in Holmes County, Ohio, had installed solar panels in their homes. She wondered if Heidi Troyer's house had the advantage of solar power. It would certainly make it easier to cook meals and run appliances. She couldn't imagine trying to operate her catering business without the advantage of electricity.

The more she'd read, the more intrigued Lisa became with the way this group of Plain people lived. She couldn't believe they had no electrical appliances in their homes or that they used gas lanterns or battery-operated devices in the evenings for lighting. *How amazing!* Lisa scratched her head. *They seem almost like pioneers in our modern day. And yet, this Amish lady can still give cooking classes.*

Lisa hoped to learn some things about Amish cooking during the six classes and incorporate them in some of the meals she offered to her clients. She couldn't say her business was booming, but over time and through word of mouth, Lisa trusted her income from the catering business would increase. She did advertise in the local paper but intended to branch out to papers in neighboring towns. Or perhaps she would create a website, if she could find someone to help her design it.

Lisa picked up the comb and ran it through her short blond hair. Regardless of how tired she looked, it was time to go.

Chapter 4

Walnut Creek

Lisa gripped the steering wheel and studied the mailboxes as she watched for Heidi Troyer's address. Approaching the right one, she jumped when a horn honked from behind. "What in the world?" She glanced in the rearview mirror and saw a flashy-looking red sports car following much too close.

Signaling her intent to go left, Lisa turned up the driveway. The other vehicle did the same. She was about to pull in next to a pickup truck, when the sports car zipped past her and took the spot.

Lisa gritted her teeth. *What's wrong with that driver, cutting me off like that? And in someone's driveway, no less! Whoever it is, they don't seem to care about anybody but themselves.*

She found another place to park, and when she got out of the van, Lisa had to force her mouth to keep from saying something she might later regret. The sports-car driver had also exited his vehicle and was walking toward the house. He paused and turned to look at her. "Guess I was a little quicker than you. Sorry about that." He motioned to his fancy car. "That baby gets me where I want to go."

Lisa nearly had to bite her tongue to keep from saying anything sharp to the belligerent man. She trailed behind him as he hurried toward the house, like a little kid needing to be first. She had to admit the guy was quite handsome. He was tall, dark-haired, and wore a pair of navy blue dress slacks, a crisp pale blue shirt, and black well-polished shoes. He walked with a purpose and an air of confidence. Lisa envied him for that, because at the moment, her stomach felt as though it were tied in knots.

As she reached up to touch her short strands, Lisa couldn't help staring at his thick, slightly curly hair. *What some girls wouldn't give for a head of hair like that.* This man was well-groomed from head to toe, and not a hair on his head looked out of place.

As he approached the porch, he turned again, this time glancing over his shoulder, and gave a stiff nod in her direction. She forced a smile she didn't really feel, and followed him onto the porch. *I hope this fellow, wearing heavy cologne, isn't here for the reason I am. What would a guy like him be doing at a cooking class anyway? Or maybe he's not here for that. He could be selling something, I suppose.*

Heidi had let Bill Mason into the house a few minutes ago, and now someone else was knocking on her door. She told Bill to take a seat in the kitchen, then stepped into the entryway and opened the door. Heidi shook hands with a young, dark-haired man and a pretty woman with blond hair after they entered the house.

She looked a little closer at the woman, and noticed faint dark circles under her appealing blue eyes. Heidi wondered if the young woman may have had trouble sleeping. She tapped a finger against her chin. *One thing for sure, if I can put others ahead of myself, maybe I'll be too occupied to focus on my own discomfort. I wonder what I'll learn from this group of students.* Teaching her previous set of students had felt like finding hidden treasures, the way some of them shared from their past, present, or what they hoped for in the future. Each session Heidi had taught so far seemed interesting in its own way; especially when her pupils caught on to whatever she was teaching them to make and gained confidence in their abilities. Deep down, Heidi was glad her husband had suggested she teach cooking classes in their home. It had been as meaningful to her as it was to her students.

"I'm Heidi Troyer. As soon as the other students get here I'll ask everyone to introduce themselves." She gestured to the door leading to the kitchen. "Please go in and make yourselves comfortable." Heidi picked up the clipboard from her desk and put a check mark next to the name of each person who had arrived.

"Okay, thank you." The young woman stepped quickly in front of the man and hurried into the other room, fanning her crimson cheeks with one hand.

The man mumbled something under his breath and followed.

I wonder if these two know each other. Heidi's lips compressed. *Could there be some kind of problem between them? I hope things don't start off on the wrong foot for this class. I'm not up to dealing with any issues today.*

After hearing another vehicle pull in, Heidi opened the door again. A teenage girl with short brown hair got out of a dark blue car. The man driving the vehicle waved and headed out of the yard. With shoulders hunched, the girl walked hesitantly up the path and onto the porch.

Heidi smiled and extended her hand. "You must be Nicole, my youngest student."

"Yeah, that's me. Hope I'm not late."

Heidi shook her head. "Three others are already inside, but I'm still waiting for another woman to arrive." She opened the door for Nicole, and they both went into the house. Heidi led the way to the kitchen and asked Nicole to take a seat at the table. She was pleased the young lady had signed up. Most of Heidi's students were a bit older, like the ones who had already arrived.

Glancing at the clock across the room, she realized it was

five minutes after ten. Heidi was about to suggest everyone go ahead and introduce themselves, when a knock sounded at the door. She excused herself and went to answer it.

A lovely, dark-haired woman waited on the porch. "Are you here for the cooking class?"

"Yes. I'm Allie Garrett, and I am sorry for being late. I had to drop my kids off at the sitters, and then..." She paused and drew a quick breath. "My GPS wasn't picking up signals for a time, so until I saw the address on your mailbox, I thought I might be lost."

"It's okay." Heidi placed her hand on Allie's arm. "You're only a few minutes late, and we haven't yet begun."

"Oh good. That's a relief."

She led the way to the kitchen, and after Allie took a seat, Heidi stood at the head of the table. Her stomach quivered with nervous apprehension, which made no sense. This wasn't the first class she'd ever taught. Maybe it was the students' somber expressions that caused her nerves to flare up. The teenage girl avoided eye contact; the dark-haired woman picked at her cuticles; the young man dressed in clothes nice enough for church glanced around the room as though checking things out; the blond-haired woman fingered her gold-chained necklace; and the older man with partially gray hair kept looking at his watch. She hoped they weren't already bored. Or maybe everyone felt as nervous as she did right now.

Heidi cleared her throat and moistened her parched lips with her tongue. "Hello, everyone. I'm Heidi Troyer. Welcome to my cooking class. Before we begin, did everyone remember to bring an apron?"

Lisa, Allie, and Todd held up their aprons, but Nicole shook her head. "Didn't know I was supposed to bring one."

"Me neither," Bill mumbled.

"It was on your registration form," Heidi explained.

"I didn't see it. Dad filled out the paper for me, since coming here was his idea," Nicole said.

Bill's forehead wrinkled. "Guess I missed the part about the apron too."

"Well, don't worry about it. I have extra ones you can both use today." Heidi opened a drawer and took out two aprons. She handed the green one to Nicole, and the blue apron she gave to Bill. Then she returned to her spot at the head of the table. "Now I'd like everyone to introduce themselves and tell us the reason you signed up for this class." She gestured to the blond-haired woman. "Would you mind going first?"

"No, of course not." The young woman sat up a little straighter, as though gaining more confidence. "My name is Lisa Brooks. I have a catering business, and I'm taking this class to broaden my cooking skills." She turned to the dark-haired man sitting beside her. "You're next."

"Yeah, okay. My name's Todd Collins, and. . ." He paused and pulled his fingers down the side of his clean-shaven face. "Umm. . .I enjoy eating different kinds of food, so the reason I'm here is to taste, and hopefully learn how to cook, some traditional Amish dishes."

Heidi smiled, motioning to the older man who'd arrived first.

He pushed his chair aside and stood. "My name's Bill Mason, and I'm here to learn how to cook something other than hunter's stew." With no further word or explanation, he returned to his chair.

Heidi gestured to the teenage girl. "Would you please tell us your name and the reason you came to my class?"

"I'm Nicole Smith, and like I said before, my dad signed me up for the class. Guess he figured I should learn how to make something other than cold sandwiches and frozen microwave dinners. He and Tonya got a divorce, so all the cooking and cleaning falls on me now." Nicole's lips curled, and her tone sounded tart. "I'm also stuck taking care of my little brother and sister."

"Was Tonya your stepmother?" Lisa asked.

"Nope. Tonya's my real mom."

"Oh, I see." Lisa lifted her gaze to the ceiling, before looking away.

Heidi's heart went out to Nicole. It had to be hard for her, living without her mother and shouldering the responsibility for taking care of her siblings. It surprised her, though, that the teenage girl would refer to her mom by her first name.

"I guess that leaves me now." The dark-haired woman who'd been last to arrive pushed an unruly strand of hair away from her slender oval face. "My name is Allie Garrett, and as a birthday present, my husband gave me a gift certificate to take this class. He said he thought it would be something fun for me to do. I agreed to take it because I hoped I might learn how to make some different dishes for my husband and our two children." She gestured to Heidi. "Do you have any kids?"

Heidi swallowed hard. She'd hoped this touchy subject wouldn't come up today. Every time someone asked if she had children, it felt as though her heart had been pierced with an arrow. "No, my husband and I have not been able to have any children."

"Oh, that's a shame." Allie's tone was soothing, and Heidi feared if she didn't change the subject right away, she might give in to her tears, which always seemed to be just below the surface. Crying was certainly the last thing she wanted to do in front of her new group of students.

"All right then, that's enough about me." Heidi clasped her hands together. "I hope you will all enjoy the class. And now, let's begin, as I share with you a few helpful hints about cooking."

"What are we gonna learn how to cook?" Bill leaned forward with his elbows on the table.

Allie resisted the temptation to roll her eyes. *Does the*

man have to be so impatient? He should at least give the teacher a chance to speak.

"The recipe I'm going to teach you how to make this morning is baked oatmeal. But first, I'd like to give you a few handouts with some tips for the kitchen." Heidi passed out a sheet of paper to each of them. "Before you all go home today I'll give everyone a three-by-five card with the recipe you learned to make this morning."

"Good thing, 'cause with the way my brain's been workin' lately, I'd probably forget everything you told us by the time I got home." Grinning, Bill's gaze traveled from person to person sitting around the table.

Allie studied the first handout Heidi gave them. It listed everything from how to keep hot oil from splattering out of the frying pan, to the best way to store dried pasta, rice, and whole grains. There was also a tip about how to get onion odor off your hands, but with the exception of that, most of the other things she knew already, since she'd been cooking since she was a teenager.

While Heidi offered some measuring tips, Allie shifted in her chair as an unexpected image of Steve flashed before her. He'd worked all night, and by the time she left for the babysitter's, her husband still hadn't come home. *Is he okay? Has Steve been hurt in the line of duty?* Allie was accustomed to Steve not always being able to get in touch with her. Many times his duties became hectic, and he often came home late. It was difficult not to worry about him.

She squeezed her eyes shut. *Get a grip; you've had these worrisome thoughts before, and Steve's been okay. Just relax and keep your concentration on learning how to make baked oatmeal.*

Chapter 5

Baked oatmeal? Eyes narrowed, Todd tugged at his shirt collar. *I signed up for this class to learn about Amish cooking, not bake oatmeal of all things. Besides, who ever heard of baking oatmeal? It's supposed to be cooked on the stove in a kettle or even microwaved in a bowl.*

He glanced at the others as they looked expectantly at Heidi while she told how to combine the eggs, sugar, and butter in a baking dish, and then add the oatmeal, baking powder and salt, stirring until blended. Everyone but Allie seemed interested. She sat rubbing her forehead while staring at the kitchen table. *Maybe she's as bored as I am. Hopefully the recipes Heidi shares during the next five classes will be more interesting than today's.*

Todd looked across the table at Lisa. She glanced at him briefly, then looked away. Since she was in the catering business, she'd obviously come here to get some new meal ideas. It was nice to know he wasn't the only one with an agenda.

He studied Lisa a few seconds—shiny blond hair, vivid blue eyes, and deep dimples in both cheeks. Her only flaw was the dark circles encompassing her eyes. Todd tried not to stare at Lisa; he didn't want to appear nosey, but he'd like to know a little more about her. Other than an interest in food, he didn't know if they had anything in common. *I wonder if she's married.* He glanced at her left hand and saw no wedding ring. She'd made no mention of a husband or children, either.

"Mr. Collins, did you hear what I said?"

Todd's head jerked as he turned his focus back to the Amish teacher. "Uh. . .no, I guess not. Would you mind repeating it for me?"

"I asked if you're ready to start mixing the ingredients for your baked oatmeal now." Heidi gestured to the bowl and mixing spoon sitting on the table in front of him.

Todd noticed the others had also been given a bowl and large spoon. He figured from their impatient expressions, they were all waiting on him. "Yeah, sure. I'm ready to begin." Todd slid his bowl closer to Lisa's, hoping to engage her in conversation. He hoped she wouldn't think he was being too forward. Todd watched as the others began measuring and putting the ingredients in their bowls. Lisa did the same, appearing confident and happy with the pleasant smile she wore. Todd tried to copy what she did, but ended up bumping her arm, causing Lisa to add too much oatmeal.

"Oops, sorry about that. I'm not used to sharing a work space like this." Todd's face heated. He wasn't off to a good start this morning—at least not with Lisa.

Her eyes narrowed. "Well, if you weren't sitting so close."

He moved to one side, pulling his bowl with him. "Don't worry. It won't happen again."

"It's not a problem, Lisa," Heidi spoke up. "Since you haven't added any liquid yet, you can just scoop out the excess oatmeal."

"Okay." Lisa did as Heidi suggested, giving Todd a side-long glance. He wanted to say something more to her but figured it'd be best to keep silent for now.

Before Allie began mixing the ingredients Heidi had given her, she pulled her cell phone out of her purse. No voice mails or text messages, so everything must be okay with Steve. No doubt she'd conjured up the earlier vision of him unnecessarily, believing he might be in some sort of trouble. Worry was a difficult habit to break.

Determined to keep her focus on the job at hand, Allie returned the phone to her purse, picked up the first egg, and cracked it into the bowl. If the baked oatmeal turned out good, she would make it for her family someday.

As she mixed the ingredients, Allie's thoughts went to Nola and Derek. *I hope they're behaving for Mrs. Andrews today.*

Allie was about to pour the runny oatmeal mixture into the small baking dish Heidi had provided, when Bill bumped her arm. Everything in her bowl spilled onto the table. She gasped, then glared at him. "I see Todd's not the only one sitting too close to someone at this table. I hope you're planning to clean up this mess."

Red-faced, Bill gave a quick nod. "Sorry about that. You're right; I shouldn't have been sitting so close."

"I guess not." Allie glanced down at her white blouse and peach-colored maxi-skirt. "It's a good thing none of it got on my clothes." A trickle of perspiration rolled down her cheek.

"Not to worry." Heidi hurried to the sink and grabbed a sponge, as well as a dish towel. "Bill, while you are cleaning the table, I'll get out some more ingredients for Allie to mix."

Allie almost said, "Don't bother, I'm going home," but she wouldn't waste the money Steve had spent for her to take the Amish woman's cooking classes. So she forced herself to smile and said, "Thanks, I'll try to hurry mixing the ingredients so I don't hold up the class."

Heidi glanced at the clock before handing Bill the towel and sponge. "We have plenty of time left before our class ends, so don't worry about holding us up, Allie." She hoped nothing else went awry today. Her nerves were already jangled, but for the sake of her students, she had to remain calm and keep a positive attitude. When the class was over, and everyone went home, she planned to check their phone shack for messages, then lie on the couch and take a nap. Lyle wouldn't be home until suppertime, so she had all afternoon to relax and do whatever she pleased.

Once the table was cleaned, and Allie's ingredients were mixed and poured into her baking dish, Heidi explained the baking process. "Since the oatmeal mixture needs to bake for thirty minutes, and I only have one oven, three of you can put yours in now. While we wait for them to bake, I'll answer questions any of you may have."

"Sounds good to me." Bill lifted his hand. "I have a lot of questions."

After several attempts to ask Heidi questions, and Todd putting his "two cents' worth" in, Bill gave up. *If this Todd guy knows so much, why is he taking this class? Maybe he should be the one teaching the class, instead of Heidi.*

Bill turned his attention to Nicole, who had been rather quiet during the class so far. A few times, he had caught her staring at him, but when he made eye contact with Nicole, she quickly averted her gaze. She was obviously the youngest in this group, perhaps even high-school age. There was something familiar about the girl, but Bill couldn't put his finger on it. Could it be that she attended the high school where he worked? Maybe she was a student there. But after working as a maintenance man all these years, the students became a sea of faces walking down the halls.

For almost thirty years Bill had been working at the school in Millersburg. He'd started out as a janitor, but along with that, he was taught other duties as well. This enabled him to be promoted to the position of managing maintenance. Of course, the men under him weren't the ones doing all the work at the school. Bill worked right alongside of them, and sometimes alone, when the need arose.

Manager. . .humph. . .a lot of good that title has done for me. His wife, Mona, now his ex, left him for someone else—a man she considered better.

Bill remembered how, during all the years they were married, his wife had been embarrassed about his job. When someone asked what her husband did for a living, she would answer, "He works at the school." This evasion succeeded for a while, especially when their son, Brent, was young. Most of his wife's friends assumed he was a teacher, until their own kids grew up and attended high school. Then they caught on. Some of Mona's acquaintances teased her about it and drifted away from the friendship, while others remained loyal and didn't seem to care what Bill did for a living. Still, when anyone turned their nose up, Mona had been affected deeply.

Bill's pay was decent, and they'd always had money to meet their bills, but it wasn't good enough for Mona. She left and married this so-called better man named Floyd. He was the owner of a huge equipment company, and they lived high-off-the-hog, so Bill hoped Mona was finally happy.

One day, Bill had made the mistake of driving by Floyd and Mona's house. It was huge, in a prominent neighborhood on the other side of town. *I hope they stay on their side of town.* Bill ground his teeth together, reflecting on how he'd felt at that moment. So far, even though he'd seen Mona on a few occasions involving their son, he'd been lucky not to cross paths when she'd been with her new husband. Bill wondered if he'd ever find love again, or if he could reach the point where he could trust another woman. It would be nice to have someone waiting for him when he got home from work. On the other hand, since the divorce, he'd become set in his ways and had come to think he could do things, including cooking, on his own. He really didn't need another wife, or even a lady friend.

Nicole tapped her fingers on the edge of the table. The aroma of food baking whet her appetite. It had been a while since she'd eaten breakfast, and the bowl of cereal she'd had didn't stick to her ribs. Her baking pan was one of the first three to go into the oven, and now the last batch had been put in. Nicole would be glad when they were done and she could go home. The cooking class wasn't as much fun as she'd hoped it would be. But then, maybe that was because she was the only teenager present. Truthfully, she felt out of place here among these strangers. *Too bad I'm not the only student in the class. It would be a lot easier if Heidi could teach just me. I have some questions, but would be embarrassed to ask them in front of the others. They might think I'm stupid.*

She glanced around Heidi's modest, but well-equipped kitchen. Everything appeared neat and in order. Nothing like the kitchen at home after Nicole finished cooking something. It was a lot easier to make a mess in the kitchen than it was to clean it all up. Of course, Nicole's mother had never kept a tidy kitchen. In fact, whenever she'd been drinking, the whole house was neglected.

As though she could sense her frustration, Heidi, who sat beside her now, reached over and touched Nicole's arm. "You've been awfully quiet today. Is there anything in particular you'd like to know?"

"No, not really." Nicole dropped her gaze to the table.

"Okay. If you think of anything, please let me know."

"I'd like to ask you something," Lisa spoke up.

"Certainly." Heidi looked in her direction and smiled. "What would you like to know?"

"Can you tell us a little about the Amish way of life, and why you do without so many modern conveniences?"

"Yeah, I'd like to know that too." Todd winked at Lisa. "In fact, I was about to ask the same question. How come there's no electricity connected to your home?"

Lisa squinted her eyes at him, then looked away. Nicole

had enough smarts to know when someone was flirting, and she had this guy pegged. It wasn't right. For all Todd knew, Lisa was married. She glanced at Lisa's left hand. *Although she's not wearing a wedding ring. I hope she doesn't fall for Todd. I know his kind. He reminds me of the jerk Mom ran off with when she divorced Dad.*

Nicole turned her attention to Heidi as she began to tell the history of the Anabaptists, and how the Amish faith was a breakaway from the Mennonites. She found it interesting when Heidi explained the reason they didn't allow TVs, computers, and many other modern things to run off electricity in their homes. Those items represented a negative distraction that could take their focus off God and family.

Nicole's thoughts went to her mother again and how she used to sit around most of the day drinking while watching soap operas and game shows on TV. When she wasn't doing that, she often hung out at one of the local bars. It was difficult to count all the times Dad had gone after Mom and brought her home in a drunken stupor. Why he hadn't been the one to file for divorce was a question Nicole had asked herself many times. Did Dad love Mom so much that he was willing to overlook the mess she'd created for herself by not seeking help for her drinking problem?

Nicole couldn't remember when her mother had quit taking care of her family or if she ever had been attentive to them. Maybe when she was a baby, and too little to remember. Mom hadn't been there for Tony and Heather, either. Nicole had been responsible for taking care of them several years before her mother left. She clenched her fingers, making a fist. *I hate that woman. She's my mother in name only, and I hope I never have to look at her again.* These days it was easier to refer to her as Tonya, instead of Mom, like her siblings still did. Dad had stressed to Nicole many times that it was wrong to hate anyone and it wasn't good to dwell on the past, but she couldn't let go of her anger. She was glad Tonya had agreed to let Dad have full custody of the children. The thought of spending time with that woman and the creep she'd recently married was enough to turn Nicole's stomach.

"So how long have you been teaching cooking classes, Heidi?" Allie's question drove Nicole's thoughts aside.

"I taught my first set of classes this past summer, so this is only my second group of students."

"How many were in the first classes?" Bill asked.

"Five—same as this time."

"Guess you wouldn't want many more than that or it might get too crazy." Bill gestured to the oven when the timer across the room rang. "Oh, good. My baked oatmeal must be done, along with Todd's." He rose from his chair, but Todd beat him to the stove, jerking open the oven door.

Nicole frowned. *How rude. Who does that man think he is? Todd monopolized much of the conversation when Bill was trying to ask Heidi questions earlier; he winked at Lisa several times; and now this? If I were Bill, I'd put that guy in his place.*

Heidi stood on the front porch, watching as the last vehicle pulled out of her yard. Nicole had been the first to leave, when her father picked her up, and Bill had been the last to go. He was quite a talker, especially when he didn't have to compete with Todd.

Heidi wasn't sure how much anyone had learned today, but at least she'd sent them all home with the recipe for baked oatmeal, as well as a meaningful scripture on the back of the card. She had done the same thing with her previous students. She'd read the verse she shared today during her devotions a few days ago. It dealt with anxiety and fear: "I sought the LORD, and he heard me, and delivered me from all my fears" (Psalm 34:4). Hopefully it would speak to someone's heart this week.

She sighed. *Well, one class is finished, and there are five more to go.* Her next class would be in early October, two weeks from today. Maybe by then Kendra's baby would be born.

Remembering she was going to check for phone messages, Heidi headed down the driveway to the small wooden building. When she stepped inside, she clicked the "message" button on the answering machine.

"Hello, this is Kendra Perkins's mother, and my message is for Heidi Troyer. I'm calling at my daughter's request. She wanted you to know that she gave birth to a baby girl this morning. The infant came a little earlier than expected, but both mother and daughter are doing fine."

Heidi sank onto the metal folding chair, holding both hands against her chest. Her heart felt as if it had been broken in two. She was happy for Kendra, as well as her parents, but, oh, how she wished the baby could be hers—a daughter to raise and cherish. Even though the infant had arrived early, Heidi would have been more than ready to care for the child. Everything had already been purchased for the nursery. Of course, it had all been put away—out of sight, but never far from Heidi's thoughts.

Tears welled in her eyes, and she blinked to keep them from spilling over. No amount of crying would change the fact—Kendra was keeping her baby, and that was that.

Heidi left the phone shack without bothering to listen to the other messages. All she wanted to do was go back to the house and sleep the rest of the afternoon. Tomorrow was Sunday; maybe things would look brighter in the morning.

Chapter 6

Heidi had no more than lain down on the couch to take a nap, when someone knocked on the front door.

Groaning, she rose and went to see who it was. When she opened the door, she discovered their mailman, Lance Freemont, holding a package.

"This was too big to fit in your mailbox, so I brought it on up to the house." As he handed Heidi the package, he leaned forward a bit, sniffing the air. "Say, what smells so good?"

"Oh, it's probably the baked oatmeal my students made during the cooking class I held this morning. Kitchen odors can linger sometimes."

Lance grinned. "Is that so? Didn't realize you taught cooking classes. How long have you been teaching people how to cook?"

"I started my first set of classes in the spring, teaching on Saturdays for six weeks. Today, I began another set of six lessons with new students." She placed the package on the entry table. "The classes aren't necessarily for beginning cooks, however. Some who come to my house already know how to cook but want to learn more about traditional Amish meals."

"I see." A lock of Lance's light brown hair sprinkled with gray, fell across his forehead. "Are the classes always on Saturdays?"

She gave a nod. "Yes, every other Saturday."

"Have you got room for one more student?"

"There are five in the class—and I could include another—but don't you deliver the mail on Saturdays?"

"Sometimes, but my schedule changes, and beginning next week I'll only be working every other Saturday. As luck would have it, I'll be off on the same days you hold classes."

"Well, you're welcome to join the class then, week after next." Heidi quoted the price, taking a little off, since Lance had missed the first day. "When you come in two weeks, I'll give you the recipe for baked oatmeal my students learned to make today."

"That'd be great." There was a twinkle in his hazel-colored eyes she'd never noticed before. "What time does class start?"

"Ten o'clock."

"Can I wait to pay you until then? I'd do it now, but I need to get back on my mail route."

Heidi smiled. "Next class is fine. I'll give you the same form to fill out like my other students received. Also, if you can, you'll need to bring an apron with you." She stepped over to her desk, grabbed a white form and handed it to him. "It has the dates of each class and my phone number, in case you have any questions. Just leave a message, and I'll get back to you."

"Okay, sounds good. I'll see you then." Lance turned, and as he started down the driveway, swinging his arms, he began to whistle.

Heidi covered her mouth to stifle a giggle. Lance's personality would be a good fit with her other students—perhaps balancing out some of their negativity. His positive attitude had helped Heidi feel a little more uplifted than she had after receiving the news that Kendra's baby had been born. She felt sure Lance's jovial spirit would bless her other students too.

I need to send Kendra a congratulations card and maybe get something for the baby. Heidi tapped her chin. It was the least she could do to offer support and let Kendra know there were no hard feelings. Before she'd moved out, the young woman had given Heidi her parents' address and phone number, in case she'd left anything behind or needed to get in touch with her.

Heidi glanced at the package Lance had delivered and wondered who it was from. She hadn't ordered anything, but maybe Lyle had and just forgot to mention it.

She picked up the box and smiled when she saw the return address. It was from her aunt, Emma Miller, who lived in Shipshewana, Indiana.

Heidi took the package to the kitchen and placed it on the table, then sliced the lid open with a paring knife, being careful to avoid damaging whatever was inside.

Pulling the cardboard flaps aside and then removing several layers of white tissue paper, Heidi gasped as she lifted out a beautiful blue-and-white quilt in the ocean waves pattern. A note was pinned to the material. "Happy Anniversary, Heidi and Lyle. Lamar and I wish you many more good years together. Be blessed! Love, Aunt Emma and Lamar."

Tears welled in Heidi's eyes as she clutched the quilt close to her chest. The different shades of blues Aunt Emma selected were perfect. *How thoughtful of my dear aunt to remember today is Lyle's and my ninth wedding anniversary.* They'd gotten cards with money inside from both of their parents yesterday, and they would celebrate the occasion this evening by going out to supper at one of their favorite restaurants. Heidi looked forward to going. Even more so than she had this morning.

Inhaling the aroma from inside the box, Heidi almost felt like she was standing in her aunt's kitchen. *She must have been baking the day she got the package ready to mail, because this quilt smells like cinnamon and other spices.*

Heidi ran her hands over the material, then draped the lovely covering over the kitchen chair. When she picked up the box it had come in, she discovered something else inside. She smiled, lifting out a plastic container, tucked neatly at the bottom. Heidi had a pretty good idea what was inside as she opened the lid and inhaled, delighting in the sweet fragrance wafting up to her nostrils. On top of the plastic wrap was another note from her aunt about the pumpkin cookies she'd made and wanted to share. Heidi pulled up the cellophane and saw over a dozen perfectly shaped cookies lined neatly in small rows.

Think I'll sample one of these right now. Heidi licked her lips, then took a bite of the plump, spicy cookie. *How sweet of Aunt Emma to remember our anniversary by making us a quilt. Such a lovely gift and labor of love. I can hardly wait till Lyle gets here so I can show the beautiful covering for our bed to him.* She looked down at the cookies. *He'll certainly enjoy eating these tasty* kichlin *too.*

New Philadelphia

Allie had only been home a few minutes with the children when she looked out the window and saw Steve's car pull up. Relieved to see that he was okay, she ran to the door and swung it open. The minute her husband stepped inside, Allie threw her arms around his neck and gave him a tight squeeze.

"I appreciate the hug, but you're holding me so firm. Is everything okay?" He patted her back.

"I–I'm fine." She pulled slowly away. "But I've been worried about you today."

Steve's brown eyes darkened further. "How come?"

Her muscles tensed. "How come? Your job is dangerous, Steve, and I had a mental picture of you this morning. It left me feeling as though you had been hurt."

He shook his head slowly. "If anything had happened to me, you'd have been the first to know."

She sighed. "That's a small consolation, dear. I wish you had a desk job, instead of being out on the streets where anything could happen."

He placed his hand on her shoulder and gave it a squeeze. "I'm doing what I feel called to do. You knew that when I decided to get training to become a police officer soon after we were married. You said you were okay with it."

Allie couldn't argue. She wanted her husband to be happy, despite knowing full well his life could be in jeopardy. Here lately, though, with the children growing and needing their father around, Allie had become paranoid about his safety. She'd never make it if something happened to Steve. She counted on him, not just for his financial support but to be there whenever she and the children had a need. She relied on him for moral and emotional support too. Along with their children, Steve was the love of her life.

Allie thought about the verse of scripture Heidi had written on the back of the recipe she'd given them today. "I sought the Lord, and he heard me, and delivered me from all my fears." She squeezed her eyes shut. *Oh, how I want to believe that. If only my fears could vanish like vapor, but I don't need to seek the Lord for that. Maybe the cooking classes I'm taking will help me learn to relax.*

Steve bent and gave Allie a kiss. "Enough about me now. How'd your first cooking class go this morning?"

She opened her eyes and shrugged. "Okay, I guess. We learned how to make baked oatmeal, but I was hoping for something more exciting than that."

"There are five more classes, though, right?"

She gave a slow nod, reaching up to run her fingers through his dark, short-cropped hair.

"No doubt you'll learn to make plenty of other things."

"I hope so. I'd like to be able to fix something Derek and Nola would enjoy."

He quirked an eyebrow and grinned. "You don't think they'd like baked oatmeal?"

She swatted his arm playfully, feeling more relaxed. "What do you think, silly?"

"Speaking of the kids. . . What are they up to this afternoon?"

Allie gestured toward the living room, at the same moment as the children started bickering. "They're watching their favorite cartoons. Or at least they were." She lifted her gaze to the ceiling and groaned.

Steve gave Allie another quick kiss. "Yeah, I hear Nola and Derek now—loud and clear. Think I'll go surprise the kids and join 'em." He wiggled his brows. "I love cartoons."

Allie gave his arm a light tap. "Okay, you big kid. While you're doing that, I'm going to feed Prissy; then I'll make us all a snack."

Allie heard Nola and Derek scream with glee when Steve entered the living room. She smiled and headed for the utility room to take care of the cat. *Those kids sure love their daddy. When I'm done, maybe I'll join Steve and the children for a while. Some microwave popcorn would be a good snack. I'll check to see if there's any left in the cupboard.*

Watching cartoons wasn't exactly Allie's favorite thing to do, but it was always nice to spend time with her family.

Dover

Lisa sat at the kitchen table, drinking a cup of tea while trying to relax. Two weeks until Heidi's next class seemed like a long way off, and she was eager to go again, hoping next time Heidi would share a more exciting recipe. Not that the baked oatmeal was bad; it just wasn't anything she'd be likely to use in her catering business, unless someone hired her to fix a breakfast meal for a special event.

Blaring music caused Lisa to jump. Ever since she'd gotten home from the cooking class, her nerves had been on edge. The renters in the unit attached to her duplex had the volume on their TV up so loud it could be heard through the wall separating her half of the duplex from theirs. When Lisa agreed to let the Browns rent the unit, she'd never expected them to be so noisy. But the loud music was better than listening to Bob and Gail argue—something else Lisa couldn't help overhearing whenever they went at it.

She poked her tongue into her cheek and inhaled a long breath. The young couple had only been married a year, but they had some marital problems that seemed to be getting worse as time went on. She'd been praying for Bob and Gail. Even invited them to attend church with her, but they showed no interest.

A few weeks ago, Gail had asked Lisa if they could get a dog. Nothing was in the contract they'd signed about pets, so Lisa felt she couldn't deny them one of their own. She liked dogs too, and thought at first having one might ease the strain between the couple. Unfortunately, it was wishful thinking. So far, their puppy had done nothing but frustrate Lisa.

When her neighbors were at work, the little thing whined and howled all the time. The poor pup was lonely, and Lisa couldn't help feeling sorry for it—especially when those sorrowful yowls went on and on. It was heartbreaking to hear.

As if that wasn't bad enough, there were times when Lisa noticed her flowerbeds had been messed up. Flowers and stems got broken, and one time she'd seen the remains of a flower lying in the yard on the Browns' side of the duplex. Lisa worried if she approached them about these issues, it would create tension between them as neighbors. They'd always paid their rent on time and spoken politely to Lisa, so she was uncertain what to do.

Lisa loved working in her flowerbeds. Getting her hands into the soil was a source of solace. The colorful mums and marigolds had been blooming so beautifully, until the pup did its damage. This was the last thing she wanted to deal with, and her patience was waning. Maybe it would be better to do some hanging baskets with flowers instead of having them in the flowerbeds. At least the neighbors' new pet couldn't bother those. She would need to figure out how many baskets would work out front, and where they could be hung so no one would run into them. Perhaps she would stop by the hardware store soon to see what was available. Since her renters were obviously not going to get rid of the puppy, she would have to do whatever was necessary to protect her property from damage.

Lisa was reminded of the sermon her pastor had preached last Sunday on how believers should let their light shine so others would see Jesus. She closed her eyes and prayed: *Lord, please help me to set an example so people, like my neighbors, will come to know You personally.*

Chapter 7

Walnut Creek

I sn't this beautiful, Lyle?" Heidi looked down at her aunt's quilt, which she had spread out on their bed the night before after returning from their anniversary meal at Der Dutchman restaurant.

Smiling, Lyle nodded. "There's no doubt about it—your aunt Emma is a gifted quilter. She makes good cookies too."

"Jah. Her thoughtful gift surely added a bright spot to our anniversary." Heidi blinked, hoping no tears would come. "It's hard to admit, but after hearing that Kendra had her baby yesterday, I began to feel sorry for myself again."

Lyle pulled Heidi into his arms, gently rubbing her back. "Would you like me to contact the adoption lawyer again and see if he can find another baby for us to adopt?"

Heidi found comfort in her husband's arms, and even more so in his willingness to adopt. For so long he hadn't even considered it an option for them. She leaned her head against his chest, feeling comfort in his strong arms. "I still want a boppli, but I'm not sure I could handle another disappointment."

"Not every mother who agrees to put her baby up for adoption changes her mind at the last minute, Heidi. We have to trust God to give us the right child."

She pulled away and looked up at him, stroking his bearded face. "You're right; I'm just not ready right now. Maybe we can talk about it again after the first of the year."

She pointed at the clock on the small table beside their bed. "Right now we need to finish getting ready for church. I'm eager to hear what our ministers have to share."

Millersburg

Nicole stepped into the living room, where her dad sat reading the Sunday paper, while Heather and Tony watched TV. "If you don't need me for anything, Dad, I'm going outside for a while."

He looked up and gave a quick shake of his head. "Go right ahead. The three of us are well-entertained."

"Are you comin' back to fix our lunch?" Tony looked over his shoulder.

Nicole grunted. "Is food all you ever think about?"

Heather snickered and bumped her brother's arm. "Before Mom left, she used to say Tony had a hole in his leg 'cause he was always hungry."

Nicole balled her hands into fists. "Of course he was hungry. Tonya neglected all three of her children."

"I've told you before, Nicole—you shouldn't refer to your mother by her first name." Dad reached up and massaged the back of his neck. "It's disrespectful."

Nicole folded her arms, remembering how her mother had shown up at her sixteenth birthday party—drunk as a skunk, and flashing her new engagement ring. "Humph! She was disrespectful to all of us—you most of all, Dad. I can't believe you're defending her."

"I am not defending her. What she did was wrong, but she's still your mother, and—"

"I'm goin' outside now, but I'll be back in time to fix lunch." Nicole whirled around and dashed out of the room.

I don't get Dad. Why doesn't he understand? After all the horrible things Tonya did, he should be angrier than I am. Nicole grabbed her drawing tablet and colored pencils, before going out the back door. When she stepped out, she nearly tripped over her brother's dog, Bowser. The critter lay on the porch in front of the door. She had to admit Bowser was kind of cute. He was part beagle, half mutt, and full of nothing but trouble. Nicole hated it when he got into barking mode, though. Bowser didn't seem to know the meaning of the command, "Be quiet!" *I suppose I should be grateful the mutt's sleeping. Just wish he'd find some place to nap other than by the door.* She couldn't count all the times she'd tripped over the dog when he was dozing on the welcome mat.

"You lazy pooch. Go find someplace else to snooze." Nicole nudged him with the toe of her sneaker.

Bowser merely grunted, then rolled over onto his side. Nicole stepped around him and sprinted toward the back of their property, where their yard met the woods. She didn't get much time alone these days, so it would be nice to be by herself for a while.

She took a seat on a log and placed the drawing tablet in her lap. They'd had a cold snap a few mornings this past week, and some of the leaves were starting to turn. Nicole liked this time of year, when the cooler weather set in. She remembered when she was a child, crunching through the leaves on her way to school during autumn mornings. Now that Nicole was in high school, she caught the bus. The only time she got to frolic in the leaves was after school and on weekends when she had time to be outside, which was rare. It was too bad the leaves didn't stay pretty longer, for it wouldn't be many weeks before the trees would all be bare.

Opening the box of colored pencils, she began sketching a squirrel sitting on a tree branch several feet away. She hoped the little critter would sit still long enough for her to get its outline done. Squirrels could be pretty skittish, so she had to sketch quickly.

Woof! Woof! Woof!

The squirrel leaped to another branch as Bowser came running and nearly slammed into the tree.

"Oh great! So much for a little peace and quiet." Nicole set her drawing aside and clapped her hands. "Go home, Bowser! You're nothing but a pest." She'd never get the drawing of the squirrel down now.

Looking up at the tiny critter, the mutt kept yapping. The squirrel found a different branch, and finally jumped into another tree. Of course it didn't discourage the dog. Nicole covered her ears as the barking continued.

Nicole's lips pressed together, her irritation increasing by the minute. In exasperation, she reached inside the log, where she kept another notebook. This one wasn't for sketching, though. It was a tablet full of letters to her mother. Not nice letters, either, but ones Nicole kept to herself. They were condemning, scolding letters; Nicole's way of getting back at her mother for all the hurt and shame she'd caused their whole family. Nicole had no plans of giving the letters to Tonya, but it made her feel better to write them. She saw it as a way to vent, but without telling anyone her troubles.

From pen to paper, Nicole finished pouring more of her emotions out. After the squirrel escaped through the trees, Bowser came over to where Nicole sat and stood staring up at her. She stared right back at him. *Stupid mutt.*

The dog tipped his head as though he'd heard something. She watched the nutty hound, who now seemed fixated on a nearby hole. Bowser growled and started digging like there was no tomorrow. The mutt appeared frantic as dirt tossed up and onto Nicole's lap. "Hey! Stop doing that, you goofball!" Nicole gritted her teeth.

Bowser, in his doggie state of mind, continued his endeavor until a poor ground mole was withdrawn from its burrow and carted off from sight. The pathetic prey squeaked for its life.

Still holding her writing tablet, Nicole jumped up, chasing after Bowser. "You let that poor critter go!" She waved the notebook several times, and even swatted the dog's behind. Sheepishly, Bowser finally gave in and dropped the mole. It scurried away and back down its hole.

Nicole looked at her tablet, noticing that the binding had given way, and frowned. The papers fluttered to the ground. "Bowser, this is all your fault!" She knelt and picked up the fallen sheets of paper. "Guess I should have let the sleeping dog lie," Nicole muttered.

After she'd claimed everything, Nicole tucked the papers together as best she could and put them back into the log. Then she picked up her drawing tablet and colored pencils. "Come on, mutt, let's go!" Maybe sitting on the back porch to do some sketching would be her best chance for peace and quiet.

When Nicole stepped onto the porch, she discovered Heather's cat, Domino, flaked out on the wooden bench.

"Go on, scat, dumb cat!" She picked up the feline and placed him out on the grass. "Go chase a mouse or find someplace else to sleep. Sure don't need you getting hair all over me."

It might not be right to take her frustrations out on her siblings' pets, but Nicole got tired of the messes they made, not to mention being unable to do anything just for herself. She thought about the cooking classes Dad had signed her up to take. Apparently he believed it was something she would enjoy, but the first class had been boring. And the fact that the Amish woman had written a Bible verse on the back of the recipe card she'd given Nicole only fueled her frustration. She was still angry at God for ignoring her pleas concerning her mother's drinking problem and horrid behavior. All the prayers Nicole had said went unanswered. If there really was a God, He should have done something about the situation.

Nicole looked up at the sky, shielding her eyes from the glare of the sun peeking through the clouds. *At the very least, You could open my mom's eyes to the truth; she needs help and should go somewhere to get it.*

Speaking this way to God, even in her mind, did nothing to make Nicole feel better. *If You are real, God, then why don't You answer my prayers?*

Canton

Releasing a noisy yawn, Todd grabbed the Sunday morning newspaper and flopped into his favorite brown, leather easy chair. He'd stayed up late last night, writing down his thoughts about the cooking class. Todd planned to write an article about taking lessons from the Amish woman, but not until he'd finished the last class. By then he'd have a lot more information, and could even include a recipe or two. It would generate interest and maybe take the sting out if he wrote anything negative about the Amish way of life or the types of meals Amish women served.

Laying the paper across his chest, Todd closed his eyes, to better reflect on what had happened during the first class. A mixed group of people had come to Heidi Troyer's to learn how to cook some traditional Amish dishes. Todd hoped whatever they made in the next class, which wouldn't be for another two weeks, would be a bit tastier than the baked oatmeal Heidi had taught the class how to make. It was probably okay for someone who enjoyed eating oatmeal, but he'd never liked it, even as a kid when his mother doctored it up with plenty of brown sugar and raisins. Truth was, when Todd got home yesterday, he'd thrown the baked oatmeal in the trash. He could only imagine what his mother would say if she'd seen him do such a thing. *"Todd Collins, did I not teach you better than that? Tossing out perfectly good food is wasteful. Why, do you know how many people are starving around the world and would give anything to have eaten the food you saw as nothing but garbage?"*

Todd didn't care; he'd just go by his favorite coffee shop in the morning and order a tempting creation to eat with his latte. *What my mom doesn't know won't hurt her.* He chuckled, still relaxing and enjoying himself in the overstuffed chair.

Todd opened his eyes. He felt relief that his parents still lived in Portland, Oregon, where he'd been born. He only saw them a couple of times a year and was always glad when they went home. Dad was okay, but Mom got on his nerves with her constant nagging and asking twenty questions. The one thing she quizzed him about most was whether he'd found a nice girlfriend yet, and if so, was he ready to settle down? She wanted to know all the aspects of Todd's life, and even called frequently to ask him questions. Mom was like a bloodhound, sniffing for any little evidence to gather and involve herself in Todd's life.

Todd's parents had gotten married when they were in their early twenties, and here Todd was twenty-eight years old, with no serious girlfriend, much less any plans to be married. It wasn't that he didn't want a wife. He just hadn't found the right woman yet. Of course, he admittedly was a bit picky. *And with good reason,* he thought. *I chose wrong once and won't make that mistake again.*

Pushing his thoughts aside, Todd focused on the newspaper and his column, where he'd given a negative critique of a restaurant in town. It wasn't a fancy place—kind of a hole in the wall, really, but he'd hoped for some good food when he went there, since it had been advertised as "Just like Mom's tasty home cooking."

"Tasty home cooking, my eye." Todd gave a disgusted snort. "I've eaten a better burger at the fast-food restaurant down the street from my condo."

He folded the newspaper and tossed it on the end table close to his chair. *If enough people read my thoughts about the new place, maybe the owners will sell out or vacate the building. I don't know these people, so what does it matter? Then hopefully someone who knows what they're doing will take over the restaurant.*

Todd grabbed hold of the armrests and lifted himself out of his chair. *Think I'll drive over to Akron and try out some other restaurant today. Good or bad, it'll give me an opportunity to do another review.*

Chapter 8

Berlin, Ohio

On Monday, Heidi decided to do some shopping. She needed groceries, and with all the shops to choose from in Berlin, she could hopefully find something nice for Kendra's baby too. It had been a difficult decision, but Lyle had agreed to hire a driver this coming Saturday so they could go to Akron and visit Kendra, rather than merely mailing the card and gift.

I want to do the right thing, and if there's a pocket-sized New Testament in one of the stores, I'll buy it as well. The Bible can be for the baby when she's older and is able to read, Heidi told herself as she headed down the baby aisle in one of the stores. Even though Kendra's parents had invited her to move back home so they could help raise the baby, her relationship with God was weak. Whatever Heidi did or said could help strengthen the young woman's faith, but if Kendra took it the wrong way, Heidi's words might have the opposite effect. Heidi didn't want to create an obstacle between Kendra and God.

As Heidi approached the baby clothes, she spotted Loretta Donnelly coming from the opposite direction.

"Hello, Heidi." Loretta smiled. "It's good to see you. Are you buying clothes for the new arrival?"

Swallowing against the constriction in her throat, Heidi barely managed a brief nod. "Only it won't be Lyle's and my child wearing the baby outfit, because we will not be adopting Kendra Perkins's child after all."

Loretta tipped her head. "But I thought. . ."

Heidi explained about Kendra changing her mind and ended by saying Kendra had given birth to a baby girl last week.

"Oh, she had the baby already?"

"Yes. Apparently it came earlier than expected, but both mother and daughter are doing fine." Heidi took a deep breath, hoping she wouldn't break down in front of her friend.

"I'm sorry to hear you won't be raising the baby. I know how much you'd been looking forward to it. You and Lyle would make wonderful parents." Loretta's brows lowered. "How will Kendra take care of a child by herself?"

"She's moved back with her folks, so they will help with the baby."

Loretta placed her hand on Heidi's arm, giving it a gentle pat. "How are you dealing with this?"

Heidi's posture sagged. "I'm disappointed, of course, but it's a situation I cannot change, so I am trying to accept it as God's will."

Loretta nodded soberly. "When things are out of our control, acceptance is always the best. God's way is not always our way."

"True. Now how are things with you these days? Are you still making plans to join the Amish church?"

"Yes, I am, and once I become a member, I suspect Eli will ask me to marry him. He's hinted at it several times."

Heidi gave Loretta a hug. She needed to hear some good news. "That's wonderful. I'm happy things are going well for you."

Loretta's wide smile reached all the way to her coffee-colored eyes. "*Danki.*"

"Where are your children today?"

"They're staying with a neighbor. I needed to get some serious shopping done, and it's hard to do it with Abby and Conner along—especially when they start begging for things they shouldn't have or don't need."

"Do the children know about your decision to become Amish?" Heidi shifted her weight.

"Yes, and they're happy about it. Abby and Conner love Eli, and he's made it clear that the feeling is mutual. I feel blessed to have met him during your cooking classes. I truly believe God brought us together."

"I couldn't agree more." Heidi felt blessed too, knowing she'd had a small part in bringing two of her students together in such a special way. She thought about her current group of students and wondered if anything said or done during the upcoming classes would make a difference in any of their lives.

Millersburg

"Mr. Mason, may I speak with you a minute please?"

Bill set his broom aside and turned to face Debra Shultz, one of the high school English teachers. Debra was in her sixties and had never married. It didn't take a genius to know why, either. The woman was a complainer, always looking for something to pick about. At least that's how Bill felt whenever she started in on him. Last week, during a cool morning, it was the vent in her classroom, and how the heat wasn't coming out of it correctly. The week before that, she complained about her floors—said they hadn't been cleaned properly. As far as Bill was concerned, Ms. Shultz should have retired years ago.

"What is it, Ms. Schultz?" He tapped his foot impatiently, as she stood with arms folded, looking at him over the top of her metal-framed glasses with narrowed mousy brown eyes. Bill resisted the urge to add *this time.* He tried to remain polite and calm.

"I wanted to remind you to make sure the garbage cans in my classroom get emptied today." A muscle in her right cheek quivered. "You must have been in a hurry last Friday, because when I entered my classroom this morning, the garbage can by my desk was still full of trash."

"Sorry about that. I'll take care of it now if you like." Apparently the custodian who emptied the trash had missed one of her cans. Bill would speak to him about it, but for now, it was best to simply do the job himself.

She shook her head vigorously. "I have one more class yet today, and I don't want to be disturbed. When you're finished doing your cleaning at the end of the day, you can empty the garbage."

"Sure, no problem." Bill picked up the broom and began sweeping the hallway again, where several pieces of wadded-up paper lay. She apparently didn't realize he wasn't a regular janitor anymore. No question about it—today was definitely Monday. He hoped he didn't encounter any more picky teachers.

As Bill moved on, he stepped aside for a group of students coming out of the lunchroom. He recognized one of them right away. It was Nicole Smith, whom he'd met at Heidi Troyer's cooking class a week ago Saturday. She glanced his way, but when he nodded, smiled, and said "Hello," she turned her head the other way.

He frowned. *Surely she must recognize me. Maybe Nicole doesn't want anyone to know she's acquainted with a lowly janitor and is taking cooking classes with him outside of school.*

Bill reflected on how she'd acted the day of the cooking class. Come to think of it, the girl hadn't said much, and barely made eye contact—not just with Bill, but with the other students as well.

She could be a bit snobbish. Bill moved on down the hall. He noticed she wasn't walking with anyone right now. Nicole Smith might be a loner, or maybe she had trouble making friends.

Earlier today when Bill had started sweeping the halls because the other custodians were busy with different things, he'd slowed and stopped to listen after hearing a teacher mention Nicole's name in one of the classrooms. A water fountain was right next to the door, so as not to appear obvious, he'd stepped over to it and taken a long drink. He couldn't help overhearing the teacher tell Nicole she wasn't doing well with her grades, and then he'd listened as Nicole tried to explain.

Wiping his shirtsleeve across his wet mouth, and down on his chin, where water had dripped, he'd watched as Nicole practically flew out of the room. Bill's quick sidestep had kept the girl from plowing into him, but it appeared she hadn't even noticed he was there. He'd remembered how Nicole introduced herself at Heidi's. The poor girl had a lot of responsibility to shoulder.

Watching as she went down the hall now, Bill continued sweeping. *Maybe I ought to make an effort to get to know her better during the cooking classes.* He gripped the handle of his broom as the idea set in. *Yep. I think that little gal might just need a friend.*

Nicole walked briskly down the hall toward her history class, her mouth twisting grimly. She'd had a lecture from Mrs. Wick, her English teacher, earlier today, about not getting her lessons in on time. Nicole had a feeling this would happen, with her being on overload at home. Now this was on her plate to deal with, on top of everything else. And unless she could talk her teacher out of it, her dad would soon be involved. She couldn't let that happen. It pained Nicole to have Dad know about her failing grades. He'd not only be upset, but disappointed in her too. Her teacher didn't mince any words about the situation, and Nicole felt worse than ever with what she'd said.

"You have failing grades in this class," Mrs. Wick warned. "If you don't bring them up, you won't pass my class. Perhaps you should stay after school a few days a week, for some private tutoring."

After trying to explain her situation at home, Nicole instantly regretted telling her teacher anything. Then Mrs. Wick suggested a conference with Nicole's father, to see if something could be worked out. The teacher said if Nicole failed one more test, she would contact her dad and suggest a one-on-one conference with him at his earliest convenience. Nicole definitely didn't want to involve Dad. He had enough to worry about. She'd begged the teacher to give her another chance, saying she'd work extra hard to get her grades up. Mrs. Wick ended the conversation by saying she was concerned for Nicole, and the matter needed to be addressed.

Nicole didn't mind English so much. In fact, she liked her teacher. It could have been worse if she'd been stuck with some other English teacher, like stuffy old Ms. Shultz. She'd heard some of the students talking about how Ms. Shultz gave no one any slack. Nicole, no doubt, would have failed the class by now, and she felt thankful for Mrs. Wick's patience. But Nicole was out of options and didn't want to fail the class. Her teacher cared; Nicole heard it in the tone of Mrs. Wick's voice as she'd explained the situation to her. Despite having a nice teacher, Nicole was still in a dilemma. She didn't have time to get all her homework done. History, English, algebra, and biology—they were all hard subjects, requiring extra study for tests and homework assignments. It seemed so overwhelming.

I don't see how Mrs. Wick thinks I'm supposed to keep up with everything she assigns when I have so many things at home to do. She scrubbed a hand over her face. *I can't believe she suggested I stay after school for tutoring lessons and wanted to have a meeting with Dad. He doesn't get home until six o'clock most evenings, and I need to be there for Tony and Heather, not to mention cooking supper every night. Who knows what kind of mischief those two would get into if I came home even a few minutes late?*

To make matters worse, when Nicole left Mrs. Wick's

classroom, she'd almost bumped into the head janitor. She couldn't believe he was attending Heidi Troyer's cooking classes, and she sure hadn't wanted that guy to know she attended the school where he worked. Worse yet would be if he found out how bad she was doing with her studies and blabbed it around the school. She wondered if janitors were friends with teachers. Did they talk or take lunch together? Nicole didn't need all these extra things to worry about.

Her face tightened. *Life is not fair. I hardly ever have any time to myself. If I do flunk out, it won't be my fault.* She let out a puff of air. *I could use some help right now. Why couldn't I have had a study hall period, or an elective class like art or music?*

Nicole dabbed on some lip balm from her purse, thinking once again about her mother. *Tonya shouldn't have run out on us. She should have stayed and straightened up so she could take care of her family. If I ever get married, which is doubtful, I'll never run out on my husband and children.*

Chapter 9

Canton

"Are you sure you want to go through with this?" Lyle asked, as he and Heidi sat in the back of their driver's van.

Heidi gave a slow nod, fidgeting nervously with her fingers against the package she held. "Paying a call on Kendra is the right thing to do."

"It might be the right thing for her, but is it for you?"

"Jah, I believe so."

Lyle reached over and clasped Heidi's hand. "I don't mean it in a prideful way, but I'm proud of you for this decision you've made. You and Kendra became quite close during the time she was living with us, so I'm sure our visit will be meaningful to her. She will hopefully know there are no hard feelings."

"I hope so." Heidi closed her eyes and sent up a silent prayer. *Heavenly Father, please help me to get through this without breaking down, and give me the right words to say to Kendra.*

After hearing Lyle draw in a deep breath, Heidi looked over at him. "What is it, Lyle?"

"Just enjoying this time of the year." His endearing gaze reached hers. "Can you smell and feel the fresh hay?"

"Jah." Heidi looked toward a field where hay had been recently cut and baled. "It's not October yet, but you can almost smell autumn's essence. Soon its brilliant colors will be quilting the land."

He grinned. "You have such a nice way with words. I could

never have put it that way. But you're absolutely right—it's God's perfect balance, don't you think?"

Heidi gave a slight nod. *The land may be in perfect balance but not our lives.* Children would balance hers and Lyle's lives completely. Even if it only turned out to be one child, the hole in Heidi's heart would finally close.

A short time later, their driver, Ida, pulled up to a large, two-story house. "According to my GPS and the numbers on this house, we're at the right place," Ida announced. "If you'll be a while, I can go somewhere for a cup of coffee. Or would you rather I just wait here in the van?"

"We shouldn't be more than an hour or so," Lyle replied. "If you want to go for coffee, that's fine. No point in you sitting here in the driveway, waiting."

"Okay, sounds good. I'll be back in an hour, but if you're not done visiting, no problem. Please, take your time." She reached across the seat and picked up a book. "I brought some entertainment."

Grinning, Lyle got out of the van. Heidi did the same, remembering to take the package she'd brought for the baby. As they stepped onto the Perkins' porch, Heidi blew out a series of short breaths.

Lyle tipped his head to one side. "You okay?"

"I'm fine." Heidi quickly rang the doorbell, before she lost her nerve.

A few seconds later, a teenage girl with long brown hair answered. "Hi, I'm Chris, and you must be the Troyers." She smiled, revealing a set of braces on her top and bottom teeth. "I heard you were coming."

Heidi smiled too, feeling a little more relaxed. She reached out her hand. "It's nice to meet you, Chris. Kendra has told us a lot about you and your sister, Shelly."

Giggling, Chris rolled her eyes. "I can only imagine. You probably heard about all the times we pestered our big sister."

Heidi shook her head. "Kendra only shared the good

things about growing up with you and Shelly." She chose not to mention that Kendra had also mentioned how, when her father first asked her to leave his house, he'd instructed her sisters to have nothing to do with Kendra. It had been a difficult time for the young woman.

"Well, that's a relief." Chris spoke in a bubbly tone as she held the door open wider. "Come on in. My folks aren't here right now, but Kendra is anxiously waiting." She led the way down the hall. "Shelly's not here, either. Our church is having a fall craft show today, and she's helping Mom with one of the tables."

Heidi was disappointed she wouldn't get to meet Kendra's parents, but maybe it was better this way. It might be easier to visit with Kendra if Mr. and Mrs. Perkins were not present. She wasn't sure how much Kendra had told her folks about her and Lyle, but they might be a bit standoffish toward them—even wondering why an Amish couple would want to adopt their grandchild.

When they entered the house, Heidi noticed a few pictures hanging on the wall in the entry. The frames were antique gold and held what appeared to be oil paintings of scenic views. It surprised her not to see any family pictures on display. Many other English homes she'd visited had photo albums sitting out and often had several family pictures on the walls.

Heidi glanced down, noticing how the hardwood floors gleamed—especially here in the hall. The scent of baby powder filled Heidi's nostrils as they walked behind Chris. Moisture gathered in the corners of her eyes when they entered the living room and she saw Kendra sitting in an upholstered rocking chair, holding her baby.

"Oh, Heidi, I'm so glad you're here. You too, Lyle." Kendra's eyes were wide and glowing as she nuzzled her tiny daughter.

That could be me, holding my child. Heidi remembered how she'd had a vision of holding a baby while stirring food in a bowl on the table. Her chin trembled slightly as she tried to regain her composure. "Hello, Kendra. It's good to see you. How are you and the baby?"

"We're both doing great. Come see for yourself." Kendra motioned for Heidi to move closer.

As Kendra's sister left the room, Heidi placed the gift on the coffee table and made her way over to the bold flower-patterned chair. Lyle held back, taking a seat on the leather sofa. Heidi figured her husband wanted her to have the opportunity to speak with Kendra first.

She couldn't help noticing how Lyle leaned forward, looking intently at the large black piano sitting on the far side of the room. Kendra's parents had a lovely home, but Heidi was more interested in seeing the precious baby than studying this house's interior.

Heidi's lips parted slightly as she gazed at the tiny bundle of sweetness in Kendra's arms. The little girl's skin was pale and dewy, and her baby-fine hair was an auburn color, just like her mother's. The infant's wee eyes were closed in slumber, and her tiny, rose-colored lips made little sucking noises. She looked so sweet in her defenseless sleep.

"She's beautiful," Heidi murmured. "I'm happy for you, Kendra."

"Thanks." Kendra looked down at her baby and sniffed. "I never dreamed it would feel so wonderful to hold my own child. Little Heidi is my whole world, and I love her more than I ever thought possible."

Heidi tipped her head. "Her name is Heidi?"

"Yeah." Kendra looked up and smiled. "I hope you're okay with that."

Heidi nearly choked on the sob rising in her throat. All she could do was nod. When she looked over at Lyle, he gave her a reassuring smile.

"Wanna hold her?" Kendra asked.

Fearful she might break down if she held her namesake,

Heidi replied, "Well, I—I don't want to wake her."

"It's okay. She's been sleeping awhile. If she wakes up, she'll go right back to sleep. My sweet little Heidi is such a good baby. Did you know, she almost came three weeks early?"

"Yes, your mother mentioned that in the message she left us."

Kendra went on to explain how she'd had contractions in the grocery store, but after getting checked out at the hospital, the doctor confirmed it was only false labor, but then a few days later the real thing happened.

Struggling against tears threatening to spill over and trying to absorb all that Kendra had said, Heidi leaned down and took the baby from her. As she stood holding the precious little girl, an image of the dream she'd had popped into her head again. *Why do I keep visualizing myself holding this boppli?* It was wrong to wish Kendra might change her mind and let Lyle and Heidi adopt her daughter, after all, but Heidi couldn't seem to control her thoughts.

Walnut Creek

Lance had barely gotten home from delivering the mail, when the phone rang. He hurried to the kitchen and grabbed his cell phone from its charger. "Hello."

"Oh, good. I'm glad you're home, Dad. Uncle Dan's been trying to get a hold of you most of the day, and he called me in desperation."

Lance shifted the phone to his other ear and took a seat at the table. "Desperation? What's that brother of mine want, Sharon? Is Dan hurt or having some kind of trouble?"

"He didn't say, but I don't think it was an emergency. Uncle Dan just said he needed to talk to you right away and wished you'd answer your cell phone once in a while."

"I left it home this morning. The battery was almost dead

and it needed to charge."

"Don't you have a charger to use in your car?"

"I did, but I lost it."

"Dad, you really ought to—"

"So what's new with you, honey? How's Gavin? And are the kids doing okay?" Lance got up from the table and ambled over to his fish tank in one corner of the room. The goldfish, his only pets, had been fed this morning, and swam around the tank without a care in the world.

"Everyone's fine, Dad." Sharon groaned. "And I wish you wouldn't change the subject whenever you don't want to talk about something."

"Well, there isn't much to say on the topic. I'll buy a new charger for the car when I get the chance. In the meantime, I'll give my brother a call and see what he wants."

"Sounds good, but before you hang up, I want to extend an invitation to you."

"What's up?"

"Gavin and I are having a few people over for dinner after church tomorrow, and we'd like you to come."

"No can do. This Sunday's my time to spend with your sister and her family. I was at your place last week, remember?"

"Of course I remember, Dad, and I've already talked to Terry about this. She's fine with you coming to our house again tomorrow."

Lance rapped his knuckles on his knee. Sharon was up to something, no doubt about it. "Okay, what's the reason you want me at your house so bad? You're not trying to fix me up again, I hope." A year after Lance's wife died, both of his daughters began to think it was their job to find him a suitable wife. Well, they could forget the notion. No one could ever replace Flo. Lance and Florence had been high school sweethearts, and gotten married when they both turned nineteen. They'd had a good marriage and been soul mates, until the Lord took Flo home three years ago.

"I'm not trying to set you up, Dad, but there are two nice single ladies from church we should all get acquainted with. They moved here a few weeks ago, and—"

"Sorry, honey, but count me out. I'm having dinner at Terry's tomorrow like I said." Lance put the phone back to his other ear. "I'd better go now so I can give Dan a call. Oh, and I'll also call Terry to let her know I'm still coming."

"Okay, Dad. I'll see you tomorrow at church. Have a nice evening."

When Lance hung up, his conscience pricked him a bit. He knew Sharon was disappointed, but the last thing he needed was to spend the afternoon with not one, but two spinster women who might be eagerly looking for a man. He wished he could make his caring daughters understand that he had no intention of getting married again and was perfectly happy trying to be a good father and grandfather. Eventually they might get it, but until then, he'd keep dodging all invitations that involved single ladies.

It was bad enough how, on some Sundays after church, a few of the older unmarried women approached Lance, hinting about invitations to their place for dinner. Some men might like the idea and jump at the chance for a lady's affection, but Lance always came up with a reason he couldn't oblige, with the hope these women would take the hint.

Even some of the widows on his mail route had found out he was single again. They'd be waiting for Lance by their mailbox near the road, or on the porch where their mail container hung. Some had homemade cookies for him, while others made fudge and other types of desserts. They all had one thing in common. Like a fish taking bait, they used their sweet smiles and tantalizing treats in the hope of reeling him in. But Lance was one fish that was never getting hooked. His heart had belonged to Flo—and it always would.

Remembering his daughter's message, he picked up the phone again and punched in Dan's number. His brother answered on the second ring. "Hey, Lance, I was hoping I'd get a hold of you before the day was over. I'm in a bit of a bind right now, and need a favor."

Lance grimaced. His brother always seemed to need something. "What's up?"

"You know the townhouse I bought after Rita died?"

"Yeah."

"Well, I'm remodeling the whole place, and every room is torn up." He paused. "So now I don't have anywhere to stay."

Lance thumped his forehead. *Great. I bet Dan wants to stay here with me. There goes my peace and quiet after work and on Sundays.*

"Anyhow, the place won't be move-in ready for several weeks, so would it be all right if I bunk with you till it's done?"

"Um, yeah, sure, that'd be fine. The guestroom's always ready for unexpected company. Bring over whatever you need; I don't have anything planned and will be home all evening."

"Thanks, Lance. And don't worry, I'll treat you to a few meals out, 'cause I owe you big."

"No problem." Lance said goodbye and clicked off his phone. He didn't look forward to having his life disrupted, but since it was for only a matter of weeks, he'd make it work.

Lance stood and ambled into the kitchen to get something to eat for supper. There wasn't much in the refrigerator, and he didn't feel like cooking, so he grabbed the container filled with leftover macaroni and cheese.

As Lance heated his supper in the microwave, he thought more about Flo. *I'm sure she would approve of me helping Dan out. She was a hospitable woman.* His eyes misted. He missed her sweet smile and wished she was with him right now. *Maybe with my brother here in the house I won't feel so lonely.*

Chapter 10

Walnut Creek

Heidi's eyelids fluttered as she struggled to stay awake, while sitting on a backless wooden bench inside Eli Miller's woodshop where church was being held today. After she and Lyle returned home from seeing Kendra and her baby yesterday afternoon, Heidi, determined not to give in to self-pity, had looked for things to keep herself busy. Holding Kendra's baby and hearing the child had been named after her caused Heidi's emotions to jump all over the place. Consequently, she'd stayed up late doing things that probably didn't need to be done and hadn't gotten enough sleep. Her conscience said she'd done the right thing by going to see Kendra, but her heart told her otherwise. It was hard not to grieve for something she wanted so desperately. If only God had said yes to her prayer.

Along with some cute pink booties and a New Testament she'd gotten at one of the stores, they'd given Kendra the small quilt Heidi's aunt Emma had made when they'd first told her they were planning to adopt. Kendra seemed pleased with the gifts.

Heidi shifted on the unyielding bench, trying to find a comfortable position. *Who wouldn't be pleased to receive such a special item as a handmade baby quilt?*

When the final hymn began, Heidi became more fully awake, eager to go outdoors for a bit to breathe some fresh air. Due to her musings, plus a struggle to stay awake, she'd missed most of the final sermon and felt guilty about it. She hoped no one had caught her on the verge of drifting off.

Lance was almost out the door of the church he attended when his daughter Terry approached him. "Say, Dad, can I talk to you a minute?"

He halted. "Sure, what's up?"

"I know you were planning to come over to our place for dinner today, but something unexpected came up, and I need to cancel. Can we make it next week instead?"

"Next Sunday will be Sharon's turn to have me over." Lance's eyebrows squished together as he touched the base of his neck. "What's going on that you have to cancel?"

"Nick's mother isn't feeling well, so I'm taking dinner to her and Nick's dad today."

Lance pulled his glasses down and looked over the rims. "Is there something going on here, Terry?"

She shook her head. "Of course not, Dad. Why would you think there was anything going on?"

"I thought maybe you were in cahoots with your sister. She wanted to have me over for dinner today so she could set me up with one of the new ladies from church." His forehead wrinkled. "I've told you both before that I'm not interested in a relationship with another woman. Your mother was the only lady I'll ever love, so there's no point even bothering to play matchmaker."

She tipped her head back, eyeing him curiously. "Is that what you think I'm doing?"

"Well, aren't you?"

"Absolutely not. Nick's mother is genuinely sick. I would never make up a story like that. I only suggested you go over to Sharon's this afternoon so you wouldn't have to spend the day alone. Besides, you're not the world's best cook, so I would think you'd appreciate a home-cooked meal."

Lance drew a quick breath, feeling heat rush to his cheeks. He felt like a heel. "S–sorry, Terry. Guess I'm a little paranoid these days. Am I forgiven?"

"Of course." She gave him a hug. "So are you going over to Sharon's for dinner?"

He shook his head. "Not today. Think I'm gonna grab something at a fast-food place on the way home and spend the rest of the day visiting with your uncle Dan and helping him find places in my guestroom for the rest of his things."

Terry's head tilted to one side. "Why is he putting things in your guestroom?"

Lance explained about Dan's townhouse being remodeled and ended by saying it would be a temporary situation.

She smiled and patted his arm. "It'll give you a chance to spend a little time with your brother. I'm sure you'll both enjoy yourselves."

He nodded slowly. *Sure hope it works out that way.*

Dover

Lisa rolled over sleepily, but when she glanced at the clock on the bedside table, she sat straight up. "Oh, no, it can't be afternoon already!" Lisa hadn't wanted to sleep this late, or miss church, either. When she didn't make it to church, her day seemed to lack a positive outlook, and it was harder to get through the week. But the night hours had been sleepless for her. And what a night it had been too. After she'd gotten home from catering a baby shower, she had gone straight to bed. Lisa had been so tired, she hadn't even bothered to remove her makeup, taking time only to quickly brush her teeth.

She should have slept like a baby after all the work she had put in for the occasion, but the puppy next door howled most of the night. During the brief time the pathetic little critter wasn't carrying on, its owners' voices kept Lisa awake as they hollered at each other. She'd slept with two pillows pressed against her ears. It was worse than any nightmare. How two people who'd only been married a year could scream at each other the way those two did, made her wonder why they'd gotten married in the first place. *If I ever get serious about anyone, I'm going to make sure not to rush into anything. I'll get to know them well before we make a lifelong commitment.*

The sun streamed in through a crack in the blinds, and Lisa clambered out of bed. Yawning, she padded down the hall to the bathroom. One look in the mirror told Lisa it was a good thing she hadn't gone to church. Her hair was a tangled mess, and her eyes were so puffy she could barely keep them open. She could never make herself presentable enough to be seen by anyone today.

Sighing, she tucked a lock of hair behind her ears. *What I need is some fresh air. Think I'll get dressed and take a walk. When I get back home, I'm going to have a little talk with my renters. They have to do something about that pup or else look for somewhere else to live.*

New Philadelphia

After Allie picked her kids up from Sunday school, she headed straight for the mall. Nola needed new shoes, and Derek a pair of blue jeans. Some people might think it wasn't right to shop on Sunday, but since Allie worked at the dentist's office during the week, she needed weekends for shopping and running errands. Besides, what did it hurt to shop on Sundays? It wasn't like the day was sacred or anything.

Allie glanced at her children in the rearview mirror. They both looked nice in their Sunday clothes. *My son and daughter are so precious. I love them more than life itself.*

She flipped on her turn signal and made a right. *Someday, when Nola and Derek are older, will their lives be better from going to church and learning memory verses? Should I consider going to Sunday school with them, rather than dropping them off and finding something else to do by myself?*

Allie had attended Sunday school when she was a girl, which was why she felt the need to see that her children went too. But she'd quit going during her teen years and didn't feel it was necessary for her anymore. She did pray sometimes, however—especially when Steve was working and didn't come home when she expected. It was either pray or spend the whole time worrying. Besides, where had any amount of worry gotten her?

As Allie pulled her minivan into the mall's parking lot, she spotted two police cars parked side-by-side. Nearing the vehicles, she realized one of the drivers was Steve. In the other police car sat a blond-haired female cop Allie had not met before. She was obviously new on the force, but it seemed strange Steve had made no mention of her. Usually, when someone new was hired, he told Allie about it right away.

A pang of jealously shot through her. The people Steve worked with saw more of him than she and the kids did these days. Today was supposed to be his day off, but once again, he'd covered for someone on the force who needed, or maybe simply wanted, time off.

Allie's heartbeat quickened when Steve got out of his vehicle and took a seat in the passenger's side of the other patrol car. *I wonder what he's doing. Should I find a spot near their vehicles and find out for myself?*

"There's Daddy!" Derek shouted from the back of the van.

"Yes, Son, it sure is your dad."

"What's he doin'?"

Allie gritted her teeth. "I don't know. Looks like he's talking to another police officer."

"Are we gonna say hi to Daddy?" The question came from Nola.

"Yes, we definitely are." Allie found a parking space in the row behind the squad cars, pulled in, and turned off the ignition. "You two sit tight. I'll be right back with your dad."

She hesitated at first, wondering what she should say. Allie didn't want to come off as being a jealous wife. Sometimes that spurred another woman on. And she didn't want to sound like a nag, either. That might push Steve right into the arms of another woman.

When Allie approached the second patrol car, she rapped on the passenger door. Steve jumped, looking at her with lips forming an O and eyes wide open. "Allie," he mouthed.

She gave no response—just stood waiting for him to exit the car.

He said something to the blond woman, then opened the car door. "What are you doing here, Allie?" Steve's cheeks looked flushed.

"I brought the kids to buy some new clothes. How come you're here? Was there some kind of disturbance at the mall today?"

"No, I, uh. . ." He rubbed the back of his head. "I heard Officer Robbins was in the area so I met up with her to talk about some things."

Allie leaned down slightly, glancing in the window. The woman inside gave her a nod. Even with her police hat on, the woman's beauty could not go unnoticed. Her hair was tied back in a long ponytail, thick with spiral curls. She had flawless skin with vivid blue eyes. No wonder she needed so little makeup.

Absentmindedly, Allie reached up to touch her own hair. At least she'd taken the time to style it this morning. "Is Officer Robbins new on the force? You've never mentioned her before."

"Yeah, Lori came on a few weeks ago."

"I see." *I wonder what kind of things you would need to talk about with her.* Allie pointed at the minivan. "The kids are waiting. They both want to say hello."

"Okay, sure, but let me introduce you to Lori first."

Allie shook her head. "No, that's okay. Maybe some other time."

"Okay, sure." Steve told the other officer he'd talk to her later, got out of the car, and sprinted over to the van.

Allie gave the blond officer a backward glance before following Steve to their car. She tried hard not to let wandering thoughts creep into her head but couldn't help wondering if Lori was the reason Steve was working on his day off. *Has he really been covering for someone else on the force all these times, or has Steve been using it as an excuse to work the same schedule as Lori Robbins?*

Allie was on the verge of asking Steve a few more questions but changed her mind. She didn't want to start anything in front of the kids. This evening, though, if the opportunity arose, she would question her husband more about Officer Robbins.

Chapter 11

Walnut Creek

When Lance pulled into his driveway Wednesday afternoon, he spotted his brother's sports car parked in front of the garage door. *Oh, great. How's he expect me to put my rig inside now?*

Lance wasn't in a good mood anyway. He'd had a rough day. It all started this morning when he dropped a bag of mail and had to scramble to pick it up before it started to rain. Things went downhill after that, and now this. His normally cheerful mood had gone by the wayside.

He knew his brother needed somewhere to stay, which meant making some adjustments on his part, but already, he couldn't help feeling some regret. Dan had moved his things into Lance's place Saturday evening, and for the past three days, he'd blocked the way into the garage. On top of that, Lance's brother was good at making messes and didn't bother to pick up after himself. No doubt he'd been used to having his wife clean the house when she was alive and figured he didn't have to pick up his clothes, do the laundry, or gather up the things he'd left in the living room after watching TV. Apparently Dan also thought he owned the driveway here.

Lance turned his vehicle off and got out. He shoved the set of keys in his jacket pocket and looked up when he felt a few drops of rain hit his arm. Maybe it wouldn't amount to more than a sprinkle. They'd had enough rain this morning to last a week.

When he entered the house, Lance found Dan sprawled out on the couch with the television blaring. Lance positioned himself between the TV and his brother. "So what have you been doing all day?"

Dan sat up and yawned. "Did a few loads of laundry, but not much else." He pulled his fingers through the ends of his silver-gray mustache. "Oh, and I fed your goldfish."

Lance ground his teeth together. "I did that first thing this morning. Remember when we were having coffee before I left for work, and I told you I'd fed the fish?"

"Oops. Sorry about that. Must have forgot."

"There's no need for you to feed the fish at all. They're my responsibility, so I'll take care of them from now on. Okay?"

"Yeah sure. Whatever you say." Dan stood and ambled toward the kitchen. "I'm goin' after a glass of milk. Can I get you anything?"

"No, I'm fine right now. I may get something to drink after I change my clothes."

"Speaking of your clothes, there's a pile of clean laundry on your bed."

Lance's eyebrows rose. "You washed my clothes?"

Dan grinned. "Sure did. Thought it was the least I could do to say thanks for letting me stay here till my townhouse remodel is done."

"Okay, thanks. I'm going to my room now to change. See you in a bit."

When Lance entered his bedroom, the first thing he saw was the pile of clothes on his bed. None of them were folded, which meant either having to iron the items or run them through the dryer again to get the wrinkles out.

He picked up one of his favorite shirts and gave it a shake, then dropped it to the bed in disbelief. It was at least a size smaller than it had originally been. *What'd that brother of mine do—wash all my clothes in hot water?*

Gripping the shirt, Lance marched out of the room

and went straight to the kitchen. With a hand on his hip, he glared at Dan. "I'm sure you meant well, but from now on, just worry about your own laundry, and I'll do mine, 'cause I can't afford to be losing any more clothes." He held up the item in question.

Dan's cheeks colored. "Oh, oh. Guess this is my day for blunders. I won't let it happen again. If you'll tell me what color and size you want, I'll buy you a new shirt."

"Don't worry about it. What's done is done." Lance flopped into a chair at the table. As far as he was concerned, Dan's townhouse couldn't get done soon enough.

"Say, how 'bout this. . . We'll go out for a bite to eat—my treat. That way you won't have to cook anything, and you can come home afterward and relax for the rest of the evening." Dan rinsed his glass and set it in the sink. "So what do you say, Brother? Do you wanna go out to supper with me?"

Lance tapped his fingers on the table, mulling things over. After a day like he'd had, it would be nice not to worry about what to fix this evening. "Yeah, sure, a meal out will be nice. Just give me a few minutes to change and get ready. Then we can head out."

"No problem. I'll get a jacket and wait for you in my car." Dan ambled out of the kitchen.

Lance pushed away from the table and carried his withered-looking shirt to his room. "This was one of my favorites," he mumbled under his breath. *Guess I may as well throw it in my bag of rags. It's not good for much else. Sure hope nothing like this happens again.*

Millersburg

Nicole entered the house, tossed her schoolbooks on the coffee table, and flopped onto the couch. It had begun to rain again, and she was relieved to be indoors. Heather and

Tony's bus should be dropping them off any minute, so she was glad she'd made it home before they did. The last time they got home before she did, they'd fixed snacks and left a mess in the kitchen. Ever since Nicole's mother walked out on the family, the kitchen had become Nicole's domain, even though she didn't know how to cook that well. Maybe after a few more lessons from Heidi Troyer, Nicole would be able to make some decent meals. Dad deserved some tasty dishes—that was for sure. After what Tonya did to him, he ought to have only good things.

Nicole had been given a ton of homework today, but she was in no hurry to get it done. All she wanted to do was get out her sketch pad, sit outside on the patio, and draw something from nature. Her dream was to have her own art studio someday. But of course, it wasn't likely to happen. "Nothing good ever happens for me," she mumbled.

"Who are you talking to, honey?"

Nicole jumped, her eyes widening when her father stepped into the room. He wore a pair of sweat pants and stood rubbing his head with a towel. "Dad, what are you doing here?"

"I live here, remember?" He chuckled. "Got off early today and just finished taking a shower."

"I didn't see your car out front when I came in."

"It's in the garage."

"Oh."

He glanced around. "Are Tony and Heather home yet?"

"Nope. Only me."

"How was school?" He took a seat in his easy chair and propped his feet on the footstool.

Nicole shrugged. "Same as usual."

"How are your grades? Are you keeping up with things?"

"I'm doin' okay." Nicole looked away from him. It wasn't right to lie to her dad, but she didn't want to worry him. She would catch up eventually. At least she hoped she would.

"Well, that's not what the email I got today from your

English teacher said." Dad's forehead creased. "According to her, your grades are close to failing." His voice grew louder. "Don't you think you should have let me know about this?"

Nicole sat quietly, looking down at her hands. *I shoulda known I couldn't trust Mrs. Wick. I thought she would give me another chance.*

Dad tapped his foot. *Thump! Thump! Thump!* "Well, young lady, what do you have to say for yourself?"

"I probably should have said something, but I didn't want to worry you." She looked up at him, tears pricking the back of her eyes.

His eyes narrowed. "Well, it's too late for that. . . . I'm worried now! You can't afford to fall behind, Nicole. Your education is important, and I want you to graduate from high school."

"I know." Nicole blinked and swallowed hard, hoping she wouldn't break down.

"We'll have to make some adjustments so you have more time to study and do your homework."

"What kind of adjustments?"

"For one thing, Heather can take over doing the dishes while you study."

"She doesn't do them as good as I do. The last time she washed dishes I found some dirty ones in the dish drainer and had to do them over."

"If she doesn't get the dishes clean, she will have to rewash them, not you." Dad paused, swiping a hand across his forehead. "I'll be checking my emails more regularly. The one I found today came in a day or two ago."

Sighing, Nicole nodded. "Okay, Dad." *Boy, what was I thinking? I should have figured Mrs. Wick would contact Dad anyway.* Her fingers curled into the palms of her hands. *Why didn't I come clean with him about this the day it happened?*

"I'm sorry for not confiding in you," she said tearfully. "I promise from now on there will be no more secrets."

Dad stepped over to Nicole and pulled her into his arms. "You know how much I love you, don't you?"

She gave a slow nod.

"And even though I don't say it often enough, I appreciate everything you do around here." He patted her back. "You're a good daughter, and an equally good sister, always putting Heather and Tony's needs ahead of your own."

Nicole pressed her cheek against his chest. "Thanks, Dad. It means a lot to hear you say it."

A horn honked behind Bill as he sat in his vehicle, waiting to pull out of the school's parking lot. He glanced in the rearview mirror and frowned. It was the picky English teacher. "Oh, don't be so impatient, Ms. Schultz. I can't pull onto the street when there's a car coming."

Bill waited a few more seconds, then once he saw that all was clear, he pulled onto the road. The sky was filled with dismal-looking clouds this afternoon, and it had begun to rain. It was a bit of a drive back to New Philadelphia, and he hoped traffic wouldn't be too bad. Sometimes, when the tourists headed out of Berlin, Walnut Creek, or Sugarcreek, it took longer than normal to get home. He looked forward to getting there today, since he had plans to meet one of his buddies for supper this evening. Of course, their main topic would focus on the big fall hunting trip they'd been planning for months. Even if Bill didn't bag a deer this year, it would be fun to spend time in the woods and sleep in his cabin.

Bill let out a deep, gratifying sigh. There was nothing better than sitting in his tree stand, watching nature prepare for winter. Except for his orange hat and vest, Bill dressed all in camouflage, right down to his boots, making it difficult for any animal to tell what he was. Even his hat and vest had a design etched through the bright orange that helped break up his image to anything looking his way. But when something did, their curiosity piqued. A few times Bill had to sit real still when a little nuthatch flew and sat on his leg. The bird remained there a few seconds and then scurried down the length of his leg, pecking at the tree pattern in the camo material of his pants before flying off.

Bill's buddies often teased him about the extent to which he would go to make his presence unknown in the woods. Before he left for hunting camp, he washed his hunting clothes in soap that smelled like autumn leaves. He also showered and washed his hair, using a scent-free soap. Lastly, to make sure there was no human odor, Bill sprayed the bottom of his boots and gave a squirt to his clothes with another type of de-scenting liquid. *Sure, let my friends laugh at me, but they won't be laughing if I bag a buck first.* It didn't really bother Bill if he did or didn't get the first deer, but it had become a contest between Russ and Tom, wagering on who would get theirs first.

The squirrels found Bill interesting too. He snickered, remembering last year when a squirrel sat on a dead tree's branch that hung close to where he sat. As it ran up and down the brittle limb, the bushy-tailed critter chattered and scolded, trying to get Bill to move. Then the branch broke, and fell onto another dead branch, breaking it as well. It was like a domino effect as the squirrel fell to even lower branches, breaking them too. Before crashing to the ground, the squirrel rolled up in a little ball, and when it hit the leaf-covered floor, it took off running, and Bill never saw him again.

Yes, there were plenty of good reasons Bill enjoyed getting out in the woods. Unlike some hunters, it wasn't about the kill, but about everything else that encompassed hunting season. Going to his cabin couldn't get here soon enough, even if he did have to do all the cooking. Bill hoped by the time they got there, he'd have learned some better recipes to try out on his friends. In just a few more days he'd be back at Heidi Troyer's place taking his second cooking class.

He flicked on the radio for some music to keep him company the rest of the way home. *I wonder what she'll teach us to make this time.*

Walnut Creek

When Heidi stepped onto the porch to shake out some throw rugs, she saw Eli Miller riding into the yard on his bike. Earlier it had rained hard, and dark clouds still hung in close.

Heidi watched as Eli set the kickstand on his bicycle. "Hello, Eli," she called to him. "I can sure tell it's fall by the way the days are growing shorter and from all this rain we keep getting."

Nodding, Eli stepped onto the porch. "Is Lyle here?"

"No, he's auctioneering again today. Was there something you needed?" Hearing Rusty barking from inside the house, she quickly opened the door, knowing the dog wouldn't quit if she didn't let him out to greet their visitor.

Eli reached down and patted the Brittany spaniel's head.

Heidi smiled. "Rusty sure likes you, Eli. He always seems to know when you're around."

"He's a good dog, for sure." Eli grinned when Rusty plopped down by his feet. "I'd hoped to see Lyle today, but it's nothing that can't wait." He shuffled his feet a few times, lowering his gaze. If Heidi didn't know better, she'd think he was hiding something.

"I don't expect Lyle will be home until suppertime. If you'd like to come back around six o'clock we'd be pleased if you joined us for the evening meal."

"Sure appreciate the offer, but I can't tonight." Eli's hand anchored casually against his hip as his lips turned up. "I'm goin' to Loretta's house for supper."

"I see. You've been seeing a lot of her lately, jah?"

His ears turned pink as he nodded. "I'm glad she's planning

to join the Amish church."

Heidi smiled. "I'm happy too. Loretta's a good friend. It will be nice to have her in our church district." She hung the rug she still held over the porch railing. "Mind if I ask you a personal question?"

"Course not. What would you like to know?"

"Are you getting serious about Loretta? I mean, would you be thinking about marrying her?" Heidi couldn't help herself. Since Loretta had already mentioned things were getting serious between her and Eli, Heidi assumed he'd be asking for Loretta's hand in marriage.

The rosy hue coloring Eli's ears spread quickly to his cheeks. "Well, we have been courting."

"I'm aware. That's why I wondered if maybe. . ." Heidi ended her sentence. "Sorry, Eli. It's none of my business, and I didn't mean to pry."

"It's okay—no problem. I'd better get going. Would you please tell Lyle I dropped by?"

"Certainly." Rusty pawed at the hem of Heidi's dress, and she knelt to pet the dog's furry head.

Eli turned, and as he headed for his bike, he began to whistle, swinging his arms easily at his side.

Heidi quit petting the dog, picked up the first rug, and gave it a good shake. *I wouldn't be a bit surprised if Eli and Loretta don't start planning their wedding the day after she joins the church. He was probably too embarrassed to tell me. Bet the next time he sees Lyle, he'll let him know. Maybe that's why Eli came over here today.*

Chapter 12

Near Strasburg, Ohio

Todd looked at the clock on his dash and groaned. It was a quarter to ten, and he was only halfway to Walnut Creek. *Looks like I'm gonna be late. And to top it off, it's raining harder than when I first pulled out of my driveway.*

Until he'd gotten up this morning and looked at the calendar, Todd had forgotten today was the second Saturday of October, and he was supposed to attend another cooking class. Between working on his column for the newspaper, trying out a couple of new restaurants in the area, and keeping up with his social life, he'd had a busy couple of weeks.

To make matters worse, Todd's mother called a few days ago, pestering him to visit them. He didn't have time for a vacation. And if he were to take one, it wouldn't be to Portland, Oregon. He'd grown up there and, after graduating from college, had been eager to move from the Pacific Northwest and be on his own without Mom looking over his shoulder, scrutinizing everything he said or did.

Todd gripped the steering wheel and tried to focus on something else. It was hard being an only child and having your parents complain because they didn't get to see you often enough. "Well, if Mom wasn't afraid to fly, they could come visit me here in Ohio more often. I shouldn't have to always be the one to put forth the effort."

Todd's most recent trip to Oregon had been last

Thanksgiving, but this year he planned to stay by himself at home. Whenever he went to his folk's place, Mom always plied him with questions about his social life, and of course, kept on him about whether he'd met anyone he might consider marrying. A few times she'd even tried to set him up with the daughter of one of her friends.

Mom doesn't even know the type of woman I'd be interested in. Todd glanced at himself in the rearview mirror. "What is it about mothers thinking their sons aren't happy unless they find a wife?" he muttered. "If I do ever decide to get married, it'll be to a woman of my own choosing. Right now, my career comes first."

Walnut Creek

As Lisa turned her van onto the road leading to Heidi's house, her excitement mounted. Even with the wet weather, she looked forward to attending the second cooking class and hoped she would learn something new today that she could incorporate in her catering business. Things were going well, and she had a wedding reception to cater next Saturday. But the opportunity to secure more clients was what she continually needed. She didn't enjoy driving places that didn't involve business in the van she used for her catering services, but money was tight, and until she was making more of it, Lisa couldn't afford to buy a smaller vehicle to use strictly for pleasure.

Lisa's cousin, Jim, was a successful lawyer, making a lot more money than she'd probably ever see. It was hard not to be envious, but he'd worked hard to get where he was, so he deserved his achievement. His wife, Carlie, and their two children, Annette and Cindy, had everything they could possibly want. Lisa, on the other hand, had yet to find a man she'd consider marrying, successful or not. She often wondered if she would ever have any children. For now, at least, she'd made growing her business a priority.

I'll just bide my time, Lisa told herself. *If I keep working hard and do my best to help the business flourish, someday it'll be a success. I may never make anything close to what my cousin does, but I enjoy my job, and if I can make a decent living, that's good enough for me.*

Heidi had begun setting out the ingredients for Amish friendship bread, when she heard a vehicle pull in. Glancing out the window, she saw Nicole get out of her father's vehicle and run quickly to the house. Too bad it had to rain again today. Heidi sensed during the last class that the young girl was deeply troubled, but she wouldn't pry. If Nicole wanted to discuss her situation at home, she would open up either during class or sometime when she and Heidi had a few minutes alone. Since no one else had arrived yet, perhaps Nicole would be more talkative.

Heidi set the sack of flour she held on the kitchen table and hurried to open the door. "Good morning." She smiled when Nicole stepped in with rain dripping off her jacket. "It's good to see you again. Just hang your wet coat on one of the wall pegs." Heidi motioned toward them. "How have you been these last couple of weeks?"

With a nonchalant shrug, Nicole stepped inside. "I've been okay, I guess."

"You're the first one here, so why don't you come with me to the kitchen? We can visit while I finish getting things set out."

Silently, Nicole followed Heidi into the kitchen and plunked down in a chair at the oversized table.

"Would you like something cold to drink? There's a pitcher of lemonade in the refrigerator."

Nicole shook her head. "No thanks."

It didn't take a genius to realize the girl wasn't eager to carry on a conversation, but Heidi felt compelled to keep trying. "Have you done any cooking these past couple weeks?"

"I cook every meal at my house, but none are very tasty." Nicole's forehead wrinkled. "At least that's what my brother and sister say about the things I fix for them. They don't appreciate anything I do."

In an effort to make Nicole feel better, Heidi touched the girl's shoulder. "Sometimes people appreciate what we do but forget to say thanks."

"Yeah, maybe. My dad says thanks once in a while, but he's got a lot of other stuff on his mind." Nicole puffed out her cheeks. "Oh, and by the way, I forgot to bring an apron again."

"It's fine. You can wear one of mine." Heidi was on the verge of saying more, when another vehicle pulled into the yard. She glanced at the clock. It was five minutes to ten. Soon everyone would be here and her second cooking class would begin.

Once everyone else arrived and had removed their wet outer garments, Heidi asked them to take seats at the kitchen table. "Today we will be making Amish friendship bread." She went on to explain that in order to make the bread, a starter must first be prepared. "You will be able to keep part of the starter and give part of it to a couple of friends." Heidi picked up a bowl that had been covered with plastic wrap. "You will notice by the texture and smell that this starter is slightly fermented." She showed each student the fresh batch from the bowl in her hands.

Bill wrinkled his nose. "If I fed that putrid-looking stuff to my hunting buddies, they wouldn't be my friends very long."

Heidi bit back a chuckle. "No one's expected to eat the starter. Only a small portion of it will be added to the other ingredients to make the friendship bread." She set the starter down and handed out all the necessary ingredients, along with small bowls and utensils for everyone.

Looking at each of the students, she smiled. "When you leave here today, in addition to the bread you will make, I'll give all of you a small amount of starter."

Todd's brows furrowed as he leaned his elbows on the table and stared at the yeasty-smelling dough. "What are we supposed to do with the stuff when we take it home?"

"We're gonna use it to make more friendship bread." Bill tapped Todd's shoulder. "If you don't have any friends you can make some new ones by giving them a loaf of the tasty bread."

Todd scowled at him. "How do you know it's tasty? We haven't even made it yet."

Bill puffed out his chest. "I have every confidence that our cooking teacher would not give us any recipe that wasn't good."

"Thank you, Bill." Heidi was pleased he had such confidence in her. Hopefully everyone's bread would turn out well.

Lisa glanced around the table. Except for Todd, who looked thoroughly disgusted, everyone else seemed eager to learn how to make friendship bread—although Allie appeared preoccupied.

She'd never say anything to Heidi, but Lisa was a bit disappointed. She had hoped that today they would learn how to make a casserole or some type of supper dish she could use in her catering business. And to be truthful, Lisa never liked getting involved in chain-type letters, which this friendship bread reminded her of—passing the starter from one person to another.

Hopefully during the next four classes, they'd be given something better to make. She stared at the starter. *Maybe I could make this recipe for the holidays, to give family members or someone from church.*

Lisa held her fist to her mouth, hoping to stifle a yawn.

She wondered if the rainy weather added to her feeling extra tired this morning.

Sitting up straighter and leaning forward, she tried to concentrate. She'd slept pretty well the first part of last night—until four thirty this morning, when the puppy next door started howling. If this went on any longer with her tenants, Lisa had made up her mind to say something. She'd been hoping the situation would have remedied itself by now, but it was worse than ever. The poor puppy needed more attention and exercise after being locked up all day alone. When Lisa arrived home the other evening, she saw Gail open her front door and let the dog out by itself. With no supervision of any sort, the puppy sniffed around for a while and did what it had to do. Lisa was glad it stayed away from the street. How sad it would be if the pup got hit by a car. When the poor thing wanted in, it sat on their door step barking and yipping to no avail. Finally, after what seemed like forever, the dog was let back inside.

Now who would leave a little puppy outside all by itself? Lisa would surely never do that. *Some people just shouldn't own pets.* Her neighbors were proving to be irresponsible, and she regretted having rented to them.

Lisa looked over at Heidi's dog, lying by the kitchen door. It was content in sleep and appeared to be oblivious to everyone in the room. Rusty was well-behaved and always listened to Heidi's commands. Lisa watched as the dog stretched, opened his eyes, and closed them again. *Now there is a dog that is obviously loved and well cared for.*

Everyone laughed at something Heidi had said, and Lisa snapped to attention. *I'd better listen to what is going on, so I don't miss something important and end up doing something stupid and make a fool of myself.*

Chapter 13

Allie had a hard time concentrating on the cooking lesson. She kept thinking about Steve, and how she'd seen him in the mall parking lot on Sunday with the cute little blond patrol officer. She'd planned to talk to him about it but changed her mind. He'd probably say she was overreacting or had become paranoid. *Well, if I am, there's good reason. My insecurity or vulnerability being married to an officer of the law could be rearing its ugly head right now.*

Steve had accused Allie of overreacting many times—especially where his safety was concerned. *When did he start filling in for a coworker and working later hours or volunteering to work on his days off? Was it when Lori Robbins started working on the force?* Allie wished now she'd made a mental note of it but felt bad after thinking things through a bit more. She didn't want to draw any conclusions or become suspicious about her husband. A good marriage should involve trust. She'd need to make sure she didn't sound accusing if she and Steve had a discussion about this. Allie had a tendency to say the first thing that came to her mind, which often got her in trouble with him.

Maybe it's me. Have I let myself go? Am I putting on weight that I just don't see? Allie reached up and brushed her hair back off her face. *I could probably use a fresh style, or maybe a complete makeover like I've seen on one of those TV shows, where they take a plain-looking woman and transform her into a beauty queen.*

Forcing her contemplations aside, Allie tried to focus on what Heidi was saying. Unfortunately, making friendship bread held little appeal. Allie had hoped for a new supper dish she could make for Steve and the children. She wouldn't say anything to Heidi, however. It wouldn't be right to hurt her feelings. Maybe, when they came to the next class, Heidi would show them how to make something Allie could fix more often. *Guess I can share a loaf of friendship bread with some of my friends at work. I don't want that starter to go to waste.*

Bill put his loaf pan full of dough into the oven, placing it next to Nicole's. *I wonder what would happen if I gave a loaf of friendship bread to the irritating English teacher at the high school.* He puckered his lips. *If it was from anybody else, she might appreciate the gesture, but coming from me, I bet she'd throw it in the trash. That feisty old lady probably wouldn't accept anything I offered, even if it was served on a fancy gold platter. Don't know why she has it in for me. I've always been polite to her, even when she got under my skin.*

Bill returned to his seat at the kitchen table to wait for his bread to bake. He glanced over at Lance, who sat beside him and smiled. "Bet with you bein' a mail carrier, you'll have plenty of people you can give friendship bread or starter to."

Lance shrugged. "Yeah, maybe so. I may make some for my two daughters, though. I think they'd enjoy sharing this recipe and bread with their families, as well as passing it along to others. My brother might even enjoy it."

"How many brothers do you have?"

"Just the one. Dan's a few years older than me, and right now he's living at my house. It's only temporary—just until his townhouse is fully remodeled. I have a younger sister too." Lance motioned to Bill. "How 'bout you? Do you have any siblings?"

"I don't have any sisters, but I do have three brothers."

Bill blew out his breath. "They all live in Cleveland, and we don't see each other much."

"That's too bad."

"It's okay." Bill shrugged. "I have some good buddies who live near me. We do a lot together throughout the year. In fact, we're heading out to do some camping at my cabin in Coshocton soon."

"Sounds like fun."

"We have a good time, but it would be nice if even one of my brothers would join us sometime." Bill frowned. "None of 'em are the outdoorsy type, though. You're lucky to have a brother living close to you. I wouldn't mind if one of my brothers lived with me, even if it was only temporary. It might give me a chance to turn them on to hunting."

"Yeah," Lance gave a quick nod.

Bill figured none of his brothers would be interested in the friendship bread, but he wished he had a daughter to give a loaf. His only child, Brent, was single and also lived in Cleveland, but he probably wouldn't want any friendship bread. Since Bill was divorced, he really had no one to share the recipe with. Someday, maybe his son would get married and he could give the recipe to Brent's wife.

Bill's jaw clenched. *It'll have to be Brent's wife if he ever marries 'cause I'm sure not getting married again. I'm doin' fine by myself.*

He thought about his hunting buddies. If the friendship bread tasted good, he'd make a few more loaves and give one each to Tom, Russ, and Andy. *That oughta show those fellows I can make something other than the same old hunter's stew.* Bill brushed away some flour clinging to his apron. *I wonder what it was like for the cooks back in the Wild West during one of those trail drives. I bet those cowboys weren't as picky as my longtime friends who like to complain about minor things.*

Bill looked across the table, where Nicole sat with her head down as though studying something on the floor. The teenage girl hadn't said more than a few words since Heidi started teaching the class this morning. What was her problem anyway? Was she thinking about the troubles she had at school, or could Nicole have some serious difficulties at home she had to deal with?

Sure wish there was something I could do to help her. Trouble is, I can barely get the gal to look at me.

Nicole tried to concentrate, but all she could think about was the test Mrs. Wick sprung on them Friday in English class. Nicole shouldn't have been surprised though, since the teacher had hinted several times about reading certain chapters. She'd been staying after school for help from Mrs. Wick, then coming home and working on the assignments while it was still fresh in her mind. Nicole had a lot to do yet to get her grades up—not just in English, but in other classes as well. It was partly her fault for not seeking help before.

Nicole sighed deeply, then looked around quickly to see if anyone noticed. The last thing she wanted was for anyone in the class, or even Heidi, to ask her if anything was wrong.

She realized something had to be done about her grades, and Nicole sure didn't want to retake any of those classes. But how could she devote more time to her studies with all the responsibilities she had at home? Her dad had been trying to come home earlier so she could study more, and he'd made her siblings do a few duties around the house to lessen Nicole's load. In fact, he'd even made a list for Heather and Tony that included some housecleaning and picking up after themselves. He was trying to help her have more time to get her grades up, but she still was stuck with cooking all the meals.

Sure wish I could be like so many other kids my age who have two normal parents. They don't realize how lucky they are.

Mondays were the hardest, going back to school, when she had to listen to fellow students talk about their weekends.

Nicole and her family rarely went anywhere exciting or did fun things together; it was normally the same old routine. So sometimes while sitting there listening to her classmates, she would envision herself doing what they talked about during their weekend. It didn't help much.

Maybe getting an interesting book to read would help take me away from my real life. Guess I could go see what our school library has to offer during lunch one day.

Nicole thought about all the events going on at school, such as the football games that took place most Friday nights. When there wasn't a game, a dance was held in the school's gymnasium. On Saturdays, some of the students liked to hang out at the sub shop located on the corner near the school. The homecoming football game and dance were coming up, but Nicole wouldn't be going to those events, either. She thought the world of her dad, as well as her brother and sister, but all because of her so-called mother, Nicole was missing out on the best years of her life.

For now, Nicole had to figure out a way to keep Friday's test results from her dad. She didn't have to be a rocket scientist to know she'd failed the test miserably. *I will have to study harder for the next test. Guess I'll be getting another talking to from Mrs. Wick after class on Monday. I sure hope she doesn't email Dad again or ask to speak to him in person.*

When the oven door was opened, releasing a sweet cinnamon aroma, Heidi's whole kitchen smelled so good, it made Todd's mouth water. He looked at all the golden loaves, with hot steam rising off their tops, and licked his lips in anticipation of eating a piece. The bread reminded him of the type of thing he often ordered to go with his latte at the local coffee shop.

Once everyone's loaf of friendship bread had been taken from the oven and placed on the counter to cool, Heidi gave each of them a three-by-five card with the recipe for the bread, as well as a small amount of starter. Curious to see if there was another scripture verse on the back, Todd turned his over. Sure enough, there it was: "I will instruct thee and teach thee in the way which thou shalt go: I will guide thee with mine eye" (Psalm 32:8).

His brows furrowed. *I don't need the Lord to guide or teach me how I should go. I'll set my own course, thank you very much.* Todd wasn't even sure there was a God, let alone a need to call upon Him for anything.

Heidi stood at the head of the table, facing everyone. "Before you all leave today, I would like to share a few more helpful hints with you. When freezing foods, label each container with its contents and the date it was put into the freezer. Always use foods that have been cooked and then frozen within one to two months."

Allie bobbed her head. "Those are good points which I'm already aware of."

"Mind if I add something to the topic of freezing foods?" Lisa asked.

Heidi smiled. "Not at all."

"You should never freeze cooked egg whites, because they will become tough."

Todd turned to face her. "Is that something you learned the hard way in your catering business?"

She gave a slow nod. "I'll admit, I've had a few bloopers along the way, but for the most part, things have gone well with my enterprise."

"Do you cater a variety of events?" The question came from Nicole, which was a surprise, since she'd been quiet most of the class.

"Yes, and in fact, I'll be catering a wedding next Saturday night. I'll be working on the cake for it this coming week." Lisa's dimples deepened as she gave a wide smile. Todd thought she was kind of cute. He still didn't know if she was married and needed to figure out the best way to find out. He sure wasn't going to make a play for her if she had a husband, or even a boyfriend.

"That's wonderful," Heidi said. "Will you be taking pictures of the cake?"

"Yes, definitely."

The mention of a wedding caused Todd to recall that he'd been invited to attend the wedding of an acquaintance next week. It was the owner of a restaurant he'd written a good review about. The guy's name was Shawn, and after getting to know Todd from coming into his restaurant several times, they'd become fairly well acquainted. Now Shawn and his business partner, Melanie, were getting married.

Todd leaned his elbows on the table. The parents of Shawn's future wife were quite well-to-do. *I bet whomever they hire to cater their daughter's wedding will be some top-notch caterer with a lot of experience behind them. The food will probably be worthy of a five-star review.*

Chapter 14

Dover

Lisa had worked hard all week, finalizing the wedding reception she was catering this evening. All weddings were important, and she treated each as such. So far, those she had been hired to do had turned out pretty well. In fact, each one seemed to get better. Lisa continually worked to improve her catering business, and this evening's reception would be no exception.

She felt pleased after she'd set everything up. The food tables were arranged in a buffet-style setting. The bride and groom had requested a few items they both enjoyed eating: Chicken fingers, several kinds of chips, and a sandwich platter as well. Lisa had also provided macaroni and potato salads. Fresh vegetables were arranged on a huge platter surrounding a ranch dip. Pineapple, cantaloupe, and honeydew, along with orange and apple slices had been neatly arranged on a three-tiered sterling silver fruit stand that belonged to the bride's grandmother.

The cake was the last thing Lisa set up, and everything seemed to be perfect until the unexpected happened. After getting the first three tiers of the beautifully decorated cake in place, she'd just positioned the fourth tier, when one of the front table legs gave out. Thankfully, Lisa stood close to that corner of the table and was able to react quickly enough before it collapsed.

Now what am I going to do? Lisa steadied the table, praying the cake wouldn't topple off. *I must look silly standing here holding this table up.* Of course, there was no one else in the room at the moment, so she only looked silly to herself. The one saving grace, which amazed her, was the cake was still in place, even though the tablecloth had bunched up. Lisa only had one more tier to add, plus the pair of doves at the top, in order to finish this five-tiered cake. But how in the world could she do it while balancing a three-legged table?

Biting her lip, Lisa came up with an idea. She only hoped it would work. First, she used her one leg, stretching it out under the table. *Maybe I can hook the leg of the table and pull it back in place.* After she tried a couple of times, and was unable to see what she was doing underneath, Lisa started to sweat. "Whew!" She blew air up over her forehead. "This is going to be harder than I thought."

She wondered if she could get on her hands and knees and balance the table using her back. Then she could see underneath and try to figure out what the problem was. But after pondering the situation further, she realized she'd have to pull up the tablecloth to see under the table. Plus, once she was under there, how could she keep an eye on the cake to make sure it didn't fall? Lisa's last resort was to call out and hope someone was in the next room and would hear her plea for help.

"Is anyone there?" *Oh, please, Lord, bring someone to rescue me.* In less than half an hour, this reception room would be filled with lots of people, and she certainly didn't want to be standing here feeling ridiculous as she held up the table.

"Looks like you might need some help over here."

Lisa jumped when a male voice came up behind her. "Todd, w–what are you doing here?" Even though he was the last person she expected to see, much less answer her plea for help, she felt thankful someone had arrived to help her with this precarious situation. At Heidi's cooking class last week Todd had mentioned he'd be attending a wedding soon, but she'd had no idea it would turn out to be the same wedding she'd been asked to cater.

"I'm a friend of the groom. In fact, he owns a restaurant where I like to eat." Todd took over and held the table in place, then instructed Lisa on what to do. "Check the leg and see if it's still connected underneath the table."

"Okay, but be careful the cake doesn't tip." Lisa got down on her knees and pulled up the white tablecloth. "The leg's still connected, but I bet it wasn't locked in place." Lisa pulled the leg out straight and clicked it into the slot. "I think it's okay now. Thanks, Todd. I owe you a debt of gratitude." Heat crept across her cheeks as she crawled out from under the table.

Grinning, he offered her a thumbs-up before taking a step closer. "No problem. Glad I showed up when I did."

Lisa stood and smoothed out the flare of her pretty pink dress. Then she put the final tier on top of the cake, along with the little turtledoves. Lisa ran her hand over the tablecloth to get out the wrinkles and stood back to look at the cake. "There, that should do it."

"Looks like everything's okay now. The cake looks great, by the way. I assume it's your handiwork?"

"Yes."

Todd took a few steps toward the guest tables, but stopped and turned around. "You look really nice tonight, Lisa. If you're not here with anyone, would you save a dance for me?"

"No, I came alone."

"No husband or boyfriend to help you out with the cake?" He looked at her curiously.

She shook her head. "I'm single."

"Same here. See you on the dance floor." He winked before walking away.

Now what was that all about? Lisa watched as Todd found his name card at the table where he'd be seated, but she stopped wondering about him when, minutes later, the flurry of activity started. Guests began to file in and find their seats, waiting for the bride and groom to arrive from the church. The wedding party was announced first, followed by the bride and groom.

As all eyes watched the doorway, an older man announced, "And now let us welcome the newlyweds, Mr. and Mrs. Shawn Goss."

Everyone clapped, and once the wedding couple was seated, the best man and maid of honor took the microphone to offer short speeches and toasts. Members of the wedding party had food served to them at their table. Then the rest of the guests went through the buffet line, one table at a time. All the while, Lisa scurried about, making sure everything ran smoothly. She wished she could afford to hire an assistant, because by the time she went home tonight, she'd be exhausted.

After the cake was cut, and everyone had eaten, all the lights were turned low and the dancing started. The bride and groom must have loved country music, for they'd hired a live country-western band to accompany the dancing. Lisa stood off to one side and watched. It was fun to watch the fancy footwork when the line dancing started. Even Todd seemed to be a pro at cowboy dancing, as he clicked his heels and stomped his feet, doing the two-step around the floor with a pretty, auburn-haired woman. Lisa wished she could join the fun, but she still had work to do.

After taking care of the leftover food, she boxed up the top of the cake for the newly married couple to enjoy on their first wedding anniversary. Glancing up, she saw Todd, wearing a charming smile, walking toward her.

"I'm here for that dance, if you'll join me." He held out his hand. A slow dance had begun, and the lights were dimmed even lower.

"O—okay." Lisa's mouth went dry as she followed him to the dance floor. She thought he'd only been kidding when he'd mentioned dancing with her earlier.

When Todd took Lisa into his arms, her heart did a little flip-flop. It made no sense. She didn't even like Todd.

At least she'd thought she didn't. Now, she wasn't so sure. He had come to her aid in time to rescue the cake, but was that any reason to let her emotions take over?

As they swayed to the music, Lisa looked into Todd's vivid blue eyes, sparkling in the low light. He truly was good looking—enough to turn any woman's head. "Thank you again for coming to my aid earlier," she whispered, finding it hard to swallow. "If you hadn't shown up when you did, I would have looked pretty silly standing there holding the table when everyone arrived."

"No problem. Glad I could help."

At first, they danced at arm's length. Then Todd pulled Lisa closer.

"Don't you just love country music?" His lips were close to her ear now, and he held Lisa's hand against his chest. "'I Cross My Heart' does seem to be the perfect song at a wedding."

"I always did like this song." Lisa found it difficult to think. Todd was a good dancer, as he smoothly swayed to the music. She had no trouble moving along with him.

"Everyone seems to be having a good time."

"Uh-huh." She caught her trembling lips between her teeth as Todd moved his head closer to hers. Was he about to kiss her? Did she want him to? Her scrambled emotions made no sense. It must be the music.

"And at least the cake was good."

Lisa stopped dancing, no longer hearing the music. "What do you mean, 'at least?'"

"Well I didn't think there was anything special about the food." Todd's nose wrinkled, like some foul odor had descended on the place. "I don't know who catered the food for this reception, but the bride and groom would have done just as well ordering everything from a fast-food restaurant."

Lisa backed up, anger flaring in her nostrils. "Is that so?" With no explanation, she spun around and stomped off.

It was good Lisa had previously packed all the leftover

food in containers and put them in the kitchen's refrigerator for the family to take later. Her job was done here, and she left in a huff, anxious to get home and out of Todd's sight before she said something she might regret later.

Lisa climbed into her van and started the engine. Gripping the steering wheel, she muttered, "Who does Todd think he is, talking to me that way? Didn't he realize I catered all the food, not just the cake? Didn't he see me hustling around making sure all the serving platters were kept filled?"

It was true that the two times Todd had approached Lisa, she was taking care of the cake. First, when she'd been balancing the table while putting the tiers together. Second, when she was boxing up the top of the cake for the bride and groom. *Maybe he forgot when we were introducing ourselves at the first cooking class that I mentioned my catering business.*

"Well, what does it matter what Todd thought? He's no expert on food." Lisa backed out of her parking space. The important thing was, Shawn and Melanie where pleased with everything Lisa had prepared to make their reception perfect. Even the parents of the newly married couple made it a point to compliment her. But somehow Todd's negative remark overshadowed the rest. In fact, it put a damper on Lisa's whole night. *When I see Todd at the next cooking class, I have half a mind to tell him what I think of his rude remark about my cooking.*

She drew a deep breath and tried to calm down. She would play like a duck and let his negative comment roll right on over her. Well, maybe she would—if she could stop thinking about his curt remark and arrogant expression.

Canton

When Todd got home that evening, the first thing he did was take off his shoes and flop on the couch. His feet were killing him, and it didn't help that he'd worn a new pair of shoes to the wedding and spent too much time on his feet, dancing the night away.

He studied his left foot. "Oh great. I have a blister forming near my little toe. What else could go wrong tonight?" Todd winced, thinking about his dance with Lisa. He realized now why she'd gotten so huffy when he mentioned the less-than-desirable food someone had catered for the reception. She'd left him standing in the middle of the dance floor, staring after her until he got his wits again. Of course, by then, the music had ended and the lights were turned up, signaling that the dancing was over for the night.

Todd had attempted to find Lisa, but to no avail. After trying to make his way through the people going back to their tables, he'd scanned the room, looking for her. Where had she gone in such a hurry? He'd even run outside to look for her, but Lisa was nowhere to be seen.

When he headed back inside, Todd was in no mood for celebration. Seeking out Shawn and his new bride, Todd wished them well and said he was heading home. He closed his eyes, replaying the conversation he'd had with the wedding couple before he left.

"Before you leave," Shawn said, "have you seen Lisa? We lost sight of her after she danced with you."

Todd wasn't sure how to answer, so he simply responded, "Guess she wanted to head home."

"Okay. Melanie and I will get in touch with her later."

"You haven't paid for her making the cake yet, huh?"

"No, it's not that. We paid in advance for the cake, plus all the food she supplied. Melanie and I wanted to tell Lisa thanks, and say how much we appreciated everything she did. The food was exactly what we asked for."

Todd felt more than a twinge of guilt now that he realized

Lisa had also catered the food. She'd done it according to Shawn and Melanie's wishes too. *Each to his own. Guess everyone's taste buds are different*, he thought.

He couldn't help envying the happy couple, their faces gleaming, as they'd looked into each other's eyes, then turned to face him again. "Anyway, Todd, my wife and I appreciate you coming to help celebrate our happy occasion."

"Glad I could be here. Best of luck to the both of you." Todd gave Melanie a hug and shook Shawn's hand. "Enjoy your honeymoon in the Bahamas. It'll be a great weeklong getaway for you."

"Yes, we are looking forward to it. We'll be flying out in the morning." Melanie slipped her hand into her husband's. "Our flight time got changed, but that's okay."

"Well, again, congratulations, and have a safe trip." Todd stepped away from the couple. He wasn't considering a real relationship at this time, but if there was a special woman in his life, he'd like to be as happy as Shawn and Melanie seemed to be.

"Thanks, Todd," the couple said in unison.

Todd said goodbye, sauntered out the door, and stepped up to his shiny red sports car. He paused to admire how gorgeous his vehicle looked sitting there, freshly washed and polished. "I've got good taste," he said, opening the car door. He climbed into the driver's seat and checked his appearance in the mirror. "Of course, if it had been my wedding, I would've picked out some better food for the reception. What were Melanie and Shawn thinking? Well, at least the band they hired was good."

Allowing his thoughts to return to the present, Todd rubbed his sore feet. Since Lisa had mentioned during the first cooking class that she owned a catering business, he should have realized she'd provided all the food for the couple's reception.

Todd slapped the side of his head. "I said too much. Open

mouth—insert foot. I really blew it, didn't I?"

He pulled the throw pillow down from the back of the couch and gave it a punch. *It wasn't the best food I've ever eaten, but it wasn't the worst, either. It just didn't meet my expectations. When I see Lisa at next week's cooking class I'd better apologize to her.*

Chapter 15

Walnut Creek

Lance rolled over in bed and grabbed his second pillow—the one Flo used to lay her head upon. On nights like this when he had trouble sleeping, he found comfort placing her pillow on his chest. It wasn't the thunder sounding in the distance that kept him from sleeping tonight, however. It was the noise from the TV in the living room down the hall. Lance had always been a light sleeper, and his brother's constant need to watch television grated on his nerves—especially when he planned to rise early tomorrow morning to get ready for Sunday school and church. The only time Lance missed going to church was when he was sick. Even during the vacations he and Flo used to take, they always found a church to attend. Sunday was the Lord's Day, and Lance enjoyed fellowshipping with other believers. He wished he could talk Dan into going with him, but every time he brought up the subject, his brother said he wasn't interested in sitting in a stuffy building with a bunch of hypocrites who used religion as a crutch.

Lance didn't see it that way. People, even those who went to church and called themselves Christians, were human and made mistakes. Lance remembered how his dad used to say, "Church is the place for sinners, saved by grace. It's not a fancy hotel for saints."

Lance wondered if his brother thought he was a hypocrite

too because Dan never excluded him from the select group of people he disliked so much at church. *Maybe I need to check my own spiritual walk and be sure I'm setting the proper example to win someone like Dan to the Lord.* Lance would pray for God to show him how and direct his life fully, in order to spiritually help his wayward brother or someone else who couldn't find their way. *Sure wish I could make Dan understand the importance of committing his life to Christ.*

Lance, Dan, and their younger sister, Evelyn, had been raised in a Christian home. But Dan strayed from God, and nothing Evelyn or Lance said or did seemed to get through to him. Lance tried extra hard to set a Christian example to his brother, but having Dan living here was testing the limits of his patience. Between the loud TV, dirty dishes in the sink, clothes strewn all over the floor of the guest room, and the laundry fiasco, Lance struggled to keep from losing his temper. At least Dan had started parking his car on the street until Lance came home and put his vehicle in the garage. If the other things that bothered Lance didn't improve soon, he may be forced to ask his brother to leave. But if he did, Dan might stray even further from God, believing his brother to be a hypocrite too.

Lance hugged the pillow tighter to his chest. *If Flo was here right now, what would she say or do? I bet she'd get out of bed, go into the other room, and politely ask Dan to turn the volume down because she couldn't sleep. Guess that's what I oughta do too.*

Rolling out of bed, Lance slipped on his bedroom slippers and padded down the hall in his pajamas. A streak of lightning lit up the hall, and an ear-piercing crack of thunder followed, causing him to jump. This time of year they didn't get many storms, but with the change of seasons and cold fronts pushing warm air out, some feisty storms developed.

"Say, Dan," Lance said when he entered the living room and saw his brother flaked out on the couch, "would you mind turning the volume down a bit?"

Dan cupped a hand over his ear and scrunched up his nose. "What'd you say?"

"I said, would you mind turning the volume down a bit?" Lance spoke a little louder this time, making a twisting motion with his fingers. "It's keeping me awake."

"It's not that loud."

"It is to me." Lance wondered if his brother's hearing was going bad.

Dan pointed to the window behind him. Now the late autumn storm was directly overhead. "The thunder and rain are a lot louder than the TV. Are you sure it's not the weather keeping you awake tonight?"

"No, it's the TV. I'm not used to having it on when I'm in bed trying to sleep. Besides, you shouldn't have the television on when there's a storm like this. Lightning could strike and blow the whole tube out."

Dan got up and turned off the TV. "Okay, okay, I get the point. If my watching television at night is such a big deal, I'll only watch it during the day when you're out delivering mail."

"Thanks, I appreciate that." Lanced turned toward his room. "Good night, Dan," he called over his shoulder. "See you in the morning."

"Sure thing." And then his brother added, "You should get rid of this dinosaur television set and get yourself a new flat screen TV with a remote. Oh, and don't bother cooking me any breakfast in the morning. I'm going out to eat with a friend."

"Okay. Night, Dan." Lance was tempted to comment about the age of his TV, but kept his mouth shut. He even thought of mentioning church, but thought better of it too. No point in starting a discussion that could end up in an argument. The best thing to do was just go to bed. Hopefully, with the TV off he could sleep.

"It's getting late. Are you ready for bed?" Lyle lifted himself from his easy chair.

Heidi held up the notebook in her hand and remained on the couch. "You go on ahead. I'm going to stay here awhile and finish working on my list for the cooking class next week."

Lyle tipped his head. "I thought you had everything figured out."

She sighed. "I thought so too but after the way some of my students responded to the friendship bread I had them make during last Saturday's class, I changed my mind."

"What's wrong with friendship bread? I've always enjoyed the variations you've made with the basic recipe." Lyle smacked his lips. "I especially like when you add raisins or chocolate chips."

"I think some of the students were okay with my choice, but others, like Allie and Lisa, seemed disappointed. Allie was probably hoping for a dish she could serve her family, and I'm guessing Lisa was looking for something to use in her catering business." Heidi fiddled with the pen between her fingers. "Neither one of them said anything, but I could sense it. And Todd. . .well, annoyance was written all over his face too."

"So what are you going to teach them next week?"

Heidi shrugged. "I'm not sure. Probably a main dish of some sort, or maybe a salad."

Lyle glanced at the grandfather clock across the room. "Well, it's getting late, and we should be heading to bed, so can you wait till Monday to decide what dish to choose for your next cooking class?"

"You're right, Lyle. My eyes are getting heavy too." Heidi yawned and set the notebook aside. "Truthfully, I could probably sit here all night and not come up with what to teach my class. Maybe by Monday I'll have a clearer head."

Heidi remained seated a few moments, thinking about Kendra and her baby. *I wonder how they're fairing this evening*

125

with the wicked storm and all its noise. Hopefully they aren't being kept awake because of it. The weather was proving to be a bit unnerving, with the rumbling right above the house and bolts of lightning shooting about. *I'm sure if the baby gets fussy, it will test Kendra's new motherly skills in trying to comfort her precious daughter.*

Heidi stood, and as she followed her husband across the room, a flash of lightning lit up the entire living room. She flinched, and their dog howled when the boom of thunder hit. She could almost feel the vibration beneath her feet. Heidi's dog lay shaking near the fireplace. She bent down and gave his head a gentle pat. "It's okay, Rusty. This terrible noise shouldn't go on too much longer."

Rusty looked up at her and whined.

"Oh, all right, boy, you can sleep in our room tonight." She looked at Lyle to get his approval, and when he nodded, she clapped her hands and told the dog to come along.

Heidi followed Lyle into their bedroom, and once Rusty was inside, she closed the door behind them. She hoped by morning the storm would pass. It was never fun to travel anywhere with the horse and buggy in stormy weather, and tomorrow, church would be held in a home a few miles away.

New Philadelphia

Bill hung up the phone after talking with his friend Andy Eglund. They'd been discussing their upcoming camping trip and talking about who, including Russ and Tom, would bring what.

It had been a tradition for the guys to leave on Thanksgiving, after having the meal with their families. It had been one of the things Bill's ex-wife complained about, but her fussing all those years never changed a thing. Nothing kept Bill from spending time with his friends. Going camping was a big deal. His ex just didn't understand.

Now that Bill was a free man, he usually arrived at camp Thursday afternoon. Since he wouldn't be having a Thanksgiving meal with anyone, there was no reason not to leave early. Andy, Russ, and Tom usually arrived Thursday evening or early Friday morning. They would spend the next three days getting the cabin cleaned up, and going out to scout where each of them would hunt. Sometimes Russ would bring a few board games along. He liked the friendly competition and said it was something fun to do after eating their supper in the evening.

At least Russ had the good sense to leave his dog at home. When he'd brought up the idea of bringing the mutt, Bill had put the kibosh to it.

The Monday after Thanksgiving was opening day of deer season. With his excitement building, Bill never got much sleep the night before the big day. There was nothing like sitting in his tree stand and watching the morning unfold— something he never tired of. Blue jays chattered, squirrels gathered nuts, and if luck would have it, a buck would sneak through the area Bill hunted. He'd been told there were bears in the woods near his cabin, but to date, Bill had never seen one anywhere he hunted.

Bill started a list of what he would need to purchase for their long weekend. He got tired of eating a bunch of unhealthy snacks when they all went up to the cabin. The junk he and the guys usually ate was full of artificial colors and preservatives, not to mention too much sugar. It wasn't even fit for the squirrels. Bill didn't want to keep adding to his girth, and it wasn't easy watching his buddies eat like that. Maybe he would bring some healthy things, like some kind of a salad and cut-up veggies to have on hand.

He hoped to surprise his friends this year with some newer tasty meals he'd be learning from Heidi. So far, for breakfast one of the mornings, he planned on making baked oatmeal. Then Bill would serve a loaf of friendship bread to go along with the spaghetti meal he planned on making for one of their suppers.

As he thought about what else he could make, the phone rang again.

"Bet it's either Russ or Tom calling to discuss more about our Thanksgiving trip." Bill reached over and picked up the phone from the small table next to the chair where he sat. "Hello."

"Hi, Dad. It's Brent."

It had been a while since Bill heard from his son, so this was a nice surprise. "Hey, Son, how are you doing?"

"I'm good. And you?"

"All's well at this end."

"Say, I won't keep you, but I was wondering if you had anything going on either the last weekend of October, or the second weekend of November? I was thinking of coming down for a few days to see you. Maybe arrive on Friday night, and spend the weekend with you. Would that be okay?"

"That sounds good, Brent." Bill smiled, eager to see his son. "I have both of those weekends free, so whatever is good for you is fine by me."

"Okay. How about the second weekend of November?"

"Yep, that's great. I'll be anxious to see you."

"Same here."

They talked about several other things. Brent told his dad Aunt Virginia and Uncle Al had invited him for Thanksgiving dinner. "I remember that you leave for deer camp on Thanksgiving, so I thought it was okay to accept Aunt Virginia's invitation."

"I'm glad you did. If my memory serves me right, she puts out a real nice spread for Thanksgiving."

"You're right about that."

"Before you called, I was talking to my friend Andy. We were making our usual deer-hunting plans." Bill cringed when a clap of thunder sounded, rattling the windows. "Well, I'd like to talk longer, but we're having a pretty bad storm right now, and the lights just flickered, so I'd better hang up before the power goes out."

"Sure, Dad. We can catch up with each other when I come to visit in two weeks."

"Sounds good. See you then."

After Bill clicked off the phone, he picked up his tablet, flipping his camping list over to start a new page. He couldn't wait to visit with Brent, and he started writing things down he knew his son liked to eat. *Maybe I'll make my son a loaf of that friendship bread, after all. Brent might enjoy it, and he can take what's left of the bread when it's time for him to go home.*

Canton

Kendra felt her chest tighten as raindrops pelted the roof and thunder cracked overhead. She'd never liked storms and used to cower under the covers when she was a little girl to try and calm her fears. Tonight, she felt like a child again, needing the comfort of her mother. But she was a mother now and didn't feel up to the task. At least, not tonight.

Another clap of thunder sounded, and little Heidi started crying. *Waa! Waa! Waa!* The noisy storm had no doubt wakened the poor baby.

Kendra turned on her bedside lamp and crawled out of bed. Then she hurried across the room and took her little girl out of the crib. "It's okay, sweet baby. Mama's got you now."

Waa! Waa! The infant continued to howl. Kendra felt sure Heidi wasn't hungry; she'd fed her just an hour ago. She checked the baby's diaper, but it was dry. It must be the storm causing her child to fuss. She couldn't blame her for that.

"Like mother, like daughter," Kendra murmured against the infant's ear. "Hush, little one. The storm will be over soon."

Another clap of thunder sounded, and Kendra's muscles tensed. It was hard to calm her baby when she, herself, felt nervous. Walking back and forth, from the crib to her own bed, Kendra patted little Heidi's back, but to no avail.

A few seconds later, her bedroom door jerked open, and Dad stepped into the room. "What's going on in here? Why's the baby crying?"

Kendra stiffened at the sharp tone of her father's voice. She couldn't get over him barging into her room like that, either. "She's afraid of the thunder, and I really can't blame her."

"Well, you'd better find some way to get her calmed down. We all have to get up early for church in the morning, and none of us can afford to lose any sleep." His brows furrowed. "If things are going to work out with you living here again, you'll have to be considerate of other people's needs."

"I am trying, Dad. I'm sure she'll stop crying once the thunder and lightning stops." At moments like this, Kendra wished she still lived with the Troyers. At least there, she was spoken to kindly and felt a sense of peace. But she'd made her choice when she decided to move back in with Mom and Dad and let them help her raise little Heidi. So she would make the best of it and try to keep the peace. She hoped Dad would let up a bit and not be so demanding. After all, Heidi was his granddaughter, not some stranger Kendra had brought home to stir up trouble.

Dad gave a quick nod, mumbled, "Good night," and left the room, closing the door behind him.

I wish Mom would've come into my room to find out what was happening, instead of Dad. He sure doesn't have much nurturing in his character. Kendra patted the baby's back. At times like this, she wished she and little Heidi could move out of this house. But they really had no other place to go.

Kendra breathed a sigh of relief when the storm abated and the baby settled down. Tomorrow would be the first Sunday to take her daughter to church, and she was a bit nervous, wondering what people would say. Of course, everyone knew Kendra had given birth to a child and wasn't married. But when she showed up tomorrow with the baby in her arms, it could cause some tongues to wag.

Well, I don't care if it does. Kendra placed the baby into her crib and gently stroked her soft cheek. *If anyone says anything unkind, I'll remind them what the Bible says about judging. "He that is without sin among you, let him first cast a stone at her."*

Chapter 16

As Kendra sat on a church pew with her parents and sisters, she breathed deeply, trying to ignore those staring at her. Were they surprised to see Bridget and Guy Perkins's wayward daughter here today, or could they be admiring her sweet baby daughter? Well, what did it matter? Like a dutiful daughter, Kendra had come here today to keep the peace, since Dad had insisted she accompany them, even though she'd been up half the night trying to calm little Heidi. It wasn't that she didn't want to attend church—just not today. She felt tired from lack of sleep and utter annoyance at her father for being so grouchy last night about her baby crying.

Kendra fussed with the baby's outfit, and then she fiddled with her necklace nervously. She could almost feel people's eyes staring at her and wondered if her family felt it too. Kendra thought back to when she was a little girl and sat on these pews, under this same ceiling. She glanced upward, appreciating the workmanship that went into creating such a beautiful sanctuary. The ceiling was crafted of wood—which type, she wasn't sure—but the patterns in each section were a masterpiece of designs. Like a snowflake, no two pieces were the same; each was unique and had a beauty of its own. Huge beams hung strategically along the ceiling's length. Kendra remembered how, even as a child, she'd found them interesting, since they were salvaged from a local barn torn down many years ago.

This church has been here such a long time. These walls have seen a lot of weddings and other happy events, and also many funerals.

Kendra fixed her eyes on the beautiful stained-glass window close to the peak of the wall in the front of the church where the congregation faced. It was a mesmerizing piece of art, with the Lord Jesus kneeling by a rock, hands in prayer, and a heavenly beam of light shining on His serene face.

Kendra's gaze returned to her baby daughter, nestled snuggly in her arms. Living with her parents, Kendra's situation wasn't perfect, but at least she and little Heidi had not been separated like she thought they would.

Looking back up at the image etched into the window, Kendra mouthed a silent, *Thank You, Lord.*

She turned her focus on the chorus the congregation had begun to sing, but her eyes grew heavy. Kendra had almost nodded off when the baby started to fuss. She lifted Heidi over her shoulder and patted the infant's small back. It didn't help; the baby began to wail. *Oh, no. Not a repeat of last night, I hope.*

Chris cast a sidelong glance in Kendra's direction. "You'd better do something quick or you'll hear about it from Dad," she whispered.

Kendra pulled the pacifier from the diaper bag and put it in the baby's mouth. After Dad's response to Heidi's cries last night, she knew full well what he must be thinking now. While her father had agreed to her moving back home so they could help with the expense of raising the baby, Kendra felt certain he'd never completely forgiven her indiscretion with Max. As a board member in good standing with the church, Dad saw what Kendra did as an embarrassment to him, as well as the rest of the family. Kicking Kendra out of the house was the way he'd chosen to deal with things when she'd first told him and Mom she was expecting a baby.

She had a hunch the only reason Dad let her come home

was to please Mom. The first night she'd returned, her sister Shelly had confided to Kendra that their mother had been miserable since Dad forced Kendra out of the house. While Mom had never said anything in front of the girls, she may have pleaded with Dad to bring Kendra back. Whatever the reason, Kendra accepted the offer in order to keep her child. Even though she was sure the Troyers would make good parents, she would have always felt like a part of her was missing if she'd gone through with the adoption. For some unwed mothers, adoption was the best way, but given the opportunity to raise her child, Kendra had jumped at the chance.

Relieved that the baby had stopped fussing, perhaps from the quieter song they were now singing, Kendra allowed herself to relax. There was a time, not long ago, when the bitterness she felt toward Max and her own father would have kept Kendra from darkening the door of any church. Now, even though she felt a bit uncomfortable, at least she could enjoy the service.

Dover

When Lisa returned home from church, she was surprised to see her renter's dog in the yard with no supervision. Of course, this wasn't unusual these days. From what she could tell, the poor little pup was sorely neglected. The dog started barking as soon as Lisa got out of her van. She figured with all the racket, one or both of the pup's owners would come out, but their front door remained shut.

"What's the matter, boy? Are you lonely?" Lisa bent down and stroked the animal's silky ears. The dog leaned into her hand, eyes closed and tail barely wagging. "You're starved for attention, aren't you?" Lisa couldn't figure out why anyone would get a pet and not spend time with it. A dog, or even a cat, made a good companion. *If I had a dog I'd make sure it was well cared for and give it plenty of love.*

Lisa started to walk toward her own duplex unit, when the puppy looked up at her and whined. "Sorry little fella, but I can't stay here in the yard and pet you all afternoon. I'm hungry and need to eat." She leaned over, picked up a small stick, and gave it a fling. When the pup ran after it, she hurried up the steps, unlocked her door, and stepped inside.

After placing her Bible on the coffee table, Lisa went to the kitchen for a glass of cold water. Since the room faced the front of the house, she couldn't help hearing the dog's continual yapping. She hurriedly made herself a ham and cheese sandwich, then took it to the dining room where it was quieter. She could still hear the pup faintly, but the sound didn't get on her nerves like it had previously. At least she could eat in peace.

When Lisa finished her sandwich, she went back to the kitchen and put her dishes in the sink. She would stick them in the dishwasher later, because right now she was going back outside to see why that pathetic dog was still carrying on.

She found the critter in one of her flower beds, digging a nice little hole. "Oh, no you don't, mister. You're going back inside to pester your owners." Lisa picked up the pup and marched over to the other unit. She was about to knock on the door when she saw a note stuck near the door knocker with tape. Squinting, she read it aloud: "To Lisa Brooks: This is to inform you that we can't pay the rent this month, so we moved out this morning while you were at church. We are moving in with my folks, but can't take the dog with us, so I hope you'll either take him in or find the mutt a good home."

Lisa slapped her forehead and groaned. It was bad enough the young couple had moved out with no advance notice, but to leave the dog behind, expecting her to take care of it was unbelievable. *I wonder what state they left the place in. I'll need to get the key and let myself in so I can take a good look around each room.* She held the pup securely in her arms. *What were those people thinking? How could they abandon this poor little thing?*

With a sigh of resignation, she headed back to her place. For now, she would keep the critter, but as soon as she could find him a good home, he'd be gone. She had no time or patience for a pet.

When Lisa entered the house, an idea formed. This coming Saturday she'd be attending her third cooking class. Perhaps one of Heidi's other students would like a dog.

⚬⚬⚬

Canton

Todd yawned and stretched his arms over his head. He'd slept in this morning and had spent the afternoon watching TV. It felt good to do nothing and answer to no one once in a while. The past week he'd tried out a couple of restaurants and written his review of each one. The first place he'd visited served French cuisine, and the other was a bistro a friend had told him about. He'd seen a young woman there who reminded him of Lisa Brooks, only her hair was a lighter shade of blond. Ever since his friend's wedding, when Lisa walked off the dance floor, Todd had thought about her. He wondered if he ought to look up her number and give her a call to apologize for his remark about the food at the reception. According to the bride and groom, Lisa had rushed off without even saying goodbye.

Todd got up from his chair and ambled out to the kitchen for a cup of coffee. Maybe he would go out later to look for some new shirts or a pair of slacks. Todd liked the attention he always got from the female store clerks. Of course, in all likelihood, they were only trying to get him to part with his money. Todd preferred the specialty shops tucked away in the mall. Catering to himself could almost always pull Todd out of the doldrums. He'd put Lisa out of his mind for the time being and concentrate on other things. He would see her at the cooking class this coming Saturday; then he could apologize for his unkind remarks. *Maybe I'll arrive early for class and wait in my car until Lisa gets there. Sure hope she's willing to talk to me.*

Chapter 17

New Philadelphia

"Hey, how are you, and what brings you by my place this evening?" Bill's friend Andy gave him a big grin and opened the door wider.

"Came to give you this." Bill handed Andy a loaf of friendship bread, along with a jar of starter. "I learned how to make this at the last cooking class and wanted to share a loaf with you. Was planning to give it to you and our other hunting buddies on Thanksgiving weekend but decided to come on over and give it to you now."

"I appreciate the bread, but what's in here?" Andy squinted at the jar.

"It's the starter, so you can make more bread if you want."

Andy shook his head vigorously. "You know I don't cook."

"Well, maybe one of your daughters might be interested in making the bread."

"Yeah, could be." Andy motioned with his head. "Come on in and stay awhile. I'll put on a pot of coffee and we can have some of this bread."

"Sounds good." Truth was, Bill wanted to discuss a few things with his friend about their upcoming plans to go hunting. Sunday evenings were always kind of boring for him, so he was glad he'd found his friend at home.

Andy led the way to the kitchen and told Bill to take a seat at the table, while he placed the friendship bread and starter on the counter. "I'll get the coffee going before I cut the bread."

"I have a better idea. I'll cut the bread while you make the coffee." Without waiting for his friend's response, Bill grabbed a cutting board and knife and sliced several thick pieces of bread. He placed them on a plate and set it on the table.

"Do we need butter or jelly to go with it?" Andy questioned.

"Only if you want some. The bread's plenty moist, and as far as I'm concerned, there's no need to put anything on it." Bill glanced over at Andy and grinned. "I'm kinda glad Heidi taught me and the other students how to make this bread; you're in for a treat."

A short time later, they both sat at the table, drinking coffee and eating friendship bread. "You were right. It is good bread, and it's plenty moist." Andy smacked his lips. "I hope my daughter Jenny uses the starter and makes another loaf or two. Maybe I oughta share it with one of our buddies."

"You can if you want to, but I'm planning to serve some of the bread when we all go hunting Thanksgiving weekend."

Andy's forehead wrinkled. "Uh…about our plans…" He paused and took a swig of coffee. "I can't make it this year."

Bill's jaw clenched as his shoulders slumped. "How come?"

"Well, the thing is…" Andy paused once more and picked up another piece of bread. "I've been invited to eat with my daughter April and her family so—"

"Not a problem. You can come up to my cabin after the meal, just like you always do."

Andy shook his head. "You didn't let me finish."

"Sorry. Go ahead."

"We won't be eating at April's house this year. Her husband booked flights for all of us to go to Disney World."

Bill's neck muscles tightened as he tipped his head to one side. "You're going to Orlando for Thanksgiving?"

His friend gave a nod. "I would've said something sooner, but I just found out about it yesterday when April dropped by to see how I'm doing."

Bill squeezed his fingers into a fist until his hand ached. He was tempted to ask Andy if he'd consider saying no to the plans his son-in-law made, but it wouldn't be fair. Andy's family had always been tight-knit—even more so since his wife, Nadine, died. Many times Bill felt envious of this; especially since he and his son rarely saw each other. *Guess I should be glad Brent is coming to visit me next month. But at least it's not on my hunting weekend.*

Andy leaned forward, his elbows resting on the table. "You okay with this, buddy? You look sorta down in the mouth right now."

"It took me by surprise, that's all." Bill lifted his shoulders in a brief shrug. "It's been a tradition for all of us to meet at my cabin on Thanksgiving weekend, but don't worry about it. Your family comes first. I'm sure the rest of our hunting buddies won't let me down."

Walnut Creek

"What are you doing?" Lyle asked when he entered the living room with two mugs full of hot apple cider. He handed one to Heidi and took a seat beside her on the couch.

She smiled and placed it on the coffee table. "I've been going through yesterday's mail. Found a letter from Ron Hensley mixed in with the bills and advertisements."

"Is that so? It's been a while since we've heard from Ron. What's he up to these days?

"He's working part-time at the Walmart store in his hometown. Best of all, he's made amends with his children and even apologized to his ex-wife for everything he did to hurt her in the past." Heidi pointed to Ron's letter lying on the small table beside her coffee cup. "He says even though there's no chance of him and his wife getting back together, at least they can be cordial to each other from now on."

"Good to hear. Is he still seeing a counselor to help with his postwar trauma?"

"Jah. He mentioned that too." Heidi reflected on how things were when Ron first showed up at their house asking for a place to park his motor home. She'd been surprised when he'd decided to join her first group of students for lessons in Amish cooking, and even more surprised when, several weeks later, she'd learned that Ron had stolen some things from their house and barn. Thanks to a scripture Heidi had written on the back of a recipe card she'd given her students after one lesson, Ron found forgiveness for the hurtful things he'd said and done to many people after leaving the Marine Corp, following his tour of duty in Vietnam. Several others who attended Heidi's first set of classes had also been affected by the scriptures she'd shared, not to mention a bit of mentoring from her along the way.

Of course, Heidi took no credit for any of it. If lives were changed, the glory went to God, for only He could change a person's heart and give them a new lease on life. She felt thankful for the opportunity to share God's love with others, and even more appreciative when someone responded to His calling. With this second group of students, she'd not seen any progress in a spiritual sense yet. But that wasn't to say it wouldn't come, for they still had four more cooking classes to get through. During those weeks, anything could happen.

———— ⚬⚬⚬ ————

Millersburg

"You look tired, honey. Why don't you go on up to bed?" Nicole's dad leaned down over the couch and tapped her shoulder.

Nicole held up her history book. "I can't go yet. Gotta test to take tomorrow, so I need to study awhile longer."

His brows furrowed. "Shouldn't you have done that

sooner? You've had all weekend, and it's not good to wait till the last minute to cram for a test."

Her teeth clamped together with an audible click. "I haven't had all weekend, Dad. I've been busy with other things—like cooking meals, washing clothes, and keeping my sister and brother entertained so they didn't get on your nerves while you were watching your favorite TV shows." It irritated Nicole that Dad couldn't see how hard she'd worked over the weekend, with so little time to herself. "Now that Heather and Tony have gone to bed, this is the first chance I've had to crack open my history book."

"If you'd said you had homework sooner, I'd have taken the kids out somewhere to give you a break."

Before Nicole could comment, the doorbell rang. Dad rose from his chair. "I'll get it."

A few seconds later, he marched back to the living room, eyes narrowed and ears flaming red. Nicole cringed when she saw who'd walked in with him. "Tonya. What are you doing here?"

"Came to see you and my other two kids. And don't call me Tonya." Nicole's mother's words slurred as she staggered toward the couch. "How have ya been Nicki?"

Nicole sat up, folding her arms tightly across her chest. "My name's not Nicki." She hated the nickname her mom had given her. It made her feel like she was a little girl. *Well, I'm not. I am practically a grown woman, and I'm doing your job, Tonya.* Nicole bit her tongue to keep from spewing the words out in her mother's face.

"You've obviously been drinking, Tonya." Dad moved closer to her. "You're not supposed to show up at this house unannounced. What brought you here anyway?"

"I just told ya. Came to see my kids." She plunked down on the end of the couch by Nicole's feet.

"Tony and Heather are asleep." Dad moved toward the door leading to the stairs, as if to block the way in case Tonya decided to head in that direction.

She released an undignified belch and didn't even bother to excuse herself.

Nicole wrinkled her nose when the smell coming from her mother's mouth reached her nostrils. The odor of alcohol was so disgusting. Nicole sat up and turned her head away. A desire to flee the room was intense. She'd always hated it whenever her mother drank—not just because of the putrid odor, but because of how Mom acted when she'd had too much to drink. She became obnoxious and loud, often cursing and sometimes slapping the kids for no good reason.

"I don't care if Tony and Heather are sleeping." Tonya's voice raised a notch. "I have a right to see my kids whenever I want."

Dad shook his head. "No, you don't. You gave up that right when you ran out on your family. Do I need to remind you that when you filed for divorce, you agreed to give up all rights to the children?" His nostrils flared. "I've been kind and let you visit some weekends, but only when you're sober. You should not have come here tonight."

Tonya's face flamed, and she leaped to her feet. "Is it any wonder I left you, Mike? You're a mean man." Teetering back and forth, she lost her balance and fell back onto the couch.

"Dad's not mean." Nicole felt the need to defend him. Tonya had no right coming here and pointing fingers at Dad. He was a good parent, doing the best he could to raise his children. Tonya, on the other hand, didn't deserve the title of *Mother*.

Nicole's mom sneered at her. "You stay out of this, young lady." She blinked several times. "And why aren't you in bed, missy?"

Nicole pointed to her history book. "I'm studying for a test." Holding her nose so she wouldn't gag, she added, "Your breath smells terrible."

As if she hadn't even heard, Tonya turned away from

Nicole and focused on Dad again. "Are you gonna get Tony and Heather outa bed so they can give their mother a kiss, or not?"

He shook his head, looking more determined than before. "I want you to leave, Tonya, and don't come back to this house unless you're sober."

Nicole struggled to keep from shouting, "Don't come back at all!"

Tonya lifted her chin, baring her stained teeth—teeth that used to be pearly white before she started smoking and drinking. "Don't tell me what to do, Mike. You are not my boss. Y–you have no control over me anymore."

"I never did. If I had, you wouldn't be in the mess you're in right now. You would have gone for help, like I wanted you to."

Dad's last statement seemed to enrage Tonya, for she hauled off and slapped his face. When it looked like she might hit him again, he grabbed hold of her wrist. "Enough, Tonya. It's time for you to go."

"Yeah, Mom, please go." Nicole spoke softly, hoping to calm her mother down. The last thing they needed was for Heather and Tony to wake up. They shouldn't see their mother acting this way. For that matter, as far as Nicole was concerned, they shouldn't see her at all. She wished Tonya would leave and never come back. All she ever brought with her was trouble.

Dad took Tonya by the arm and led her firmly to the front door. "Do you have a driver who's sober, or should I call you a cab?"

She sneered at him. "Arnie's waitin' for me in the car."

"Okay, good. And the next time you want to pay the kids a visit, please give me a call."

Nicole felt relief when her mother went out the door. The whole episode had shaken her badly. She set her history book on the coffee table. There was no point in trying to study anymore. All she wanted to do was go to her room and hope that things would look better in the morning after a good night's sleep. Of course, it was doubtful. Short of a miracle, nothing would ever seem right in Nicole's life—not with the way her mother was. The best she could hope for was that Tonya and her new husband would move out of town and never be heard from again. She sighed deeply. *But that will probably never happen. Tonya is so mixed up and miserable. I think she wants to pull us all down so we'll be unhappy right along with her. Well, I'll show Tonya. I don't know how, but I'm gonna make something out of my life someday, and I don't need a mother to do it.*

Chapter 18

Dover

Using her key to the other half of the duplex, Lisa opened the door and stepped inside. The evening shadows had darkened the entryway, so she flipped on the light switch. With the exception of a few scratch marks near the bottom of the front door, everything looked okay.

She made her way to the kitchen, but when she entered the room and turned on the light, Lisa's mouth dropped open. In addition to the refrigerator door hanging wide open, there was food on the table and dirty dishes in the sink. Her renters had not bothered to clean out the refrigerator or clear the table before moving out, and didn't even care about leaving grimy dishes behind. Since she'd rented the place furnished, Lisa was anxious to see what condition the living room and bedroom had been left in.

Upon entering the living room, she leaned against one wall and groaned. The leather couch had several holes; the carpet was stained; and the rocking chair, which she'd bought used but in good condition, was missing an arm.

Her jaw tightened. It seemed the young couple with exceptionally loud voices didn't care any more about the furniture in this home than they did their marriage. Several old newspapers were stacked on the coffee table, and when Lisa picked them up, she noticed a large scratch gouged in the finish. It would take considerable sanding and varnishing to fix a mark that deep.

She ground her teeth together. *How could anyone be so careless and disrespectful of someone else's property? I certainly made a mistake renting to them.*

Moving on to the bedroom, Lisa found it also to be in disarray. The linens and bedspread, which had also been included with the furniture, had been stripped from the bed and lay in a tangled heap on the floor. The mirror above the dresser bore a huge crack, as though someone had intentionally thrown something at it. The bedroom carpet was also stained, and what appeared to be fingernail polish had been spilled on one of the nightstands.

Shaking her head in disbelief, Lisa clicked her tongue against the roof of her mouth. She'd have to do a lot of cleanup and perhaps pay for some work to be done before she could rent the unit out again. And then there was the yappy pup she'd left tied up in her yard. Lisa hoped once more that she could find the little fella a good home, because she certainly couldn't keep him, even if he was a cute dog.

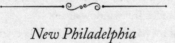

New Philadelphia

Allie stood in front of her bedroom window, staring at the blackened sky. It seemed like the stars were hung on invisible threads. Like so many other Sundays, she and the children had spent the day without Steve. Why couldn't he get the weekends off once in a while to be with his family? Didn't he care enough about her and the kids to want to spend time with them?

Her thoughts went once again to the female officer she'd seen Steve with a couple of weeks ago. Allie couldn't help thinking the pretty blond had something to do with him working so many hours. *I wonder how he'd respond if I asked.* She gripped the windowsill until her fingers felt numb. *Even if it were true, I'm sure he would deny it. Steve would most likely make up some excuse.*

Allie glanced at the clock on the table beside their bed. It was almost ten o'clock. *Steve should be home by now. Should I be worried about his safety or concerned that he's up to no good?*

The bedroom door clicked open and shut, causing Allie to jump. She whirled around in time to see her husband stroll across the room. He slipped his arms around her waist and nuzzled her neck with his cold nose. "Sorry I'm late."

Allie breathed a sigh of relief. Steve was back home, safe and sound. But now the other doubts replaced her fears.

"How'd your day go, honey? Did you and the kids do anything fun?"

"No, not really. After I picked them up from Sunday school, we had an early lunch. Then Nola and Derek spent the rest of the day watching TV while I read a mystery novel." Allie's voice quavered. "The day would have been a lot more fun if you'd been here to share it with us."

"Sorry. You know I had to work."

No, I don't know that. I only know you said you had to work. She turned to face the window again.

Steve put his hand on her shoulder. "Is everything okay?"

How could it be okay when you're hardly ever at home? Allie merely shrugged in response to his question. There was no point going over this again. Steve knew how she felt about him working long hours—often when it wasn't necessary.

As he stood quietly beside her, she heard his heavy breathing against her ear.

Gathering her nerve, she turned to him and voiced a question that needed to be asked. "Do you still love me, Steve?"

"Of course I do, Allie. Why would you even ask me that?"

The words stuck in her throat, and she shrugged again. Truth was, as much as she wanted to know if he was having an affair, she feared the answer. If Steve had been unfaithful, would he want a divorce? How would the children be affected if their parents split up?

"I'm not scheduled to work next weekend, so maybe we can do something fun with the kids."

She looked at him hopefully. "Really? What if someone wants you to cover for them again?"

"I'll say no."

Allie hugged her husband tightly, her doubts disappearing, at least for the moment. She could only hope Steve meant what he'd said and would stay true to his word.

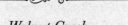

Walnut Creek

As Lance stood in front of the bathroom mirror, preparing to brush his teeth, he paused to look at the red heart-shaped tattoo on his right arm. His wife's name was featured in the middle of the heart, done in dark blue ink. Every time Lance looked at the tattoo, he was reminded of how much he missed Flo. He missed her all the time, but even more since Dan had moved in with him. Flo would have been a buffer.

A muscle on the side of Lance's neck quivered, thinking about his latest irritation. Dan had a habit of raiding the refrigerator at night, after Lance had gone to bed. Lance would get up in the morning and find dirty dishes in the sink, and sometimes food would be left on the kitchen counter or table. Growing up, he hadn't realized his brother was such a slob. Of course, back then, either Mom or their sister, Evelyn, did the cleaning. No doubt they picked up after Dan, so Lance hadn't noticed his brother's messy habits.

He curled his fingers around his toothbrush handle. *Well, I'm noticing them now, and if it were anyone else but my flesh-and-blood brother, I'd ask him to leave—pronto!*

To make matters worse, Dan came home the other day with one of those new-fangled flat screen TVs. "I am no more interested in one of those things than I would be with a smart phone," Lance grumbled out loud, as if it would make him feel better. His old TV may be old-fashioned, but it worked fine. Now he'd have to call someone to have it removed and the new one hooked up. Maybe he would suggest Dan return the new flat screen. But then, that would probably hurt his brother's feelings.

Lance clenched his jaw. At last report, Dan's townhouse renovations weren't even half done. So unfortunately, it would be a while before he moved out of Lance's house.

Lance squeezed the rest of the toothpaste from the tube and went over his teeth again for good measure. *Unless I can think of someplace else for my brother to live, guess I'm stuck with him awhile longer. Now if I could just come up with some way to cope.*

Chapter 19

With only one more week left in October, Heidi couldn't believe it was almost time for her students to arrive for the third cooking class. Today she would be teaching them to make Chicken in a Crumb Basket—a favorite main dish that had been passed down from her husband's family and enjoyed by everyone Heidi had prepared it for since she'd married Lyle.

Heidi spread the recipe notecards on the table, taking the time to write the verse she'd chosen to share on the back of each card. "If we love one another, God dwelleth in us, and his love is perfected in us" (1 John 4:12). She wasn't sure who among her students this scripture was meant for, but God had laid it on her heart to choose this particular verse to go with today's lesson.

Pausing from her work to glance out the kitchen window, Heidi focused on the haze sliding over the landscape. The colors of the few leaves remaining on the trees in their yard appeared muted by the morning fog. It was nothing unusual for Holmes County—especially this time of the year. Mist formed at night and in the early morning hours, when the temperatures dipped and the air became filled with moisture. Heidi didn't mind the fog, except for the unpleasant feel of cold and damp, combined with visibility restrictions. Fog, or even a light mist, could play with a person's sense of direction and make landmarks unrecognizable. This is what she feared the most whenever Lyle took the horse and buggy on the road in blurry weather conditions. Fortunately, her husband's driver had picked him up this morning to oversee another auction event. With bright beams on his truck to guide the way, she wasn't nearly as worried as she would have been if Lyle was out with the buggy.

Heidi tapped her chin with the end of her pencil. *I hope none of my students are late this morning due to the fog. Depending on the severity of it in various locations, maybe some of them will decide not to come today.*

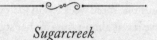

Sugarcreek

As Lisa passed the road leading to the Carlisle Inn, the fog became thicker. She turned on her high beams, but that didn't help much. In fact, it made seeing through the dense haze even worse. It was hard to focus on the road when she could only see a few feet in front of her.

She kept her speed down, gripping the steering wheel with such force the veins on the back of her hands became more noticeable. *Sure hope I don't run into the rear end of a car—or worse yet, an Amish buggy.* With all the hills, it was sometimes hard to spot a horse and buggy until right on top of it, even when the weather was clear.

As moisture stuck to the windshield, Lisa gave herself a pep talk and turned on the wipers. *You still have plenty of time to get there, so try to relax and concentrate. No need to hurry. Just take it slow and easy.*

The closer she got to Walnut Creek, the denser the fog became. Lisa feared she might miss the road where she was supposed to turn for Heidi's house. She'd carelessly left her cell phone at home, so she had no way of activating her GPS to help navigate the way. If she hadn't been bothered with feeding the pup this morning and then locking the little guy in her laundry room, she probably would have remembered the phone. But the puppy she'd named Trouble needed to be someplace where he couldn't do any damage while she was gone. The little rascal was kind of growing on her, but if she could find him a good home, it would be better. With her business growing, Lisa didn't have time to train or care for a dog.

Straining to see the road signs, she pulled over to get her bearings and hopefully calm her nerves a bit. She'd only been sitting on the shoulder of the road a few seconds when another car pulled in behind her. Curls of hazy air currents kept her from observing what kind of vehicle it was. She figured the driver might also be having difficulty seeing the road.

As Lisa looked out her side mirror, the skin on the back of her neck prickled. The figure of a man had gotten out of the vehicle and was approaching her van. She quickly locked all the doors. A moment later, a face she recognized stared in at her through the window. *Oh, no, it's Todd.*

Todd knocked on the driver's-side window of the van parked in front of his car. Even through the thick fog, Todd knew right away that the vehicle was Lisa's. He'd thought he wouldn't get the chance to speak with her privately today, but as fate would have it, he'd been given the opportunity to talk to her with no one else around to interrupt or overhear what he had to say.

He lifted his hand and rapped on the window again. She stared at him a few seconds, then rolled the window down. "Hey, Lisa. Is everything okay?"

"Of course. Why wouldn't it be?" Her tone was terse, and she barely made eye contact with him.

"Well, I just thought. . . Seeing your van parked here, I wondered if you were having trouble with your vehicle."

"I'm fine. Just stopped for a minute to get my bearings. This horrible fog is like driving through pea soup, and I wanted to be sure I was on the right road." Her voice didn't sound quite so snappish, but now she was talking too fast.

He shifted his weight, leaning against her door. "Mind if I come in a minute so we can talk?"

She pulled her fingers through the ends of her shiny blond hair and gave a brief shrug. At least she hadn't said no.

Todd hurried around to the passenger's side and climbed into the van. "How have you been, Lisa?"

"You needed to get in my van to ask me that?"

Todd moistened his lips with the tip of his tongue. This wasn't going as smoothly as he'd hoped. "I really wanted to talk to you about why you ran off the dance floor in such a huff the night of my friend's wedding."

Lisa pulled at her jacket collar. "I figured you'd know the answer to that."

"I do, and I—I'm sorry."

"If you didn't like the food I prepared for the wedding reception, you could have at least kept your opinion to yourself."

"But I thought you'd only made the cake."

"I run a catering business, which I mentioned during our first cooking class." Folding her arms, she looked at him through half-closed eyes. "But maybe you weren't listening."

Todd rubbed the back of his neck. "Yeah, I remember, and as I said, I was aware that you'd made the cake. I just didn't think—"

"Whether you didn't realize I'd made the food for the reception or not is immaterial. You said it was horrible." Lisa's chin trembled.

"No." Todd shook his head. "What I said was that I didn't think there was anything special about it."

"Same difference. You obviously didn't like the food, and it hurt my feelings."

"I'll admit, it wasn't my favorite cuisine, but it wasn't all that bad, either." He placed both hands on his knees, gripping them firmly as he spoke. "Look, I'm truly sorry I offended you. I sometimes speak before I think. Can we forget the whole thing and start over?"

"I—I suppose." Her face relaxed a bit.

"Good." He smiled, then glanced at his watch. "Now that we have that settled, we'd better get back on the road or we'll be late for the cooking class. I can hardly wait to see what Heidi wants us to make today." Todd wrinkled his nose. "Hopefully it'll be something better than the crazy bread she taught us to prepare two weeks ago. I threw the starter out as soon as I got home that day."

"You did? How come?" Her vocal pitch rose, as she looked away from him, then back again.

"Because it smelled funny. Besides, I had no reason to make more bread. I have no one to give it to."

"It's friendship bread. Couldn't you have given it to a friend?"

Todd rubbed his chin. Truth was, he didn't have many friends. Since Shawn and Melanie were still on their honeymoon, he couldn't give it to them. Besides, they were more acquaintances than friends.

Ignoring Lisa's question about the bread, Todd opened the van door. "We'd better get going now, or we're gonna be late. I'll pull my car in front of your van and lead the way. That is, if it's okay with you."

She slowly nodded.

"Okay then. Toot your horn if you can't see my car or feel like you're lost in the fog." Todd stepped out of Lisa's van and climbed back into his car. He still wasn't sure if she was really his type, but it would be fun to find out. *Who knows? Maybe before the end of our class today I'll have an opportunity to ask her out on a date. Bet Mom and Dad would like Lisa. They'd probably be impressed that I found someone who's not only beautiful but has a head for business too.*

Chapter 20

Walnut Creek

Lisa relaxed a bit as she followed Todd's car. It helped being able to see his taillights leading the way to Heidi's house. Todd was going nice and slow, which made driving less tense. Over and over she thought about the conversation they'd had minutes ago.

She pursed her lips. *I wonder if Todd truly meant it when he apologized for his remark about the food I catered for his friends' wedding. Or was he only trying to save face?* The bride and groom seemed pleased with what she'd fixed at their request, so that's all that really mattered. Lisa didn't know why she even cared what Todd thought. She'd only known him a short time, and they were not well acquainted, at that. For some reason, though, she wanted to know him better. On the one hand, he irritated her; on the other hand, she found him quite attractive and charming. Of course, a solid relationship should never be built on looks. Outward appearances could be deceiving, whereas a person's character and behavior was what made them likable.

Lisa gave her head a quick shake. *Stop thinking about Todd and concentrate on your driving. I'm sure he has no interest in me, and even if he did, I don't have time for love or romance in my life right now. I've got my hands full with my business, plus getting the duplex next door ready to rent again.* She groaned. *Not to mention a puppy to take care of if I can't find it a good home.*

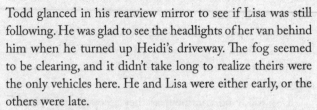

Todd glanced in his rearview mirror to see if Lisa was still following. He was glad to see the headlights of her van behind him when he turned up Heidi's driveway. The fog seemed to be clearing, and it didn't take long to realize theirs were the only vehicles here. He and Lisa were either early, or the others were late.

Good. That'll give me a little more time to visit with her. Todd felt a tingling in his chest. Lisa probably wasn't his type, but he wouldn't know for sure until he spent more time with her. *I might even do a review of one of the dinners she caters sometime in the future. If it's a good review, it could help her business, which in turn might put me in her good graces. Then again, if Lisa read the review she might think I only did it to get on her good side. Probably the best thing to do is try to see her more often and let things go from there.*

Todd turned off the ignition and got out of his car. He stood by the driver's side and waited for Lisa to exit her van.

"Were you able to see my taillights okay?" he asked when she joined him a few minutes later.

"Yes, and it helped a lot." Lisa rubbed her hands down the side of her beige slacks. "The only thing I dislike more than driving in snowy weather is fog. Unfortunately, in my business I'm often stuck driving in foggy conditions during the fall, and then the winter months often bring snow."

"Ever think about relocating to a warmer climate, like Arizona, Southern Florida, or one of the Hawaiian Islands?"

She shook her head vigorously. "Oh, my, no. My family lives here in Ohio, and it's where I call home."

"I think I could live about anywhere as long as I had a job I liked." Todd started walking beside Lisa toward Heidi's house.

"What about your folks? Do they live close by?"

"Nope. Mom and Dad live in Portland, Oregon, and since I have no siblings, there's no family living near here."

Lisa tipped her head, looking at him through half-closed eyes. "If your parents live on the West Coast, why would you want to live in Ohio?"

"I have a job here, and I like my independence. When I lived in Portland, Mom tried to run my life." Todd scrubbed a hand down the side of his face. "She scrutinized nearly everything I did."

Lisa made no comment as they stepped onto Heidi's front porch. Todd had a hunch she didn't have a clue about the way he felt. No doubt Lisa was in pretty tight with her family. They probably didn't try to tell her what to do or say.

She raised her hand to knock on the door, but he put his hand in front of hers. "Uh, before we go inside, there's something I'd like to ask you."

"Oh?" Her lips parted slightly.

"If you don't have plans for this evening, how about letting me take you out for supper at the restaurant of your choice? I'd like to make up for what I said about the food you catered at Shawn and Melanie's wedding reception."

"You don't have to make up for it. You've already apologized."

He cleared his throat, while shuffling his feet. "Umm. . . yeah, I know, but I'd still like to take you out. It'll give us a chance to get better acquainted."

"Okay, but—" Before Lisa could finish her sentence, the front door swung open.

Smiling, Heidi greeted Lisa and Todd. "I'm glad you both made it okay. With the fog so thick today, I wasn't sure anyone would be able to find our home."

"It's lifting in a few places, so I'm sure the others will make it here too." Todd glanced over at Lisa, gave her a quick smile, and then looked back at Heidi.

"I'm glad to hear it's improving. It was pretty thick for

a while this morning." Heidi stepped aside. "Please, come in. You can take a seat in the living room while we wait for everyone else to arrive."

The sound of Heidi's shoes clacking on the polished hardwood floors echoed in the hall. Todd and Lisa followed her into the living room and both took seats on the couch, while she seated herself across from them in the rocking chair. Heidi found it interesting how Todd leaned slightly forward, with one hand on his knee, as though anticipating or eager for something. Surely he couldn't be that excited about taking another cooking class. Lisa, however, sat with her mouth in a straight line, clutching her purse tightly to her chest as though it were a shield.

Heidi started the rocking chair moving. *Neither of them acted this way the first time they were here. I wonder if anything's wrong.* It wouldn't be right to ask, of course, so she engaged them in conversation. "In case either of you are wondering what I'll be teaching you to make today, it's an old family recipe called Chicken in a Crumb Basket. It's quite tasty, and I think you'll enjoy it."

Lisa's eyes lit up. "That sounds interesting. It might even be something I could offer to some of my potential clients who are looking for something a little different in a meal they want catered." She glanced at Todd. "Does Chicken in a Crumb Basket sound like something more to your liking than what I served at the wedding reception last week?"

Todd's ears turned pink, and his stomach growled noisily. His hand went quickly to his midsection. "I can't say for sure, since I haven't tried it yet, but I'm eager to find out what it's all about. I've never heard of chicken crumble in a basket before." He thumped his stomach when it rumbled again. "As you can tell, I'm a little hungry."

"Crumb basket," Lisa corrected. "That is what you said, isn't it, Heidi?"

Heidi gave an affirmative nod. Remembering the baking

dish in the oven, she excused herself and went to the kitchen. From the way Todd and Lisa kept stealing glances at each other, she had a hunch something might be going on between them—something more than two people sharing a desire to learn how to make a few of her favorite recipes.

She smiled to herself. *Wouldn't it be something if another romance developed between two of my new students like it did between Eli and Loretta during my first set of classes?*

Chapter 21

Berlin

"You seem kind of grouchy this morning. Is something wrong?" Nicole's father asked as they headed to Heidi Troyer's cooking class. "It's not the dismal weather, I hope."

Nicole clenched her fingers. *Something is always wrong, Dad. Don't think anything in my life will ever be right again.* "No, the fog doesn't bother me that much. I'm just tired."

"You've been working hard, and I appreciate all you do." He reached across the seat and squeezed her arm. "Your brother and sister may never say it to your face, but I'm sure they appreciate the things you do for them too."

With a slight shrug, Nicole sat silently, mulling things over. While it was nice to be appreciated, it would be a whole lot nicer if she had less work to do at home so she could spend more time on her schoolwork, not to mention making new friends and going to some of the school functions. She wanted to tell Dad her grades were still slipping but was afraid to say anything, fearful he'd get upset. Since there was nothing he could really do about it but scold her, there was no point in bringing it up.

"There's something I've been meaning to talk to you about." Dad squinted and turned on the windshield wipers. It seemed like the closer they came to Walnut Creek, the worse the fog got.

"Uh, what's up?"

"We haven't really talked about the unexpected visit your mother paid us last Sunday night."

"There's not much to say." Nicole looked in his direction. "Tonya hasn't changed, and she's still nothing but trouble. I wish she and that loser she ended up with would move out of town and we'd never have to see or hear from them again."

"As nice as that would be, it's probably not going to happen." He frowned. "But the next time she comes knocking on our door unannounced, I won't let her in. Same goes for you. Under no circumstances is she to come into our house when I'm not home."

Nicole grunted. "You'd better tell Tony and Heather that, 'cause there's no way I'd ever let Tonya in, even if you were at home, Dad."

"Good to hear, but I'd still prefer you stop calling your mother by her first name."

"But, Dad, she's so disgusting. I'm ashamed of her."

"Still, she is your mother."

"Okay, whatever." They'd had this discussion before, but Dad hadn't stopped reminding Nicole to quit referring to her mother as Tonya. Nicole would try not to say it in front of him anymore, but only to others outside their family, and of course, in her own head. She vowed she would never acknowledge that woman as anything else but Tonya.

Walnut Creek

Lance looked forward to this morning's cooking class. It would be a nice break from the constant drone of the TV, always turned up too loud. He gave his truck's steering wheel a sharp rap with his knuckles. Weekdays weren't quite so bad, since he was at work most of the day, but unless he went out somewhere, the weekends were unbearable. He'd tried his best to be patient with his brother, but it became harder with each passing day. In fact, it had gotten to the point that Lance had begun looking for places he could go in order to get out of the house for a while.

The real clincher was when he got home two days ago, and walked into the living room. There sat Dan with a big ole smile on his face, pointing to the flat screen TV. It was mounted on the wall where one of Lance's favorite pictures used to hang.

Lance shook his head, wondering how he'd remained speechless when his brother showed him how to use the remote. It was a wonder Lance didn't blow his stack right then and there. Somehow, he'd managed to keep his cool, even when Dan went on to explain how he'd made arrangements for a local charity to come take the old television set away. *The nerve of some people!*

"Too bad the cooking classes don't last all day," Lance mumbled, turning up the Troyers' driveway. He'd no sooner parked his vehicle when Bill's SUV pulled in. They got out of their rigs at the same time and walked up to the house together.

"Sure is nasty weather today," Bill mentioned.

"Yeah, I fought the fog most of the way."

"Same here, but at least we made it okay." Bill gave Lance's shoulder a tap. "How'd your week go?"

Refusing to go into detail, Lance casually answered, "Okay, I guess. How about yours?"

"Not bad at all. I took a loaf of friendship bread to a friend, which felt kind of nice. But the best part of my week was hearing that my son will be visiting me in a couple of weeks." Bill gave a wide grin. "There's nothing quite like being with family."

Lance stared at his feet as he shuffled up the stairs and onto the porch. "Yeah, right."

Allie drew her mouth into a straight line, biting her lower lip. The fog had been so dense when she left home this morning, she'd considered turning around and heading back home. But she had already dropped the kids off at the babysitters, and her eagerness to take another cooking class drove her on. About halfway there, the fog had begun to lift, but now, as she approached Walnut Creek, her minivan seemed to be swallowed up again in more of the thick haze. This increased Allie's anxiety. Since she was getting close to Heidi's house, determination kept her going.

Sure hope the fog's lifted by the time I go home. Allie gripped the steering wheel a little tighter. *It's times like this when I wish I was rich and could hire a driver to take me everywhere.*

She thought about Heidi and all the other Amish people who lived in the area. Most of them weren't rich, but they hired a driver whenever they went somewhere too far to take the horse and buggy. *I don't think Steve would be too happy if I did that. He'd say it was a waste of money, when I'm perfectly able to drive.*

Normally, Allie had no problem driving, but when the weather became nasty, she tried to plan her errands around Steve's work schedule so he could take her. Of course, with him working more hours than usual lately, he was rarely available to act as her chauffer.

Squinting into the haze, Allie saw a movement along the shoulder of the road, but was unable to make out what it was. As the fog shifted, and her eyes focused, Allie's scalp prickled. *Is that a dog?* Turning into the Troyers' driveway, before she had time to think or react, the critter darted in front of the van. She slammed on her brakes, but it was too late. The horrible thump put no question in her mind that she'd hit whatever it was. From what Allie could see through the misty air, the animal lay in the middle of Heidi's driveway, unmoving.

Chapter 22

Allie's knees quivered as she stepped down from the minivan and knelt beside the animal. At first she thought it was a small dog, but then she noticed the animal's bushy tail and realized it was a red fox. She felt bad she'd hit the critter, but at least it wasn't someone's dog. Just to be sure, Allie nudged the fox's leg. There was no doubt about it—the poor animal was dead. *I'm glad my kids aren't with me right now. They'd both be upset—even worse if it was someone's dog.*

Allie thought about the last time she'd taken Derek and Nola to the mall. They'd stood in front of the pet store with their noses pressed against the glass. Steve said the children were too young for a pet, but maybe owning one of their own would teach them responsibility. Prissy, the persnickety cat, was the only animal in the house, but she was Allie's pet and didn't care much for the children.

Allie recalled her little dog, Rascal, when she was growing up. The two of them were inseparable, and oh how it hurt when Rascal grew old and started having problems with his hips. Her dog wasn't a purebred, but he was smart and seemed to understand everything she said. If he could have talked, Allie knew he would have all kinds of interesting things to say.

In the end, after all the medication and treatments her parents did for ole Rascal, Allie's heart broke when the vet said there was nothing more they could do for him. That was the worst part about owning a pet—having to say goodbye. Did she want to put her children through the grief she felt when that happened? Besides, Prissy had a mind of her own and might not get along with a dog.

I can't worry about that right now. I need to get up to Heidi's house, because I'm already late for class. I'll see if one of the men will dispose of the dead fox.

Hearing a vehicle approach, Heidi looked out the living-room window. "Oh, good, Allie's here now, so we'll be able to start the class as soon as she comes inside."

"Well, it's about time." Lance folded his arms and grunted. "The rest of us managed to get here on time. I wonder what her excuse is."

Heidi was surprised by Lance's attitude. He was usually soft-spoken and polite. *Something might be going on his life right now to make him edgy.* She hurried to the door to let Allie in.

When the woman stepped inside, Heidi couldn't help noticing her flushed cheeks and wide-eyed expression. "Is everything all right? You look a bit flustered."

Blowing out a series of short breath, Allie twisted her gold wedding band. "I–I'm sorry I'm late. There was a lot of fog, so I drove slowly. Then, to make things worse, a fox ran out in front of my car when I was turning up your driveway. Unfortunately, I hit it." She paused and drew another breath. "Do you think one of the men could go out and take care of the fox? I hate the idea of it lying there for some scavenger or bird of prey."

Feeling the need to comfort the distraught woman, Heidi placed her hand on Allie's arm. "Let's go in the living room where the other students are waiting. I'm sure someone will take care of the fox."

When they stepped into the living room, and Heidi

explained the situation, Bill got up from his seat with no hesitation. "No problem. I'll take care of the animal right now." He grabbed his jacket and hurried out the door.

"Are you kidding me?" Nicole flopped against the sofa pillows with a groan. "Couldn't that have waited till after our class? At the rate things are going, we'll never get started. And I even remembered to bring an apron today."

"I'm sure he won't be long. While we're waiting, we can sit and chat." Hoping to ease the tension, Heidi took a seat and posed a question. "Do any of you have anything you'd like to ask concerning what we learned in our last class?"

Todd's hand shot up.

Heidi nodded in his direction. "What is it you'd like to know?"

"I'm curious why you included a Bible verse on the back of the recipe card like you did the previous week." He leaned slightly forward. "I thought we came here to learn how to make some traditional Amish recipes, not attend Bible study or feel like we just came from church."

Heidi fidgeted under his scrutiny, rubbing her forearms to dispel a sudden chill. "Well, I, uh. . ." She paused to moisten her parched lips. "I began doing it during my first set of cooking classes because I wanted to share a bit of God's Word. I'm sorry if you found it offensive or preachy."

"It's neither of those," Lisa was quick to say. "I enjoyed reading the verses you put on the first two recipe cards and hope you continue doing so." She looked at each person. "Everyone needs a little help along the way—myself included. As far as I'm concerned, the Bible is like a roadmap for life. It teaches us how to deal with all the things that are thrown at us."

"Yes, indeed." Lance bobbed his head. "The Good Book is full of wisdom, and it points the way to God's Son."

Heidi smiled. She couldn't have said it better, and appreciated two of her students' input. From the dubious expression on Todd's face, not to mention Nicole's, Heidi figured they weren't believers. She wasn't sure about Allie, who said nothing, either. *What a shame. I won't stop including scriptures on the back of the recipes cards—not unless God directs me to stop. I'm 100 percent sure that everyone in this class needs the Lord's wisdom.*

Chapter 23

A s everyone sat at Heidi's kitchen table, waiting for her to hand out today's recipe cards with directions, Lisa remembered she hadn't said anything about the puppy that needed a good home.

She cleared her throat. "Before we get started, I have something I'd like to share with everyone."

Heidi smiled. "Certainly, Lisa. Go right ahead."

"Well, the thing is. . ." Lisa didn't know why she felt so nervous all of a sudden. Maybe it had something to do with the way Todd kept staring at her so intently. She also felt guilty taking up time meant for cooking to talk about the pup.

"What did you want to say?" The question came from Bill.

"It's just that I have a puppy I need to give away, and wondered if any of you might be willing to take it." Lisa quickly explained about her renters moving out and leaving the dog for her to deal with.

Bill shook his head. "I own a black lab, and I don't think he'd take too kindly to me bringing another dog on the scene."

"I have several goldfish to care for, and that's enough for me right now," Lance put in.

"I have a dog too," Nicole mumbled. "At least it seems like it's my dog, since I'm the only one who takes care of it."

Lisa glanced at Todd.

He lifted both hands in the air. "Don't look at me. It's doubtful I'll ever own a cat or dog. Pets are too much trouble, and I don't want to deal with their hair everywhere."

"I have a cat named Prissy, but my kids would sure like a dog." Allie touched the collar of her creamy white blouse. "I can't believe I'm saying this, but could I bring them by your place later this afternoon to take a look at the puppy?"

"Of course." Lisa leaned back in her chair, feeling a sense of relief. Within the next few hours, the little abandoned pup might have a new home.

Todd alternated between watching Lisa, wearing a dimpled smile, and Heidi, showing everyone the ingredients for Chicken in a Crumb Basket. This particular recipe intrigued him—partly because he liked chicken—but mostly because it was an unusual dish. Certainly worth writing about if it turned out halfway decent.

Todd's mind wandered as he thought about taking Lisa to dinner this evening. He hoped she'd agreed to go. If Heidi hadn't opened the door and interrupted their conversation, he'd know for sure. *Sure wish I hadn't made a comment about the food at my friend's wedding. From now on, I'll be more careful what I say about anything—especially food—to Lisa. I'd like the chance to see where our relationship might take us. She seems like a nice person—unlike some women I've met in the past.*

Todd's thoughts went to his previous girlfriend, Felicia, and how she'd spread rumors about him, saying he had been seeing other women during the time they'd been dating. Lisa didn't seem like the type to spread rumors, so he felt safe in giving their relationship a try.

"Hey, wake up! Aren't you listening to what the teacher said?"

Todd jumped when Bill poked his arm. "Huh? What was that?"

"Heidi said we're supposed to mix all the ingredients she gave us in a bowl and then line the bottom and sides of a greased casserole dish with it, forming a basket."

Todd stared at the items set before him. He hadn't even realized she'd placed them there, much less asked him to do any mixing or lining the casserole dish. *Guess that's what I get for letting my thoughts run wild.*

He poured everything into a bowl, grabbed a wooden spoon, and started mixing. Looking around, Todd saw everyone else already had their casserole dishes lined with the "basket."

"Okay now, you'll need to take turns baking the baskets." Heidi gestured to Lisa and Allie. "Why don't you ladies go first? As soon as yours is done, Bill and Nicole can go next, then Todd and Lance will do theirs. They will only need to bake for fifteen minutes, so it shouldn't take long to get them all done."

Todd plopped his elbows on the table, watching Lisa carry her casserole dish over to the oven. She seemed so confident—a natural in the kitchen. While the first two baskets baked, everyone sat around the table and listened to Heidi explain how to mix the cut-up chicken and other ingredients for the filling. After it was cooked in a white sauce, it would be added to the crumb basket and baked another thirty to forty minutes.

When the pleasant aroma of the first two baking baskets filled the room, Todd's stomach rumbled even louder than before. He'd been in a hurry this morning and hadn't taken time for more than a cup of coffee and a bagel. *Sure hope there's enough time for us to eat what we've made before we have to go home.*

"Say, Lisa," Lance spoke with a gleam in his eyes, "didn't you mention that the duplex you rented is empty now."

"Yes, it is, but I need to get some work done, and some pieces of furniture must be fixed before I can rent or lease it again."

"Hmm..." Lance rapped his knuckles on the table. "My brother needs a place to stay while his townhouse is being remodeled. Would you consider renting on a month-to-month basis to him?"

Lisa tilted her head from side to side, as if weighing her choices. "I suppose I could, but I'm really looking for a full-time renter. Besides, as I explained, the place isn't ready yet."

"When it is, could you please let me know?" Lance took a small notebook from his shirt pocket, wrote down his phone number, and handed it to her.

"Of course." Lisa put the piece of paper in her purse.

Once Allie and Lisa's dishes were taken from the oven, it was Nicole and Bill's turn. When Nicole picked up her glass dish, Lance bumped her arm. Nicole's chicken in a crumb basket slipped from her hand and landed on the floor with a *splat*!

Turning away from the others, she gripped the sides of her head. "Why does everything bad always happen to me?" Gulping on a sob, she crumpled to the floor beside the mess. "That's it—I'm done!"

Chapter 24

B ill watched in sympathy as Heidi comforted Nicole, saying it was okay, that she could mix a new batch of ingredients, and it shouldn't take long to bake. Heidi pointed to the broken casserole dish. "Don't worry about that, either. It's an old one and can certainly be replaced."

Nicole, still hunkered down on the floor, continued to sob. Bill hated to see the girl have a meltdown like this, but maybe something good would come from it. Holding one's feelings in and trying to be strong all the time were not good for anyone. He wished there was something he could say or do to draw Nicole out and make her open up, although he was fairly sure she wouldn't do it with all of them sitting here staring at her.

"Come, take a seat. I'll get you a glass of water." Heidi helped Nicole, still sniffling, to her feet. "We've all dropped things at some time or another."

Nicole sat in the chair beside Lisa and lowered her head to the table. When Heidi brought her a glass of water, she looked up again. "Th–thanks."

After Nicole finished the drink, she sat a few minutes, taking in deep breaths, while Lisa patted her back.

"It–it's not just the mess on the floor and broken dish that has me upset." Nicole paused and blew her nose on the tissue Heidi handed her. "Things are horrible for me at home, and they're getting worse all the time."

"In what way?" Allie asked.

"For starters, I'm getting behind at school and almost failing in some of my classes."

"You ought to study more and do something for extra credit. That's what I did when I was in high school." Todd looked over at Nicole.

She shook her head slowly. "You don't understand. There's a reason I can't get my homework done or spend enough time studying for tests."

Everyone sat silently as Nicole poured out her heart, telling how the responsibility of cleaning, cooking, and overseeing her siblings had fallen on her ever since her parents' divorce. "My grades are failing because I don't have time to study or get all my homework done." She sniffed deeply, dabbing at her tears with the tissue Heidi had given her. "I have no life of my own anymore."

"Why doesn't your dad hire someone to come in and clean the house at least?" The question came from Lance.

"He doesn't have enough money for that. Dad moans every time another bill comes in. Even though he's a plumber, Dad's barely making enough to keep up with all our expenses."

Bill fiddled with the buttons on his shirt. He wasn't wealthy, by any stretch of the imagination, but he made a decent living. Other than his hunting expenses, Bill didn't spend much on unnecessary things. There was no reason he couldn't help out by providing the money for Nicole's dad to hire a housekeeper. He just had to figure out a way to do it without her finding out, because he was almost certain she would see it as charity.

Nicole's cheeks, already pink, turned a deep shade of red. "As if things aren't bad enough at our house, Tonya—my mom—came by last Sunday evening, and she was drunk. I'm glad my brother and sister were in bed. They'd have been really upset if they'd seen her staggering around and heard the way she was carrying on."

Bill grimaced. *Poor Nicole. She has too much on her shoulders and is being forced to grow up before her time. I can't do anything about her mother, but I'm definitely going to do something to help ease Nicole's burden and give her more time to spend on schoolwork.*

Canton

"Are you sure you don't want me to watch the baby while you go to Mt. Hope to visit your friend Dorie?" Kendra's mother asked when Kendra began filling the diaper bag.

Kendra shook her head. "The reason I'm going to Dorie's is so she can see the boppli."

Squinting, Mom tipped her head at an odd angle. "What does boppli mean?"

"It's the Pennsylvania Dutch word for baby. I learned a few Amish words while living with Heidi and her husband."

Mom's lips pressed together. "I'm certainly glad they won't be raising my grandchild. The baby would have been raised Amish and never had the privilege of experiencing all the things you grew up with." Her nose wrinkled. "Can you imagine having to live without electricity, traveling by a horse and buggy, and dressing in Plain clothes?"

Kendra clasped the handles of the diaper bag tightly. She didn't like the way this conversation was going. "For your information, Mom, I enjoyed staying with the Troyers, and I wouldn't have minded if little Heidi had been raised in the Plain lifestyle and ended up joining the Amish church when she was older."

Mom's mouth formed an O as she leaned against the baby's crib, facing Kendra. "I can't believe you would say that."

"Why not? The Amish are good people, with strong moral values. They believe in God and putting Him first. Isn't that what our church teaches?"

"Well, yes, but. . ." Mom turned and covered little Heidi's

feet, where she'd kicked the covers off. "I don't want to argue with you, Kendra. I'm just glad you decided against the adoption and came home to be with your family."

"Yeah, well, let me remind you, before you got up the nerve and convinced Dad to let me come home, you knew I was pregnant and yet you were perfectly fine with wherever and whoever I was living with. In fact, it was not even six months ago when you said, and I quote, 'Your child will be better off with adoptive parents.' So please don't tell me your version of how much better it is living here. You don't even know the Troyers and what wonderful people they are. And I'm going to make sure they are in my daughter's life, whether you and Dad like it or not."

Little Heidi started to whimper, but calmed down when Kendra scooped her up. "There, there, my little sweet baby. It's okay. Everything is all right." She looked at her mother, who stood speechless. "There's been enough said about the Troyers, so please don't say any more negative comments about them."

Before Mom could offer a response, Kendra walked out of the room. After living with Heidi and Lyle for several months, she'd begun to feel as if they were her family. She felt thankful for the help they'd given her when she had no place else to go. Deep in her heart, Kendra still wondered sometimes if her daughter would be better off with the Troyers, but she'd made her decision to keep the baby, and it would be too hard to give her up now.

Walnut Creek

That afternoon, after everyone had gone home. Heidi sat down to eat a delayed lunch. Between Allie arriving late for class and then taking time to listen to Nicole unburden her soul, the class lasted longer than usual. Even though it was good to see Nicole open up and share her burdens, Heidi felt sorry for the girl and would remember to pray for her. She hoped somewhere down the line things would get better for Nicole and her family. Heidi's own parents had always been kind and loving. She couldn't imagine what it must be like for Nicole to deal with an undependable mother who got drunk.

Heidi had finished eating her sandwich and soup and was placing the dishes in the sink, when she heard a vehicle pull into the yard. She dried her hands on a dishtowel and hurried to the front door to see who it was.

When Heidi opened the door, she was surprised to see Kendra getting out of a car. She stood on the porch and watched as Kendra reached inside the backseat and took out her baby.

Heidi's heart pounded. For a fleeting moment she thought maybe Kendra had changed her mind and was bringing little Heidi for her and Lyle to raise, after all. But then seeing only a small diaper bag slung over Kendra's shoulder, logic took over. If she had changed her mind about letting them adopt the baby, she would have called to discuss it with them and set it all up with the lawyer again. And Kendra would have brought more than just a diaper bag along.

Kendra smiled as she stepped onto the porch. "I've been to Mt. Hope to see my friend Dorie, and since I was so close, I decided to stop by here and see if you were home. Are you busy right now, or do you have time for a short visit?"

Heidi nodded. "I taught another cooking class this morning and just finished having lunch, so I'd enjoy visiting with you for however long you can stay. If you haven't eaten, I'd be happy to fix you something." While speaking to Kendra, Heidi couldn't help gazing at the sweet bundle in her arms.

"It's nice of you to offer, but I had lunch with Dorie."

"Well, come in, and I'll fix you something to drink." Heidi opened the door, and motioned for Kendra to follow her inside. "Let's have a seat in the living room. It's more comfortable there."

Kendra shifted the baby from one arm to the other, glancing around the room. "Nothing's changed. Your place still looks as cozy as ever."

Heidi smiled. "Why don't you take a seat over there? I'm sure the baby will like being rocked." She gestured to the rocking chair.

"I have a better idea; why don't you sit and rock your little namesake while I go and fix us something to drink?" Kendra grinned. "After living here a few months, I know my way around your kitchen pretty well."

"True." Heidi lifted the baby into her arms and took a seat in the rocker, while Kendra headed for the kitchen. As she sat staring at the infant's delicate features and holding her tiny hand, a lump formed in her throat. *If she could only be my boppli, I'd be the happiest woman in Holmes County.*

Little Heidi opened her eyes briefly, then closed them again. Her breathing was sweet and even. Although Heidi was pleased Kendra had stopped by, seeing and holding the little girl who'd once been promised to her was bittersweet. Raising this child would have been such a blessing.

I don't understand why some women, like Nicole's mother, don't care about their children, while others, like me, who would give anything to be a mamm, go through life with a sense of emptiness.

Heidi blinked back unbidden tears threatening to spill over. It was wrong to feel sorry for herself and dwell on what would never be. This special baby was a blessing to Kendra, and she deserved the opportunity to raise her own child.

She put the baby over her shoulder and gently patted her small back. Closing her eyes, Heidi allowed herself to fantasize. *Maybe Kendra and little Heidi could live here with us, and even though Lyle and I wouldn't be the baby's parents, we could at least help raise her.*

"Here you go. I made us some hot tea."

Heidi's eyes snapped open. "Thank you, Kendra. You can set it there on the coffee table." She gestured to the baby. "Do you want to take her now?"

"No, that's okay. You can hold her as long as you like. Unless you'd rather not."

Heidi sighed, brushing the top of the infant's head lightly with her fingers. "I could hold your baby all day, but I guess I should drink my tea before it gets cold." Truthfully, Heidi felt if she didn't let go of Kendra's daughter now, she might never be able to let her go.

Kendra stepped up to the rocking chair. "I'll put her on the couch by me while we both drink our tea."

Heidi's arms felt empty when Kendra took the baby and found a seat on one end of the couch, placing the child close to her. "How are things going for you?"

"Okay. As good as can be expected." Kendra reached for her cup of tea.

"Are your folks enjoying their new role as grandparents?"

"I guess so." Kendra took a sip of her tea. "Sometimes the baby's crying gets on my dad's nerves, and he becomes irritable or impatient." She sat quietly for several seconds, looking at her daughter. "I think the only reason he agreed to let me come home was for my mom's sake. I found out from my sister Shelly that even though Mom stood by Dad's decision when he kicked me out of the house, she was brokenhearted and wanted me to move back home. Dad probably would have turned his back on me and little Heidi indefinitely if it hadn't been for Mom."

"That's too bad. Maybe after he spends more time with his granddaughter, he'll come around."

Kendra shrugged her slim shoulders. "I hope so, but I'm not holding my breath. Even so, I'm grateful they gave me this chance to keep my child. Things aren't the way I'd like them to be, but the good Lord above kept me and my baby together."

As they both sat in silence, watching baby Heidi, Kendra spoke again. "Remember when I told you how little Heidi almost came early?"

Heidi nodded.

"Well, when the pains got worse some really nice people at the grocery store helped me out, and even called the paramedics."

"It's good you were surrounded by compassionate strangers."

"I sure was, but get this—before the ambulance arrived, while I was still lying on the floor, this man—and I only got a fleeting glimpse of him—had been watching me, before he turned and went out of sight."

"Who do you think it was?"

"I thought it looked like my dad." Kendra frowned. "And I wondered why, if it was, he didn't come see if I was okay."

"Did you ask him later?"

"After I got home from finding out it wasn't true labor, I questioned Dad about it." Kendra sighed. "Well, it was him I saw, and he just gave me some lame excuse. He justified it by saying he had stopped to pick up a snack to take to a church meeting he was already late for, and that the woman he'd seen on the floor of the store looked like me, but he didn't think it actually was." Kendra sagged in her chair. "Can you believe that? Wouldn't you think he could have at least come over and checked?"

Heidi nodded slowly. She certainly would have checked if she'd seen someone in trouble and thought she knew them. For that matter, she'd have offered help even to a stranger. It was hard to understand how Kendra's dad, a churchgoing man, could be so unfeeling.

After a pause, Kendra continued. "I don't believe for one minute that Dad didn't know it was me, but I chose not to say anymore to him about it." She lifted her hands and let them fall to her lap. "I mean, what was the point? He's still embarrassed about me, and I'm sure he didn't want to be seen with his pregnant, unwed daughter there in the store."

"I'm sorry, Kendra." Heidi simply couldn't imagine

Kendra's father treating her that way. Feeling the need for a change of subject, Heidi told Kendra how Loretta had decided to join the Amish church."

Kendra chuckled. "I'm not surprised. I'll bet she and Eli are planning to be married soon after she joins."

Heidi smiled. She hadn't talked to Loretta recently. She would have to pay her a visit soon and ask how things were going.

They visited another half hour, then Kendra said it was time for her to go.

Heidi rose to her feet and walked to the door with Kendra and the baby. "Feel free to drop by anytime you're in the area." She reached out and gently stroked the infant's head. "I would like to visit with you again and see how much the baby has grown."

Kendra smiled. "Sounds good. I'd enjoy seeing you again, too."

When Kendra left, Heidi returned to the rocking chair. Her hands went limp as she lowered her head, giving in to the tears she'd been trying so hard to hold back. Spending time with the baby had only fueled her desire to be a mother. If the pain would only subside.

"I need to get busy and keep my mind occupied." She pulled herself upright, dried her eyes, and headed to the laundry room to put a load of towels in the wringer washer. If they didn't dry outdoors in the few hours left of daylight, she'd bring the towels inside and hang them in the basement.

Heidi yawned. She felt done in from the day's activities and wished she could take a nap. But Lyle would be home soon, and she needed to get supper ready. Maybe later this evening they'd fix hot apple cider and sit by the fire and talk. She would share with him all the events of the day, including the visit with Kendra.

Chapter 25

Dover

When Allie stepped onto Lisa's front porch, she began to have second thoughts. Bringing a puppy into their house might not be a good idea after all. Prissy would see the dog as an intruder, and the pup may not care for the cat. But it was too late to change her mind now. She'd already told her kids if they liked the dog they could have it. Nola and Derek stood beside her now, giggling and bouncing on tiptoes.

When Lisa opened the door, Allie introduced her to the children.

"It's nice to meet you. The puppy's in the kitchen. Follow me. I'll lead the way."

When they entered the room, Allie spotted the pup inside a small cage. The children saw him right away too and dropped to their knees in front of the enclosure.

"Can we take him out?" Derek looked up at Lisa expectantly.

"Sure, but let me close the kitchen door first. I don't want the little stinker running all over the house." Lisa wrinkled her nose. "Trouble—that's what I call him—has been known to make messes when left unattended."

Allie groaned inwardly. In addition to worrying about how the cat and dog would get along, she'd have to work at getting the puppy housebroken and trained not to chew on everything in sight. Then there was the issue of what to do with the animal during the day while she and Steve were at work and the kids were in school. *I should have thought all this through before I opened my mouth—first to Lisa, saying we'd come look at the pup—and then to Derek and Nola, offering to let them have the dog.* Allie wondered if her common sense had gone out the window lately.

After Lisa closed the kitchen door, she lifted the latch on the cage. The pup bounded out and headed straight for Nola. As soon as the child reached out to pet the dog, he slurped the end of her nose. She giggled. "Look, Mommy, the puppy likes me."

In all the excitement, the puppy made a wet spot on the floor. "Oh, oh." Nola looked sheepishly up at Lisa. "Sorry he did that."

"Oh, don't worry about it." Lisa went to get a paper towel. "This little pup is still a baby and will need some training."

Allie was on the verge of changing her mind about taking the puppy home, but she remembered her childhood dog. Her parents had been so patient with the little mistakes Rascal made, but everyone was happy when Allie eventually got the puppy trained. At least she had to give her children a chance and see how they handled this new responsibility.

"Mommy," Nola said quietly, "does the puppy making a mess mean we can't take him home?"

"I'm still thinking about it."

Nola clung to Allie's hand. "Please, Mommy. I like the dog."

"You realize that you and your brother will have to take care of Trouble and help me get him housebroken as soon as possible."

"Oh, we will Mommy," Nola shouted.

"We promise." Derek got into the act, clapping his hands and calling for the pup. Wiggling and wagging his tail, Trouble nuzzled the boy's hand and then crawled into his lap.

Derek grinned, looking up at Allie. "I think he likes us,

Mommy. Can we take him home now?"

Nola's head bobbed up and down as she reached over and stroked the puppy's head.

Allie pinched the bridge of her nose. It looked like she had no choice. "If it's okay with Lisa, then Trouble will have a new home at our house."

Lisa smiled. "Sounds good. I'm sure he'll be much happier there, with children to play with, then he would living here with me."

As they were getting into the van a short time later, Allie's cell phone rang. Looking at the caller ID, and seeing it was Steve, she quickly answered.

"Hi, hon. Just wanted you to know not to expect me for supper this evening."

"Oh? How come? You said this morning that you'd be home early today."

"I thought so then, but something's come up, so I will be working later than I thought. I'll grab something to eat before I head home. Oh, and if you get tired waiting for me, go on to bed. I'll see you in the morning."

In the morning? Allie positioned herself behind the steering wheel, grabbing it tightly with both hands. *I wonder if Steve's with that female officer again. Is he really working, or could they be having an affair?*

───── ◦◦◦ ─────

Walnut Creek

After Lance left Heidi's, he'd run a few errands in Berlin and stopped to eat lunch at the Farmstead Restaurant. He wasn't in a hurry to go home but couldn't stay away any longer because he wanted to work on the photo albums he'd been putting together to give his daughters for Christmas. He'd set a box of pictures on his desk in the kitchen before he left for the cooking class this morning and planned to go through it this afternoon before starting supper. He especially wanted to find some pictures of Flo, beginning with when she was a girl, all the way up to when she'd married him. He was sure Terry and Sharon would treasure the albums filled with memories of their loving mother.

Lance pulled into his yard and hit the remote to open the garage door. It was nice to be able to pull right into the garage again. After having that talk with Dan, he was no longer blocking the garage door with his vehicle. Now if he could just convince his brother to move into Lisa's duplex when it was ready, things would be better all the way around.

When Lance entered the house, his nose twitched. *Do I smell paint?* The odor permeated the house, but seemed to be stronger the closer he got to the kitchen. He stepped into the room and halted, mouth hanging open. The kitchen walls had been repainted a drab beige. If the stench and putrid color wasn't bad enough, the box of photos was no longer on his desk. Everything that had been hanging on the walls now lay on the table. There was no doubt who'd done it, either. The question was why?

Following the sound of the new TV, Lance marched into the living room. Holding the remote in one hand, and a can of soda pop in the other, Dan sat on the couch with his feet propped on the coffee table.

Lance's jaw clenched as he squinted at his brother. "What possessed you to paint my kitchen without my permission?"

"It needed painting, so I figured I'd surprise you."

"Oh, I'm surprised all right." Lance slapped his hands against his hips. "Flo liked the cheerful yellow color in our kitchen, and so did I."

Dan blinked rapidly. "Sorry if I overstepped my bounds. I thought it was time for a change, and those yellow walls seemed too bright."

"I like it bright. So did Flo."

"Okay, okay. . . . Don't panic." Dan held up both hands,

as if to surrender. "I'll paint it back. In fact, I'll start on it tomorrow while you're in church."

"I'd hoped you might go to church with me."

Dan shook his head. "You know how I feel about church. Have ever since we were teenagers and someone in the congregation got really upset because the new carpet wasn't the color they wanted. They were so mad they ended up leaving. Then someone else left, and pretty soon half the church members were gone."

Lance clenched his teeth. "That's a dumb reason to quit going to church. People are people, and not everyone attending church is perfect. In fact, none of us are. We're all humans with bad habits and differing opinions."

Dan lifted his pop can to his lips, took a drink, and placed it on the side table. "Say what you like, but I'm not goin' with you tomorrow. Besides, there's a football game I want to watch."

"How are you gonna do that if you're repainting the kitchen?"

"I'll paint during halftime, or turn up the TV so I can hear the score from the kitchen."

Lance figured he wouldn't get anywhere with his brother, so he left the living room and headed to his bedroom to hopefully get away from the paint smell. The last thing he wanted was to say something to Dan that he might regret later on, but now Lance was more determined than ever for his brother to move out. *Think I'll give Heidi a call and leave a message, asking if she'll give me Lisa's phone number. If I have to, I'll go over to the duplex she wants to rent and help her get the place in shape so Dan can move in.*

Remembering the pictures he'd left on his desk this morning, Lance returned to the living room. "What'd you do with the box of photos that were on my desk in the kitchen?"

Dan sat staring at the television as though he hadn't heard a word Lance said.

Lance's jaw and facial muscles tightened as he positioned

himself between his brother and the television.

"Hey! What'd you do that for?" Dan's eyes narrowed. "You're blocking my view of the TV."

"I'm standing here to get your attention, because you didn't answer when I asked a question." Lance crossed his arms, refusing to budge from his spot.

Dan's forehead wrinkled as he leaned his head to one side, as if hoping to see around Lance. "What was your question?"

"I asked what you did with the box of photos that were on my desk in the kitchen. I set it there this morning so I could work on the albums I'm making for my daughters."

"Let me think. . ." Dan scratched his head. "Oh, yeah, now I remember. I put the box in the utility room, on top of the dryer. Didn't want to get any paint on the pictures, so I figured I'd better get them out of the kitchen."

"Okay; good thinking." Well, at least his brother had done one thing right. If those pictures had gotten ruined, Lance would feel sick.

Then Dan added, "I hope you don't mind, but I ended up looking through the pictures and sorted them by category for you. You know, family, places you've been—that sort of thing."

"What?" Lance never felt so exasperated in his life. "Didn't you look on the back of those photos?"

"No. Why would I?"

"Well, I have the year the photo was taken written on the back of each one." Clutching his shirt collar, Lance inhaled a long breath. "Now I'll have to re-sort them again, by the year. That's how I wanted them." Lance watched for his brother's reaction, but Dan gave none. "Oh, never mind." *No use trying to get through to him.*

"Are you done now? Can I finish watching my show?"

"Sure, Dan, we'll talk later." Lance plastered a smile on his face, but inside, his anger boiled like a pot of pasta cooking on the stove. *Who does my brother think he is, anyhow? He has no respect for my things at all.*

Lance wanted to talk to his brother about moving into Lisa's duplex right away, but since he was a bit overwrought right now, he figured this wasn't a good time. Dan was already giving him an icy stare, and if he missed any more of his TV program, he'd probably blow his top.

Lance entered his room and flopped onto the bed. *Sure hope I have better luck getting Dan to move out than I have with getting him to go to church.*

<hr>

Charm, Ohio

"I hope you like Bavarian-style food." Todd pulled his sports car into Chalet in the Valley restaurant's parking lot and smiled at Lisa. "I've been here once, but not since they got a new cook, so I'm anxious to try the place out again." After the cooking class today, Todd had asked her again if he could take her out. Against her better judgment, Lisa agreed and had even let him choose the restaurant.

"If you haven't been here in a while, how do you know they've hired a new cook?" she questioned.

"Oh, I don't know. Guess someone must have mentioned it to me." Todd got out of the car and hurried around to help Lisa before she could exit on her own. She wasn't used to getting in or out of such a small vehicle, so she appreciated his gesture. In fact, ever since Todd picked her up in Dover, he'd been the perfect gentleman.

Guess I ought to give him a chance, Lisa told herself as they walked to the restaurant's entrance. She wasn't sure why, but she'd taken extra care with what to wear this evening, and had even put on a little extra makeup. She'd chosen a simple, dark blue dress, which brought out the color of her eyes. Lisa also added a matching silver necklace, adorned with a heart-shaped blue sapphire that sparkled when the light hit it.

As they entered the building, Todd rested his hand gently

against the small of Lisa's back. He was certainly a gentleman this evening. Perhaps he wasn't as self-centered as she'd originally thought.

Once inside, the hostess, wearing a Bavarian-style dress, showed them to a table near the window. The restaurant, as well as the town, seemed quaint and appealing. If not for the need to be closer to the bigger towns for her catering business, Lisa thought she could be happy living in a small community like this. There was something about the area here that reminded her of pictures she'd seen of Switzerland in magazines and travel brochures. Someday it would be fun to travel to Europe and see the real Switzerland for herself. Until, and unless, that day ever came, she'd be content to visit a place such as this, here in the scenic Doughty Valley.

"You look very pretty tonight."

Lisa's cheeks grew warm. Todd's compliment caught her off guard. "Thanks." *You look nice too* she wanted to add but couldn't bring herself to say it.

He grinned at her from across the table. "So what appeals to you?" Todd pointed to Lisa's menu.

"I'm not sure yet." Lisa perused the list of dinner choices. She hadn't eaten lunch today, so at the moment, nearly everything appealed. Lisa noticed near the bottom of the menu it stated that the chef used local products in many of the deliciously authentic recipes.

"The wiener schnitzel sounds good to me." Todd took a drink of water. "Think I'll have that."

Lisa continued to study the menu, then decided on a ham-and-swiss sandwich, with a side order of sauerkraut.

After placing their orders, they talked about the cooking class and how things had gone that morning.

"We're certainly a group of diversified students." Lisa took a drink from her glass of water.

Todd bobbed his head. "I'll say. What'd you think of Nicole's meltdown?"

"I feel sorry for her. Sounds like she's having a hard time dealing with her family situation."

"Yeah, it's too bad 'cause she's still just a kid and shouldn't have to shoulder so much responsibility."

Lisa was pleased to hear the compassion in Todd's tone of voice. Maybe he was nicer than she'd originally thought. With his good looks and intelligence, she was surprised he wasn't married, or at least romantically involved with someone. If Todd was seeing another woman, surely he wouldn't have asked her out or danced cheek-to-cheek with her at his friend's wedding reception. Or would he? Some men liked to play the field. Todd might be one of them.

When their food came, Lisa pushed her thoughts aside. "When I'm eating out, I always pray like the Amish do—silently," she said, smiling at Todd.

His brows lowered a bit, but then he nodded. "Fine by me."

Lisa bowed her head and thanked the Lord for the food set before her. She also offered thanks for this opportunity to get to know Todd better.

As they ate their meal, she noticed how Todd seemed to critique everything he ate, and even made a few comments about their young waitress. Here they were on a date, yet he was suddenly paying more attention to the food than her. Todd had been quite talkative on the drive here, but now his only comments were about the items on his plate or how attentive the waitress was or wasn't. She thought it was odd. But then, many things about Todd seemed a bit strange. One minute he was the perfect gentleman, saying kind and courteous things, and the next minute, Todd made off-handed remarks. He was a complicated man.

Lisa took a sip of her hot tea. *Maybe I should invite him over to my place sometime and cook a nice meal. Perhaps then he'd be more attentive. Or would he end up critiquing my dinner, and maybe even me?*

Chapter 26

Walnut Creek

By Monday, Lance still had not heard from Heidi about getting Lisa's phone number, so he decided to stop by her house. If she was there, he would speak to her during his mail delivery, rather than putting the Troyers' mail in their box near the road.

As he neared the house, he spotted Lyle standing near the buggy shed, hitching his horse. "Morning, Mr. Troyer. Is your wife at home?"

"Yes, she's getting ready to go into Berlin with me. We both have dental appointments this morning."

"Oh, well, I won't keep you. I just wanted to ask Heidi a quick question."

"You can either knock on the door or wait here. I'm sure she'll be out soon."

"Think I'd better knock." Lance headed to the house and had barely stepped onto the porch when Heidi came out the door.

"Good morning, Lance. Do you have a package for me?"

He shook his head. "Not today, but I was wondering if you have Lisa's phone number. I need to talk to her about the duplex she has for rent, and it can't wait till our next cooking class."

"Of course. I'll see if I can find it." She turned and went back inside.

Lance leaned on the porch railing, waiting for Heidi's return. Several minutes went by, and he began to pace. *Sure hope I don't cause her to be late for the dental appointment. Guess I should have said I could stop by later for Lisa's number.*

Lance reflected on yesterday's happenings. He'd gone to church by himself, of course, and when he got home Dan had half the kitchen painted yellow. It wasn't the exact color as before, but at least it wasn't beige anymore. He'd changed his clothes and helped his brother finish the job. Afterward, due to the paint odor, they'd gone out for lunch, leaving a few windows open to air the place out and help the paint dry. When they returned home, Dan watched TV while Lance worked on his daughters' photo albums in the dining room. He'd managed to get all the pictures back in date order and had enjoyed reminiscing as he looked at each one.

Redirecting his thoughts, Lance glanced at Lyle, still standing beside his horse and buggy. "Your wife went to get a phone number for me," he called. "Sorry if I'm holding you up."

Lyle started walking toward Lance, but before he reached the front steps, Heidi came out of the house. "Here you go." She handed Lance a slip of paper.

"Thanks. I'll give Lisa a call during my lunch hour. I'll see you a week from Saturday. Oh, and I hope things go well at the dentist." Lance gave a quick wave and headed back to his vehicle. With any luck, Dan would be moved out before this week was over.

New Philadelphia

Allie tapped her fingers against the steering wheel as she waited at a stoplight while on her way to work. She'd dropped the kids off at school a few minutes ago and felt glad to be free of their chatter about the new pup. The name Lisa had given him was appropriate—he was a bundle of Trouble. At least that's how Allie saw it. Nola and Derek were enamored with the little fellow and thought everything he did was cute.

Yesterday while the kids were at Sunday school, Allie had accidentally left the door of the pup's cage unlatched, and he'd gotten out while she was in the living room visiting with Steve. When she returned to the kitchen, she found Trouble chewing on the throw rug by the sink. On top of that, he'd piddled on the floor near the back door. Then Prissy came in for a drink of water and something to eat from her dish, but the puppy wanted to play and ended up spilling cat food all over the floor.

When Allie went back to the living room to ask for Steve's help, he'd mumbled, "It wasn't a good idea to get that pup for the kids." Then he went back to reading his newspaper.

The skin around Allie's eyes tightened. To make her weekend worse, when she'd asked Steve why he'd gotten home a few minutes before midnight the night before, he gave some excuse about being called out for a domestic dispute, then quickly changed the subject. Allie felt sure he'd lied to her, but she didn't make an issue, since she had no proof. She was driving herself crazy thinking Steve may have been with another woman. When she came right down to it, the whole idea sounded ludicrous, but then, when she thought about all the facts, what else could it be? If things kept up, she may come right out and ask if he was having an affair. As much as it would hurt, knowing the truth would be better than living with her suspicions. One thing was for sure—Allie would not give up without a fight in order to save her marriage.

Millersburg

Struggling to keep her eyes open, Nicole tried to focus on the test her English teacher had given the class. She'd stayed up late last night studying for it, but now she could barely stay awake. This morning, she'd overslept, so that didn't help things any as she rushed around getting breakfast ready and lunches made for her siblings, as well as herself. Dad left early for work, which meant, as usual, all the responsibility fell on Nicole.

She rolled her shoulders, trying to get the kinks out, and reached up to rub the back of her neck. *Use an apostrophe and s to form the possessive of a noun not ending in s. Girl's. Use an apostrophe alone to form the possessive of a plural noun ending in s. Girls'.*

Nicole bit the end of her pencil. *Or is it the other way around?* She opted for the first one and hoped for the best.

When Nicole looked up from her paper, she realized all the other students had turned in their tests. Earlier, before the exam started, the teacher told everyone when they were finished, they could read a book or start working on the next lesson, as long as they didn't disturb other students who were still working on the test. Nicole pursed her lips. *So, great—I'm the last to finish.*

She glanced at her watch and frowned. *Fifteen minutes left to get the test done, and I still have ten more questions to answer.*

The next question involved sentence structure, and when a comma should or shouldn't be used. By the time Nicole finished taking the test, she had a full-blown headache. She could only hope she had enough answers right and wouldn't fail the exam.

As Bill headed up the hall to replace a light in the auditorium, he spotted Nicole coming out of her English class. He gave her a friendly wave, but her only response was a brief nod, then she looked the other way. Seeing her downturned facial features, Bill figured she'd had a bad morning so far.

He paused, pinching the bridge of his nose. *I still haven't done anything to help the girl, and I need to take care of that right away. As soon as I get home from work today, I'll make good on the promise I made to myself last Saturday. Like all young women her age, Nicole deserves the chance to be happy and enjoy a little time to herself.*

"Mr. Mason." A voice from behind brought Bill out of his thoughts. "May I have a word with you?"

Oh brother. Now what? Bill lifted his eyebrows as he turned to face Ms. Shultz.

"There are cobwebs in the corner of my classroom, which means there could be a spider lurking about." She stood looking at him with her arms crossed. "And I'll not put up with that."

"Now what's wrong with a little ole spider?" Bill grinned, wondering what she'd do if he put the big rubber spider he had at home in one of her desk drawers. He'd pulled a prank like that when he was a boy, and his teacher nearly fainted.

Guess I won't press my luck with Ms. Shultz today. He gave a placating nod and stepped into her class.

Chapter 27

Dover

Monday evening, as Lisa was getting ready to fix supper, her cell phone rang. She didn't recognize the number, but decided to answer anyway. "Hello."

"Is this Lisa Brooks?"

"Yes, who's calling?" She thought she recognized the deep male voice but wasn't sure where she'd heard it before.

"It's Lance Freemont from the cooking classes. I got your number from Heidi Troyer."

Lisa took a seat at the kitchen table. "Oh, I see. If you're calling about the duplex, the unit I rent out isn't ready yet."

"I figured it wouldn't be but thought maybe you could use some help with it. I'd like my brother to take a look at the place as soon as possible too."

"Are you offering his assistance to clean and fix things up?"

"No. Thought I'd help you with that myself. Of course if he's willing. . ."

She raised her eyebrows. "Really? How come?"

Lance cleared his throat. "Figured if I helped out, you'd get the job done twice as fast."

"But don't you have a mail route during the week?"

"Sure, but I only work five days a week. A sub fills in on my days off."

"Oh, okay. Well, I suppose we could work something out." Lisa paused. "But don't you think you should bring your brother by first, to make sure he's interested in moving here?"

"Right. That's a good plan. Can I come over sometime tomorrow to help out? It's my day off and I have nothing else planned. I'll bring Dan with me so he can see the place. Then if he likes it, we'll both help out. He likes to paint, so if you're needing that done, Dan's your man."

"Sounds good. Why don't you come over around ten? I have an errand to run at eight thirty, but I should be back by then."

"Great! See you then."

Lisa said goodbye and put her cell phone on the counter. Her stomach rumbled, and she gave it a pat. It was definitely time to start supper.

Canton

After supper, Kendra's sisters cleared the table and did the dishes, so Kendra took little Heidi to her bedroom to change and feed her. Once that was done and the baby lay sleeping in her crib across the room, Kendra pulled a cardboard box out of her closet. She was surprised it was still there—especially after she'd been kicked out of the house in the early part of this year. When Kendra returned home at her parents' request, she'd half expected to discover all of her old things had been thrown out.

The box was full of old papers and memorabilia from her high school days, and she wanted to make sure there was nothing left in it to remind her of Max. When he'd chosen not to acknowledge Kendra's pregnancy and had cheated on her, she'd vowed to erase him from her life. That included getting rid of any pictures of him that may still be floating around. The last thing she wanted was for her little girl to know anything about her biological father when she grew up.

Kendra took a seat on the floor and took everything out

of the box. Then, one by one, she began sorting through each item. So many mementos she'd saved in those days. It was hard not to laugh at them now. First, there was a ticket stub to a school play she'd gone to. Why she'd saved that had her perplexed, because as Kendra remembered, she'd gone there alone. Then there were the pictures of some of her classmates she'd never bothered to put in her wallet. When she came to the yearbook from when she was a sophomore, she paused to look through the photos and read a couple of pages. She'd managed to get a few signatures and autographs from teachers and some of her fellow students. Kendra had to laugh when one of them had been signed, "*To a girl who will go far in life.*"

"Yeah, right." Pushing her hair off her face, Kendra criticized her situation. "Here I am coming up on my twenty-first birthday, still living with my parents, a single mother, and no job." She heaved a sigh. "If those kids I went to school with could see me now, they'd wish they had written something different in my yearbook."

Halfway through the book, Kendra's gaze came to rest on the senior class pictures. She hadn't known many of the senior students, but recognized a few who were either involved in sports or held some position on the student body council. She recognized one of the guys—a tall, good-looking fellow named Brent. He was captain of the football team and also president of the senior class. As she recalled, Brent always had a group of silly girls around him, vying for his attention.

Then she glanced in the box and saw something else. Folded, in the shape of a triangle, was an old gum wrapper. Picking it up, she had to smile, remembering the night, like it was yesterday.

Kendra had been standing on the sidelines, cheering her school's football team as they ran out on to the field. She'd been with a group of other students when she saw a piece of paper fall out of Brent's uniform. She'd kept an eye on where it fell. Then, when everyone went back to the bleachers while the team was doing the coin toss to see who would get the ball first, Kendra hurried over and picked up the small paper and stuffed it in her pocket. It was this very gum wrapper she looked at now that had been in Brent's pocket that day.

She smiled, placing the yearbook aside, then went to the waste basket to throw the wrapper away. Ironically, to this day, she still bought that brand of chewing gum, all because of a high school crush.

I bet Brent's got a wife and a couple of kids by now. A guy like him, who had it all together, would never have given someone like me a second glance. Sure wish I could have found somebody better to date than Max. He was a loser from the get-go. I was just too dumb to see it.

<hr />

Millersburg

"How'd things go at school today, kids?" Nicole's father asked as she and her siblings sat at the kitchen table eating the pepperoni pizza he'd picked up on the way home. It was a treat for Nicole, not having to cook.

"School was okay," Tony said around a mouthful of food. "I'd rather spend the day outside riding my bike or playin' basketball, though."

"Those are things you can do when you get home from school, Son." Dad looked at Heather. "How was your day?"

"It was good. I found a new book in the library I like. It's about a. . ."

"Hey, where's the milk?" Tony bumped Nicole's arm with his bony elbow. "I thought you were gonna put it on the table."

"I asked you to take the milk out, remember?" Nicole gestured to the refrigerator. "Why don't you get off your lazy bones and get it?"

"You're not my boss." Tony glared at her. "Only Mom and Dad can tell me what to do."

Nicole swatted at the air. "Dad's your boss, but in case you've forgotten, Mom's not here. And even when she was..."

Dad held up his hand. "Okay, you two, that's enough. Tony, please get out the carton of milk. And don't forget four glasses."

"Okay," Tony mumbled, pushing his chair away from the table.

Dad looked at Nicole. "How was your day at school? Didn't you mention you had a math test to take?"

"No, it was English."

Nicole cringed. She was almost certain she'd gotten at least half the answers wrong. Between lack of sleep and not studying long enough, her brain couldn't absorb all the questions on the test, let alone come up with right answers. "It's too soon to know how I did on the test." She waited for Tony to set the milk on the table and hand her a glass, then she poured herself some. No way was she going to admit she'd probably flunked the test. Dad would probably come unglued.

The telephone rang from the living room, and Dad left his seat at the table to answer it. When he returned several minutes later he wore a closed-lipped smile. "Good news, kids—especially for you, Nicole. An anonymous donor has paid for us to have our house cleaned weekly for the next six months."

"What?" Nicole's eyebrows shot up. "Why would someone do that?"

Dad lifted his shoulders in a quick shrug. "The woman who called has her own cleaning business. All she said was that she'd been paid in advance to come here and clean weekly until the last day in May. She will start this Saturday."

"Yeah!" Tony clapped his hands.

"The last day of May is when we get out of school, Dad." Heather grinned. "Nicole won't have to start cleaning again till then. Of course, I'll help her, since we won't have any schoolwork to do during the summer."

Barely able to take it all in, Nicole thought about all

the people they knew. She couldn't imagine who would care enough to hire a housekeeper for them or who had that kind of money. She hoped she could find out someday who the donor was so she could thank that person for it. Even though she'd still have cooking and other chores to do, not having to clean the house every week would give her more time to study and hopefully get all her homework done on time. For the moment, at least, things were looking up.

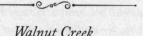

Walnut Creek

Heidi glanced at the kitchen clock. It was almost six, and Lyle wasn't home yet. After their dental appointments, which had turned out well for both of them, he'd dropped her off at home and headed out to conduct an afternoon auction. Heidi spent the next few hours catching up with some mending and making a list of all the ingredients she would need for her next cooking class. Although it wouldn't take place until a week from this Saturday, she liked to plan ahead and be prepared.

Heidi's mouth watered as she lifted the lid on a kettle of stew and inhaled its savory fragrance. She was tempted to eat without Lyle, knowing he probably wouldn't mind, but she didn't want to sit at the table alone. She'd done it on too many occasions.

She turned away from the stove and gazed out the window. After nine years of marriage, there should be children playing in the yard, eager to come in when she called them for supper. Instead, the only thing Heidi saw was her dog, Rusty, running across the lawn. The Brittany spaniel was a loyal pet, but he could never take the place of a child.

Heidi moved from the window and shook her head. *You're doing it again—feeling sorry for yourself. When am I ever going to accept things as they are?*

The words of Psalm 103:2 crossed her mind: *"Bless the*

LORD, *O my soul, and forget not all his benefits.*"It was a timely reminder of God's faithfulness and the hope she had in Him. Heidi remembered one of their ministers saying recently that every believer should spend time naming the ways God had been good to them. This act would offer encouragement during times when things appeared bleak. He also said, "As God has been faithful to us in the past, His love for us will continue in the future. Reminding ourselves of God's goodness will keep us filled with His peace."

Heidi bowed her head and closed her eyes. *Heavenly Father, thank You for the reminder of Your faithfulness and love. Help me remember all the blessings You have bestowed on me in the past and will continue to provide in the future. Amen.*

She was on the verge of having a small bowl of the stew, when a noisy ruckus broke out on the lawn. *Groink. . .Groink . . .Arf! Arf! Arf!*

She hurried to the window and gasped. Rusty and six hefty hogs ran in circles through the freshly mowed grass. "*Ach*, the neighbor's pigs must have gotten out of their pen!"

Heidi turned off the stove, grabbed two apples from the fruit bowl on the table, and rushed out the back door. She'd seen her father lure pigs into their pen a good many times when she was a girl. Hopefully, using fruit like he did would entice them to follow her back to their owner's home.

Chapter 28

Heidi was halfway to the neighbors' house with the pigs when she saw Lyle's horse and buggy coming down the road. He must have spotted her then too for he pulled over to the side of the road, hopped out, and tied the horse to a fence post. "What's going on?" he called, cupping his hands around his mouth.

"The neighbors' pigs got out. Rusty was chasing them all around our yard." Moving toward Lyle, Heidi showed him the apples she held. "I'm luring them home with these."

He chuckled, slapping his knee as he got behind the pigs and cheered them on. Soon, they were back where they belonged and locked securely in their pen. Since the neighbors weren't home, Lyle said he would tell them about it in the morning. He smiled at Heidi and motioned to his horse and buggy. "Hop in, and I'll give you a ride back home."

She did as he suggested, reaching over to touch his arm after he'd untied the horse and they'd both taken a seat. "Danki for your help with the *sei*. Those rambunctious critters can be a handful when they're all stirred up, and our faithful dog didn't help things any with all the barking he did."

"Where's the *hund* now?" Lyle glanced around before clucking to the horse to get him moving down the road.

Heidi pointed in the direction of their house. "As soon as you showed up with the horse and buggy, he made a beeline for home."

Lyle snickered. "Guess he figured I might holler at him for being out of the yard."

"That's quite likely," Heidi agreed. "So how'd things go at the auction?"

"They went well, and there was a good turnout. How was your day?"

"Okay. I got lots done, and I hope your *hungerich*, because I made a pot of stew, and it's keeping warm on the stove."

Lyle thumped his stomach and grinned. "You know me . . . Always ready to enjoy a good meal."

Heidi placed her hand on his knee and gave it a tender squeeze. Her husband's humor and pleasant attitude were reminders that she'd chosen well when she married him.

"Say, this is a pretty good meal. What's it called?" Lance's brother smacked his lips.

"It's Chicken in a Crumb Basket. The Amish woman I told you about taught me how to make it during the last cooking class." Lance put some coleslaw on his plate and handed the bowl to Dan. "There's something I need to talk to you about."

"Oh? What's up?"

"There's a young woman named Lisa who's also taking the cooking classes, and. . ." Lance paused and took a quick drink of water. "Anyway, Lisa owns a duplex in Dover. She lives in one side and rents the other one out."

Dan grabbed a pickle and plopped it on his plate. "That's nice, but why are you telling me this?"

"The thing is. . . Well, Lisa's previous tenants moved out unexpectedly, and now she's looking for someone else to rent or lease the place to."

"I'm still not sure why you're mentioning this."

Lance clutched his fork tightly. Did he need to draw his brother a picture? "I thought you might want to take a look at it—maybe rent the duplex."

Dan's brows furrowed. "What for? I own a townhouse, you know."

"Yeah, but it won't be ready for several more months."

"That's okay. Thanks to your generosity, I have a place to stay."

Lance briefly closed his eyes, taking a deep breath. This wasn't going as well as he hoped. Should he come right out and tell his brother that he wanted him to move, or would it be better to let Dan figure it out himself? All Lance knew was he couldn't put up with his brother's irritating habits and inconsiderate actions much longer.

He drew a quick breath and decided to try again, using a more direct approach this time. "I think it might be better for both of us if we weren't sharing the same house."

"I shoulda known this was coming." Dan slumped in his chair. "You're still mad 'cause I painted the kitchen beige without asking you, huh?"

"It's not just the kitchen or the TV you replaced my old one with. We don't see eye-to-eye on many things, and it'd be best if we had our own space."

Dan pressed his lips together. "Wow, I've only been here a short time, and have already worn out my welcome." He pushed his chair back and rose from the table. "Well, don't give it another thought. I'll find someplace else to live till my townhouse is ready. Sorry I've been such a bother to you."

Lance groaned inwardly. He'd offended his brother, and now he felt like a heel. "Listen, Dan, you're not a bother."

"Sure sounds like it to me."

"Okay, look, I'll be the first to admit, I'm set in my ways. Since Flo died I've established somewhat of a routine, and havin' you here has upset my applecart. If you don't want to look at Lisa's duplex, that's fine by me. We'll continue with our arrangement until your place is ready."

Dan gave a firm shake of his head. "No, you're right. It'd be better if we weren't sharing a home. We may be brothers, but we've always been different as nighttime and daylight. If you want to set up a day and time with your friend Lisa, I'll take a look at her place."

Lance wasn't sure if Dan had given in merely to keep the peace, or if he actually felt he'd be better off living on his own. No matter, though. Dan had agreed to look at the duplex, so tomorrow morning they'd head over there and see if anything could be arranged. One thing Lance hadn't mentioned, though, was that he'd promised to help Lisa with anything that needed to be fixed. He'd make sure Dan knew about it before they got to Lisa's place, though, because he figured his brother should help too.

Lance tapped his chin. *On second thought, it might be better if I wait till we get to Lisa's to mention the work that needs to be done. It'll be harder for Dan to say no in Lisa's company.*

* * *

Canton

Todd had finished eating a fried egg sandwich for his evening meal, when his cell phone rang. Seeing it was his mother, he almost didn't answer. But if he ignored her too long, she'd only keep calling and leaving him long messages, which really got on his nerves.

Todd swiped his thumb across the front of his phone. "Hi, Mom. How are you?"

"I'm well, and so is your father. We haven't heard from you in a while and wondered how you're doing."

"Doin' okay. Keeping plenty busy with work and other things."

"I figured as much." There was a brief pause. "Listen, the main reason I'm calling is to see if you plan to be here for Thanksgiving weekend."

Todd glanced at his calendar. Thanksgiving was still a few weeks away. "Probably not, Mom."

"How come?" He could hear the disappointment in her voice.

"I have other plans."

"Oh, I see. So what are your plans for Thanksgiving?"

The truth was, Todd had no holiday plans but hoped he and Lisa might get together that day. He wanted to go out with her a few more times before he asked, though, and didn't want her to think he was moving too fast. The last thing he wanted to do was lay out money for a plane ticket to see his folks and spend Thanksgiving listening to Mom pick apart everything he said and did. Her constant badgering was one of the reasons he'd moved away. The offer to write a food column for the newspaper here had come at just the right time.

"Todd, did you hear what I said?"

"Yeah, sure, Mom. You asked what my plans are for Thanksgiving."

"And?"

"I'm seeing someone I met recently, so. . ."

"You're dating again?"

"Yeah. Sort of."

"I'm happy to hear this, Son. After the breakup with Felicia, I wasn't sure you'd ever want to date again."

Todd put the phone on speaker and moved over to the sink to rinse his dishes. "Can we talk about something else? I'd rather not rehash all that went down with my ex-girlfriend."

"Whatever you wish. Is it all right if I ask a few questions about your new girlfriend?"

"Sure, but right now we're just friends. I'm not sure how she feels about me yet."

"Then why are you spending Thanksgiving with her?"

Todd lifted his gaze to the ceiling. If he didn't hang up soon, this could turn into a session of twenty-plus questions. "I enjoy Lisa's company, and—"

"Lisa who? What's her last name, Todd?"

"Brooks."

"Did you meet her at work, or is she another woman you met on one of those Internet dating sites?"

"I haven't been doing anymore online dating. Once was enough. I met Lisa at a cooking class I've been taking, hosted by an Amish woman who lives in Walnut Creek." Todd moved back to the table and took a seat.

"Cooking classes? An Amish woman?" Mom's voice raised nearly an octave. "Since when did you decide to learn how to cook, and why take lessons from an Amish woman? I'm sure she's not a gourmet chef."

"Of course not, but she's an excellent cook and is teaching us to make some traditional Amish dishes."

"How many others are taking the class?"

"There are six of us. Three men and three women. We meet every other Saturday for a total of six classes."

"Hmm. . . Interesting."

Todd glanced at his watch. In three minutes one of his favorite shows would be coming on TV. "Sorry, Mom but I have to hang up now. Thanks for calling, and tell Dad I said hello."

"All right, Son. I'll talk to you again soon. Oh, and it'd be nice if you called us for a change."

"Okay, Mom. Bye." Todd clicked off the phone. He wished his mother hadn't brought up the topic of his breakup with Felicia. It was a bitter pill, and he wanted to put it behind him. Hopefully, if he and Lisa's relationship developed further, she wouldn't betray him the way Felicia had.

Chapter 29

Dover

"Thank you both so much. I appreciate all the help you gave me this morning." Lisa smiled at Lance and his brother as they sat at her kitchen table, eating the lunch she'd prepared. When they'd first gotten here and she'd shown them the duplex, Dan hadn't seemed that interested in the place. Now, however, as he gobbled down some of her homemade chicken noodle soup, he talked about moving in and said he looked forward to being able to spread out.

Dan glanced at Lance with eyes slightly narrowed. "This way I won't be in anybody's way."

Lance ignored the comment and grabbed a roll, slathering it with butter.

Sensing a bit of discord between the men, Lisa handed Lance a jar of apple butter and changed the subject. "Are you looking forward to our next cooking class with Heidi?"

His eyes brightened as he nodded. "The last recipe she taught us to make was good, but I'm hoping for some kind of dessert I can make for Thanksgiving or even Christmas."

"That would be nice. I cater a lot of parties during the holidays, so I'm always looking for new pie, cake, or cookie recipes to try."

"Bet your business is doing well." Dan wiped his mouth on a napkin. "Because this chicken soup you made is sure good."

"Thank you. It's an old family recipe, handed down from my great-grandmother."

"My wife, Flo, used to make good soup. She taught our daughters how to cook well too." Lance rubbed his hand against his chest, where his heart would be. "Sure do miss her."

Lisa felt like leaving her seat and giving him a hug, but she held back. Except for the times they'd met at Heidi's classes, she didn't know Lance well and thought he might not appreciate a hug from a near stranger. "Loss is hard," she murmured. "It's good you have other family around."

"Yeah." He bumped Dan's arm with his elbow. "I may not always show it or think to express my feelings, but I do appreciate you, Brother."

"Same here. Even though we have our differences, when the chips are down, I know I can count on you."

Lisa's cell phone rang from the living room, so she excused herself to answer it. She took a seat on the couch. "Hello."

"Hi, Lisa, it's Todd. I hope you aren't busy."

"I was having lunch with Lance and his brother, Dan."

"Lance Freemont from our cooking class?"

"Yes. He brought Dan over this morning to look at my rental, and since they helped me with a few repairs, I fixed them lunch."

"Wow, if I'd known having lunch with you would be the reward, I'd have volunteered to come help myself."

She snickered. "And miss work?"

"You're right, I do need to write an article for the paper, but I get a lunchbreak, which I'm taking right now, in fact."

"If you were closer to Dover, I'd invite you to join us."

"That'd be nice, but since I'm not, how about dinner tonight?"

"You want to join me here for dinner?"

"I was thinking of taking you out for another meal." He laughed. "I'm a pretty direct person, but I'd never invite myself to anyone's house, expecting them to cook for me."

"Actually, I'd be happy to fix you a meal, but tonight I'm busy."

"Oh, I see." She heard the disappointment in Todd's voice.

"I'm catering a friend's baby shower this evening, so I won't even have time for a decent dinner myself." Lisa heard laughter coming from the kitchen and smiled. It sounded like the brothers were getting along well, and she was glad. She'd be most happy to have a brother or sister. She hoped Lance and Dan knew how fortunate they were.

"Are you still there, Lisa?"

"Uh, yeah. I need to finish eating, but can we get together for dinner some other night this week—maybe Friday or Saturday?"

"Saturday would work for me."

"Okay, see you at six o'clock that evening. Oh, and plan on eating here this time. I'll fix something special."

"Sounds good, Lisa. See you Saturday."

When Lisa hung up, she sat several seconds, thinking about Todd. Based on some things he'd said during one of the cooking classes, she wasn't sure if he was a Christian or not. She needed to find out soon, before their relationship went any further.

New Philadelphia

After leaving work that afternoon, Allie picked the kids up from school, then went to the bank. As she headed for home, with Nola and Derek talking quietly in the backseat for a change, her thoughts went to Steve. She couldn't believe he'd worked past midnight both Sunday and Monday. Allie had tried talking to him about it this morning, before she took the kids to school, but he'd been evasive. Something had to be going on, and she was determined to get to the bottom of it, once and for all. It wasn't fair of Steve to cause her to worry and wonder like this. Tonight, when he came home—no matter what time it was—she would insist they sit down and have a little talk.

"Mommy, can we take Trouble for a walk when we get home?" Derek's question pushed Allie's thoughts aside.

"We'll see. I need to put a roast in the oven for supper, and you two need to change into your play clothes before we do anything else."

"Can we have cookies and milk?" Nola asked.

"Yes, we'll take time for a snack. Afterward, you can play in the yard with the dog until I'm free to take a walk with you."

"Okay, Mommy," the children said in unison.

Allie smiled. It was good to see them both in pleasant moods, with no teasing or quarrelling. There were times when the kids sat in the back of the van picking on each other until they reached their destination. Nothing got on Allie's nerves more than that.

The grocery store was up ahead, and Allie decided to stop and pick up a few things she needed. "Let's go kids." Allie parked the van and opened the door. "We are going to make a quick trip inside, then we'll go straight home and take care of Trouble."

Once inside, Allie and the kids scooted down each aisle. She was glad her children kept up with her. Rounding the cart to the next aisle, Allie spotted another mother whose daughter was in her son's class. *Oh, fiddle. I was hoping I wouldn't run into anybody. I don't want to take the time for idle chitchat.*

Allie tried to look away, in hopes she wouldn't be seen, but it was too late. Tammy Brubaker approached her cart.

"Nola and Derek, I want you each to pick out a box of cereal you'd like to get while I say hello to Mrs. Brubaker." Allie didn't want to be rude, and hopefully she could make this conversation short.

"Hi, Allie." Tammy smiled. "I haven't seen you in a while."

"Hi, yourself. And yes, it has been a while."

"How are you and your family doing?"

Allie gave a quick rundown and mentioned the puppy she'd recently gotten for the kids. Then Tammy asked how Steve was doing.

"He's good, but his job keeps him from home a good deal of the time."

"I'll bet. Having a job as a police officer, well... I'm sure there is never a lull." Tammy pushed her long auburn hair away from her face.

"You're right about that." Allie wished she could find a way to end their conversation, but it would be impolite. The last thing she wanted to talk about with Tammy was Steve or his job.

"Come to think of it," Tammy continued. "I saw Steve recently, when I went to get a cup of coffee at the little café in the mall."

"Oh?"

"Yes. I was parking my car, but didn't get a chance to talk with him, though. He was leaving with a fellow officer. A nice-looking lady with blond hair." Tammy pulled a jar of pickles off the nearest shelf and placed it in her shopping cart. "She looked too young to be a police officer, but then, these days it's hard to tell a person's age."

Allie tensed up, and no words would come. Call it good timing, but she was thankful when the children came running back with their choices of cereal. Did Tammy suspect something was going on between Steve and Lori? If so, Allie hoped she wouldn't mention it to anyone.

"I'm sorry Tammy, but we really have to run." Allie put the cereal boxes in the cart. "The puppy has been home alone all day, and I'm sure we'll have a mess to clean up in his cage." As she pushed the shopping cart toward the front of the aisle, Allie looked over her shoulder and hollered, "It was nice talking to you."

Allie didn't care about the curious expression on Tammy's face. All she wanted to do was get out of that store, take the kids home to care for Trouble, put the groceries away, and start supper. The busier she kept, the more it would help her anger to keep from bubbling over. The last thing Allie had wanted to hear was news of Steve being seen with that blond—especially learning such a thing from someone else.

After making sure the kids were buckled in, Allie got into the minivan. *Now calm down,* she told herself. *It doesn't do any good for you to get so upset—especially when you have no proof of anything.* But the image of Steve and his blond partner having coffee in that cute little café remained in Allie's head.

* * *

Millersburg

As Bill headed across the school's parking lot to his truck, he spotted Nicole walking in the direction of the buses waiting to pick kids up. For the first time since he'd met the young woman, he noticed a spring to her step. It was an even bigger surprise to see her walking beside another teenage girl, talking and laughing.

I bet she's in a good mood today 'cause she found out some of her workload will be lifted by having a weekly housekeeper. Bill grinned. It felt good to do something nice for a person in need, even if he didn't know her well. It had been hard to part with the money Bill had been saving for a trip to Alaska he wanted to take, but he had waited this long to go and could wait awhile longer. Besides, he had his upcoming hunting trip to look forward to and the hope of bagging a big buck this year. Bill could almost see a beautiful pair of antlers hanging on the wall in his cabin in Coshocton.

He turned back toward the buses and saw Nicole wave to her friend. Then she started walking down the sidewalk. Bill was tempted to go talk to her, but thought better of it. She might be embarrassed to have anyone see her talking to the school's head janitor. Well, that was okay. He'd talk to

Nicole at Heidi's next cooking class. He was curious to hear how things were going for her in school now that she'd been given more time to study.

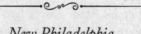

New Philadelphia

Allie finished putting the roast in the oven and had gone to the kitchen window to check on the kids and the dog, when she saw Steve's SUV pull into the yard. Over and over she told herself, *Keep calm, Allie. Keep calm and don't say anything out of anger or start making accusations.*

When Steve came in, the first thing he did was give Allie a kiss. But before she could ask him any questions, he told her about an unwed woman he'd arrested today for child abuse.

Steve shook his head. "It was sad to see her three kids taken from her, but they'll be better off in foster care."

"What a shame." Allie felt bad for those unfortunate children, as well as for the mother who desperately needed help. Every child deserved to grow up in a stable, happy environment.

Steve ambled across the kitchen and poured himself a cup of coffee. "There are so many kids in the system these days who need good foster parents. Too bad we're not able to take one or two children in."

Allie nodded. "It would be nice, but with both of our jobs, plus caring for our own kids, it's not feasible."

"You're probably right." He drank his coffee and set his mug in the sink. "I talked to the kids before I came inside. They want us to take them and the dog for a walk. Are you free to go with us?"

"I did tell them I would walk the dog, but now that you're here, I'd like us to talk for a bit."

"No problem. We can do that while we're walking."

She shook her head. "What I have to say is not for the kids to hear."

He leaned against the cabinet, folding his arms. "Okay. What's up?"

"I want to know why you're always working late. And I want you to explain—"

Steve held up his hand. "I work late because I have to, Allie. We've had this discussion many times, and unless you want to start an argument and ruin the whole evening, there's nothing more to say—end of story. Now let's get our jackets on and join Nola and Derek."

She heaved a sigh. "Give me a few minutes to change into my sweatpants, and I'll be ready to go."

When Allie walked into the bedroom, she stared at her image in the mirror. Pulling her thick, curly hair away from her face, she secured it with a clip. "I'm not a bad-looking person," she mumbled to her reflection. Running her fingers over her cheekbones, it pleased Allie to have such soft skin. Having an olive-tone complexion, with no wrinkles other than a few laugh lines around the corners of her eyes, gave her a younger-than-thirty appearance. *Steve should be satisfied with me. I'm a good mother, and I do my best to look nice for him.*

She massaged her temples, trying to gain relief from a headache. *Why does Lori Robbins have to be so cute? She can't be much younger than me. Does Steve find her more attractive than I am? Would he rather spend time with Lori than his wife and children?*

Allie turned sideways and ran her hand over her flat stomach. One would never know she had two children. Her arms and legs were toned too.

She drew a deep, cleansing breath. *Why am I doing this to myself? What am I afraid of? Steve and I have a good marriage and two wonderful kids. I need to stop dwelling on all this, or I'll end up causing problems in our marriage. I knew soon after I married Steve, his being a police officer would not be easy.* She pinched her cheeks. *Come on, girl—toughen up.*

"Hey, Allie, hurry up! The kids and puppy are raring to

go," Steve yelled from downstairs.

"I'm on my way!" With one last look in the mirror, Allie stuck her tongue out at herself and, as if she were a child needing to be scolded, added, "Shame on you. Now go enjoy the evening with your family. Isn't this outing what you've been hoping for?"

Allie felt a little better when she headed outside to go for their walk. If Steve refused to listen to her concerns, there wasn't much she could do. But one thing was certain: Allie planned to keep an eye on things. It truly wasn't Steve she was worried about, though. It was the blond-haired cop. She had too much at stake to let some other woman steal her husband away.

Chapter 30

Walnut Creek

After Heidi got the mail Saturday morning, she decided to stop at the phone shack to check for messages that may have come in since last evening. She was pleased to find one from her mother, inviting her and Lyle to Middlefield for Thanksgiving. It had been a while since Heidi visited her folks, and she looked forward to going. Hopefully, Lyle hadn't already made plans with his parents for that day. She would wait and check with him before responding to Mom's phone message.

She listened to the rest of the messages and wrote down those that were important, then stepped out of the phone shack, pausing briefly to breathe in the fresh morning air.

Heidi was almost up to the house when a car pulled in. She recognized the vehicle, and waved when Kendra got out and took the baby from the car. How wonderful it was to see them again.

"I was hoping you'd be home." Kendra smiled when she joined Heidi near the front porch. "Do you have time to visit?"

"Of course." Heidi gestured to the infant held snuggly in Kendra's arms. "How's my little namesake doing?"

"She's getting along well—gaining the weight she should too. And as long as she's fed and diapered regularly, my sweet little Heidi is a satisfied baby."

"That's good to hear." Heidi gestured to the house. "Let's

go inside where it's warmer."

Kendra followed Heidi into the house, and they found seats in the living room. With a great sense of longing, Heidi gazed at Kendra's precious daughter. *I will not allow myself to feel jealous.* "How are things going now with you and your parents?" she asked. "Any better?"

"Unfortunately, about the same as when I was here before. Dad's still impatient, and Mom—well, she keeps reminding me to keep the baby quiet when Dad's in the house because Heidi's crying gets on his nerves." Kendra's shoulders lifted as she released a deep sigh. "I wish I could get out on my own, but there's no way I can afford to rent a place right now. Maybe when I'm feeling strong enough to look for a job, but then there's the matter of finding someone to watch the baby while I'm at work."

"Won't your mother take care of her granddaughter?" Heidi couldn't imagine Kendra's mother being unwilling to watch the baby. Most grandmothers she knew looked for excuses to be with their grandchildren.

"She probably would take care of the baby, as long it was during the day, when Dad's at work. If I worked during the evening hours, it could be a problem, though."

Heidi was tempted to ask Kendra why her father had agreed to let her move back home if he had no patience with a little one. Instead, she held out her arms. "May I hold the baby?"

"Sure." Kendra handed the infant to Heidi.

She moved from the couch to the rocker and got it moving back and forth as she stroked the infant's silky head. *I shouldn't do this,* Heidi told herself. *Holding Kendra's daughter only increases my desire for a child and makes me wish this little girl was mine.*

Heidi sucked in her bottom lip. It wasn't right to envy, but despite her best efforts, she couldn't seem to help herself. Then the words of Hebrews 13:5 came to mind: *"Let your conversation be without covetousness; and be content with such things as ye have: for [Jesus] hath said, I will never leave thee, nor forsake thee."*

Heidi paused to thank God for the reminders found in His Word, for she certainly had much in her life to bring contentment—a wonderful husband, loving parents, good health, and special friends. Those were the things she needed to focus on and feel thankful for.

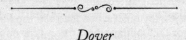

Dover

Lisa rushed about the kitchen, getting things ready for dinner with Todd. She felt relaxed and at ease with the world today. Having a renter in the other half of the duplex again would be nice, and since Dan had no pets, she wouldn't have to worry about the place becoming a mess.

Lisa lifted the lid on the crockpot and inhaled the zesty aroma. "Yum. If this tastes even half as good as it smells, I think Todd will be impressed."

Her cell phone rang, and thinking it might be Todd, she hurried across the room to pick it up. Seeing in the caller ID window that it was her mother calling, she quickly answered. "Hi, Mom. How are you?"

"I'm fine, honey. How are things going with you?"

"Doing well." Lisa put the phone in speaker mode and began to set the table.

"Are you busy right now? I hear some clinging and clanging going on."

Lisa laughed. "Todd's coming over for dinner this evening, and I'm setting the table."

"Oh, I see. One of these days you'll have to bring your new fellow by the house so your dad and I can meet him."

"How about Thanksgiving? It would be a good chance for you both to get to know him." Lisa rubbed an itchy spot on the side of her nose. The truth was, she didn't know Todd all that well yet, either.

"You haven't invited him to join us yet, I hope."

"No, Mom, but I thought—"

"In all honesty, I would prefer it just be our family this year. I hope you understand."

No, I don't understand. Her mother's request made no sense to Lisa. In times past, they'd invited many different guests to share their Thanksgiving meal. Why should it be any different this year? "Okay, that's fine," she murmured. "Todd may have other plans for the holiday anyway, and I haven't mentioned Thanksgiving to him."

"I'm glad you're agreeable. We'll see you then, and feel free to come a little early." Mom's tone sounded chipper. Since Lisa kept so busy with her business, she didn't get to see her folks as often as she used to. Maybe that was the reason they wanted her all to themselves this holiday. If her relationship with Todd kept going, Lisa would make sure Mom and Dad got to meet him.

When Todd entered Lisa's kitchen, he lifted his nose and inhaled deeply. "Something sure smells good in here. What have you got cooking?"

She smiled, pointing to the crockpot on the counter. "I made lemon chicken, a tossed green salad, steamed brown rice, and brussels sprouts cooked in coconut oil and fresh garlic."

He jiggled his brows. "Sounds pretty good so far."

Lisa poked his arm. "What do you mean, so far?"

He gave her a kiss on the cheek. "I'm wondering about dessert."

"I made a banana cream pie. How's that sound to you?"

"I like banana cream pie, but I bet it won't taste half as good as your sweet lips." Todd kissed her again, this time a gentle kiss on the mouth. He'd been right. Lisa's kiss was sweet as honey.

Her cheeks colored, and she pushed him gently away. "You're such a big flirt."

"I'm not flirting; I'm serious."

"I'm flattered by the compliment, but now it's time to eat." She gestured to the table. It had been set with fancy dishes and shiny goblets. There was even a scented candle in the middle, surrounded by a small autumn-colored wreath. "Now, if you'll please take a seat, I'll serve the meal."

"Is there anything I can do to help?"

She shook her head. "It won't take me long to set things out, so just sit and relax."

Todd obliged. Being here in Lisa's kitchen was nicer than going out to a restaurant, and much more relaxed. He could get used to spending time with her like this.

After everything was on the table, Lisa took the seat beside him and bowed her head. "Would you like to say the blessing, or should I?"

Todd squirmed uncomfortably in his chair. He hadn't expected she would ask him to pray. Truth was, he wouldn't know what to say. "Uh. . .why don't you do the honors?"

Todd sat with his eyes partially open as Lisa offered a prayer, thanking God for the food and the opportunity to be with Todd this evening. He couldn't help feeling a bit guilty for sticking her with saying grace, but he had not offered any kind of a prayer since he was a boy. And then it was only when he'd spent time with his grandparents, who prayed at every meal. Todd still remembered how Grandma used to make everyone at her table take turns saying a prayer. When it was his turn, he would hurriedly say a little prayer he'd memorized. "God is great. God is good. And I thank Him for this food. Amen." He'd feel pretty foolish if he recited that prayer in front of Lisa, though. It was best that she offered the blessing.

As they ate their meal, Todd's taste buds came alive. The succulent chicken all but melted in his mouth, and the brussels sprouts were done to perfection. "I'm duly impressed with your culinary skills." He gave her a thumbs-up. "Everything tastes superb."

Once more, Lisa's cheeks turned rosy as she nodded her head. "Why, thank you, sir. I am pleased that you like what I cooked for you this evening."

"I'm sorry I misjudged your abilities based on what you fixed for my friends' wedding."

She wrinkled her petite little nose. "Please, let's not go there again."

"Okay." He winked at her and reached for another helping of chicken.

After the meal was over, Todd helped Lisa clear the table and load the dishwasher. Then they went to the living room and spent the next couple of hours visiting.

"Are you ready for some pie?" Lisa rose from the couch. "And how about a cup of coffee to go with it?"

Todd smacked his lips. "Both sound good. Need some help getting it out?"

"Thanks anyway, but I can manage. While I'm in the kitchen why don't you turn on the gas fireplace? It's a little chilly in here, and a cozy fire is always nice during an autumn evening."

"Sure thing. I like the whole 'flick a switch and instant flames' thing. It beats dealing with messy wood and ashes you have to clean out of a wood-burning fireplace, like my grandparents have."

She took a few steps toward the kitchen, but paused and turned to look at him. "Do they live in the area?"

"Nope. Both sets of my grandparents live in Oregon, not far from my folks."

"I bet you miss them."

"Yeah, but I enjoy my independence, so the positive outweighs the negative."

Lisa turned and headed to the kitchen. Todd figured she probably thought it was strange that he'd chosen not to live close to his family. A slight muscle jumped in his cheek as he moved across the room to turn on the fireplace. *Well, if she knew my mom, she might understand. Not everyone has a good relationship with their family.*

Once the fire was going, and he'd set the remote for it to a nice, even temperature, Todd took a seat on the couch again, to wait for Lisa. She returned shortly, carrying a tray with two pieces of pie and coffee mugs, which she placed on the small table in front of the sofa.

"Here we go. Please, help yourself."

Todd didn't have to be asked twice. Just looking at the banana cream pie, he knew he was in for a treat. After taking his first bite, Todd smiled and took hold of Lisa's hand. "This pie is awesome. Not quite as sweet as your lips, but a close second."

She lifted her gaze to the ceiling. "You're incorrigible."

He snickered. "Just trying to be honest."

As they ate their pie and drank the coffee, Lisa told Todd a little about her family. They also visited about the cooking classes and agreed that they'd be sorry to see them come to an end. While the classes might be winding down soon, Todd hoped he'd have the chance to keep seeing Lisa. She was different than any woman he'd ever met, and he wanted the opportunity to see if their relationship could deepen.

When it came time for Todd to leave, Lisa walked him to the door. With no hesitation, he pulled her into his arms for a lingering kiss.

"Before you go, I have a question to ask," Lisa said breathlessly.

"Sure. Ask me anything you like."

"I was wondering if you'd like to attend church with me tomorrow morning. Maybe we can go out for a bite to eat afterward."

He bit down on his bottom lip. *Oh, great. Now why'd you have to go and ruin our nice evening? Do I try to weasel my way out of going or cave in and give church a try?*

"Todd, did you hear what I said?"

"Umm. . .yeah."

Lisa tipped her head and looked up at him. "Yeah, you'll go to church, or yeah, you heard my question?"

"Both."

She smiled and gave him a hug. "I'll see you tomorrow then. Church starts at ten thirty, so if you could pick me up at ten, that'd be perfect. Unless you'd rather I give you the church's address and we can just meet there."

He shook his head. "No, I'd rather pick you up. See you then." He leaned down, gave her another kiss, and rushed out the door. *I must be out of my mind.*

The next morning, when Todd took a seat on a church pew with Lisa, he looked around the sanctuary and cringed. *How did I get talked into this? The only reason I agreed to come here is so I could spend more time with Lisa. Plus, I didn't want her to think I'm not interested in religion, which she obviously is. Why'd I have to choose a woman who's into spiritual things?*

Todd stuck a finger inside his shirt collar to loosen it a bit. Looking at all the people with their holier-than-thou expressions made his stomach tighten. He'd gone to church a few times with his previous girlfriend, and where had that gotten him? A kick in the teeth—that's what. Felicia, with the sweet smile and pearly white teeth, may have pretended to be a Christian, but her actions proved louder than her words. Would Lisa do the same?

Todd glanced over at her, sitting beside him with a pleasant smile, while reading the church bulletin they'd received from an elderly greeter when they first entered the church. Was she a true Christian in every sense of the word?

I need to quit thinking about this, and let Lisa prove herself. Todd didn't know why it bothered him so much, because he was far from being a Christian, but anyone who professed to

225

be one should act like it.

Turning his attention to the front of the room, Todd forced his thoughts aside and tried to concentrate on the announcements being made. According to what was written in the bulletin, they still had singing, scriptures, offering, and a sermon to get through. He gave his shirt collar a tug. *Sure hope I can sit here that long.*

As they drove toward the restaurant of Lisa's choice after church, Lisa watched him, wondering what was going through his mind. He hadn't joined in when the songs were sung during the service today. Todd seemed distracted, glancing at his cell phone several times throughout much of the pastor's message. Was he bored, preoccupied, or just didn't enjoy the kind of worship service she was used to? Lisa wrapped her fingers around her purse straps, squeezing tightly. *Maybe I shouldn't have invited him to join me today.*

Looking out the window as they drove outside of town, she was finally able to relax as she gazed at the countryside. It was the end of October, and winter would soon be creeping in. Today's weather reminded her of that. It had dipped into the twenties overnight, and so far, she realized, glancing at the thermometer reading on the car's dashboard, it was barely in the thirties.

Todd's vehicle had tight quarters and no backseat, but it was nice and cozy in his little car, since it heated up faster than her minivan.

Continuing to watch out the passenger window, Lisa admired the huge farm they were passing. Cows stood bunched together around a feeding trough, and vapor coming from their nostrils resembled smoke drifting into the air. The good news was, according to the local weather channel, this cold spell would be short lived. Even though she loved the holidays, Lisa wasn't sure she was ready for winter.

She reached across the seat and gently tapped Todd's arm. "Can I ask you a question?"

"Sure."

"Did you enjoy being in church with me today?"

A muscle on the side of Todd's neck quivered. "I enjoyed being with you. Just not in church."

She pulled her hand back. "How come?"

He sucked in his bottom lip. "I should have been straight with you before, Lisa. I'm not a religious man."

"Are. . .are you an atheist?"

"No, but I don't believe in prayer and all that sort of thing. I think religion is for people who can't stand on their own." He lifted his chin. "I'm a self-made man, and I don't need any help from God in order to make it through life."

"I see." A shiver ran up the back of Lisa's neck as the words of 2 Corinthians 6:14 came to mind: *"Be ye not unequally yoked together with unbelievers."* She should have suspected Todd wasn't a Christian because he'd shown no evidence of it. He was good looking, charming, intelligent, and said all the right things to turn a woman's head, but that wasn't enough—not for Lisa, anyway. She needed a man who loved God as much as she did and wanted to serve Him with his whole heart.

Lisa drew in a deep breath. "So if you feel this way, why'd you agree to go to church with me this morning?"

"I wanted to be with you, and I didn't want you to think—"

"Todd, I don't think we should see each other socially anymore."

He looked at her, then turned his head back to the road ahead. "You're shutting me out because I can't buy into religion?"

"I'm not shutting you out. I just don't want to continue in a relationship that can never go anywhere."

"That's stupid. I like you, Lisa—a lot, in fact, and I'm pretty sure you feel the same about me."

She couldn't deny the feelings she'd begun to have for Todd, but a clean break was the best, for both of them. "Sorry, but I won't be going out with you again." Lisa was glad now that her mother had discouraged her from inviting Todd to Thanksgiving dinner. *I wonder if Mom suspects the guy I've been dating is not a Christian.*

Chapter 31

Walnut Creek

With arms folded, Heidi looked at the calendar on the kitchen wall. Today was the first Saturday of November, and she would soon be teaching the fourth cooking class in this series. With her fluctuating emotions during the first three classes, she hoped she'd made herself clear enough and that everyone had understood the directions she'd given them for the recipes they'd made so far. More than that, Heidi hoped the verses she'd written on the back of each person's card had been meaningful to one or more of them. She hadn't done much actual mentoring during the classes—at least not the way her Aunt Emma did during her quilting classes. But if the scriptures Heidi had shared helped anyone at all, she would be satisfied.

Heidi tapped her chin. *Of course, how will I know whether anyone's been helped, unless they say something to me? I certainly can't come right out and ask. That would be like fishing for a compliment, and it would be prideful.*

"I'm ready to head for Millersburg now, Heidi. Is there anything you need me to get while I'm there?"

Lyle's question pulled Heidi out of her musings. "No, I can't think of anything." She snickered. "Something will probably come to mind after you've gone, though. Isn't that the way it usually goes?"

"Jah, it's true." He pulled Heidi into his arms and gave her a firm kiss. "I hope everything goes well with your class today."

"Danki. I hope so too."

Lyle grabbed his straw hat from the wall peg and slapped it on his head. "See you sometime this afternoon," he called over his shoulder as he headed out the door.

Smiling, Heidi moved over to the cupboard where she kept her baking supplies. Then she took out the ingredients needed to make the apple corn bread she'd be teaching her students to make today. It was an easy recipe and quite tasty—a nice addition to any autumn supper.

After watching out the window as her husband's buggy went down the driveway, Heidi glanced around the section of yard within her vision. So many leaves still needed to be cleaned up, especially where the wind had piled them in corners. "Guess I'll have to get out there soon and get some raking done. Not today, though."

She moved away from the window. The leaves in her flower beds could stay there until the first warm days of spring. It would give the flower bulbs an extra blanket until the coldest weather was done for the season.

She glanced toward the trees in their yard. The only leaves still clinging were on a white oak, which dropped its leaves in the spring. At least the weather had warmed up a bit, and the recent cold snap was over. But with winter coming, things would soon change.

Heidi set everything out on the table, and was about to pour herself a cup of tea, when a knock sounded on the back door. She glanced at the clock. It wasn't quite time for her students to arrive, and normally they wouldn't use the back door.

She hurried to answer it and was surprised to find Loretta Donnelly on her porch in tears. Heidi clutched her friend's hand, leading her inside. "Loretta, what's wrong?"

"It—it's Eli."

"What's wrong with him? Is Eli sick, or has he been hurt?"

Sniffing, Loretta shook her head. "We. . .we had our first

disagreement, and I'm afraid my response may have ruined things. Even though I joined the church last Sunday, it might be over between us."

"Come sit down." Heidi hoped none of her students would arrive early and interrupt their conversation, because Loretta obviously needed to talk.

After Heidi fixed a second cup of tea and handed it to her friend, she joined her at the kitchen table. "Now tell me what happened between you and Eli."

Loretta took a sip of tea, then set her cup down. "I had him over to my house for supper last night, and he compared the meat loaf I fixed to one his wife used to make."

Heidi leaned forward, resting her arms on the table. "Is that all there was to it?"

"No. I became upset when he said her meat loaf was similar to mine, but hers was juicier. Eli said his wife was a great cook and he'd never had better meat loaf." Loretta paused long enough to take another sip from her teacup, then she resumed. "This isn't the first time Eli's compared me to her, either. And if he's doing it now, I can only imagine how it would be if we got married." She rolled her shoulders, as if to release some of her tension. "I don't compare Eli to my first husband. Even if I did mentally, I would never say anything to Eli's face. When he makes comparisons between me and his deceased wife, I feel as if I'm not good enough—like I don't measure up."

"Have you explained this to him? Told him the way you feel about things?"

Loretta shook her head. "I was afraid he wouldn't understand my feelings or might not want to talk about it. He's a man of few words, you know."

Heidi placed her hand on Loretta's arm and gave it a loving pat. "Lyle and I have come to know Eli pretty well. I'm almost certain you can share your feelings with him about this."

Hands clasped beneath her chin, Loretta spoke in a

trembling voice. "I'll take your advice and try—as soon as I can work up the nerve."

Heidi smiled. "I'll be praying for both of you."

"Thank you. Or should I say, 'Danki?'"

Heidi nodded. "Yes, that's the right word." She was pleased her friend had been making an effort to learn Pennsylvania Dutch. It would certainly help since she was now part of the Amish church.

A knock sounded on the front door, and Heidi jerked her head. "Oh, I bet it's one of my students."

"Sorry, I didn't realize today was one of your cooking classes. I'd better be on my way." Loretta rose from the table and gave Heidi a hug. "Once I've talked to Eli, I'll let you know how things went."

"Jah, please do." Heidi let Loretta out the back door, then she hurried to see who was at her front door.

"Good morning, Heidi. Am I the first one here?" Lance asked when she led the way to her comfortable living room. As usual, the room was tidy—just the way Flo had kept things in their home.

"Yes, you are the first to arrive, but I'm sure the others won't be far behind."

He grinned. "You know, every time I come to your door I feel like I should be delivering a package or something."

"That is how I normally find you on the front porch." Chuckling, Heidi gestured to Lyle's favorite chair. "Why don't you have a seat and relax till the others get here?"

"Thanks. Don't mind if I do." Lance took a seat in the recliner and put the footrest up. "How have you been, Heidi?"

"Fine. How about you?" She seated herself on the couch.

He stretched his arms out wide. "Never better. I feel like I'm on top of the world."

"Did something special happen since you were last here?"

He gave a nod. "You bet! My brother moved out, and I have the whole place to myself again."

"Did he move to the duplex Lisa had for rent?"

"Yep." Lance rubbed his hands together. "Dan and I went over to her place and helped with several repairs while she cleaned the place. He moved in the following day, and even bought a few new pieces of furniture to replace the ones the previous renters had ruined." His smile widened. "Never knew my brother could be so generous. Guess he took a liking to Lisa. She is a pretty sweet gal."

"That's wonderful, but what about your brother's town-house you'd previously mentioned?" Heidi tipped her head. "Won't it be completed soon?"

"Nope, it doesn't look like it. Things are still going slow with the remodel. I'm guessing my brother will stay in the duplex at least a month—maybe longer."

"I see. Then Lisa will have to look for another renter." Heidi's brows pulled in.

"Yeah, I suppose." Fidgeting in his chair, and feeling a bit guilty for putting Lisa out, Lance looked down at his feet. *Maybe I was too hasty asking Dan to move out. Guess I could have put up with him for another month or so, but our relationship was at stake.* Well, it was too late now. His brother was already moved and temporarily settled. He hoped when Dan moved out of Lisa's duplex, she wouldn't have any trouble finding another renter.

"What are we making today?" Bill asked when everyone gathered around Heidi's kitchen table.

Heidi pointed to the ingredients she'd set out. "Apple corn bread."

"Sounds good." Grinning widely, Bill thumped his belly. "I love apples and most always eat the whole apple—core and all, just not the stem. Some of my buddies tease me about

233

being related to a horse."

Everyone but Lisa and Todd laughed. They'd both been quiet since they'd arrived and had barely glanced at each other. Bill wondered if some sort of issue had developed between them. Well, it was none of his business. He came here to learn how to make something new, not worry about the problems others might be having.

He glanced across the table at Nicole. She seemed more relaxed than usual. With lips slightly parted, and eyes shining brightly, her attention was focused on Heidi's instructions.

"How are things going at school, Nicole?" Bill ventured to ask.

She turned her head in his direction. "Better than before. Think I passed the math test I took yesterday. Course it helped that I had more time to study for it."

"Good for you." Bill was well aware of the reason Nicole had more time to study. He was glad he'd eased things for her by paying for a cleaning lady to come in once a week. He saw it as a blessing to help Nicole and her family out but wondered how she would feel if she knew the gift had come from him.

"Does anyone have a question about this bread before I go on?" Heidi broke into Bill's thoughts.

Allie raised her hand. "Does it matter what kind of apples we use?"

"Not really. The type we are using today is Fuji, but most any apple will do." Heidi handed them each a recipe card. "If you'd like a sweeter-tasting corn bread, then you might want to use a sweeter variety of apple. But if you'd prefer something tarter, I'd suggest Granny Smith apples."

Bill turned over his card. As he expected, Heidi had written another Bible verse on the back. "I am the light of the world: he that followeth me shall not walk in darkness, but shall have the light of life" (John 8:12).

The scriptures their teacher had included on the cards

peaked his interest. Especially the one for today. What exactly did it mean to have the "light of life"?

While Todd waited for his corn bread to bake, he alternated between taking notes about Heidi's style of cooking and watching Lisa. His frustration mounted, because Lisa would barely look at him today. He'd said hello when she arrived shortly after he did, but all he'd gotten from her was a brief nod and a mumbled, "Hi." *Why's she so picky about me not being religious, anyway? Can't she just appreciate me for who I am? I'm willing to ignore her religious ways; she should overlook my nonreligious views.*

"What are you writing there?" Lance pointed to Todd's notebook.

"Umm. . ." Todd's face heated. "Just taking some notes."

"You took notes during our last two classes." Lance peered over Todd's shoulder. "What are you up to? Are you writing a book?"

Breathing heavily through his nose and ignoring the man's question, Todd decided to change the subject. "So what's everyone doing for Thanksgiving this year?"

"I've invited my parents, as well as my husband's mom and dad, to our house for the holiday," Allie spoke up. "I just hope Steve doesn't decide to work that day, because most of the work will fall on me if he's not there to help out."

"Won't your parents and in-laws help out?" Lisa questioned.

"I'm sure they would, but Nola and Derek don't get to see their grandparents often enough, so I want our folks to spend as much time with the kids as possible." She tilted her chin down. "Last year we went to my folks' in New York, and because it had snowed the day before, we ended up having a white Thanksgiving. The kids enjoyed being able to play in the snow. My dad even helped them build a snow fort."

"New York usually does get snow early on. Especially

if the storms are coming off Lake Erie," Lance chimed in.

Allie got a faraway look in her eyes. "When I was a young girl, I always loved the first snowfall of the year. In fact, I still do."

"Me too." Bill gave a nod. "Especially when I go up to my cabin to hunt. With snow on the ground, the cabin, the woods—everything looks like a picture postcard."

Todd hadn't expected all this conversation about snow, and he quickly got back on track. "How about you, kid?" He looked at Nicole. "What are your plans for Thanksgiving?"

Her slim shoulders slumped. "We're not having any company, and I'll probably help my dad cook the meal."

"It's good you're taking cooking classes then. Maybe you can fix the bread we're learning to make today to go with your Thanksgiving meal."

Nicole gave no reply to Todd's comment, as she sat staring at the recipe card. The girl had seemed pretty upbeat when she'd first arrived. Todd wondered what had happened between then and now to make her turn sullen.

He looked at Heidi. "The way you cook, I'll bet you're planning a big dinner with all the trimmings. Am I right?"

"Actually, my husband and I will be going to Middlefield to spend Thanksgiving with my parents. Most of my siblings and their families will be there too." A wide smile stretched across Heidi's face. "I'll take something to contribute to the meal, of course."

Todd glanced across the table, where Lance sat. "Have you made any big holiday plans?"

"Not yet, but I'm sure to get a dinner invitation from one of my daughters. They take turns each year, alternating whose house the dinner will be at."

"What about you, Lisa?" *If she won't voluntarily talk to me, I'll force her to say something. So far, she'd only been listening to everyone. Surely she won't ignore my question and make herself look bad in front of these people.*

Keeping her focus on her hands, folded in her lap, Lisa murmured, "I'm going to my parents' house too."

"Good for you." Todd gritted his teeth. *Too bad I wasn't invited. At one time you said you wanted me to meet your folks. How could you change your mind so quickly? Are you gonna let a little thing like religious differences come between us?*

"In case anyone's interested," Todd mumbled, "I'll most likely be spending Thanksgiving alone."

"That's too bad. Don't you have plans to be with your family?" Heidi questioned.

"Nope. They all live in Oregon, and I'm not going there." Todd turned to face Bill. "What are you gonna do for Turkey Day?"

"I'm going deer hunting the Monday after Thanksgiving, so I'll be heading up to my cabin on Thanksgiving Day. I usually start getting the place ready—make sure there's a good fire going in the wood stove and all. Some of my buddies will join me there, but not till the day after Thanksgiving." Bill pointed at Todd's tablet. "You never did say why you're writing stuff down. With Heidi showing us firsthand how to make whatever she's teaching, plus the recipe cards she gives us to take home, I wouldn't think you'd need to take any notes."

Todd's pulse quickened. He set his pen down and crossed his arms. "If you must know, I'm taking notes for an article I'm writing for the newspaper in Canton."

Heidi quirked an eyebrow. "You're writing about my cooking classes?"

He gave a brisk nod. "To be honest, I'm a food critic, and I decided to take this class so I could write about it in my column." There, the truth was out. Now to wait for everyone's reaction—especially Lisa's.

All heads turned in Todd's direction. Some, like Heidi, wore questioning expressions, but the reddening and tightening of Lisa's face let him know she wasn't happy hearing this bit of news.

Heidi's portable timer rang at that moment, and Todd jumped up to get his bread from the oven. *Well, who cares if she's angry or not? I'm glad the truth is finally out, because I don't have to pretend any longer.*

Chapter 32

Lisa could hardly sit in the same room as Todd without letting her annoyance show. Besides his disinterest in religious things, he was a deceiver. *How could I have been so foolish? I should have known by the way he scrutinized everything here and at the restaurants he's taken me to that he had more than a passing interest in the food. I'm glad I won't be seeing him anymore.* She shifted in her chair. *If I'm meant to have a man in my life, there has to be someone out there who's better suited to me.*

She glanced over at Todd as he removed a piece of corn bread from the pan. Not a shred of guilt on his face, or even an apology for misleading Heidi after he'd announced his true profession and admitted the reason he'd signed up for her classes. *I can only imagine what Heidi and the others must be thinking right now as they all sit staring at him.*

Unable to hold her tongue, Lisa left her seat and marched across the room to where Todd stood at the counter after placing his bread on a cooling rack. "How could you be so deceitful?" When he gave no reply, she tapped his shoulder. "The day Heidi first asked each of us what brought us to her cooking classes, why weren't you honest about being a food critic?"

He leaned away from her, creating several inches of space between them. "Don't judge me, Lisa. You're not perfect, you know."

Heat shot up the back of Lisa's neck and quickly spread to her face. "Never said I was." She pointed a finger at him.

"But I didn't lie about my reason for taking Heidi's classes. For that matter, I've always tried to be honest and upright."

His nostrils flared. "Wow, I had no idea I'd been going out with a saint. Wasn't I the privileged one, though? I'm surprised you wasted your time with a sinner like me."

Lisa planted her hands against her hips, but before she could offer a retort, Heidi stepped between them. "It would have been nice to know your true reason for being here, Todd, but no harm's been done, and I'm not angry with you."

The hair on the back of Lisa's neck prickled. *Really, Heidi? You're more forgiving than I would be. Guess I'm not living up to my Christianity today.* She pulled in her top lip. *Even if I do forgive Todd, we can never be together. We are unequally yoked.*

After everyone's corn bread had cooled sufficiently, Heidi placed a cube of butter on the table, along with a jar of honey she'd gotten from one of the local beekeepers. "Now it's time for us to sample what we made. Oh, and I have some hot apple cider to go with it."

Bill smacked his lips. "Autumn's the best time to enjoy hot cider. I always take plenty of it when I go to my hunting cabin."

Heidi handed out the prefilled mugs. "I think this cider's the best, because one of our neighbors makes it with an antique cider press."

Allie lifted her mug and took a sip. "Mmm. . .this is good apple cider."

Lance nodded in agreement.

"The apple corn bread's not bad, either," Nicole added. "Think I might make some for Thanksgiving dinner. I bet Dad would like it, and maybe my sister and brother will too." Nicole smiled at Heidi. It was nice to see her looking more cheerful again. The other three times Nicole had come to cooking classes, she'd been quiet and sullen. With the exception of Lisa and Todd, everyone seemed to be in good spirits today.

Heidi thought about her previous students, and how some of them had brought their problems to class. She wondered if she should have encouraged Lisa and Todd to air things out. Perhaps she, or one of the other students, would have some good advice to offer these two. But with them being in the middle of cooking, it hadn't seemed appropriate. Now that the lesson was over, if either Lisa or Todd continued with their disagreement, Heidi planned to say something more. If the opportunity didn't arise, she would remember to pray for Todd and Lisa, because as her bishop often said, "Prayer is a powerful tool."

"Is that today's newspaper over there?" Lance pointed to the desk across the room.

Heidi nodded. "Yes, it is."

"I didn't realize you folks subscribed to the paper." He rubbed the back of his neck. "Thought you only read things written by the Amish or specifically for the Amish."

"We read those magazines and papers, as well as the regular newspaper. Lyle likes to keep up with the local and national news."

"There's not much good in the news these days." Bill grunted. "Fact is, I quit subscribing to the paper for that reason. And I really get mad when they put things of importance way back inside the paper instead of on the front page."

"I know what you mean about the news being bad," Lisa chimed in. "Just the other day there was an article about a store that had been robbed and the owner beaten."

"Stuff like that is on the Internet and television news too," Todd interjected. "Bad stuff happens. Like it or not, it's part of the real world."

Nicole frowned. "Yeah, the real world—that's not always so great. Fact is, most of the things going on in our world stink."

"She's right." Allie's forehead creased. "Last night, when my husband came home, he mentioned three young children who were taken from their mother because of child abuse. It's sad that so many kids in Ohio are waiting for foster homes and in desperate need of someone to care for them. Some of these children are babies, but most are older kids, and many come from abusive situations." Allie slowly shook her head. "It's a shame there aren't more people willing to become foster parents."

Heidi swallowed hard. Maybe she and Lyle should apply to be foster parents to some needy child. It wouldn't be the same as having a baby of their own, but at least they'd have the satisfaction of helping some poor child in need. When he got home later today, she would talk to him about it.

Canton

After Todd got home from the cooking class, he flopped onto the couch, hoping to relax while he read the newspaper. "Yep," he grumbled, "Bill was right. There's nothing much good in the news these days."

Skimming through the paper, Todd tried to keep his mind off Lisa and how upset she'd gotten with him in cooking class today. His confession about being a food critic had not gone well with her. And now, as he played over some of the things she'd berated him about, Todd wondered if she might be right. "Guess I should have been honest with Heidi, up front." But again, Todd rationalized that he hadn't actually deceived Heidi, or anyone else in the class; he just hadn't told them the truth. His concern was not making a bad impression that first day, or revealing the main reason for attending the class. Taking Heidi's cooking lessons had actually turned into more than Todd expected. He was beginning to get to know everyone, and actually felt more comfortable with some of them than he did his own parents.

It was hard to concentrate on reading the paper. In fact, most of it had become a blur.

Skimming over the local news, though, something familiar caught Todd's attention. A restaurant he had critiqued a while back was going out of business, the article said. He remembered he hadn't given a good review of the place and had criticized several things about the food, as well as the condition of the restaurant.

He continued to read how this family establishment had been in business for a long time, and at the same location since it first opened. The article didn't say why they were closing, but it gave a date when it would last be open. Todd was surprised it would be so soon. The restaurant's final day of business would be this coming Thursday, November 10.

"Maybe I ought to go there." Todd pulled out his cell phone, to check the calendar and make sure he had nothing else going on that day. The tenth was open for him, so he wrote a note to remind himself.

Todd wasn't sure how he would handle the situation, but he was curious to find out the reason they were closing the establishment. Inside, he felt a pang of guilt and hoped his negative critique hadn't brought this restaurant to a close. It had happened one time before, when a new place of business couldn't make a go of things. They'd blamed Todd for the uncomplimentary review he'd written about their hole-in-the-wall restaurant.

"Mind if I come in?" Kendra's sister Shelly poked her head into Kendra's room, where she lay on the bed next to her precious baby girl.

"Sure, come join us." Kendra motioned to the other side of the bed.

"Okay." Shelly lay down, with little Heidi snuggled between them. "My niece sure is growing, huh?"

"Yeah. Babies don't stay little long enough."

"Mind if I ask you a question?"

"Nope. Ask away." Kendra stroked her sleeping infant's velvety cheek.

"Do you have any regrets about not letting the Amish couple adopt your baby?"

"I do have moments of doubt," Kendra admitted. "But when I'm holding the baby, all my reservations melt right away."

"I can understand why." Shelly leaned close to the baby and kissed her other small cheek. "Things are getting better around here between you and Dad, don't you think?"

"I don't know. . .maybe so. He's not barking at me all the time anyhow."

"I'm not defending his previous actions, because I thought it was awful when he kicked you out, but. . ."

"But what?" Kendra lifted her head, eyeballing her sister. "Do you think he was justified in putting his own needs ahead of mine? Do you think it's okay that he sent me away?"

"No, that's not what I was gonna say."

"What then?"

"I can understand a little of how embarrassed he felt when he found out you were pregnant. It was hard for him to acknowledge it to the other church board members."

"Yeah, I know. He was more worried about what they would think of him than me, though." Kendra fluffed up her pillow. "It hasn't been easy, but I've forgiven him for giving me the boot."

They lay silently for a while, until Shelly posed another question. "Would you have married Max if he had asked you?"

"I can't say for sure. Maybe back then I would have, but now, knowing what a louse he is, I'd never agree to marry the guy."

"Do you ever hear from Max?"

"Nope. Why do you ask?"

"Just wondered if you know where he is or what he's been up to since he went into the Marines."

"I haven't a clue."

"Don't you think Max has a right to meet his daughter?"

Kendra's face warmed as she shook her head vigorously. "No way! Max gave up the right to be Heidi's dad when he cheated on me and ran off with another woman." Her toes curled inside her stockings. "I don't want him anywhere near my little girl."

"Suppose I can't really blame you, given the circumstances."

"Thank you for that."

"Think you'll ever find someone you love enough to marry?"

Kendra shrugged. "Who knows? Maybe someday Mr. Right will come along. For now, though, I need to concentrate on being the best mom I can for my sweet little girl." She gazed lovingly at her daughter. *If I'd given you up for adoption, I would have missed out on so much. No, I did the right thing by keeping you, little Heidi. And if I have my way, your biological father will never get the opportunity to lay his snake eyes on you.*

Chapter 33

Walnut Creek

"Do we have everything filled out as required?" Lyle leaned over Heidi's shoulder, brushing a gentle kiss across her neck. They'd just finished eating breakfast and putting the dishes away.

She shivered and reached up to touch the side of his bearded face. "Jah, I believe so. I never expected there'd be this many questions, though."

He took a seat opposite her at the dining-room table. "Becoming a foster parent requires several things, including being licensed, which won't happen unless we fill out the paperwork and prove we meet all the necessary requirements."

She drew a deep breath and exhaled quickly. "I hope we get to take in a boppli."

He thumbed his ear. "A baby might not be the best idea, Heidi."

"How come?"

"Eventually, when it's time for the child to return to his or her parents or some other relative, it would be hard to say goodbye to a baby."

She pursed her lips. "It'll be difficult to say goodbye to any child put in our care, but we'll do what needs to be done when the time comes."

Lyle gave no argument. Instead, he rose from his chair, went over to the window, and looked out. "It's only November eleventh, but with the way the gray clouds are looming in the sky, and the chilly temperatures today, it looks like we might get some *schnee*."

Heidi's eyebrows rose. "Ach, I hope not. It's too early for snow."

"I agree, but unfortunately, we have no control over the weather."

She sighed. "Or anything else for that matter."

"Are you thinking of something in particular?"

"Jah. I was thinking about Loretta and Eli."

Lyle slid his chair in closer to the table. "What about them?"

"Well, Loretta stopped by the morning of my last cooking class, before any of the students arrived." Heidi paused to sip some of her mint tea. "She was upset because Eli compared his deceased wife's meat loaf to the one Loretta made when she invited him to join her and the children for supper."

"Did she talk to him about it?"

Heidi shook her head. "I told her she needs to, though. Eli probably doesn't even realize he hurt her feelings." She placed her hand on Lyle's arm. "Has he spoken to you about this?"

"No. The last time I talked to Eli he mentioned that Loretta would be joining the church and said he planned to ask her to marry him once she became a church member. I figured now that she's done that, he'd have already proposed."

"It may not be good to interfere, but would you consider talking to Eli?"

Lyle pinched the bridge of his nose in a slight grimace. "Oh, I don't know, Heidi. Eli might not appreciate me butting in. He could even tell me to mind my own business."

"But he's your friend," Heidi argued. "When a person sees their friend going through a difficult situation, they should say something, don't you agree?"

"I suppose I could drop over to see him soon. Maybe I can get Eli to open up without coming right out and telling him what Loretta said to you."

"Good to hear." Heidi's lips parted slightly. "Now let's get back to filling out the foster-parent paperwork."

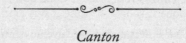

Canton

Todd had gotten up early, showered, and fixed himself some toast so he could get to the restaurant that had closed yesterday. He'd had full intentions of going there for supper last evening, but he'd fallen asleep and didn't wake up until two this morning. Surely, the owners would still be there, finalizing everything before the restaurant was vacated.

Todd parked his car and noticed a light glowing from the interior of the building. *Good. Someone's inside.*

After Todd entered the place, he was surprised when the owners, Antonio and Teresa Carboni, greeted him with a smile.

"You probably don't remember me. I'm Todd Collins. I'm a food critic, and I write a column for the local newspaper.

Antonio put his arm around his wife's shoulder and gave it a squeeze. "So what brings you here today, Mr. Collins? You know we are now closed, don't you?"

"Yes, I read about it in the paper. Your last day was yesterday." Todd looked down at his shoes. "I actually wanted to come by last evening, but didn't make it, so I hoped I could catch you here today." He looked up again, barely able to make eye contact with the Carbonis. "I—I need to know something. Was the reason you closed this establishment because of the negative review I wrote about your restaurant a while back? Did it affect your business at all?"

Smiling, Antonio patted him on the shoulder. "Business has slacked off, but it's probably our fault for not putting more money into the place to fix things up and hire a more experienced cook. And actually, son, in some ways your article did us a favor."

Todd scratched his head. "Really? How so?"

"Seeing how business was slacking off, and being too tired to keep pursuing it, Teresa and I decided to do what we've wanted to do for a good while now. In hindsight, we should have done it sooner, because it was getting to be a little much for the two of us to keep the restaurant going. That was most likely the reason you found some negative things about our place."

"I'm sorry about the article I wrote, but as a food critic, I have to be honest and write the truth, which at times, is not easy to do."

"No need to explain." Antonio went on to tell Todd a few things he didn't know. With nothing but the clothes on their backs, and a little bit of money they'd saved, Antonio's parents came to the United States to start up a family-owned restaurant many years ago. "They built this business through perseverance and hard work, and they worked here until they died." Antonio spread his arms out and pointed to the inside of the building. "Growing up, this place was more like home to me than where we actually lived.

"When my parents died, their wish was for me, their only child, to take over the business. They'd prepared me from a young age when I began helping out." Antonio grinned at Teresa, still standing by his side. "I was lucky to marry a woman who stood by me and helped to keep this place going."

"Sounds like it was a lot of hard work."

"Sure was."

Todd listened to more of Mr. Carboni's story, although he wasn't sure why the man was telling him all this.

"This restaurant my mama and papa started has been a labor of love, but it's getting too much for us now." The wrinkles in Antonio's forehead deepened. "My wife and I are in our late sixties, and we're exhausted working day and night to keep this place going."

She nodded. "My husband is right about that. Truth is,

we've never been on a real vacation or taken much time off just to relax. It hasn't been easy to make this decision, but we've both decided we're ready to move on and spend time with our children and grandchildren."

"I'm sure your parents would be proud of you for keeping this restaurant going all these years." Todd was surprised when he noticed tears in Antonio's eyes, and his own eyes started to water. "Thanks for sharing your story with me." Todd felt better after hearing the facts and all the reasons behind the restaurant's closure. "Well, I'm sure you folks have lots to do, so I'll be on my way. I wish you both nothing but the best." Todd shook Antonio's hand, and when he turned to Teresa, she gave him a hug.

On the way home, Todd thought about the Carbonis and began to question his own life. *Do I want to continue in this profession any longer? Do I want to risk possibly hurting more establishments with my negative critiques and causing hardships on the owners or their families?* He didn't know any of these owners personally or the problems they might be facing, but he wouldn't be able to live with himself if more places closed because of his opinion in an article he'd written.

Todd gripped the steering wheel with a sense of conviction. *Maybe it's time for me to make a career change.*

New Philadelphia

Bill grabbed his son, Brent, in a hug. "It's sure good to see you, Son."

"Same here, Dad. We shouldn't wait so long to get together."

"I know. . . I know." Bill led the way to the living room, and they both took seats after Brent returned from putting his suitcase in the spare bedroom. "So tell me how things are going with you these days. Are you still seeing Donna?"

Brent shook his head. "We broke up three months ago."

"Sorry to hear it. What went wrong?"

"Our relationship wasn't going anywhere, even though Donna dropped hints about us getting married." Brent tapped his foot. "I wasn't in love with her, Dad. Also, I want kids, and Donna made it clear that she doesn't."

"All I can say is, she doesn't know what she's missing."

Brent's expression was pensive. "Yeah."

"You know, Son, even though it may have been hard to end the relationship with Donna, love is important in a marriage, as is a shared desire to have a family. So you probably made the right decision."

"Thanks, Dad. I appreciate your support." Brent shifted on his chair. "Now tell me what's new with you."

"Well, I told you about the cooking classes I've been taking."

"Right. I'm glad you're learning new things and getting out so you can meet some new people."

"Same here. It's been a blast." Bill snapped his fingers. "Say, I have an idea. I'd like to take you over to the Troyers' so you can meet my cooking teacher. How about we drive over to Walnut Creek sometime tomorrow for a short visit?"

"Fine by me. In fact, I'm lookin' forward to it."

"Are you hungry for lunch yet?" Bill asked.

"Yes, I'm actually starving." Brent rubbed his stomach, and they both laughed when it gave a loud growl.

"Good. I kinda thought you might be after the drive down here, so I'm going to make something I learned in one of the classes." Bill headed for the kitchen, with Brent on his heels. "It's called Chicken in a Crumb Basket, and I'm positive you're gonna like it."

Chapter 34

Walnut Creek

Heidi hummed as she put a batch of pumpkin cookies in the oven. They were one of her favorites, especially when she added raisins and walnuts to the spicy dough. These cookies were good any time of the year, but even more so this close to Thanksgiving.

Heidi looked forward to spending the holiday with her parents. She could hardly wait to tell them she and Lyle had decided to become foster parents. Heidi felt sure Mom and Dad would support their decision. She'd been tempted to tell them over the phone but decided it would be better to share the good news in person.

Heidi set the timer, then poured herself a cup of green tea. She was about to sit down when a knock sounded on the front door. *I wonder if it's Lance delivering another package.* He'd brought one up to the house yesterday, but it was something Lyle had sent for. Heidi was waiting for the supplements she'd ordered from an Amish-owned health food store in Indiana and hadn't been able to find locally. Perhaps that package had finally arrived.

When Heidi opened the front door, she was surprised to find Kendra on the porch, holding her baby.

Heidi smiled. "Well, this is a pleasant surprise. It's good to see you again, Kendra. Please, come in."

"Are you sure? If you're busy. . ."

"No, not at all. Just baking some pumpkin cookies."

Kendra lifted her head and sniffed. "I can tell. They smell delicious."

"Let's go to the kitchen. You can sample some from the first batch as soon as they're out of the oven." Heidi took Kendra's jacket and hung it on a wall peg; then she led the way to the kitchen. "How is little Heidi doing?"

"Fine. She's a real good baby. Would you like to hold her?"

Before Heidi could respond, the timer went off. "I'd love to hold her, as soon as I take the cookies out and get another batch put in."

"If you'd like to hold her now, I can take care of the cookies." Kendra chuckled. "Thanks to you, I've had a little baking experience."

"True." Heidi grabbed two pot holders. "I'll get the cookies out, then you can take over."

While Kendra dropped the cookie dough onto the baking sheet, she paused to glance at Heidi. She seemed more relaxed than usual, looking content as she held the baby. What a shame she couldn't have children. Motherhood would come naturally to Heidi.

As Kendra continued to take cookies in and out of the oven, they visited about a variety of things.

"Lyle and I have decided to become foster parents." Heidi stroked the baby's head. "We filled out the paperwork yesterday to begin the process. We'll also have to complete a home study, which will be conducted by an assigned licensing specialist."

Kendra smiled. "That's good news. You'll both make good parents."

Heidi lowered her gaze. "The easy part will be caring for a child, but it'll be hard to say goodbye when it's time for the child to go."

Before Kendra could respond, a knock sounded on the front door.

"That could be our mailman," Heidi said. "Would you mind answering it for me?"

"No problem." Kendra left the room. When she opened the front door, and saw two men on the porch, her mouth dropped open. "Brent Coleman?"

"Kendra Perkins?" His brows lifted as he took a step forward. "What are you doing here?" He glanced at the other man, as if looking for answers, then looked back at Kendra.

"I'm here visiting my friend, Heidi. Why are you here?"

The older man spoke before Brent could respond. "I'm Bill Mason, one of Heidi's students, and Brent is my son. I assume you two must know each other?"

"Yes, we do." Brent motioned to Kendra. "We went to high school together. I was a senior when she was a sophomore."

Kendra swallowed hard. Back then she had a crush on Brent, but he never seemed to notice her. She was surprised he remembered her at all. After graduation Brent had gone off to college, and she hadn't seen him again until now. He was tall and muscular, with dark curly hair and vivid blue eyes. Brent was still as handsome as he was in high school, but more mature looking. It was hard not to stare at him.

"Is Heidi expecting you?" she asked.

Bill shook his head. "We just dropped by, hoping to find her at home so my son could meet her."

"Yeah, Dad's told me all about the cooking classes he's taking, and he was excited to introduce me to the woman who's taught him how to make some new recipes he can try out on his hunting buddies. I got to taste one of them for lunch yesterday, and it was exceptional."

Kendra smiled. "Heidi's a wonderful teacher. I took her first set of cooking classes—that's how we met." Remembering her manners, she swung the door open wide. "Come inside. Heidi's in the kitchen with my baby."

As the men stepped into the entryway, Brent paused beside Kendra. "You're married?"

Kendra shook her head. "No. It's a long story." Lifting her chin, in an attempt to look confident, she hurried toward the kitchen.

"Well, this is a surprise," Heidi smiled up at Bill when he and Brent entered the room.

"I would have called first but didn't know how often you check for phone messages." Bill gestured to his son. "This is Brent. He's here for the weekend, and I wanted him to meet you."

Heidi stood, handed the baby to Kendra, and shook Brent's hand. "I'm glad you could drop by. I've enjoyed having your father in my class."

"Not as much as I've enjoyed being here." Bill chuckled. "My cooking was one-dimensional before I signed up for your class, and I'm looking forward to trying even more new recipes in the future. But I want you to know I made the Chicken in a Crumb Basket for Brent yesterday for lunch."

"It was sure good." Brent rubbed his stomach.

"Well, I'm pleased to know that. Would you both like to try out some pumpkin cookies, fresh from the oven?" Heidi gestured to the ones Kendra had previously placed in a canister.

Bill licked his lips. "I won't turn down a cookie or two. How about you, Son?" He turned to look at Brent, who stood staring at Kendra.

When Brent didn't answer, Bill bumped his arm. "Do you want a cookie?"

"Uh, sure. Sounds good." Brent shuffled his feet.

Bill sensed his son's unease. He was fairly sure it had something to do with Kendra—especially since he couldn't seem to take his eyes off her.

"The baby's asleep. Would you mind if I make a bed for her on the couch?" Kendra asked Heidi.

Heidi shook her head. "Of course not. Why don't we all

go into the living room so we can visit? I'll bring a tray of cookies and some hot coffee."

Bill didn't have to be asked twice. He headed for the living room, barely glancing over his shoulder to see if Brent followed. At first, Brent held back, but then he ambled in behind Bill and took a seat in the chair nearest the couch.

Kendra came in behind them with the baby and settled the sleeping child on one end of the couch. She smiled at Brent. "I'll sit here to make sure my little girl doesn't roll off; although it's doubtful, since she hasn't rolled over by herself yet."

Bill watched with interest as his son's gaze went from Kendra to the baby. "She's a cute little thing. What's her name?"

"I named her after Heidi." Kendra leaned over and kissed her baby's forehead. "I call her my precious little Heidi."

"So where's the baby's father?"

I'd like to know that myself, Bill thought, as he waited for Kendra's answer to Brent's bold question.

Face turning crimson, she mumbled, "He split as soon as he found out I was pregnant. Said he couldn't be bothered and didn't want any kids."

A vein on the side of Brent's neck bulged. Bill could almost guess what his son was thinking. He wanted to be a father, but his ex-girlfriend didn't want kids. Kendra had a child, but the baby's dad didn't want anything to do with fatherhood. Some things in life made no sense at all.

Heidi came in carrying a tray with a coffeepot, cookies, and four mugs. She placed it on the coffee table and told everyone to help themselves.

Bill waited to see what Kendra and Brent would do, but when neither of them made a move, he poured himself some coffee, grabbed a napkin, and took three cookies. The mere sight of them made his mouth water. He ate one and wiped his lips with the napkin. "Delicious, Heidi. Course, I wouldn't have expected otherwise."

She smiled. "I'm glad you like them."

"Are you gonna teach us in class how to make cookies like these?" he asked, after slurping some coffee.

Kendra and Brent still hadn't taken a cookie or poured themselves any coffee. They sat quietly looking at each other.

"I was thinking for next week's class, I'd teach you all how to make pumpkin whoopie pies," Heidi responded.

"I'm all for that. Anything with pumpkin in it sounds good to me." Bill gave her a thumbs-up.

Heidi pointed to the tray of cookies. "Kendra and Brent, don't you want to try a pumpkin cookie? You especially, Kendra, since you baked most of them."

"Oh, then if that's the case, I'd better try a few." Brent grabbed a cookie and took a bite. "My dad's right. . . . This is real tasty."

Kendra took one too, nibbling on it as she tucked the baby's blanket under her little feet.

Bill's cell phone rang, so he excused himself and went outside to answer it. He didn't feel right about taking a call inside an Amish home, where phones were not allowed.

The call was from Bill's friend Andy asking if Brent made it to his place okay.

"Sure did. He and I are at Heidi Troyer's right now. I wanted him to meet her."

"Are you having a good visit with your son?"

"Yeah, but the weekend's going too fast. Sure wish I could see Brent more often."

"Maybe you can convince him to move closer." Andy chuckled. "He could join our hunting party. You did teach him the fine art of hunting, right?"

"No," Bill mumbled. He felt bad about it now, but in all the times he'd gone hunting when Brent was growing up, he'd never taken the boy hunting or taught him how to shoot a gun or bow and arrow. The kid seemed more interested in sports and hadn't shown any interest in hunting. Bill wished he could go back and do some things differently, but it was too late.

"Listen, Andy, I should get back inside."

"You're outside talking to me?"

"Yeah."

"How come?"

Bill explained the situation and said he didn't want to be rude by taking the call in Heidi's house. "Did you call for any particular reason or just to shoot the breeze?"

"Just wondered if you're gonna be alone at the cabin on Thanksgiving."

"Most likely. None of the other guys can make it till the following day." Bill rubbed his arm as the wind whistled through the trees. The day seemed to have gotten colder, even more so, since he and Brent had arrived at Heidi's house. "Sure hope it doesn't snow."

"You mean now or on Thanksgiving?"

"I meant now, since my son has to drive home tomorrow. But during hunting season—that's a different story. I'd be eager for some snow."

"Well, I'll let you go so you can get back inside where it's warmer. I'll miss joining you and the guys at camp this year."

"Yeah, we'll miss you too."

When Bill entered the house, he was surprised to see Brent sitting on the couch next to Kendra, while Heidi sat in the rocking chair holding Kendra's baby. Brent and Kendra were engrossed in conversation, and he hated to interrupt, but figured it was time for them to get going, since he'd planned to take Brent out to lunch at his favorite restaurant in Berlin.

He took a seat, drank the rest of his lukewarm coffee, and stood. "We should get going, Brent. I'd like to get to the restaurant before it becomes too crowded. Saturdays are always busy with tourists and locals who like to go shopping and eat out."

"Oh, okay." Brent stood and handed Kendra one of his business cards. "Give me a call sometime. I'd like to keep in touch."

She smiled. "That'd be nice."

Bill and Brent said their goodbyes and headed out the door. As they climbed into Bill's truck, he turned to his son and said, "Think she'll call?"

Brent's ears turned slightly pink. "I don't know. Guess I'll have to wait and see what happens."

Chapter 35

Millersburg

Nicole was in the kitchen, gathering up her apron and notebook in readiness for Dad to take her to the fifth cooking class, when she glanced out the window and saw her mother's car pull up next to the garage. *Oh, great. What does she want this time? I hope she hasn't been drinking again.*

Holding her breath, Nicole stepped back from the window, out of sight, but positioning herself so she could still see her mother. *If I don't answer the door, maybe she'll go away.* But it was too late. She watched as Dad went out the door and walked up to Tonya. *I hope he holds his ground and tells her to leave. If she doesn't go soon, I'm gonna be late for the cooking class.*

Eager to know what they were saying, Nicole opened the door a crack and listened while peeking through the narrow gap.

"I've been going to Alcoholics Anonymous, and I'm working hard at staying sober." Tonya moved closer to Dad. "Thanks to my drinking and irresponsible attitude, I made a mess of our marriage."

Nicole clenched her fingers. *You've got that right, Tonya. You made a big mess of everything. You don't care about your family, so just go away and leave us alone.*

"I'm sorry for all the hurts I've caused, and I want to do better."

You're lying. You always lie when you want something.

Dad said nothing; just gave a brief nod. Nicole hoped it didn't mean he'd accepted Tonya's apology. Surely he couldn't be that weak where his ex-wife was concerned. Not after all the damage she'd done to this family.

Tonya touched Dad's arm. "I hope once you see that I've changed you'll allow me to spend some quality time with the children—especially around the holidays."

"We'll see how it goes, Tonya." Dad's tone held no malice. He didn't even pull his arm away. "This is not something you can fix overnight, though."

"I realize that, but please give me a chance to prove myself." Her pleading tone was pathetic.

Nicole shook her head. *Don't let her get to you, Dad. She's trying to prey on your sympathies. Do not give in.*

"Do you forgive me, Mike?"

Dad took a deep breath as his shoulders raised, then lowered. Rubbing his forehead, he answered, "Yes, Tonya, I forgive you."

Nicole's spine stiffened. *You've gotta be kidding! How can he forgive so easily? If Dad wants to be foolish where Tonya's concerned, that's up to him, but there's no way I will ever forgive that woman for all she's done.* Nicole shook her head forcibly. *Nope. I don't want anything to do with Tonya—not now, not ever!*

Nicole was relieved when a few minutes later, Dad came into the kitchen. "You all ready to go, Nicole?"

She gave a nod. "I saw you talking to Tonya outside—I mean, Mom. I assume she's gone?"

"Yes, and we'd better get going so you're not late for the cooking class."

"Yeah, okay." Nicole was on the verge of asking Dad if he believed all the things Tonya had said to him, but thought better of it. If he brought it up, she would offer her opinion. Otherwise she wouldn't say anything. No point letting Dad know she'd been eavesdropping.

Walnut Creek

Heidi was pleased when everyone showed up at her house on time. Making the whoopie pies would take a bit of time, so she wanted her students to get started right away. Once everyone was seated at her kitchen table, she explained what they'd be making and handed out the recipe cards, along with all the ingredients they would need.

"I think you will all enjoy these special cookies," she said, standing at the head of the table. "They've always been one of my family's favorites, and the pumpkin whoopies make a wonderful treat during the fall and winter months."

"I'm sure I'll enjoy them." Lance offered Heidi a big grin.

"Same here," Bill chimed in.

Heidi clasped her hands together. "Well, all right then, let's get started."

Allie stared across the table at no one in particular. She had a hard time concentrating on the recipe Heidi had given them for pumpkin whoopie pies. She'd had an argument with Steve last night, and they'd both gone to bed angry. He'd gotten up early and left before she and the kids were out of bed, so there'd been no chance to talk more or offer any apologies.

She clenched her fingers around the mixing spoon, while stirring the cookie batter. *Not that he would have offered any, and I probably wouldn't have apologized either. Seems like all we do is argue lately, but no one ever wins. Steve doesn't want to be with me or the kids anymore. If he did, he wouldn't work unnecessary shifts for others.*

"These cookies would be good for Thanksgiving, don't you think?" Lisa leaned closer to Allie.

"Yes, I suppose so." Allie hadn't even planned what they

would have for their Thanksgiving meal yet. She had originally hoped they'd be able to go to her parents for the holiday again this year, but Steve's schedule didn't allow that to happen. Instead, her folks and Steve's parents were coming to their home, but Steve wouldn't be there. He'd told her last night that he was scheduled to work Thanksgiving Day, which had led up to their argument. Allie had even been bold enough to ask if he was in love with someone else, and secretly seeing another woman, but he'd denied it and said Allie was paranoid and worried too much.

"I'll be taking a pumpkin pie to my parents' house for Thanksgiving, but I think I'll take some whoopie pies too." Lisa interrupted Allie's thoughts again. "There can never be enough desserts for a holiday, right?"

"My sentiments exactly," Bill spoke up. "Think I'll take some whoopies to the cabin with me." He chuckled. "Course I may have them all eaten before my buddies show up the day after Thanksgiving."

"I'll probably take a batch of them to my daughter Sharon's place," Lance put in. "She called last week and invited me to join her family on Thanksgiving." He gave an enthusiastic grin. "My other daughter, Terry, will be there too, as well as my brother, Dan."

Allie glanced at Todd, to see if he would say anything, but he kept stirring his cookie dough without a word. Same for Nicole. Her glum expression was an indication that she was not in a good mood today.

Well, join the club. Allie poked her tongue to one side of her cheek. *But at least I'm trying not to let it show.*

After everyone's whoopie pies were baked and cooled, Heidi suggested they go into the dining room to sample what they'd made. "I'll bring in some hot chocolate and coffee to go with the cookies. While you're eating your whoopies, I'll tell you

the decision Lyle and I made about becoming foster parents."
She gestured to Allie. "I have you to thank for bringing up
the topic at our last cooking class."

Allie's lips twitched before breaking into a grin. "That's
good news. I'm happy for you, Heidi."

Nicole and the others all nodded.

"My husband and I are looking forward to caring for a
child, but I'll tell you more as we're sharing our snacks." Heidi
opened a cabinet and took out a large serving tray.

"I'll stay here in the kitchen and help you carry things
out," Bill offered.

Heidi smiled. "Thank you, Bill."

Nicole gathered up her whoopie pies and placed them
in the plastic container Heidi had given each student. Then
she followed the others to the dining room and took a seat at
the table between Allie and Lisa. Lance and Todd sat across
from them. While everyone chatted about various things,
Nicole studied the recipe card Heidi had given them to go
with the cookies they'd made. The whoopie pies weren't too
hard to make and would probably be something her sister
and brother would enjoy. *Maybe I'll make a batch sometime
before Thanksgiving. Sure hope Tonya doesn't get any ideas about
coming over that day.*

She turned the three-by-five card over and frowned when
she read the verse of scripture Heidi had written: *"[Jesus said,]
'If ye forgive men their trespasses, your heavenly Father will also
forgive you'" (Matthew 6:14).*

Nicole shifted in her chair, crossing and uncrossing her
leg. *Why is it so important to forgive? Tonya doesn't deserve my
forgiveness. She hasn't asked for it, either.*

Growing more uneasy by the minute, she pushed her
chair back and stood. "Think I'll go see what's taking Heidi
and Bill so long."

Nicole headed for the kitchen, and was almost to the
door, when she heard Bill mention her name. He was telling

Heidi how he'd paid for a weekly housekeeper to help Nicole and her family out. "Not knowing how Nicole would take it, I decided it'd be best to remain anonymous."

Nicole stood at the door, her lips pressed together, as her thoughts scrambled to understand. Why would Bill have done this for her? He hardly even knew Nicole. *Should I go in and say something—tell him I overheard what he said?*

Blinking rapidly, she stood like a statue, barely breathing as she weighed the pros and cons. If she said something, Bill might be embarrassed. If she kept quiet, he would not be thanked for his good deed. Nicole did appreciate it, after all. Still, it upset her that anyone had to even do this for her family. If Mom hadn't bailed on them, there would have been no need. Having the housekeeper had given her more time for schoolwork, as well as the chance to do some other things. No one—especially a near stranger—had ever done anything this nice for her, and Bill deserved a thank-you.

Pushing her sweater sleeves past the elbows, Nicole was about to enter the kitchen, when Bill stepped out, carrying the tray with napkins and paper cups. Heidi came behind him with a coffeepot. Bill's eyes widened as his head jerked back. "Oh, Nicole, I didn't realize you were near the door. How long have you been standing there?"

"Long enough to hear what you said to Heidi about paying for someone to clean my dad's house." She lifted her chin and looked up at him. "I don't know what to say, except thank you."

He winked at her. "You're more than welcome. I was happy to do it."

Tears welled in Nicole's eyes, and she was powerless to keep them from spilling over. Heidi was quickly at her side, slipping one arm around Nicole's waist, guiding her into the kitchen. "Is there something you wish to talk about?"

Nicole gulped on the sob rising in her throat. Desperate to unburden her soul, she blurted out the details of her mother's visit that morning and how Tonya had told Nicole's dad she was going to AA and wanted to spend more time with her children.

A rush of heat flushed through Nicole's body. "She asked for Dad's forgiveness, and I can't believe it, but he actually forgave her. I mean, how could he be so gullible?" She sank into a chair at the table with a groan. "Tonya may have quit drinking for a while, but she'll be at it again, and probably soon. Nothing will change for the better. I can't stand her, and I wish she wasn't my mother."

Heidi took the seat beside her. "Loving people is not always easy, especially if we've been hurt by them. But when we choose to hate and refuse to forgive instead of offering love and forgiveness, it's as though we are roaming around in darkness." She paused and placed her hand on Nicole's trembling arm. "Hatred is disorienting. It takes away our sense of direction."

Nicole sniffed deeply. "I—I don't care. Tonya's done too many bad things. She doesn't deserve my forgiveness—especially when she's just gonna do it again. And people wouldn't have to be helping us out if she'd stayed home and been a real mom."

Heidi handed Nicole a tissue. "I understand—it's not always easy to forgive. Please think about it this week, and remember, I'll be praying for you."

For some reason, Nicole found comfort in knowing Heidi would be praying for her. This young Amish woman was so kind and loving—nothing like Nicole's messed-up mother. It was a shame Heidi didn't have any children of her own. She would certainly be a good mother.

Bill moved close to the table and cleared his throat. She hadn't even realized he'd joined them in the kitchen until now. She'd thought he'd gone into the dining room with the others.

"You know, Heidi, as you've been talking to Nicole, I've been thinking about my own situation. I realize now that I've never forgiven my wife for her part in what turned out to be a painful divorce." Bill shuffled his feet a few times. "I need to do that, and I'll also talk to Michelle and ask her forgiveness for my part in the breakup of our marriage. It's too late for us to get back together, because she's remarried, but at least I'll feel better knowing there's no animosity between us."

Nicole couldn't listen anymore. With head down, she went back to the dining room to join the others and wait for Dad to pick her up. If Bill wanted to forgive his wife, that was his business, but it didn't change the way she felt about Tonya.

Chapter 36

Burton, Ohio

The morning had started out with low, steel-colored clouds. But now, as Heidi and Lyle's driver neared the town of Burton, on their way to Middlefield, the wind came up, pushing the clouds to the west, and revealing a milky sun. The closer they got to their Thanksgiving destination, the more eager Heidi became.

"Look over there." Heidi pointed out the front window of their driver's van. "It looks like smoke up ahead."

"You're right it does," Lyle agreed. "But those huge puffs, resembling smoke, are nothing more than billowing steam coming off the manure being spread by that tractor over there. It's a good time of year to get it done, before the snow falls and blankets the ground."

Squinting, Heidi leaned forward as far as her seatbelt would allow. Sure enough, the man in the tractor drove the outline of the field. Then little by little, he worked his way toward the middle, leaving a steaming trail of manure behind him.

As the van continued on, she noticed all the barren trees on both sides of the road. Everything looked so dismal this time of year. Dead leaves, brown with no color left, blew across the road in the wind. Several homes they passed, with their once-green yards, now matching the color of wheat, had smoke rising out of the chimneys. Heidi hoped they might have some snow by now, to give more color to the ground and trees. In fact, with the cooler temperatures, she'd expected snowy weather might have already come, or at least that they'd see some before Christmas arrived. It was always special to wake up on Christmas morning and view the beauty of everything blanketed in pristine snow.

I can hardly believe it's Thanksgiving. Heidi shook her head. *Wherever did this year get to?* The holiday had approached so fast, and as they rode by an English man wrapping colored lights around a pine tree in the front yard, it was one more reminder that Christmas would be here soon too. Two young children stood near the man, jumping up and down. No doubt they were excited about the upcoming holiday too.

What fun it must be to have children around the holidays. Hopefully by this Christmas, she and Lyle would get to find out. But until then, Heidi had to be patient. *What a blessing it would be for us to bring a child into our home at Christmastime.*

She looked over at Lyle and placed her hand on his knee. "I wonder what Mom and Dad's response will be when we tell them about our plans to become foster parents."

"I imagine it'll be the same as my folks when we told them the other day." He smiled and placed his hand over hers, giving her fingers a tender squeeze. "Your parents will be happy for us too and probably offer encouragement, as well as words of wisdom about parenting."

Heidi gave a nod. "We are both so fortunate to have loving parents." She thought about Nicole and the situation with her mother. "Not everyone is blessed with good parents."

Zoar, Ohio

"Sharon sure lives in a dinky town," Dan commented as he and Lance drove into the historical village south of Canton.

Refusing to let his brother's negative comment rile him, Lance smiled and replied, "Zoar is more than a dinky town.

It's an interesting piece of local history."

Dan let go of the steering wheel with one hand and gestured toward Lance. "Oh? How so?"

"For starters, the people who lived here more than a hundred years ago were part of the Separatist Society."

"Is that a fact?"

Lanced nodded. "Due to religious persecution, they left their home country of Germany and fled to America."

"Hmm... Sounds similar to why the Amish came here."

"You're right, only the Zoarites were communal and didn't have their own homes. The community association here works hard to keep the spirit and lifestyle of the original village alive."

"Guess that's important."

"Yep. And since the Zoar village used to be an apple orchard, the town is known for its delicious apple dishes. Fact is, Sharon said she was gonna make a dutch apple cake for dessert today. It'll go well with the pumpkin whoopie pies I brought along."

"Both desserts sound good."

They rode in silence for a while, until Lance spoke again. "Say, Dan, before we get to Sharon's place, there's something I need to say."

"What's that?"

"I'm sorry for getting upset with you during the time you were staying at my house. I overreacted on a few things."

Dan waved his hand. "It's okay, Brother. You do things different than I do, and living together was hard for both of us. Things are better now that I'm living in the other half of Lisa's duplex, where I can pretty much do as I please."

"So everything's good?"

"Absolutely."

"Glad to hear it." Lance was tempted to ask if his brother was keeping the place picked up but didn't want to start a discussion that could lead to an argument. Even if the place wasn't being kept super clean, he felt sure Dan would not ruin any of Lisa's furniture or mark anything up. "So, on another note—any idea how long till your own place is ready for you to move back to?" He asked.

"A few more weeks. It probably won't be long after I move out before Lisa finds someone else to rent the side of the duplex I'm in now."

"I hope so. She did us both a favor renting to you—especially knowing it wouldn't be full-time."

"True, but her place is nice, and I'm sure once I move out she'll find another renter."

Lance hoped his brother was right. He would feel bad if Lisa had a hard time finding another person to move in. Most likely she relied on the rent money to supplement her income.

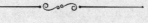

New Philadelphia

Allie put the turkey in the oven and sighed. *I wish Steve could be here to carve the bird when it's done.* The fact that her parents and in-laws would be here for Thanksgiving made Steve's absence seem even worse. Would she be able to keep a lid on her emotions and not let on how upset she felt because her husband couldn't join them? If she said too much, one or both sets of parents might figure out that things were strained between Allie and Steve. *They could even think we're headed for a divorce.*

Should I consider divorcing Steve? Allie wondered. *Would it be better for me? But what about the kids? I have to consider their needs.* She cringed, having gone over this in her mind several times before. Even though Steve wasn't around as much as he should be, Nola and Derek would miss their daddy. When he was home, the kids and their father were practically inseparable.

Tears welled in Allie's eyes. *Truthfully, I'd miss him too.* Allie had fallen in love with Steve a short time after they'd begun dating. He was everything she'd ever wanted in a man—nice looking, smart, strong, and brave. He had a pleasant personality and got along well with people too. Allie's father had taken to Steve the first time she'd brought him home to meet her folks. When she and Steve first got married, they were inseparable and communicated well with each other. But as time went on and Steve became more involved in his work, things began to change.

Before this year, Steve had always managed to get off on Thanksgiving, which made his absence today even harder. Allie felt empty as she washed the potatoes and laid them on a paper towel to dry.

Arf! Arf! The kids' puppy darted into the kitchen with Derek at its heels.

"Come back here, Trouble!" Derek shook his finger at the dog. "You need to come when I call you."

Allie glanced at the clock. "Your grandparents will be here soon, so you should put the pup in his cage now."

Derek's nose wrinkled. "Trouble don't like it there, Mommy. It's like bein' in jail." He looked up at her with a pleading expression. "You wouldn't wanna be in jail, would you?"

"Of course not, Son, but Trouble will get into mischief if he's left to run around the house all day." She leaned over and scratched the pup behind his silky ears. "You can keep him out till your grandparents arrive, but then he has to go in the cage. Understood?"

Derek nodded. "When's Daddy gonna be home?"

"Later this evening."

His lower lip protruded. Allie figured she'd better change the subject or her boy would end up whining.

"Where's your sister? Did she clear her toys out of the living room like I asked?"

Derek shrugged. "Don't know. I wasn't watchin'."

Allie lifted her gaze to the ceiling. *What else is new?* She'd go check on Nola, then come back, wash her hands, and peel the potatoes. If she got all the prep work for dinner done ahead of time, the meal would be ready by the time the parents showed up. Besides, keeping busy took her mind off Steve and how much she missed him not being here today.

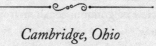

Cambridge, Ohio

Gravel crackled beneath the tires of Lisa's van as she drove up her parents' driveway. Living in a rural area, they'd never bothered to put pavement down. As Lisa approached the two-story house, she was surprised to see a vehicle she didn't recognize parked outside their garage. *Did Dad buy a new car?*

She parked next to the SUV and stepped out of the van. Since she planned to spend the night, she took out her small suitcase and the plastic container with the whoopie pies in it.

A rustling wind slid through the trees as Lisa made her way to the house. She paused briefly to look at the well-used tire swing hanging from the stately maple. She'd spent many hours in that old swing when she was a girl, daydreaming and wishing she had a sibling. But it was not meant to be. Mom had complications when Lisa was born, and a hysterectomy put an end to her childbearing days. Of course, Lisa had friends to play with, but it wasn't the same as having a brother or sister. She'd determined in her heart some time ago that, if she ever got married, she would have three or four children. Right now, however, marriage seemed to be in the distant future. She'd need to find the right man first, and at present, that seemed unlikely too.

Halting her thoughts, Lisa stepped onto the front porch and rang the bell to announce her presence. Certain that the door would be unlocked, she opened it and stepped inside. The delicious aroma of roasting turkey greeted her, and she was tempted to head straight for the kitchen. But hearing voices coming from the living room, she set her luggage in the hallway, hung up her coat, and placed the whoopie pies on the entry table.

When Lisa entered the adjoining room, she was surprised to see a young couple with two little, tow-headed boys sitting on the couch. She'd never met them and wondered if Mom had invited a new neighbor or someone from church whom Lisa didn't know.

"Oh, good, I'm glad you're here." Mom rose from her chair, and Dad did the same. They took turns hugging Lisa. Then Mom introduced their guests. "Lisa, this is Tim and Sandy Sawyer." She gestured to the children. "And these two young men are Nicolas and Wesley. Your dad and I invited them to join us for dinner today."

Lisa shook hands with Tim and Sandy, and told the boys hello. Her smile felt forced, however. It didn't seem right that after Mom had specifically told her not to invite Todd, saying today was just for family, that she would invite strangers into their home for Thanksgiving. At least to Lisa these people were strangers. If Mom and Dad knew them, they'd certainly never mentioned it, nor had Mom informed Lisa they'd invited any guests.

I suppose it doesn't matter, though, Lisa told herself, *since I'm not seeing Todd anymore. And maybe these people had nowhere else to go for the holiday. Mom's hospitable and has always reached out to those in need.*

"Lisa, please take a seat. There's something you need to know." Mom pointed to one of the recliners.

A tingle of apprehension slid up Lisa's spine. Mom's tone and expression were so serious. She hoped nothing was wrong. "What is it?" Lisa asked, lowering herself into a chair.

Mom glanced over at Tim, then back at Lisa. "There's no simple way to tell you this, except come right out and say it."

Lisa leaned forward. "Say what, Mom? You're scaring me. Is something wrong with you or Dad? Is that what you're trying to tell me?"

Mom shook her head. "No, we're both fine, and I hope you will be too when we share this news."

Lisa sat quietly, waiting for her mother to continue and watching as Mom grabbed Dad's hand. Something big was going on here, and Lisa was eager to find out what it was.

Mom cleared her throat a couple of times. "Tim is my son."

Lisa swallowed hard, touching the base of her neck. *I must have misunderstood. I'm an only child. Mom couldn't have more children, and if she had, I certainly would have known.* "Wh—what are you saying?" Lisa could barely speak. Was Mom playing some kind of a joke on her?

"I know this must come as quite a shock," Tim spoke up. "But as a baby, I was adopted. I've been looking for my biological parents for the last two years, and thanks to the Internet, I've found my birth mother." He paused and moistened his lips. "I'm your half brother, Lisa."

Chapter 37

Lisa sat in stunned silence as her mother explained how twenty-eight years ago she'd had a baby out of wedlock and put him up for adoption. It had pained her to do so, but she was young and immature, with no way to support a child. When Tim contacted her a few weeks ago, Mom invited him and his family here today so they could meet and share a Thanksgiving meal.

"Why am I just now hearing this, Mom?" Clutching the folds in her dress, Lisa tilted her head to one side.

"Your mother wanted to surprise you today." Dad spoke for the first time. "We both thought this would be a good opportunity for Tim to not only meet his biological mother, but his half sister too."

Oh, I'm surprised, all right. Shocked might be a better word for it. Lisa glanced at Tim. He had blond hair like hers, and it wasn't hard to see that they were related. Even his sons, who sat on the floor across the room, playing a game, resembled Tim, rather than their dark-haired mother. All these years of wanting a brother, and here she'd had one the whole time and didn't even know it. As pleased as Lisa was to hear this news, she felt cheated and hurt by her mother's deception. *Didn't Mom think I deserved to know the truth? Was she afraid I would think less of her because she'd given birth to a child and wasn't married?*

Lisa shifted in her chair. *Would I have been condemning?*

Would knowing Mom had put my brother up for adoption have made a difference in the way I feel about her?

She had to admit, it would have been a shock, no matter when she'd learned the truth. But it may have been easier to accept and deal with it if she'd found out sooner.

Tim smiled at Lisa. "I'm eager to get to know you. I grew up with three brothers and always wondered what it would be like to have a sister."

Lisa's throat constricted. It wasn't Tim's fault they'd been kept apart. *If Mom had told me early on that she'd given birth to another child and put him up for adoption, I could have begun a search for him, and maybe found Tim sooner.*

As the shock of it all began to wear off, Lisa relaxed a bit. Today would be a time to get to know Tim, his wife, and their children. It would be a new beginning for all of them. She truly had something to be thankful for this Thanksgiving.

———— ❧⟳❧ ————

Middlefield, Ohio

"You outdid yourself on this meal, Rachel." Lyle gave his stomach a pat. "I ate too much, and I'll probably sleep the rest of the afternoon, but it was worth every bite."

"I'm glad you enjoyed it." Heidi's mother laughed. "And you probably won't be the only one taking a nap today." She looked at Heidi's father. "Isn't that right, Irvin?"

"That's correct, because you're a good cook." Heidi's dad grinned as he stifled a yawn.

Heidi looked at all the smiling faces gathered around the extended table, as well as a smaller one for the children. She was glad her brothers, Richard and Sam, along with their wives and children, had been able to join them today. Her sisters, Naomi and Elizabeth, were also present with their families. Now that everyone was together, it was the perfect time to share her and Lyle's good news.

She picked up her spoon and gave her water glass a few taps. "Well, before anyone gets too sleepy—Lyle and I have a special announcement to make."

All heads turned in Heidi's direction, and Lyle clasped her other hand under the table.

A wide smile formed on Mom's lips. "After all these years are you expecting a boppli?"

Heidi shook her head. "It's doubtful that will ever happen, but Lyle and I are going to become foster parents."

Now everyone smiled, and several people asked questions.

"What you plan to do is a real good thing." Dad leaned closer to Lyle and gave his back a few hearty thumps. "I'm sure I speak for everyone here when I say that we support your decision."

Mom bobbed her head. Heidi's siblings did the same.

Heidi inhaled deeply. She was almost certain becoming a foster parent was the right thing to do, and she felt ever so grateful for her family's support.

Canton

Sitting alone at a table in a crowded restaurant on Thanksgiving Day was not Todd's idea of having holiday fun. *Maybe I should have booked a plane ticket and gone to Mom and Dad's place after all. It would have been better than sitting here by myself, eating bland food that doesn't even deserve a critique.* He squared his shoulders. *Well, maybe it's not really bland. It's just that nothing tastes good to me today.*

The slices of turkey on Todd's plate held no appeal, and neither did the piece of pumpkin pie the waitress had brought out with Todd's dinner. She'd said they were getting low on pumpkin and wanted to be sure he got a slice.

"Ah, Miss. . ." Todd snapped his fingers to get the waitress's attention. "Could I please have a little whipped cream with this pie?"

"Sure thing."

He nodded in thanks when she returned, shaking a can, then squirted a design of whipped topping on his dessert.

If I hadn't ruined things with Lisa, I would probably be with her right now, Todd fretted. *I bet she's having a great Thanksgiving with her folks. Why'd I have to mess things up by acting like such a jerk? I was on the brink of thinking we were establishing a relationship, but then everything went sour, and it's all my fault.*

Gazing at the pie, Todd thought about the verse Heidi had written on the back of the recipe card for pumpkin whoopie pie cookies. It was about forgiveness. Todd needed to forgive his ex-girlfriend for the things she'd said to hurt him. He also needed to ask God's forgiveness for the things he'd done to hurt others, including Lisa. He'd had a good start when he visited the Carbonis. If their reasons for closing hadn't turned out the way it did, Todd would have done something for them to make up for the negative critique he'd written about their restaurant. What that would have been, Todd wasn't sure, but in his heart, he knew, his intentions would have been sincere. He could feel his heart soften and shift in another direction. He wanted to take a better path from now on. Trouble was, Todd didn't know where to start when it came to God. He had never established a relationship with the Lord, but when the realization hit him, Todd knew what he had to do. The only place he could think to begin this connection was by going to church. Surely the pastor, or someone there, could show him the way.

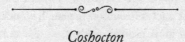

Coshocton

Bill arrived at his hunting camp early, and after getting a warm fire going in the fireplace and eating a quick breakfast, he was bound for the woods to do a little pre-hunt scouting. When he got back to the cabin, he'd clean things up, set up the foldaway cots, and make sure everything was ready for when Russ and Tom arrived tomorrow. He also wanted to hang his orange blaze hat and hunting vest out on the porch. This way, by Monday morning, the items would have pulled in the natural smells from the woods. Today, though, since Bill wasn't hunting, he'd dressed in camouflage clothes.

Bill couldn't help but think how different it would be this year without Andy joining them. Going to Orlando this time of year certainly didn't interest Bill. It wouldn't feel much like the holidays, being in a warm climate without any anticipation of snow. But since Andy wanted to be with his family, he couldn't blame his friend for that. Bill had to admit he felt a bit envious too, for it would certainly be nice to have Brent here with him at the cabin.

When he got to the area where his tree stand was located, Bill checked it over thoroughly, and all seemed secure. Climbing the ladder, and putting a camouflage cushion on the seat, Bill sat down to enjoy the scenery and watch for any deer activity. After pulling his thermos from the backpack he had brought along, he opened the lid, poured some out, and sipped the steaming brew.

"Sitting here in my tree stand with a good cup of coffee, now what could be better than this?" Bill grinned and raised his thermos lid in a toast to nature. He loved being up here this time of year. The silence and surroundings were pure delight.

After Bill sat there awhile, his feet grew cold and his legs started to cramp up. He stood and stretched them a bit, but there was not a lot of room on the small wooden platform, so he couldn't move around much.

"I oughta have a bigger tree stand built," he muttered. "There's barely room for me up here, let alone my hunting buddies."

It had rained a bit when Bill first got here this morning, but the downpour stopped after a few hours. The earthy scent from fallen wet leaves lying all over the ground wafted up to greet him. If he had a new stand built, he'd make sure it had a roof and was twice the size of this old one, or maybe even bigger. The tree stand had been here when Bill bought the property, and since he didn't use it all the time, he'd made do. Maybe next year, after he'd built up his savings, he'd see about replacing it. In times past when his buddies were here, they'd traded off—two of them sitting on the platform in tight quarters, while the other two hunted from the ground.

I can't wait till Monday morning. Bill smiled in anticipation. Opening day was always exciting. When would the first shot be heard? Would he get a chance to bag a big buck? Who'd be lucky enough to get the first deer, and would any of them go home empty-handed? It really made no difference to Bill if he got a deer or not; it was the experience of it all that he enjoyed. But once his buddies arrived and they got to talking, Bill knew he'd get excited about getting a deer too.

As steam from his breathing escaped Bill's mouth, he reminisced about previous years on opening day, climbing up here before it got light. His eyes would adjust, and as dawn began to break, he'd see shadowy images of deer sneaking through before it was legal to shoot. Bill had witnessed some beautiful sunrises from up here too, and he always looked forward to it, coupled with the thrill of watching wildlife begin to stir. His friends had different ideas about the whole hunting experience and tended to be a bit more competitive.

Bill sat back on his canvas camping chair and tried to relax. At least it was fairly comfortable if he didn't sit there too long. No sign of any deer yet, though. Were they all bedded down, or just avoiding this area because he, the intruder, was near? Bill had forgotten to de-scent his clothes with the special spray he'd brought along, but hopefully any odors from breakfast didn't linger on his hat, shirt, pants, or jacket.

In the distance, Bill heard a few shots. Most likely, someone was sighting in their rifle, which was common to hear this close to opening day. He hoped that's all it was, since shooting a deer wouldn't be legal until Monday.

If nothing came his way in the next hour or so, he'd head back to the cabin to fix supper. Bill had brought potatoes, carrots, and onions from home as the basis for a savory stew. He'd also packed a loaf of apple corn bread he had made yesterday, and that would be his Thanksgiving meal. Bill didn't mind being alone in the woods. He enjoyed the solitude. But with today being a holiday when he normally got together with his buddies, he felt kind of lost.

Wish my boy could have joined me today. Bill shifted on his chair. *It would have been good to have a little more father-son time together. The three days Brent and I shared two weeks ago went too fast. No wonder Andy chose to go with his family, even if it meant being in an environment as warm as Florida.*

Bill's attention came to a peak when a rustling noise reached his ears. He turned his head slowly in the direction it was coming from and sat forward in anticipation. *Maybe it's a deer sneaking through after hearing the gunfire a few minutes ago.* He wished he would have put his camera in the backpack, but it was too late to worry about that now. Bill watched and waited and hoped it would be a big buck. It would be nice to know one was in the area and hopefully get a chance to see it on opening day.

The sound grew closer, and when the animal appeared, Bill's eyes widened and his mouth dropped open. Slowly, Bill sat back against the tree as close as he could get and tried not to move a muscle. Down below, a few feet from the tree, stood an enormous black bear. Bill had heard there were bear in the area, but after years of hunting and never seeing any, he'd thought it was only a rumor, or one of those stories people liked to tell while sitting around a campfire. But here was a bear, as big and bold as you please, and he was a beauty.

Bill blinked his eyes rapidly as they began to water. *I cannot believe what I'm seeing. The guys will never believe this.*

Boy, do I wish I had my camera.

As the bear stood on all fours, looking around and sniffing the air, Bill was glad he had gone unnoticed. A few times, the bruin looked up in his direction, however with Bill wearing his camo clothes, the material blended in well with the tree's bark. He had read one time, though, that a bear's hearing was exceptional. *I hope he can't hear my heart beating, because it feels like it's about to pop right out of my chest.* Bill released air through his lips as quietly as he could. He tried to swallow, but his mouth felt too dry.

Oh brother, what am I going to do now? I hope the bear leaves soon, or I'll be spending the night up in this tree stand. Bill took short, quiet breaths, so the big creature would not hear him. Barely breathing, he watched the bear stick his nose in the air, as though trying to get a scent of something. *I should have stayed back at the cabin. How long is he going to stand there like that?*

It was cool out, but by now, Bill was drenched in sweat. When the bear started walking around, he could hear the intake of air going through its nostrils as it investigated every stick, sniffing every leaf and what seemed like every blade of brush grass. Then it walked over to the ladder Bill had climbed up on and took a few sniffs of the lower rungs. When the bear stood and looked up at Bill, eyes on each other and unblinking, time seemed to stand still. *Please don't climb this ladder.*

Then as if someone had stuck him with a needle, the bear jumped back and became alert. Just that quick, the animal took off running in the opposite direction. How something that big, could run so fast, Bill could not comprehend.

He stood up to watch, but saw no sign of the bear. All he could hear were sticks breaking and the crunching of leaves, as the lumbering sound grew farther away. After sitting there a few minutes longer, and not hearing anymore noise, Bill hoped it would be safe to leave the tree stand.

By now, it had started spritzing, and as Bill turned to go down the ladder, he heard some cracking noises above his head. He froze, and his scalp prickled when he looked up and saw some dead limbs high above that had begun to rot. The last thing he needed was a tree limb hitting him on the noggin. *This big old oak tree probably needs to be taken down soon.* Bill grabbed his seat cushion, put his thermos in the backpack, and gave the area one last look. *I'm getting back to the cabin where it's safe.*

By the time Bill got to the bottom rung, a steady rain had begun to fall. This time a lot harder than earlier today. He grimaced when the raindrops splattered his face and dripped down the back of his neck.

He'd only made it a few feet from the tree when—*crack!*— the rotting limb broke off and dropped to the ground with a sickening *thud.* Letting out a yelp, he shuffled backward, stumbled on a rock, and landed on the seat of his pants. *Whew, that was too close for me! If I hadn't gotten down from the tree stand when I did, that old limb could have smacked me on the head.*

Bill's heartbeat raced as he clambered to his feet. *If the falling branch had hit me, I could be unconscious or even dead. It's probably not a good idea to be out here by myself. I shoulda waited till the guys could join me tomorrow to do some early scouting. So much for me wanting to brag about seeing a deer when Tom and Russ arrive, but at least I can tell 'em about the bear. Sure wish I had picture to prove it, though.*

Bill's leg muscles spasmed with each step he took as he hobbled toward the cabin. Although not seriously hurt, both knees throbbed. Bill made a mental note to rub some joint cream on them when he got back to the warmth of the fire. On top of that, his teeth chattered from the moisture seeping through his jeans and the opening of his jacket. More importantly, Bill was concerned about putting distance between himself and that enormous bear. This would be a memorable Thanksgiving, although not in a good way. At the moment,

Bill didn't care if he bagged a deer Monday morning. All he wanted was to seek refuge and warmth inside the cabin, get out of his wet clothes, and have something to eat. Come morning, he might feel differently—especially once his buddies showed up.

Millersburg

Nicole sat beside her sister at their Thanksgiving table, while Tony sat opposite of them, next to their father.

"The ham turned out good, Dad." Nicole smiled at him. "I like it better than the turkey Tonya used to make."

Dad's forehead wrinkled. "How many times must I tell you to stop calling your mother that? You need to call her Mom."

Nicole lifted both hands in surrender. "Okay, whatever."

"I thought Mom's turkey was fine," Tony spoke up. "She made good mashed potatoes too." He looked over at Heather. "Don't you think so?"

A cat-like whimper escaped Heather's lips. "I miss Mom so much. Holidays don't seem the same without her."

"You know, kids, your mother is working on getting better," Dad said. "And when she does, you may be able to spend some time with her."

Heather's face brightened. "Really?"

"Yes. Would you like that, honey?"

Heather and Tony both nodded.

Dad looked at Nicole. "How about you? Would you be agreeable to seeing your mother now and then?"

Nicole pursed her lips. "We'll see." Truthfully, she had no intention of spending any time with her mother, but seeing how happy her sister and brother were about the idea, Nicole kept her feelings to herself. There was no point in spoiling the day for her siblings.

Later, while washing the dishes, Nicole glanced out the window from time to time, but her thoughts focused on something Heidi had said during the last cooking class. Was she wrong in refusing to forgive? If Mom meant what she said, and really was trying to get better, shouldn't she be allowed another chance? It wasn't as if Mom would be moving back to their house. She'd only come for visits, or maybe Tony and Heather would go to her place sometime. Nicole didn't want to go, but she wouldn't say or do anything to sway her siblings or turn them against their own mother.

Nicole's chin trembled, and then her shoulders began to quake. For the first time in a long while, she bowed her head and offered an earnest prayer. *Lord, please help me get rid of the anger I have felt since Mom left, and fill my heart with forgiveness toward her.*

Chapter 38

Coshocton

Bill looked up at the clock above the fireplace, wondering when his buddies were going to show up. It was eight thirty Friday morning, and he'd been up since the crack of dawn. Thinking at least one of them would be at the cabin by now, he'd made a fresh pot of coffee, mixed pancake batter, and also fried some maple-flavored bacon. When no one showed up by eight o'clock, Bill ate breakfast alone.

Being used to the quiet, he jumped when his cell phone rang. Bill hoped it wasn't one of the guys saying they weren't coming after all or had been delayed. When he picked up the phone he realized it was his son.

"Hey, Brent, how was your Thanksgiving?"

"I ate too much, but otherwise it was good. How about yours, Dad? Did you see any deer when you went scouting?"

"Nope, but I did see a big black bear."

"Really? So it's not just a rumor about bears being seen in the area?"

"Apparently not, 'cause I saw the creature with my own two eyes."

"It must have taken you by surprise. Glad you're okay, Dad."

"Yeah, me too." Subconsciously, Bill rubbed the top of his head. "It wasn't just the bear I had to worry about either."

"What do you mean?"

"I may have to take down the old oak where the tree stand is."

WANDA & BRUNSTETTER

"How come?"

"I noticed some dead branches above where I sit, and I came pretty close to getting clunked on my head when one broke off and fell."

"Wow! You're not going to hunt from the tree stand Monday morning, I hope."

Bill heard the concern in his son's voice.

"Definitely not. I'll look for another spot tomorrow, when the guys and I do more scouting. If they ever get here, that is." Pressing the phone tighter against his ear, Bill huffed. "It's not what I want to do, but to be on the safe side, I'll be hunting on the ground this year. I fear the oak tree is too dangerous now."

"Smart move, Dad." Brent sounded relieved.

"It's disappointing, but yeah, it's the wise thing to do."

"Say, Dad, I don't mean to change the subject or anything, but I'd like to ask your opinion on something."

"Sure, go ahead." Bill took a seat in front of the fireplace and put his feet on the coffee table. The heat from the burning logs sent warmth throughout the room.

"You know that day you took me to meet Heidi Troyer, and Kendra Perkins was there?"

"Yeah."

"Well, I've been thinkin' about calling her to see if she'd like to go out with me sometime."

"I see." Bill picked up his coffee mug and took a drink.

"Do you think it's a good idea?"

"Well, that all depends."

"On what?"

"On whether you're looking for a serious relationship or just want to establish a casual friendship."

"I don't know right now. But I'll never find out if Kendra and I don't spend some time together."

"True." Bill set his mug on the coffee table and slouched in his chair. "You don't need my approval to go out with Kendra, but I would like to offer a few words of advice."

"Such as?"

"For starters. . . She has a baby. Are you prepared to raise another man's child if your relationship develops into something serious?"

"I don't know. Maybe. I've never really thought about it." This time Bill heard a hint of doubt in his son's tone. That was good. It meant he was being cautious.

"It's something you ought to think about."

"I suppose."

Bill massaged the back of his neck. "If you decide to pursue a relationship with Kendra, I'd move slow. You don't want to make a mistake you'll be sorry for later."

"Are you thinking of yours and Mom's relationship?" Brent asked.

"Yeah. We had a few things in common when we first got married, but as time went on, our differences pulled us further apart."

The rumble of a vehicle told Bill to look outside, so he rose from his chair. Peering out the front window, he saw Russ getting out of his vehicle.

"Sorry, Son, but I've gotta go. One of my hunting buddies just pulled in."

"Oh, sure, no problem, Dad. I'll talk to you again soon."

"Sounds good. Oh, and be sure to let me know how things go between you and Kendra."

"Will do." Brent chortled. "And if I decide to marry her, you'll be the first person I tell." Before they hung up, Brent added one more thing. "Oh, and Dad—good luck Monday morning. Stay safe and watch out for that bear."

Canton

Kendra had just put little Heidi in the crib when her cell phone rang. When she answered it, she was surprised to hear

Brent's voice. She really hadn't expected to hear from him. Kendra had called Brent the other day but got his voicemail, so she'd left a message, giving him her cell number.

"Hey, Kendra, how's it going? Did you have a nice Thanksgiving?"

"Yes, I did. How about you?"

"Good. I ate dinner at my aunt's place, and even though the food was great, there was too much of it."

She laughed. "I know what you mean."

"Say, uh. . . I got your message, and was glad to hear from you. I was wondering if you'd like to go out to dinner with me tomorrow evening."

Blinking rapidly, Kendra tightened her grip on the phone. It had been so long since anyone had asked her on a date, she wasn't sure how to respond. "I'm pleased that you asked, and I'd really like to go, but I'll have to see if my mom or one of my sisters is free to watch Heidi for me."

"Sure, no problem. When do you think you'll have an answer for me?"

"Umm. . . Can I call you back this evening? I should know something by then."

"This evening's good."

"Okay, great. I'll talk to you later, Brent."

Kendra's stomach fluttered as she clicked off the phone. *I hope someone's available to babysit Heidi for me. I'd sure like to spend more time with Brent.*

Cambridge

Lisa sat beside Tim on the couch, engrossed in what he'd been telling her about his childhood. It was amazing how many things they had in common. They both enjoyed cooking, were active in their churches, liked many of the same foods, and spent much of their free time outdoors. Of course, there was also the similarity in their looks. Their hair was about the same shade of blond; however, Tim's eye color was a darker blue than Lisa's. Why she hadn't noticed that when they first met, Lisa wasn't sure, but thank goodness, they did meet.

While she and her half brother got to know each other better, Mom and Dad had taken Tim's wife and the boys shopping. No doubt they wanted to play grandma and grandpa and spoil the children a bit. Lisa couldn't blame them. Finding out Mom had two grandsons, plus a daughter-in-law she'd known nothing about, had been an added bonus to the reunion with Tim. Lisa couldn't remember when she'd seen her mother look so happy. She'd worn a smile throughout the entire Thanksgiving meal yesterday.

Tim tugged on his ear. "You know, I like what I've seen of Ohio so far. If I could find a job and housing, I'd move here in a heartbeat."

Lisa clasped her hands together. "Really?"

He nodded. "I think my wife and boys would like it here too, and it would sure be nice to live closer to you and your folks."

"What about the parents who raised you?" Lisa asked. "I'm sure they'd be upset if you packed up your family and moved away from them."

Tim shook his head. "You don't understand—my parents are deceased. They were killed in a car accident five years ago."

Lisa brought her hand to her mouth. "I'm so sorry, Tim. That must have been quite a shock."

He dropped his gaze to the floor. "It was a tough time, but with God's help, and the encouragement of our church family, my brothers and I made it through."

Lisa swallowed hard. She could almost feel Tim's pain. "I wonder sometimes how people who don't put their faith in God make it through difficult times." Her thoughts went to Todd. He thought he could do everything in his own strength, but he was so wrong. She hoped one of these days his eyes would be opened to the truth.

Focusing once again on Tim, Lisa turned to him and smiled. "If you should decide to move, I have a two-bedroom duplex I'd be happy to rent at a deep discount. There's someone living in it now, but he'll be moving out soon."

Tim clasped Lisa's hand. "Thanks, Sis. I'll talk to my wife, and we'll give it some thought—sprinkled with lots of prayer, of course."

Moistening her lips with cautious hope, she gave his fingers a tender squeeze. Lisa still couldn't believe she had a brother. How grateful she was that she'd come to her parents' for Thanksgiving. It was one holiday she would always remember. And if things went the way she hoped, she'd have her newly found brother living close by. What a blessing it would be to spend time with Tim, his wife, and their cute little boys. If they moved into her duplex, they'd be living right next door. The only thing that could make Lisa's life any better right now would be if God provided her with a Christian boyfriend.

Chapter 39

Coshocton

Bill, Russ, and Tom started walking toward the cabin after doing some morning scouting. "That's some deer you got a picture of there." Tom thumped Bill's back as they stood looking at the digital camera.

"Yep. I came across this windfall to sit up against, and it seemed like a good spot, since the tree stand is no longer an option." Bill grinned at the photo of the six-point buck he'd taken earlier today, from the new area he'd found to hunt. He'd remembered to take his camera along when he left the cabin this morning. "I watched that deer for a good fifteen minutes as he rubbed his antlers on a tree." Bill leaned slightly forward. "Sure hope I see him again Monday morning. But if not, at least I got a good picture."

"Tom and I haven't seen a thing after traipsin' through the woods all morning," Russ chimed in. "I was hoping to see a deer after we got here yesterday. Now here it is Saturday, and still no luck. I hope that bear you saw on Thanksgiving didn't chase them out of the area. Too bad you didn't get the bear's picture."

"Didn't have my camera with me." Bill gestured to Russ and Tom's orange hunting coats and hats. "Maybe you two should have worn all camouflage today." He pointed to his own clothing. "The buck never saw me this morning, and I was only a few yards away from him. That's why my orange hat and vest are hanging here on the porch. Really don't need them till Monday morning."

"I didn't have a choice, since I forgot my camo jacket." Tom grunted. "Think I shoulda stayed home this weekend." He plunged both hands into his jacket pockets. "The only thing I've gotten so far is a chill seepin' all the way into my bones. Sure hope this isn't an indication of how Monday morning will be."

Russ blew out a breath so strong it rattled his lips. "You should have brought some hand warmers like Bill and I did."

"That's right, and we dressed warm enough." Bill gestured to the cabin as it came into view. "Maybe you should stay inside the rest of the day. You can sit by the fire, drink a cup of coffee, and eat some of the friendship bread I brought to give you fellas. There's also a few pumpkin whoopie pie cookies left."

Tom shook his head vigorously. "And miss the chance of getting a glimpse of a big buck, should one come along? No way! I can drink coffee and try out the bread and cookies when we all go inside, but then I'm heading back out."

Bill chuckled and thumped Tom's shoulder. "Now that's the spirit, my friend."

"It is a bit disappointing about the tree stand, though." Russ looked out toward the woods. "I always liked hunting from up there."

"Don't worry," Bill assured him. "We'll find another, healthier tree, and build an even bigger stand. Maybe one large enough for all of us to be up there together, and we'll put a roof on it, to keep us dry when it rains or snows." Just talking about the plans for a new tree stand gave Bill a sense of anticipation.

"Yeah, I like the idea already." Tom bobbed his head.

"I have a lot of good memories from up there in the old tree stand, but this morning, before I went scouting, I went over to the oak tree and took a good look at things." Bill's forehead wrinkled. "It's a good thing too because I discovered some wood dust around the base of the trunk, and that can only mean one thing—carpenter ants."

Grunting, Russ shook his head. "Oh, boy, that's not good."

"Don't know how I missed it yesterday." Bill grimaced. "And if I hadn't gone over to take a look this morning, I may not have noticed it today, either. Guess it must have happened for a reason, though."

He thought about some of the Bible verses Heidi had written on the back of the recipe cards she'd given him and her other cooking students and wondered if God's hand might have been in the situation that spared his life. It was something to ponder all right.

"Building a new tree stand sounds like something we could all work on this coming year." Tom rubbed his hands together, grinning enthusiastically. "I'll bet Andy will be interested in hearing about this too."

"I agree. It's something we can look forward to." Bill gave a small slap to Tom's back. "Well, let's go inside for a while so we can warm up a bit." He opened the cabin door. "I'll put some fresh coffee on and we can chow down on the rest of the bread and pumpkin whoopies I brought along. You guys are gonna like 'em." While the desserts Bill had brought to share with his friends were not particularly "health foods," they weren't full of artificial ingredients, like some store-bought treats were. Bill had remembered to bring some cut-up veggies for snacks and meals, and he'd made a big tossed green salad to go with their supper tonight.

"Sounds good to me." Tom thumped his belly. "And I can hardly wait to see what you've got planned for lunch. Your cooking's sure improved since you started those classes."

Bill couldn't argue with that. He wished he could continue to learn from Heidi beyond the six classes. But at least he would have the recipes she'd taught them, along with a notebook Heidi gave everyone with helpful tips for the kitchen.

Canton

Kendra stared at her reflection in the bedroom mirror. She wasn't sure what restaurant Brent would be taking her to but hoped she was dressed appropriately. Kendra had chosen a rust-colored skirt and creamy white blouse, which brought out the color of her auburn hair. Dressing up wasn't really her thing, but she wanted to look nice for her date this evening.

Tap. Tap. Tap.

Kendra turned toward the door. "Come in."

Mom poked her head inside. "Well, don't you look nice? Are you going somewhere?"

"Yeah. I have a date with Brent Mason. You said you'd watch Heidi for me, remember?"

"Oh, oh." Mom touched her parted lips. "Sorry, I forgot."

Kendra could hardly believe her mother had forgotten so quickly. It had only been twenty-four hours since she had told her Brent called, and she'd asked if she would watch the baby. "Brent should be here in the next thirty minutes, so are we good?"

Mom shook her head. "Sorry, Kendra, but your dad's boss is having a get-together this evening, and it wouldn't look good if he went without me."

Kendra frowned. "How long have you known about this?"

"Your dad told me this morning." Mom glanced at the baby, sleeping in her crib. "I would suggest that you ask one of your sisters, but they've both gone to the roller-skating party the church youth group is having tonight."

"That's just great." Kendra clenched her teeth. "I wish you had told me about your plans sooner. I would have cancelled my date with Brent." She glanced at the clock on her nightstand. "It's too late now. He's probably on his way here already."

Mom sighed. "Guess I'd better stay home then and watch

Heidi." She turned toward the door. "I'll give your dad the news."

"No, that's okay. Your place is with Dad, and you need to keep him happy. When Brent gets here, I'll tell him I'm not able to go out to dinner after all." Kendra figured if Mom gave up her plans this evening to watch the baby, Dad would be upset—probably more with Kendra than Mom, of course. Even though he'd allowed her to move back home, he'd never really accepted the situation and wasn't as attentive to his granddaughter as Kendra would like him to be. The last thing she wanted was to be the cause of more irritation for him. Hopefully, someday her father would wake up and realize what he had right here before him. Until, and unless, that time ever came, Kendra would continue to try and keep the peace.

Mom turned back around. "Say, I have an idea. Why don't you take the baby with you this evening?"

Kendra pinched the bridge of her nose. "That's not a good idea. Heidi might get fussy, and it would be hard for Brent and me to visit if I have to take care of her while I eat and carry on a conversation. Besides, he's expecting this to be a date, not an evening of watching me keep the baby entertained."

"If you feed her now, before he gets here, she'll probably sleep most of the evening."

"I'd rather not chance it." Kendra shook her head. "Go on now, and have a good time with Dad. With any luck, Brent will ask me out again some other time."

"Okay." Adopting a slumped posture, Mom opened Kendra's bedroom door and shuffled out of the room.

Mom obviously felt bad, but that didn't solve Kendra's problem. Raising her hands, she lifted her head toward the ceiling. "How come nothing ever works out for me?"

Chapter 40

The doorbell rang. With regret, Kendra went to answer it, knowing it must be Brent. Sure enough, she found him on the porch, holding a bouquet of red carnations, mixed with pretty feathery-looking greens. He'd obviously gotten them from a florist, since carnations weren't blooming in anyone's yard this time of the year. Grinning, he handed it to her. "These flowers are for you. Hope you like them, and sorry I'm a bit late."

Kendra blinked. Was this guy for real? In all the time she'd been seeing Max, he'd never given her flowers—or much else, for that matter. And her ex-boyfriend had never apologized for being late. "Thanks, Brent. They're beautiful. Carnations are one of my favorite flowers."

"Glad you like 'em." He eyed her with a curious expression—one she couldn't quite read. Did he think she wasn't dressed appropriately for their date? "You about ready to go?"

She drew a quick breath. "I hate to tell you this, but I won't be able to go out with you tonight after all."

Brent's brows furrowed as he tipped his head to one side. "How come?"

She explained about her mother not being able to babysit after all and that both of her sisters had gone out for the evening. "So I have no one to watch little Heidi."

"Not a problem." He leaned closer, his hand on one knee. "You can either bring the baby along, or we can get takeout and eat here."

Now why didn't I think of that? Kendra inhaled quietly. "You wouldn't mind eating here?"

"Nope. Not a bit."

She pressed a palm to her chest. *This guy is really something. Nothing like Max, that's for sure.* She smiled and stepped aside. "Come on in, Brent, and thanks for being flexible."

"No problem. Now that I think about it, eating here would probably be better anyways, because it'll be easier for us to visit in your house than it would be in a crowded, noisy restaurant."

She gave a nod. "Good point." *I'm glad Brent's so agreeable.*

Brent followed her into the living room. After she took his jacket and hung it up, he found a seat on the couch. Glancing over at Heidi, lying in the portable crib, he smiled. "She's a cute little thing. You're lucky to have her."

Kendra leaned over the crib and stroked her daughter's soft cheek. "I know. I feel very blessed."

He got up and stood next to her, staring down at the child. "Someday I'd like to have a house filled with kids."

She turned to face him, lips parted slightly. "You're kidding, right?"

"Well, maybe not a whole houseful, but two or three, that's for sure. Do you want more children, Kendra?"

A warm flush crept across her cheeks. "Yeah, I guess so. Not till I fall in love and get married, though. I made one mistake with Max; I'm not gonna make another."

"I understand." Brent pulled out his cell phone. "What should we order? Are you up for pizza?"

"Sure. I can eat pizza most any time." Kendra glanced at her skirt and blouse. "Even if I am overdressed for it."

"You look really nice." Brent stared at Kendra so hard it made her toes curl.

"Thank you." *Could this be the beginning of a new relationship?* she wondered. *If so, am I ready for it?*

After they had the pizza, and little Heidi was fed and lay sleeping in her crib again, Kendra and Brent relaxed in front of the TV. Neither one of them watched it, though, as they chatted about their current lives, as well as the days they'd attended the same high school. Kendra felt as comfortable with Brent as she did wearing a cozy flannel nightgown and her fuzzy bedroom slippers. She'd never felt this way with Max. She'd always been on edge, for fear she'd say or do something to rile him. Thinking back on it now, she wondered how she could have given herself to a guy like Max. He was hot-headed and demanding, always making her feel guilty if she didn't do things his way. Some of her desire to be with him could have been rebellion, and part of it was a need to feel as though someone truly cared about her. Of course, she realized that Max had never truly cared, but when he held her in his arms and whispered words of love, Kendra had weakened and let her emotions and physical desires take over.

Kendra took a quick breath to steady her nerves and admitted to Brent the feelings she'd had for him back in high school. "You didn't even know I existed, of course. But I can't blame you. I was only in tenth grade when you were a senior."

"This may surprise you, but I do remember you from our school days." Brent's eyes looked so sincere, it made Kendra's heart do a little flip-flop. "You were that cute little redheaded sophomore I saw standing on the sidelines, cheering our team at the football games. In fact, after one of those games, during half-time, because I was looking at you instead of what the coach was saying, I ended up swallowing my gum."

Kendra giggled. "Really? I had no idea. And by the way, would you care for a piece of gum now?" She reached into the pocket of her skirt, and pulled out a package.

Raising his brows, Brent took it from her. "Spearmint huh? This is my favorite flavor of gum."

Kendra smiled. "I know. It's the kind I like best too." She didn't tell him that she'd saved one of his old gum wrappers. He might think she was weird or had acted like some silly schoolgirl who'd never gotten over the crush she'd had on him. Her breathing slowed, as the memory took over. *Well, maybe I haven't gotten over that crush. If I had, then why's my heart racing right now?*

Walnut Creek

Heidi sighed contently as she snuggled on the couch beside Lyle, rubbing her bare foot along their dog's silky back. How nice it was to relax for a while before bed and enjoy this quiet time with her husband. Between his busy schedule with auctions and chores, as well as her work around the house, and the time spent preparing for her cooking classes, they didn't get as much time together as she'd like. But then, keeping busy was important for both of them.

"Just think," Heidi commented, "in a few more weeks we'll officially become foster parents. Are you as excited as I am, Lyle?"

"Sure am. I'm also anxious to find out whether we get a *buwe* or *maedel*."

"Either a boy or a girl is fine with me. My only concern is whether he or she will like it here. It's quite likely they have never met an Amish person before and certainly won't have lived in an Amish home. What if the child doesn't like it here? What if. . ."

Lyle placed his fingers gently against Heidi's lips. "Now don't start fretting about things that may never occur. The child may adjust to our way of living with no trouble at all."

"I know. I need to trust the Lord in all things and wait to see what happens." She kissed his fingers. "The best part of all in the joy of waking every day is that it gives us a chance to begin anew. So even if things aren't as we want them to be the day before, we're given another chance to make things right," Heidi quoted from a recent message given by one of their ministers.

"So true," he agreed, "and with tomorrow being Sunday, we'll have the opportunity to worship God with other believers and begin our new week."

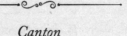

Canton

Todd stood in front of his bedroom mirror and straightened his tie. He couldn't believe he was going to church this morning, but it was time for him to turn over a new leaf. At first he had looked in the paper at the different churches he could attend here in town. But in the end, he'd decided to go back to Lisa's church in Dover, where he'd been before. Since Todd had already gone there once and met the minister, he felt semicomfortable about attending there again. Even if Lisa didn't like him showing up at her church today, maybe if he explained his reasons for being there, she would understand.

As Todd put on his overcoat, his cell phone rang. He pulled it out of his pocket and swiped it on with his thumb.

"Hello, Son. It's your mom."

"Hi, Mom." Todd tapped his foot, glancing at his watch. He didn't have much time to get to church, so he'd have to make this brief.

"How was your Thanksgiving? Did you have a nice time with. . . I think you said her name was Lilia?"

"No, her name is Lisa, but I'm not seeing her anymore, and I ended up having Thanksgiving by myself, in a restaurant of all things." Todd braced himself. *Here it comes; Mom's gonna have more questions.*

"Oh, Todd, what happened with you and Lilia—I mean, Lisa?"

"It's complicated, and I don't have time to go into it right now."

"You know, you could have flown home, instead of being there by yourself."

"Mom, I have to go. Church service starts soon, and I'll be late if I don't leave now."

"Church service? Where are you going to church?"

"I'll tell you later. Say hi to Dad for me. Bye for now, Mom." Rushing out the door, Todd quickly hung up and stuffed the cell phone in his coat pocket. *Sure hope I'm not gonna be late. I probably shouldn't have taken Mom's call.*

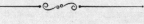

New Philadelphia

"Mama, I can't find my church shoes!" Nola shouted from her bedroom upstairs.

Rubbing the back of her neck, Allie lifted her gaze to the kitchen ceiling. She should have left ten minutes ago to take the kids to Sunday school, and if they didn't leave soon, they'd be so late, they may as well stay home.

She stepped into the hallway and cupped her hands around her mouth. "Did you look in your closet?"

"Not there!"

"How about under the bed?"

"Huh-uh."

Allie groaned. "Ask Derek to help you look for them."

While she waited for her daughter's response, Allie took her teacup to the sink and rinsed it out. She'd wash it, as well as the breakfast dishes, when she got back to the house after dropping them off. Steve was working again, of course, and it would be nice to have some quiet time by herself.

The kids' puppy whimpered and brushed against Allie's leg. She bent down and gave him a pat on the head. "Hey, Trouble... What do you want, boy?"

The dog barked twice, then raced to the back door.

"Oh, I see. You need to go outside." Allie opened the door and stepped aside as Trouble darted out and made a beeline for the fenced-in yard. *Cute little pup. He's learning fast.*

She closed the door and hollered at Nola again. "Did you find your shoes?"

"No, Mama."

"Then you'll either have to stay home or wear your sneakers today." Allie tapped her foot, her impatience mounting. If Nola had gotten her shoes out last night like she'd been asked to, they could have looked for them then if she'd realized they were missing.

She glanced at the clock and was about to go upstairs to check on things, when the telephone rang. "Now what?" She was going to let the answering machine get it, but decided to pick it up in case the call was important. "Hello. Garrett residence."

"Allie, this is Sergeant Bowers. I'm afraid I have some bad news."

Her heart started to pound, and she leaned against the kitchen table for support. "Wh–what's wrong?"

"Steve's been shot, and is being taken to the hospital in Dover."

A sudden coldness spread through Allie's body as the room began to spin. Every time Steve went out the door to report for work, his life was in danger. Tightening her grip on the phone, she feared the worst. Could her husband's wound be fatal? Would she ever see him again? The fearful thoughts shook her clean to her toes.

Allie covered her ears in an attempt to stop the agony raging in her soul, but it did no good. She needed to get to the hospital right away!

Chapter 41

Canton

K endra was almost finished getting the baby ready for church when her dad came into the room. Since the door was open, she figured he thought it was okay not to knock.

"Can I talk to you a few minutes before it's time to leave?" he asked.

Kendra, feeling hesitant and not wishing to deal with whatever he wanted to say, shrugged her shoulders. "Well, it might make us late."

He shook his head. "We have ten minutes yet before it's time to leave, and I don't want to go until I've said what's on my mind."

"Okay." Kendra buttoned the baby's pretty pink dress. It was a gift from her friend Dorie.

Dad took a seat on the end of her bed, watching as she finished dressing little Heidi. A few seconds passed. Then he cleared his throat. "I've been doing a lot of thinking lately, and spending some time in prayer."

Oh, great. I suppose he's gonna tell me he made a mistake letting me move back home and now he wants me to find someplace else to live. She bit her trembling lip. "What are you trying to say, Dad?"

He stood and moved over to stand next to her, in front of the changing table. "I owe you an apology, Kendra."

She tipped her head in question but said nothing. *Did I*

305

hear him right? As far back as she remembered, her dad rarely apologized to anyone—at least not to his wife or daughters. She was even more surprised to see tears well up in his eyes. Was it possible that her father truly felt remorse?

He placed his hand on her arm. "My attitude has been wrong where you are concerned. I shouldn't have demanded you leave the house when you told your mother and me that you were pregnant. I should have been there to offer support and help you make the right decisions concerning the baby. I've been harsh and unfeeling. Will you forgive me, Kendra?"

Her mouth felt dry, and she swallowed hard, barely able to say the words. "I—I—yeah, Dad, I forgive you. Will you forgive me for bringing shame on our family by giving in to my desires and sleeping with Max?"

Dad slipped his arm around Kendra's waist and drew her up close. "Yes, I will, but you need to seek God's forgiveness too."

A lump formed in her throat, and her voice cracked when she spoke. "I already have."

"That's good." Dad patted her back. "I've done the same." He paused. "I've also apologized to your mother. It hasn't been fair to her being stuck in the middle of all this due to the way I've been acting. I shouldn't have made her feel guilty if she didn't want to take my side."

Kendra felt a sense of relief such as she'd never felt before. For the first time in a long while, she knew without reservation that Dad loved her. All the anger and bitterness she'd felt toward him for so long, melted away.

She looked at him and smiled through her tears. "I love you, Dad."

He lifted his hand and dried the dampness from her cheeks with his thumb. "I love you too, Kendra, and I'm proud of you. You're a good mother to sweet little Heidi." Tenderness laced his words, like a soft blanket against rough skin. Then, glancing down at the baby, he added with a smile, "And I feel blessed to be the grandfather of such a precious little girl."

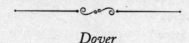

Dover

Drawers on medicine carts sliding open and then banging shut grated on Allie's nerves. Even a simple thing like someone's newspaper rattling put her on edge. Her chair creaked as she tried to find a comfortable position. She glanced at her watch. Steve had been in surgery well over two hours. What in the world could be taking so long? Why wouldn't someone come and tell her something?

She left her seat and paced the length of the waiting room. As she passed an elderly woman thumbing through a magazine, Allie stifled a sneeze. What kind of horrible-smelling cologne was the woman wearing? People ought to have better sense than to wear stuff like that.

I am being oversensitive and need to calm down. She walked to the far side of the room, poured herself a cup of hot tea, and returned to her seat. *I wish someone was with me right now. Steve's folks should have been here by now.* A raw ache settled in the pit of her stomach.

When Allie received the news that Steve had been taken to the hospital, she'd called her parents, as well as Steve's folks right away. Then she phoned her neighbor Ella and asked if she could come over to be with the children. There would be no Sunday school for her kids today. Of course, Allie's parents, living in New York, wouldn't be here for several hours. Ella had wanted to go with Allie to the hospital, and suggested her daughter, Tara, could stay with the kids, but Allie insisted on going alone. Big mistake! What she needed the most right now was comfort and someone's support. *Maybe I should have notified the pastor or somebody from the church where the kids attend. At least I could have asked for prayer on Steve's behalf.* In times like this, sometimes prayer was the only thing that could hold a person up. And right now, Allie had been doing a lot more than praying; she'd been begging God to spare her husband's life.

"How's Steve?"

Allie looked up, surprised to see Lori Robbins, the blond-haired patrol officer new to the force, looking down at her. Allie's nostrils flared as she lifted her chin. "What are you doing here?"

"I came to find out how Steve is doing. After he was shot, I had to go back to the office and fill out a report. Otherwise, I would have been here a lot sooner." Lori took a seat beside Allie.

"So you were with him when it happened?"

"Yes." Lori's facial features sagged as she held her hands together.

"Would you please give me the details about the shooting? What I've been told so far has been sketchy, and Steve was already in surgery when I got here." Despite Allie's irritation, since Officer Robbins had been with Steve at the time he'd been shot, she was the best person to talk to about it right now.

Lori leaned slightly forward, staring down at the floor. "We received a call saying there was a robbery at the mini-mart on the other side of town. When we got there, a man wearing a ski mask was running down the sidewalk. He fit the description of the robber, so Steve shouted at the guy to stop, but he kept going." Lori paused and pushed aside a wayward strand of blond hair that had come loose from her ponytail. "While I called for backup, Steve pursued the suspect. Suddenly, a shot rang out, and then Steve slumped to the pavement." Her eyes misted. "I hope he's gonna be all right. Have you had any word?"

Allie's chin quivered as she shook her head. "Nothing since they took him into surgery. I—I don't know what I'll do if

Steve doesn't make it. The children and I need him so much."

Lori placed her hand on Allie's arm. "Think positive thoughts and say a prayer for your husband. He's a good man. I've been praying for him too."

Allie was tempted to quiz Lori about her relationship with Steve, but this wasn't the time or place for an inquisition or accusations. Her focus right now was on her husband, willing him to live and hoping God would answer her prayers.

As Lisa approached the pew where she normally sat, a shiver went up her spine. *Todd. What's he doing here?* She was about to turn around and leave the church sanctuary when he spotted her.

"Lisa, don't go. I need to talk to you."

She put her finger against her lips. "Not here. This isn't the time or place."

"Can we go somewhere after church?" he whispered.

She shook her head.

"Please, Lisa. It's important." He scooted over. "If you don't have time later, then have a seat, and I'll tell you right now."

Lisa glanced around, noticing several people staring at them. The best option would be to take a seat, but with the service about to begin, she certainly wasn't going to carry on a conversation with Todd. She slipped in next to him and whispered, "We can talk in the parking lot after church."

Eyes focused straight ahead, he gave a brief nod.

Lisa shifted nervously on the bench. It was difficult sitting next to Todd, inhaling his spicy cologne and wondering what he wanted to talk to her about. His hand brushed her arm, and the brief contact made her flinch. She didn't trust Todd, and the last thing she needed was to lose her heart to this man. Heat flooded her face, like it always did when she was flustered.

When the worship team gathered on the platform, Lisa

forced her attention to the front of the room. The musicians consisted of two guitarists, a young woman playing the keyboard, and a drummer. Four vocalists led the congregation in choruses and hymns. Normally, Lisa would have relaxed and enjoyed singing along, but this morning it was hard to focus, much less unwind and feel one with the music. She'd come to church full of joy after a weekend of learning she had a brother. Now the bliss she'd felt had been replaced with apprehension.

Lisa glanced briefly at Todd, surprised to see he was actually singing along. Or perhaps he was merely mouthing the words. She couldn't be sure with all the voices around her. Todd didn't appear to be bored, like the last time they'd been here together. Was he putting on an act for her benefit, or had something changed in Todd's heart?

Chapter 42

When the church service drew to a close, Todd's hands began to sweat, as negative thought patterns took hold. What if Lisa didn't accept his apology or believe he was trying to change for the better? His thoughts spun faster than a windmill in a gale. She might think he was making it up to try and win her favor. But it was worth a shot, and he couldn't go home until he'd tried.

"Don't forget, I need to talk to you," he murmured in Lisa's ear as they walked out of the sanctuary.

"I remember. Follow me to my car."

Todd paused at the door to shake hands with the pastor and his wife. Lisa did the same and waited while he asked the pastor a question. "Do you think I could meet with you soon? I need someone to talk to." Todd pulled at the tie up close to his throat. It felt like it was choking him.

Lisa stood by and silently watched. He wished she would say something—at least give some indication as to what she was thinking.

The minister handed Todd a piece of paper with his phone number on it. "Give me a call, and we'll set something up."

"Thank you. I appreciate it." Todd shook the preacher's hand again. Then he and Lisa stepped outside.

Todd waited for Lisa to drill him with questions, but instead she remained quiet. The silence between them was deafening, except for Lisa's heels clicking against the pavement.

Out in the parking lot, by Lisa's car, Todd wiped a palm across his sweaty forehead. "I just want to say that I'm sorry for deceiving you about my job. I've made a lot of mistakes in the past, and more since I met you." He stopped talking and studied Lisa's face but couldn't tell what she was thinking. "Lisa, I need to find forgiveness." He crossed his arms in an effort to keep from touching her. What he really wanted to do was take Lisa in his arms and beg her to forgive him. "I—I figured coming to church today would be a good place to start."

Todd saw skepticism in Lisa's pursed lips and squinted eyes, but he continued. "Can you find it in your heart to forgive and give me a second chance?"

He waited, but Lisa said nothing, looking deeply into his eyes. Todd's gaze held hers as she seemed to scrutinize his face. He didn't have to wonder what she was doing, for he'd done it many times to others. She was reading him and wondering if what he said had merit.

She looked to the left as someone walked by, then turned to face him again. With her gaze fixed somewhere near the center of his chest, Lisa replied, "I forgive you, Todd, but for now, all I can offer you is friendship."

Todd wasn't sure how to respond. He had to admit, he was disappointed. But at least being friends with Lisa was a good place to start. "Having you be my friend is more than I deserve, Lisa. Thank you for that." He leaned closer and gave her a quick kiss on the cheek.

Lisa pulled back, her mouth forming an O.

His face warmed. "Sorry about that. I did it on impulse."

Her eyes narrowed, and she turned her head away. "Don't worry about it. Some things—or shall I say, some people—never change."

Todd's shoulders slumped. "Yeah, right. Guess I deserved that comment. See you, Lisa."

As Todd walked to his car, he could feel her gaze upon him. Unlocking the door, he hesitated, then looked in her direction.

Lisa looked back at him briefly, then turned, climbed into her van, and drove off.

He watched until she was out of sight. Friends? Was that all Lisa wanted? Well, if it was, then he'd accept it, no matter how much he longed for more. Lisa's friendship was better than nothing.

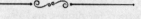

Walnut Creek

Heidi sat on one end of a bench, enjoying pleasant conversation with a group of women after the noon meal that followed their church service. When she noticed Loretta at a table nearby, she excused herself and took a seat on the bench beside her friend. The other night, Lyle had told Heidi that he'd spoken to Eli, but she would not mention it to Loretta. Her friend might see it as meddling.

"Where are your children?" Heidi asked.

Loretta gestured to her daughter, Abby, playing with a couple of young girls a short distance away. "And Conner is somewhere with Eli."

"Would you like to go outside and take a walk with me?" Heidi scooted closer to Loretta.

"That sounds nice. It's gotten kind of stuffy in here, and I could use a breath of fresh air."

"Will Abby be okay by herself?

"Jah. She's busy playing and probably won't even know I've left the building." Loretta chuckled. "My son and daughter haven't had any trouble making friends with the Amish children in this church district."

"I'm glad." Walking beside Loretta, Heidi stepped out of

WANDA E BRUNSTETTER

the barn, where church had been held that morning.

As they walked around the building and toward the pasture, Heidi was about to ask how things were going, when Loretta posed a question. "I haven't seen you for a while. How'd Thanksgiving go with your folks?"

"Oh, it was *wunderbaar*. I had such a nice time visiting with my parents and siblings."

Loretta smiled. "It's always good to be with family."

"How was your Thanksgiving?" Heidi asked.

Loretta's eyes gleamed. "Mine was wonderful too. I had Eli and his parents for dinner, and also my folks. It was the first time they'd had a chance to meet each other."

"How did that go?"

"Quite well, actually. Since my mom and dad were raised Amish, they know the Pennsylvania Dutch language. So they were able to communicate with Eli's parents in both English, as well as their Amish dialect."

"I'm pleased to hear that." The two women paused near the fence. "There's something I've been meaning to ask," Heidi added.

Loretta tipped her head. "Is it about me and Eli?"

"Jah. I've been praying for both of you, and I hope things have gotten better between you two by now."

"They have. In fact, I took your suggestion and spoke to Eli about the way I feel when he compares things I've said or done to his late wife." Loretta touched Heidi's arm. "I forgot I said I'd let you know how things turned out once I'd spoken to Eli about the situation. Sorry about that."

"It's all right. I'm eager to know, though. Did he take it okay?"

"Yes, and Eli even apologized and said he would try not to do it again. He also added that if he slipped and did make another comparison, I should tell him about it right away." Loretta placed both hands against her chest. "I believe everything's going to be all right between me and Eli."

Heidi slipped her arm around Loretta's waist. "Hearing that pleases me very much."

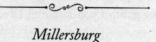

Millersburg

Nicole handed her sister a dishcloth. "Your turn to dry."

Heather wrinkled her nose. "Do I have to?"

"Would you rather wash the dishes?"

"No, washing's even worse. I wish Dad would buy a dishwasher."

"Those cost money, and Dad doesn't have extra cash floating around, you know." Nicole filled the sink with warm water and added a few squirts of liquid detergent. "So stop complaining and be glad for what we have."

They did the dishes in silence. When they finished, Nicole suggested her sister go outside and ride her bike with Tony. With both kids entertained, it would give her a chance to get some sketching done. She hadn't done any drawings for a few weeks, and it would be nice to have some quiet time to herself.

After Heather put on her hooded jacket and headed outside, Nicole went to the hall closet and took out her art supplies. "Come on, Bowser. You can stay inside for a while and keep me company." She patted the dog's head and laughed when his wagging tail thumped against the wall.

Nicole had just taken a seat at the table when the telephone rang. Since Dad was out in the garage, she went to answer it, with Bowser barking at her feet. "Shh... Now go lie down." Bowser crawled under the table and let out a whiney yawn before laying his head on his front paws.

"Smith residence."

"Nicki, is that you?"

"Yeah, it's me." Nicole didn't have to ask who the caller was; she recognized her mother's high-pitched voice.

"Is your dad at home?"

"He's in the garage. Should I go get him?"

"In a minute. Since you answered, I'd like to say a couple of things."

Nicole's gaze darted around the kitchen, wishing she could flee the room. *Oh, great. Here it comes. I'm about to hear the same old song and dance about how much my mother has changed.*

Mom cleared her throat. "I'll be the first to admit, I haven't been the best mother."

You got that right.

"But I'm really trying to clean up my life."

"Uh-huh, I know. The last time you were here, I heard you telling Dad that you're going to AA meetings."

"Yes, that's right. Why didn't you say something, or at least show yourself?"

Nicole clenched the receiver until her fingers ached. Should she tell Mom what she thought? "I didn't want to talk to you. I've been angry about the things you've done to our family, and what all I've had to go through in order to help Dad keep everything together."

"I understand. You have every reason to be upset with me, and so do Heather and Tony." There was a pause as Nicole's mother drew a quick breath. Then she started to cry. "I know it's a lot to ask, but can you find it in your heart to forgive me?"

Nicole flinched, as though Mom had reached out and touched her through the phone. She thought about the scripture written on the back of the last recipe card Heidi had given her. *If I don't forgive others, God won't forgive me.* She stood by the sink several seconds, trying to stop the flow of tears that came unexpectedly. "Yeah, Mom, I forgive you, and I hope things will go better for you from now on."

"Thanks, Nicki—I mean, Nicole. I hope things go well for you too."

Dover

Lisa curled up on the couch with a cup of hot chocolate. She'd been sitting here for a while, reflecting on the joy of learning she had a brother. She felt excited thinking how, in the near future, Tim could possibly be living next door. Lisa was eager to get to know him better, as well as his wife and boys. Even if only for a short time, she was glad Dan had been able to move into the duplex. It had helped pay the bills, but it would be nice once the place was empty and she could offer it to Tim and his family, should they decide to move to Ohio. Tim was a carpenter, and his wife a nurse, so surely one or both of them could find employment in Dover or one of the nearby towns.

Sighing, Lisa's thoughts turned to Todd. She still couldn't get over him showing up in church today. He'd truly seemed different, and hearing him speaking to the minister caused her to wonder if Todd had been serious about the things he'd said to her. Lisa had forgiven him and offered friendship, but she felt sure he wanted more.

"I'm not ready for that," she murmured, reaching for the Sunday paper. She needed to get her mind off Todd and onto something else.

She read the weather report and some of the local news, then turned to the classified section. Lisa needed a new dishwasher, and hoped she might find a good used one—not someone's hand-me-down on its last legs, but a commercial dishwasher that had been reconditioned.

Seeing nothing at all, she resigned herself to the fact that she may have to let loose of her purse strings and buy a new one.

Lisa set the paper aside long enough to take a sip of her hot chocolate, which wasn't hot anymore. She headed to the

317

kitchen to put the mug in the microwave. While it heated, she glanced out the window. Shortly after Lance's brother moved in, he'd asked permission to hang a feeder in the birch tree out back. Within a few hours, the birds discovered it and had been coming into the yard ever since, seeking food.

Lisa found it relaxing to watch and identify the different species. Some of the birds held fast to their perch, eating one sunflower seed after another, while others would take a single seed and fly off to a nearby branch and peck it open to eat. Since Dan's purchase, Lisa had gone out and bought a suet cake and cage to hang in the tree. The woodpeckers were especially attracted to that.

Along with the suet, Lisa found an interesting book to help determine the different types of birds. In the last few pages near the back of the book was a lot of space to log in the date and kind of birds she'd been able to identify.

As she continued to watch out the window, Lisa spotted a red-bellied woodpecker hanging on the suet cage. The basically pale bird had a brilliant red cap, black-and-white barred wings and back, and a slight tinge of red on its belly, for which it had been given its name.

Lisa grinned. *I should have thought of hanging out a few feeders long ago. Who knew it would be so much fun to watch these beautiful birds?* Birdwatching had become a new hobby for her, and she looked forward to seeing what birds would come into the yard when the weather turned colder and it snowed. It was a good idea to feed the birds during the frigid winter, when nature's food for them was scarce.

Putting her thoughts aside, Lisa realized that the microwave had beeped several minutes ago, so she hit it for thirty more seconds and continued to watch the woodpecker. When she heard another beep, she turned from the window and took the steaming cup of hot chocolate out, then returned to the living room.

After settling on the couch, she placed her mug on the

coffee table and picked up the newspaper. This time, her gaze came to rest on an advertisement placed by a local photographer, Charlene Higgins. The ad stated that Charlene was available to do photo shoots for businesses that wanted to advertise their products in various ways.

"What a great idea." Lisa grabbed a pen and piece of paper to write down the phone number listed in the ad. She would make the call first thing in the morning. Perhaps a bit more advertising was exactly what her catering business needed.

Allie felt relief when Steve's folks arrived and took seats near her in the waiting room. She felt even better when Lori excused herself to make a few phone calls. It was hard to look at her and not feel resentment, coupled with anger. Lori had seemed genuinely concerned, but was it for Allie, or was she frightened for herself? If the new officer was having an affair with Steve, then her concern for his welfare was for selfish reasons.

Desperate to focus on something positive, Allie thought of happy times she and Steve had spent as a family. Would they have an opportunity to spend more time together, or was her husband's life about to end?

She glanced over at Steve's mother, Jeanette, clinging to her husband's hand. Carl, Steve's father, gave his wife's fingers a squeeze, whispering words of hope, while trying to appear strong. They were worried too. Steve was their only son. If he died, they'd be lost.

Allie recalled how when Steve had decided to become a policeman, Jeanette had tried to talk him out of it. "It's a dangerous profession," she'd said several times. "A dangerous, thankless job." But Steve had made up his mind, and even said he felt that police work was his calling. Wanting her husband's happiness, Allie had neither said nor done anything to stand in his way. Now, with his life possibly hanging in the balance, she wished she could go back in time, regardless of wanting to be supportive, and beg him to seek some other type of employment. Allie had so many regrets, but they got her nowhere.

Her attention was drawn to the door when a tall, dark-haired doctor stepped into the waiting room. "Mrs. Garrett?" He moved slowly across the room.

"Yes, I'm Allie Garrett. Do you have some news about my husband?"

He gave a slow nod, then took the seat beside her.

Her body felt paralyzed with fear. She couldn't speak, couldn't move. It was bad news. She felt it at the core of her being.

Steve's parents must have felt it too, for they left their seats and came over to stand in front of the doctor, eyes wide and biting down on their bottom lips.

"We got the bullet out, and your husband is in stable condition," the doctor said. "His injuries aren't life-threatening, but he will need plenty of rest. It will be several weeks before he can return to work."

Allie pressed her palms against her eyes, sagging in her chair. Struggling to speak around her swollen throat, she rasped, "I am so relieved."

Steve's mother bowed her head, releasing a ragged breath, while his father made the sign of the cross.

"When can I see him?" Allie asked.

"He's still in Recovery, but as soon as he's settled in a room, a nurse will let you know."

"Thank you, Doctor, for all you've done."

Allie sat in Steve's room, watching his chest rise and fall as he drifted in and out of sleep. His parents had popped in earlier and were now in the hospital cafeteria getting a bite to eat. They'd offered to bring something back for Allie, but she'd declined. Food was the last thing on her mind right now. Lori

Robbins had left the hospital, after being told only Steve's immediate family could see him today. She'd asked Allie to give him the message that she'd be praying for his full recovery.

Allie fidgeted in her chair, trying to relax, but her nervousness won out. Negative thoughts regarding the blond officer continued to haunt her. Were Lori and Steve an item? How many times had Allie asked herself that question? *I need to know. I can't go on like this, conjuring up all kinds of scenarios. How would I have felt if Steve had died, knowing Lori was the last person to be with him?*

Steve's eyelids fluttered, then opened. "Allie, I. . ."

She put her fingers to his lips. "Shh. . .don't talk. You need to rest."

He shook his head. "I'm sorry, Allie. So sorry."

Her spine stiffened. This was it. Steve was about to confess. Allie couldn't bear the thought of him admitting his love for another woman. If he asked for a divorce, she would have a meltdown, right here in his hospital room. A nurse would probably come in and ask Allie to either quiet down or leave.

Steve reached for her hand. "I'm sorry for working such long hours and not spending enough time with you and the kids." Tears welled in his eyes. "I only did it so I could buy all of you something really special for Christmas this year. I was hoping to plan a trip to Disney World."

Disney World? Something special for Christmas? "Oh, Steve, I don't care about any of that. All I want is you." She sniffed, swiping at the tears rolling down her cheeks. "As much as Nola and Derek would like to go to Disney World, I'm sure they'd rather have their father, whole, and healthy, and spending quality time with them."

His Adam's apple bounced as he swallowed. "You and the kids are my only reason for living."

"What about Lori?"

Steve's brows furrowed. "Officer Robbins?"

Allie nodded slowly.

"What about her? Was she shot too?"

"No, she's fine." Allie took a tissue from her purse and blew her nose. "She was here earlier and said I should let you know that she's praying for you."

"Then what did you mean when you asked, 'What about Lori?'" Steve took a breath and let it out slowly.

"You two have been together so much, and I just assumed…" He stared at her strangely for several seconds before a light seemed to dawn. "Please don't tell me you thought something was going on between me and Lori."

Allie dropped her gaze. "To be honest, the thought had crossed my mind. More than once, in fact."

He coughed, then sputtered. "Oh, for goodness' sakes. Lori is my partner—nothing else. The times we have been together were necessary."

"What about the day I saw you two in the car at the mall?"

"We were talking about her boyfriend and the problem they were having with his folks disapproving of him dating a cop." Steve paused and moistened his lips with his tongue. "I could totally relate, since your folks, and my parents too did not approve of my line of work."

Allie released a huge breath, rocking back and forth in her chair as moisture from her eyes continued to dribble down her cheeks.

Steve brushed the tears away with his thumb in a circular motion. "I love you, Allie. You're the woman I will always call sweetheart."

"I love you too." Allie felt such relief as she watched her husband drift back to sleep. She was glad she'd been wrong about Steve and Lori, but beyond that, Allie was thrilled that Steve wanted to spend more time with her and the children. Perhaps, once Steve felt well enough, they would go to church as a family. It was the least they could do to thank God for sparing Steve's life.

Chapter 43

Walnut Creek

Even though she'd received some good news yesterday, a sense of sadness came over Heidi as she scurried about the kitchen, preparing for her students' arrival on this, their final cooking class. With Christmas fast approaching, she'd decided to teach them how to make a Christmas Crunch Salad. The verse she'd written on the back of their recipe cards this time was taken from Luke 18:27: "The things which are impossible with men are possible with God." Heidi knew this scripture well and had memorized it when she was a girl. She couldn't imagine how anyone could make it through life without knowing God personally. His presence was everywhere: in the sun, moon, and stars; on earth; throughout nature—everything was made by Him.

The good news Heidi had received was twofold—first Eli told Lyle he and Loretta were planning to be married this coming spring. Now that Loretta had been baptized and joined the Amish church, they were free to begin planning their wedding.

The second bit of news was when Kendra called and left Heidi a message early this morning. She wanted Heidi to know that her father had apologized for the way he'd treated her since first finding out she was pregnant. Heidi was thrilled with this news, and planned to call Kendra back later today. Some people might believe certain things were impossible, but God, in His infinite wisdom and mighty power, could turn even the most difficult situation into something good—something that would bring glory to His name.

Heidi paused from her introspections to separate the freshly washed broccoli, cauliflower, onions, and cherry tomatoes into piles, placing them around the table where each of her students would sit. She would wait to set out the ingredients for the dressing until everyone arrived.

While she waited, Heidi continued working on a list she'd started for the things they would need to have on hand as foster parents: extra tissues for sniffling noses; bandages of various sizes; a variety of toys, including coloring books with crayons; and of course, plenty of healthy snack foods. There were so many things to think about. But Heidi and Lyle were eager and more than ready to begin this new adventure.

Heidi tapped her pencil along the edge of the rolltop desk. *Do I need to give up teaching cooking classes now that I'll be parenting full time?* She lifted her shoulders briefly. *Well, it doesn't matter. I have other, more important things to think about now. I will make that decision when the time is right.*

The sound of tires crunching on the gravel brought Heidi to her feet. One of her students had arrived. She set her notebook and pencil aside and went to open the front door, where she saw Nicole getting out of her father's car. The next thing Heidi knew, the girl sprinted toward the house, grinning and waving a blue apron in her hand.

When Nicole stepped onto the porch, she held the item out to Heidi. "I remembered to bring it this time."

Heidi smiled. "That's good, because the old one I've let you use a few times is in the dirty laundry basket right now."

When they entered the house, Heidi paused in the hall. "I have a few things to do yet in the kitchen, Nicole. Would you like to wait in the living room until the others arrive?"

"I'd rather go to the kitchen with you. I have something

to tell you, and I'm anxious to share."

"No problem."

They headed to the kitchen, and while Nicole took a seat at the end of the table where there were no vegetables, Heidi took two glasses out of the cupboard. "Would you like something to drink? There's apple cider in the refrigerator, and also some milk."

"I'll just have a glass of water."

"Okay." Heidi filled one of the glasses with water and placed it in front of Nicole. Then she poured herself a glass of apple cider and sat in a chair next to her young student.

"Thanks." Nicole took a drink then cleared her throat. "I did like you said and forgave Tonya—I mean, my mom. I told her that when she called last week. Mom's going to Alcoholics Anonymous, and she's trying to do better, so I need to at least give her a chance." She closed her eyes briefly and released a puff of air. "I felt better after we hung up—like a sense of relief. I've been angry at Mom ever since she left, and it's made me disagreeable. Sometimes the resentment I felt made me feel almost sick."

"I'm glad you were able to forgive her. With forgiveness comes healing." Heidi's eyes filled with joyous tears as she clasped Nicole's hand. "What a wonderful thing to learn on this last day of class."

"I have something for you, Heidi." Nicole opened the manila folder she'd carried into the house. Heidi hadn't even noticed it until now. She pulled out a piece of heavy paper and handed it to Heidi. "It's a picture I drew of your dog. I wanted to surprise you with it."

Heidi gazed at the picture. "It certainly does look like our Rusty." She shook her head slowly. "I had no idea you were an artist, Nicole. This is a wonderful gift."

Nicole tucked her arms in at her sides, looking down at the floor. "It's nothing, really. Drawing is something I do just for fun. I'm not really that talented."

"Oh, but you are." Heidi placed the picture on the table and gave Nicole a hug. "I appreciate your thoughtfulness."

Bill stepped onto the Troyers' porch at the same time as Lance. "How was your Thanksgiving?" he asked.

"It was good. I spent it at one of my daughter's." Lance gave a wide smile. "How was yours?"

"I was alone at my cabin on Thanksgiving, but my two hunting buddies showed up the next day." Bill puffed out his chest a bit. "Got me a nice-sized buck on Monday, opening day, with a good set of antlers."

"You gonna hang 'em on the wall in your cabin or display them at your house?"

"Probably at the cabin. I have several others there too."

"Do you eat the deer meat?" Lance questioned.

"I have in the past, but this year I made a decision to donate the venison to a local food bank. They are always in need of meat."

"That's a nice thing to do." Lance gave him a friendly smack on the shoulder.

Bill knocked on the door. "I can't believe this is our sixth and final cooking class."

Lance nodded. "I know. I'm gonna miss coming here every other Saturday." He chuckled. "Gonna miss the good-tasting food, most of all."

"Yeah, same here. But I'll also miss the time we've spent getting to know each other, as well as our cooking instructor. Heidi's a special young woman. I have the utmost respect for her."

"Me too." Lance tugged his earlobe. "It's interesting how we all come from different walks of life, yet have found something in common—specifically our interest in Amish cooking."

Heidi opened the door and greeted them both, asking the men to join her and Nicole in the kitchen.

The minute Bill entered the room and took a look at Nicole, he knew something was different about the girl. Gone were her drooping shoulders and downturned mouth. They'd been replaced by a relaxed posture and eyes that sparkled. It had to be something other than better school grades and more time to do homework. He stood with arms folded, staring at Nicole as she fingered her glass of water. Did he dare ask what had brought on such a change?

As if she could read his thoughts, Nicole offered Bill a wide smile. "I wasn't gonna say anything, but it's only fair that you know—I'm not mad at my mom anymore. It feels good to have let it all go."

He stepped behind her and placed both hands on her shoulders. "That's good news. Life's too short to carry a heavy load of anger in our souls." Bill thumped his chest. "Ask me—I know."

"I wholeheartedly agree," Lance put in. "I've had my own share of things to deal with concerning my brother, but I think it's all good now."

"Life ain't perfect," Bill added, "but it's a lot better when we're at peace with others. I've learned a lot more than cooking from taking these cooking classes." He lifted both hands. "And who knows. . . I may even start goin' to church sometime in the future."

Heidi smiled. "That's good news."

Bill moved closer to Heidi. "By the way, I know something I think you'll want to know."

She raised her eyebrows. "Really? What's that?"

"My son, Brent, who came with me to meet you before Thanksgiving, had a date last weekend with your previous student, Kendra." Bill scratched the back of his head. "Well, they didn't actually go out on a date. Kendra's babysitter fell through, so they ended up ordering pizza, and Brent spent the evening with Kendra at her folks' house."

Heidi placed a hand on her hip. "Somehow I'm not

surprised. I saw the way those two looked at each other when you three were here that day."

"Yep." Bill snapped his fingers. "I wouldn't be surprised if Kendra and Brent don't get hitched someday."

"That would be something all right. Now, did you both remember your aprons today?" Heidi asked, looking at Bill and then Lance.

"Sorry, I forgot," Bill mumbled. This wasn't the first time he'd forgotten his, either.

"I brought mine." Lance held up the paper sack in his hands. Bill hadn't even noticed Lance had been carrying it until now.

"I don't have any clean aprons today, but I can give you a big towel to drape around your neck, if you'd like to keep your clothes clean." Heidi moved across the room and opened a drawer.

Bill waved his hand. "Naw, that's okay. My jeans and sweatshirt are old, so it doesn't matter if something gets spilled." He glanced at the piles of vegetables on the table. "What are we making today, anyway?"

"Since Christmas is only a few weeks away, I decided to show you how to put together what I call Christmas Crunch Salad. It's simple to make and quite tasty. We'll get started on it as soon as the others arrive." Heidi gestured to some empty chairs at the table. "Why don't you men have a seat?"

Lisa was getting out of her car when Todd's vehicle pulled in. *I hope he doesn't pressure me to go out with him again. I'm still not ready for that.*

She gave him a polite wave and started for the house. With Todd's long strides, he caught up to her before she reached the porch.

"Too bad this is our last cooking class." Todd stepped close to Lisa and reached out to support her elbow. "I'm gonna miss the friendly banter, and I'll especially miss seeing you." He gave her elbow a little squeeze. "Sorry if I'm being too pushy."

Lisa's purse strap slipped off her shoulder, and Todd quickly repositioned it. Her face grew warm when an electrifying sensation went through her from the touch of his hand. "I'll miss everyone too. The classes have been fun, and I've been able to try a few of the recipes for myself, as well as some of my clients." Even though her heart had begun to flutter, Lisa couldn't bring herself to say she would miss seeing Todd too.

Todd moved closer to Lisa—so close she could feel his warm breath on her cheek. "Think you might ever go out with me again?"

"I don't know, Todd. Maybe. We'll have to wait and see how it goes." Lisa stepped onto the porch and knocked on the door. Todd was so charming that it was difficult to say no to him. But she had other, more important things on her mind right now, and they didn't include dating. In addition to meeting her brother and wanting to get to know him better, she'd been asked to cater a large Christmas party next week. It would take lots of planning, not to mention preliminary prep work. And she needed to find someone who could assist her with all that, as well as help set everything up. So, with the exception of being with her folks on Christmas Day, she wouldn't make any social plans until after the New Year.

Lisa felt relieved when Heidi answered the door. No more pressure from Todd—for now, at least. She was eager to tell Heidi about the meeting she'd had this past week with one of her previous students.

Heidi greeted Todd and Lisa, leading them to the kitchen and suggesting they take a chair.

"Oh, yes, I will, but before I do, there's something I want to share with you." Lisa spoke excitedly.

"What is it? I'm eager to hear." Heidi took a few steps

closer to Lisa, as Todd pulled out a chair at the table and sat down.

"I met with one of your former students on Thursday evening. Her name is Charlene Higgins."

Heidi gave a nod. "I enjoyed getting to know Charlene. She's a sweet young woman."

"Yes, based on the phone call I had with her, she seems nice. Charlene is going to take some pictures I can use on my new website to help promote my catering business." Lisa's face broke into a wide smile. "You can only imagine how surprised we both were when the topic of food came up and I mentioned that I've been taking cooking classes from you. Then Charlene said she was a student in your first set of classes, and after that, we had a lot to talk about."

"Oh, my, that's wonderful. How is Charlene doing these days?"

Lisa leaned against the counter near Heidi's desk. "She mentioned that she'll soon be getting married to a wonderful guy. And in addition to teaching school, Charlene's started a part-time photography business." She paused to tuck a short strand of hair behind her ear. "Oh, and she also mentioned having to move her wedding date out a bit."

Heidi tipped her head. "Oh? I hadn't heard. I figured by now she and Len were already married. I believe they'd planned for a September wedding. I wonder why the delay."

"I don't know. She didn't say. She did, however, ask me to tell you hello."

"When you speak to Charlene again, please give her my regards." Heidi clasped her hands to her chest. "Charlene won a photo contest for a prestigious magazine during the time she was taking my classes. When she showed us the beautiful picture of a colt and its mother with a glorious sunset behind the animals, I knew she had talent. I'm pleased to learn she'll be using her abilities in a positive way. And I'm doubly happy to hear she and Len are still planning to be married."

"Let us know when your new website is up and running, Lisa," Lance called from across the room. "I'm sure we'd all like to check it out."

A faint blush crept across Lisa's cheeks as she joined the others at the table. "Yes, thank you. I will keep you posted."

Heidi noticed when Todd fixed his gaze on Lisa, and she gave him a brief smile. There had to be something special going on between them, even if neither of them knew it. Perhaps a new romance would come out of this class, after all. Heidi hoped if it happened, Todd and Lisa would keep her informed. It was nice keeping in touch with former students and finding out how they were doing.

No wonder Aunt Emma enjoys teaching her quilting classes so much, Heidi mused. *It's not just about instructing people how to make something; the real joy comes from getting to know the students personally and feeling like you're a part of their lives.*

A knock sounded on the door, and Heidi excused herself to answer it. She was pretty sure it had to be Allie.

A few minutes later, Heidi returned to the kitchen, with Allie at her side. After everyone washed their hands and put on their aprons, Heidi explained how to make the salad. "I also made some Christmas cut-out cookies we can have as a treat afterward," she added.

"The salad sounds good. Think I'll make it to go with our Christmas dinner." Allie smiled. "This is going to be one of our best Christmases, because my husband is alive."

Heidi's brows furrowed as she tipped her head. "What do you mean?"

Allie explained how Steve had been shot by a robber, and ended the story by saying he was going to be all right and wouldn't be working so many long hours anymore. Bill and Todd asked a few questions about the details of the robbery, and then everyone got busy cutting up their vegetables and placing them in a bowl.

"I'd like to tell you all something." Todd looked at everyone individually. "I'm sorry I wasn't honest up front with all of you about my job and the reason I took this class."

Before anyone could respond, he continued. "As soon as I finish writing my last article, which will be about the cooking classes I've taken part in, I'm going to quit my job at the newspaper as a food critic."

Heidi's mouth opened slightly. She wondered what he might say about her classes.

"I've come to realize I can no longer have a job that could rip the rug out from anyone's feet." He looked at Heidi. "Don't worry, because I will have nothing but good to say in my article about your cooking or the classes you've taught. In fact, I'm gonna give it a five star review."

Heidi smiled. "Why, thank you, Todd."

"What did you mean about ripping the rug out from anyone's feet?" Nicole questioned.

"I don't want to chance giving a negative review on a restaurant, and because of it, having the place close down. Who knows what the owner's situation might be?" He lifted his hands as if in defeat. "It's happened before, and I could not live with myself if it happened again because of me."

"What are you going to do now?" Lance questioned.

"I'm not sure. I'd like to work with food in some capacity, though." Todd stroked his chin. "Guess I'll have to start reading the classified ads and see if there's something out there for me."

"Todd, it took a lot for you to admit that to all of us, but I can see a burden has been lifted from you," Heidi commented.

"Yes, and don't fall over, but I've even started going to church." Todd smiled. "The minister there met with me this week, and he's going to help me develop a closer relationship with God." Todd heaved a sigh. "Hopefully with his guidance, and by studying the Bible, I'll be on the right path for once in my life."

As Lisa listened to Todd, she could not believe the transformation. It thrilled her to know he was seeking a relationship with God. There was something about his manner that seemed different too. Todd genuinely seemed sincere.

She also considered what he had said about finding another job and wanting to work with food. *Should I say something, or would he be offended by my suggestion? Oh well, here goes. . .* "Todd, before you look at the classified ads, we need to talk. I may have an opportunity for you."

Todd turned to face her. "Oh?"

Lisa looked around and noticed that everyone seemed to be listening. "I have a huge Christmas party to cater soon, and I'm going to need someone to help me with it. I cannot cater this party alone—it's too big for one person to handle. There will be even more guests than there were at Melanie and Shawn's wedding reception." She paused briefly. "Also, my business is slowly growing, and I'm considering the idea of teaming up with someone who might someday, down the road, want to partner with me in the catering business. We can take things slow, and see how it goes, but Todd, do you think you might be interested?"

"Interested? Are you kidding me? You bet I'm interested!" Todd bumped shoulders with Bill, who sat next to him. "I have a lot to learn about cooking and all the things I'll need to know concerning the catering business, but if you're willing to teach me, Lisa, I'm more than eager to learn."

Smiling, she said, "With your sophisticated palate and understanding of what foods go together well, we should make a great team."

Everyone clapped when Todd and Lisa sealed the deal with a handshake. Afterward, Todd got up from his chair and gave Lisa a kiss on the cheek.

The blush Lisa felt spread from her toes all the way up to the top of her head. "I'd like to also make an announcement."

All heads turned to look at her.

"My family has suddenly increased."

"Oh, how's that?" Heidi questioned.

"Well, I found out on Thanksgiving Day that I have a half brother. I'll tell you all about it when we're eating our snacks."

"Lisa, that's wonderful news. I'm eager to hear the details." Heidi's smile was deep.

"Now it's your turn, Heidi. How have you been since we last saw you?" The question came from Allie, but everyone watched and waited.

"I've been well," Heidi responded. "Lyle and I had a nice Thanksgiving with my family in Middlefield, and yesterday we got word from the caseworker helping us become foster parents that we'll be getting two foster children a few days before Christmas."

"Two kids, huh?" Bill reached for another piece of broccoli to cut up. "Sounds like you'll be kept pretty busy."

Heidi nodded. "But we're looking forward to it. Besides, this will be a good kind of busy."

"How old are the children?" Lisa asked.

"Marsha is three, and her brother, Randy, is five." Heidi clasped her hands, placing them under her chin. "The caseworker explained that the little girl hasn't spoken since her mother and father were killed in a car accident. She also mentioned that the boy has a negative attitude, so it's going to be a challenge."

Todd whistled. "Wow, I hope you're up to it. Sounds like those kids will be hard to deal with."

"If anyone can do, it'll be Heidi and Lyle," Lance interjected. "As their mail carrier, I've gotten to know them fairly well. Why, I bet within a few weeks they'll have those kids wearing smiles, big as you please."

"Thanks for the vote of confidence. My husband and I will do the best we can." Heidi relaxed in her chair. Even though she didn't know how long these children would be with them, she determined in her heart to do the best she could in caring for and offering love to Marsha and Randy. She looked forward to giving them a wonderful Christmas, and thanked God for His special blessings in allowing her and Lyle this unexpected opportunity.

Heidi thought about the scripture she had put on everyone's recipe card for this class: *"The things which are impossible with men are possible with God."* The truth of that verse was definitely being lived out in this small group.

Looking around the table, at each of her students, she appreciated being able to teach them how to make six special recipes. But more than that, Heidi felt thankful she had been given the opportunity to share the love of God and see how He was working in each person's life. She looked forward to the days ahead, and the opportunity of sharing the many blessings she had received.

―― ❦ ――

Recipes from
Heidi's Cooking Classes

―― ❦ ――

Amish Friendship Bread

INGREDIENTS:

- 1 cup starter (see recipe for starter below)
- 3 eggs
- 1 cup oil
- ½ cup milk
- ½ teaspoon vanilla
- 2 cups flour
- 1 cup sugar
- 1½ teaspoons baking powder
- 2 teaspoons cinnamon
- ½ teaspoon salt
- ½ teaspoon baking soda
- 1 to 2 small boxes instant pudding (any flavor)
- 1 cup nuts, chopped (optional)
- 1 cup raisins (optional)

Preheat oven to 325 degrees. Grease and flour two large loaf pans.

Mix 1 cup starter (recipe below) with eggs, oil, milk, and vanilla. In separate bowl, mix flour, sugar, baking powder, cinnamon, salt, baking soda, instant pudding mix, and nuts and/or raisins, if desired. Add to liquid mixture and stir thoroughly.

Dust greased pans lightly with some cinnamon-sugar mixture. Pour batter evenly into pans and sprinkle remaining cinnamon-sugar mixture on top.

Bake for one hour or until toothpick inserted in center of bread comes out clean.

Options: Use 2 boxes pudding mix. Change flavor of pudding mix. Add up to 2 cups dried fruit or baking chips (note: heavier add-ins may sink to bottom). Decrease fat by substituting ½ cup oil and ½ cup applesauce for 1 cup oil in recipe. Decrease eggs by using 2 eggs and ¼ cup mashed banana. Use large Bundt pan rather than two loaf pans.

Recipe for Starter:

¼ cup warm water	3 cups milk
1 (¼ ounce) packet yeast	3 cups flour
1½ cups plus 1 tablespoon sugar	

Day 1: Put warm water in bowl with yeast. Sprinkle 1 tablespoon sugar over it and let stand in warm place to double in size (about 10 minutes). Mix 1 cup milk, ½ cup sugar, 1 cup flour, and yeast mixture. Stir with wooden spoon. Do not use metal spoon as it will retard yeast's growth. Cover loosely and let stand at room temperature overnight.

Days 2–4: Stir starter each day with wooden spoon. Cover loosely again.

Day 5: Stir in 1 cup flour, 1 cup milk, and ½ cup sugar. Mix well. Cover loosely.

Days 6–9: Stir well each day and cover loosely.

Day 10: Stir in 1 cup flour, ½ cup sugar, and 1 cup milk. It's now ready to use to make bread. Remove 1 cup to make your first bread. Give 1 cup each to two friends, along with the recipe for the starter and your favorite Amish bread. Store remaining starter in a container in refrigerator (or freeze) to make future bread.

Apple Corn Bread

- ¾ cup cornmeal
- ¾ cup spelt or whole wheat flour
- 3 teaspoons baking powder
- ¼ teaspoon cloves
- 1 teaspoon cinnamon
- ¾ teaspoon salt
- 1 egg, beaten
- 1 teaspoon vanilla
- ¾ cup buttermilk
- 2 tablespoons cooking oil or melted butter
- 1 tablespoon honey
- 2 cups diced apples

Sift dry ingredients together in a bowl. Add egg, vanilla, and buttermilk. Blend well. Add oil, honey, and apples. Mix thoroughly. Pour into greased, 9-inch square pan. Bake at 350 degrees for 25 minutes.

Baked Oatmeal

INGREDIENTS:

- 2 eggs, beaten
- 1 cup sugar or substitute sweetener
- ½ cup butter, melted
- 3 cups oatmeal
- 1 cup milk
- 2 teaspoons baking powder
- Pinch of salt

Preheat oven to 350 degrees. Combine eggs, sugar, and butter in 2-quart baking dish. Add oatmeal, milk, baking powder, and salt. Stir until well blended. Bake for 30 minutes. May be served plain or with milk or whipping cream.

Chicken in a Crumb Basket

INGREDIENTS FOR CRUMB BASKET:

½ cup butter, melted
6 cups bread crumbs
¼ cup onion, chopped

1 teaspoon celery salt
½ teaspoon poultry seasoning

Mix all ingredients in bowl. Line bottom and sides of greased 2-quart casserole dish with mixture, forming a "basket." Bake at 350 degrees for 15 minutes.

FILLING:

¼ cup butter
¼ cup flour
½ cup milk
1½ cups chicken broth
1 cup carrots, finely chopped

1 cup potatoes, finely chopped
3 cups chicken, cooked and finely chopped
1 cup fresh or frozen peas

Make white sauce in a kettle by melting butter, browning flour in butter, then slowly adding milk, followed by broth. In separate pot, cook carrots and potatoes in water until soft. Drain. Add chicken and peas. Coat with white sauce. Pour into crumb basket and bake at 350 degrees for 30 to 40 minutes.

Pumpkin Whoopie Pies

2 cups brown sugar
1 cup vegetable oil
1½ cups pumpkin (cooked
  or canned)
2 eggs
1 teaspoon vanilla
3 cups flour

1 teaspoon salt
1 teaspoon baking powder
1 teaspoon baking soda
1½ tablespoons cinnamon
½ tablespoon ginger
½ tablespoon cloves

Preheat oven to 350 degrees. Cream sugar and oil together in mixing bowl. Add pumpkin, eggs, and vanilla. Mix well. Add dry ingredients and stir until combined. Drop by heaping teaspoon onto greased cooking sheet. Bake for 10 to 12 minutes.

FILLING:

2 egg whites
1½ cups shortening
1 teaspoon vanilla

¼ teaspoon salt
4½ cups powdered sugar

In a bowl, beat egg whites and add shortening, vanilla, and salt until combined well. Stir in powdered sugar and mix until creamy. Spread some of filling on cookie. Place another cookie on top of filling. Wrap each "sandwich" in plastic.

Christmas Crunch Salad

4 cups broccoli, cut into
   small pieces
4 cups cauliflower, cut into
   small pieces
1 medium onion, chopped
8 cherry tomatoes, halved

DRESSING:

1 cup mayonnaise
½ cup sour cream
1 to 2 tablespoons sugar
1 tablespoon apple cider
   vinegar
Salt and pepper to taste

Put cut-up vegetables in a bowl. In another bowl, combine dressing ingredients. Pour over vegetables and toss well. Cover and chill in refrigerator for 1 to 2 hours.

Discussion Questions

1. For some time after Kendra changed her mind about letting Heidi and Lyle adopt her baby, Heidi grieved. How would you deal with a situation like Heidi's? Would you try adopting another baby or be content in your marriage without children?

2. In addition to teaching her students how to make some traditional Amish meals, Heidi felt compelled to help those in her class who had emotional or spiritual problems. Sometimes, however, she was unable to get through to them. Is there ever a time we should stop trying to help someone?

3. Kendra changed her mind about letting Lyle and Heidi adopt her baby because her parents agreed to let her come home so they could help raise the child. Was it right for Kendra to break her agreement with the Troyers? Would her baby have been better off with them instead of Kendra and her parents?

4. Nicole had a lot of responsibility on her young shoulders: trying to keep an eye on her two siblings, cleaning, and cooking while her father went to work. This ended up affecting her grades because she had less time to concentrate on her studies. Do you think she should have been honest with her father from the beginning and explained that she was falling behind at school due to all her responsibilities at home? Was Nicole trying to prove something by taking on all the responsibilities her mother used to do?

5. Nicole was bitter and angry at her mother for divorcing her dad, and she struggled with her relationships with others. What are some ways we can help a person like Nicole?

6. Lance had an issue with his brother when he came to live with him for a while. Dan kept doing things that got on Lance's nerves, until Lance was fed up and sought some other place for his brother to stay. Rather than taking that approach, would it have helped if Lance had communicated better with Dan when he asked him to stop doing the things he found annoying? Have you ever had someone living in your home temporarily? How did things work out for both of you?

7. Lance was a widower, and his daughters were always trying to play matchmaker, believing their dad needed another wife. Lance was content and didn't want to remarry. How could he have better conveyed that to his daughters?

8. Allie was married to a policeman, and she became upset because he filled in for others on the force, which didn't leave much time for them to be together as a family. Have you ever had a parent or spouse who worked too much and didn't take time to be with his or her family? How did you deal with that situation?

9. Allie suspected that her husband might be having an affair. Do you think she was too hasty in making this assumption? Did Allie's suspicions have more to do with her lack of self-esteem or was it a lack of trust in her husband?

10. Bill liked to hunt and had been saving for a trip to Alaska. But he depleted part of his savings when he did something to help someone in the cooking class, even though he didn't know her very well. Have you ever made a monetary sacrifice for someone you didn't know well? How did it make you feel?

11. Lisa was attracted to Todd, even though he didn't profess to be a Christian. Is it good for people to date if they don't share the same religious beliefs? What does the Bible say about being unequally yoked with unbelievers? Does that also pertain to dating?

12. Although Todd wanted a relationship with Lisa, his dishonesty put a wedge between them. Todd also had a know-it-all attitude. Have you ever known someone like that? How did you respond, and did their attitude drive a wedge between you? Is there a nice way of telling someone who thinks they know everything that it's affecting your relationship?

13. Heidi liked to include a Bible verse on the back of the recipe cards she gave her students. Were there any verses in this book that spoke to your heart? How has God's Word helped you through a difficult time in your life?

14. Did you learn anything new about the Amish who live in Holmes County, Ohio, while reading this book? Why do you think some Amish communities differ in their rules and what the church ministers will allow their people to do?

15. Did you like how some of the characters from Book 1, *The Seekers*, were mingled into this story? Who were your favorite characters from Books 1 and 2, and what did you like about them?

About the Author

New York Times bestselling, award-winning author, Wanda E. Brunstetter, is one of the founders of the Amish fiction genre. Wanda's ancestors were part of the Anabaptist faith, and her novels are based on personal research intended to accurately portray the Amish way of life. Her books are well-read and trusted by many Amish, who credit her for giving readers a deeper understanding of the people and their customs. When Wanda visits her Amish friends, she finds herself drawn to their peaceful lifestyle, sincerity, and close family ties.

Wanda enjoys photography, ventriloquism, gardening, bird-watching, beachcombing, and spending time with her family. She and her husband, Richard, have been blessed with two grown children, six grandchildren, and two great-grandchildren.

To learn more about Wanda, visit her website at www.wandabrunstetter.com.

AMISH COOKING CLASS SERIES
By Wanda E. Brunstetter

**Lives are transformed during an Amish
woman's cooking classes in Holmes County, Ohio.**

The Seekers
Book 1

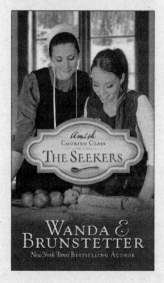

Married for eight years with no children to help fill her days,
Heidi Troyer hatches the idea of teaching classes in the art of
Amish cooking in her Holmes County, Ohio, home. During
each of the classes, Heidi teaches a variety of skills, but it is
her words of wisdom that have a profound effect on her five
students—a woman engaged to marry, an expectant mother
estranged from her family, a widowed mom seeking to simplify,
a Vietnam vet who camps on the Troyer's farm, and an Amish
widower—whose souls are healed as their stomachs are filled.

Mass Market / 978-1-63609-043-6 / $7.99

The Celebration
Book 3

Lyle and Heidi Troyer have taken in two children, orphaned when their parents were killed in a car accident. Hoping to help them adapt and make friends, Heidi decides to hold a series of cooking classes for kids. But children are always accompanied by an adult—and that is where the trouble arises. Trent and Miranda Cooper are separated and try to juggle bringing their two children to class. Denise and Velma both have overwhelming lives with husbands, kids, and stressful jobs. Darren, single dad and firefighter, and Ellen, single mom and nurse, find a few things in common. Will hearts be healed over plates of Amish food?

Mass Market / 978-1-63609-245-4 / $7.99